CW00687367

The Hacker Hunter

By Christopher Keenan

Copyright Lionwing Ltd 2011 - Published 2011
ISBN: 978-0-9570564-0-4

www.TheHackerHunter.co.uk

Intro

Dear Reader,

This book is dedicated to the memory of John (Mac) McAleese MM, who died in late August 2011 aged 62.

John McAleese was the legendary SAS hero in black who you saw on the balcony of the Iranian embassy. Mac was watched by the world as he blew the front windows off the embassy and led the SAS raid that ended up saving the lives of those held captive.

Writing the book was great fun; it allowed me to relive a few places and times and gave John, Bob, Alex, Henry and I something to talk about other than work and family for a year.

Mac was such a clever guy, I hid truths in the story and he'd always find them, he was like a SAS Sherlock Holmes. I finished the book nine days before he died, we must have spent hours on the phone talking about the ending, which he described as "The Italian Job meets Agatha Christie"!

When I felt like giving up on the book John said "listen, your grammar and punctuation is dreadful mate but I'm on the edge of my seat, keep writing". Bottom line; John McAleese wrote the training manual for modern-day spies, I wrote the fictionalised story of what they get up to, I hope you enjoy it as much as we did.

The Hacker Hunter © Copyright Lionwing Ltd 2011

I should stress, however that all characters and all the events depicted in this work are fictitious. Any resemblance to real events or to real persons, living or dead, is purely coincidental.

Thanks for purchasing the Hacker Hunter

Keenan

Christopher Keenan

Chapter 1 – The Company

A hand, well manicured but blemished with age reached into an open ice bucket; a set of silver tongs remained hooked over the rim, neglected in favour of a bohemian grasp. A moment later the hand re-emerged, now full of cubes it moved swiftly and elegantly towards two sturdy whisky glasses. The hand reached an 'all stop' to hover over one of the empty glasses for a few long seconds. The crisp, cold ice burned the old flesh but regardless of this the hand remains motionless, perhaps enjoying the sensation or perhaps the mind was blindly distracted with the contemplation of more sobering matters. A single cube of ice, as solid as glass dropped into the empty crystal cylinder, the cube danced around for a few seconds as the energy from the impact reverberated within the crystal prison. The noise from the dancing cube seemed to awaken the senses, like an alarm bell bringing the mind back to its physical intention. Two more cubes followed, the hand moved over the second empty whisky glass.

"You?" asked a mature, well spoken voice. Not waiting for a reply the hand released the remaining cubes. A few moments passed, just long enough to squeeze the top off a bottle of Scotland's finest golden liquid. As this bitter sharp nectar washed over the cracking cubes, thin, barely noticeable wisp of white vapour was released in swirls from the ice, providing a trace scent of cool Scottish air, a scent only detectable to the most enlightened nose. The glass was raised and inspected, a little shake to rattle the ice and then the drink was lowered towards a figure sat expectantly in a corner of the room. The seated man remained motionless. The host, an older gentleman in his early seventies, rattled the ice in the glass once more, with this gesture inviting the man to stand with him. However, the seated male, clearly younger, maybe in his early fifties, remained motionless. In submission the elder gentlemen walked towards him and passed the glass. The seated man extended his arm and accepted the drink. In lieu of a thank you, he spoke.

"You are an old cliché, a parody of an old school tie intelligence official, a mimic of a cold war prescription against an enemy that doesn't exist." Without even stopping for a breath he continued, but with even more distain in his voice, "You are living in a fantasy built on what you think you should be. From your leather upholstered chair to your partner's desk, right down to the musty old oil paintings hung above the wooden wall panels."

The younger man lifted the glass to half a thumb's distance from his nose and sniffed a sniff that was more like a man trying to detect poison than a quality aroma. Frozen in motion his eyes looked up, fixated on the elder man, he took a second or two to observe the distinguished but worn face of his host, the glass still under his nose. He readjusted himself, poised to take a sip and then stopped, eyes still fixed on his host he continued to talk.

"I'm surprised you have room for another snifter!" Doing little to contain the bitter tones in his voice he remarked further, "had a long lunch at your club, did you? Let me guess, life time membership to the 'spy club', better still the 'in and out club' or whatever they call it nowadays."

Stopping again the younger man paused to contemplate, his intense gaze remaining unbroken. He continued, "No, that's to clichéd, even for you. If I was to guess, you would be more akin to the Liberal club. Yes. Drinks at Whitehall Place, the irony would provide you with a smug satisfaction, would it not? "

The Hacker Hunter © Copyright Lionwing Ltd 2011

The elder of the two men calmly placed his drink down on the dark green leather padding of his old partner's desk, without taking so much as a sip. "I don't like to walk too far. You'll find the Adam Street Club provides a good meal if that's what you mean, but I prefer my own Scotch, and this is the first of the day. Don't ruin it - there's a good chap." His left hand reached for the right cuff of his impeccably tailored suit and with a sharp tug he pulled the sleeve out to reveal the cufflink. A golden cufflink, in the shape of a small coat of arms no less. It was hard to be sure which coat of arms, but this was obviously a gesture of status. Casually, he reached back towards the glass and, picking it up he softly went on.

"Let me tell you what I think. As a child you played a lot of imaginary games, you gave all the other children imaginary characters to act and made up elaborate plots for them to follow out to a conclusion that you found entertaining. I'd imagine your imagination stretched to playing army games, detective games, cowboys and Indians mainly. Anyone that did not follow the plot of your 'let's pretend' world would be expelled, ousted to play alone. In your own childish way you are still making up elaborate plots but this time in the name of national security. You've become so embroiled in your own games that reality escapes you. You clearly crave a sense of the real as much as a drowning man craves air, I dare say."

The elder man stopped talking, walking closer to his guest he seemed to gleefully savour the confrontation, leaning over he placed his mouth right next to the still seated man's ear and whispered,

"No cliché, parody or upholstered chair gets close to what I am. So, my drowning subordinate, hold on tightly to this proverbial rope," he paused as if to swallow anger and then coolly continued, teeth clenched, "I am your only excuse for playing

The Hacker Hunter © Copyright Lionwing Ltd 2011

make believe games in the real world. Learn to lose gracefully, there's a good sport."

The younger of the two men lowered his drink to the height of his belt, in the process loosening his grip on the glass to the point that it wouldn't take much for the forty year old liquid held within to spill into his lap. His jaw loosened in a similar fashion to his grip on the glass, a look of irreverence came across his face. This elder gent held all the winning cards and, all jibes to one side, his host was an extremely dangerous man. Whatever the history, and there was clearly bad history, it was time for the younger to dispense with holding a grudge.

Leaning back, the elder gent lowered his glass, breaking his gaze from his ungrateful guest he gently clinked the side of his glass with the other man's, who quickly stiffened up again. Taking a few steps back to his desk he half sat on one corner and offered a vague partial smile to break the tension. He then carried on.

"I would prefer it if you were to see me more as a guardian than... what was the term, oh yes, a cold war prescription; a guardian of our history, our culture and our influence. Take this chair," he gestured towards the old leather studded chair. "Before me this seemingly simple chair held the asses of admirals. Take this desk- before my computer graced its elegant leather inlay, civil servants of the highest grade signed some of the most important orders ever to pass on it.   My job is not to act a part in your fantasies, or mine for that matter, Robert. My job is to play a small, insignificant part in defending what is rightfully ours, what we have fought for and what we have won, irrelevant of borders."

On hearing his name Robert picked up again and replied.

"Tell me something Sir Adam, apart from providing your guests with excellent Scotch, do you also offer them the option to smoke?"

Sir Adam, as the title suggested displayed all the calm resolution of a British dignitary, a sense of superiority that left lesser men staring at their feet. However for one moment the calm seemed to break as Sir Adam started to grin at his guest. Looking down at him from his half seated position on the edge of his desk, Sir Adam played with a few observations. He knew Robert came from humble middle class stock and Sir Adam revelled in the chance to tease him about it. Robert wore an off the hanger suit, not fashioned by a Savile Row tailor as Sir Adam's was. In Sir Adam's eyes Robert needed merit, reward and recognition to feel accomplished, something Sir Adam was born with and as a side effect had no need for. Robert clearly despised the old school tie network, a network to which he clearly didn't belong. Sir Adam, detecting this hatred waved a finger and declared in a mocking tone,

"Smoking in a London office, what do you think this is, 1971? Look at the windows - five centimetres of bullet proof glass. Look at the walls- reinforced three feet thick. Look at the ceiling- solid. A bomb could go off next door and the light fixtures wouldn't even rattle, do you really think they'd build this place with a air vent to whisk away smoke or a window I could crack open for someone stupid enough to try and spark up a cigarette? You aren't doing much to impress upon me your reputation for being one of SIS's best intelligence directors."

There was a pause, Robert contemplated the fact that he had been stopped and searched before entering the room. In the process of being heavily frisked by two well built men, no doubt ex regiment boys, his pen, his wallet, his cigarettes and just about every other object in his pockets had been taken from him.

The Hacker Hunter © Copyright Lionwing Ltd 2011

He was surprised that they hadn't removed his belt and shoes as well. Robert knew that it was more likely that all his pockets had been emptied in an attempt to remove bugs or tracking devices rather than assassination weapons. Sir Adam was the man MI, Interpol, SIS and the NSA would turn to for help but be far too afraid to turn on. Sir Adam had made it into his seventies by removing the need for trust; Robert knew this only too well. Robert's track of thought changed to ponder why he had been called to this meeting and then back to wishing for a smoke, if for no other reason than for comfort.

"Churchill, Havana ok for you? One of the benefits of being a cold war cliché as you so elegantly put it. "

Sir Adam lifted a box from his desk, flipping it open he revealed the neatly packed row of finely rolled Havana cigars. Churchill, Cetros, Figurado, Toro, Nacionales, Petit, Monarca , all names used to define cigars. The idea of a cigar being named after a British wartime leader seemed to add more distain to Robert's view of Sir Adam's pomp. Robert reached into the box and picked out a cigar, rolling it between his fingers and thumb in appreciation. Robert suddenly stopped rolling, a look of questioning came across his face, he held the cigar at chest height and then pointed it at Sir Adam.

"Also one of the benefits of being the boss of the 'company' I dare say. A British limited liability company, otherwise known as an LTD. I've always found that rather amusing."

Robert made an attempt at a smile, his endeavour to make light mockery of the 'company' was clearly a sign of his gratitude for this soon to be smoked gift.

"What do you find amusing exactly Rob? The fact that a limited trading company registered with Companies House, England

and Wales, holds a limited liability rule of exemption for its directors' accountability and actions?"

As Sir Adam spoke he raised a lit flame from what looked like an old Zippo lighter but was in fact an old lighter he had taken from a German POW. The flame met with the end of Robert's cigar. The ends of the cigar had been pre cut, 'strange', thought Robert. Ordinarily that would be enough for him to put the cigar down for fear of the worst, but he knew that if Sir Adam wanted him dead, then dead he would be. So he decided to blow caution to the wind and inhale the first volley needed to fire up the end into glowing embers. A few puffs of white smoke were released into the air and then strangely vanished; there was clearly some sort of ventilation system at work. Robert look satisfied and reclined back into his seat, looking a lot more relaxed he replied to Sir Adam's statement.

"Limited liability rule for England and Wales? You mean the world. Any country can try to pursue a director of a British LTD for accountability but they will never succeed. Not if he's played by the book. Something you do very well, Sir. "

Sir Adam's facial expression didn't change.

"Tell me, Robert, how would you define artificial intelligence"?

Robert gave Sir Adam a smile. "Isn't that a question best directed to GCHQ, don't they use AI for their code cracking and threat assessment systems? For that matter, don't the Yanks use AI nowadays for logistical management of their troop supplies?"

"I'm asking you Robert." Sir Adam's tone became more aggressive.

The Hacker Hunter © Copyright Lionwing Ltd 2011

Robert took a few puffs from his cigar before answering "If I was to have a crack at defining artificial intelligence Sir Adam, I would have to say that it was the ability to teach a machine to teach itself. "

"Good answer Robert, but wrong. Let me tell you. AI is defined as the ability for a computer to guess. "

Robert, clearly in the mood for a lighter conversation to enjoy his cigar and Scotch with, replied, "A guessing computer, I'd prefer a computer that didn't need to guess but in fact got it right. After all, isn't that what computers are meant to do? "

Sir Adam took a moment to light his own cigar and then replied "Dr. Hanns, a Doctor of mathematics and a Doctor of Physics no less developed some of the earliest AI systems for British missile technology. In the early days it was simple: a missile would recognise heat coming from an aircraft engine and simply follow it to a point where it was close enough to detonate and in doing so destroy the aircraft. "

"Did your Dr. Hanns develop that? " Robert asked.

Sir Adam looked into his glass and took a sip, the cool Scotch gave a moment's bitter pleasure and then Sir Adam rebuffed "The British military definition of AI was set by the good doctor, a definition that is now being repeated by a civilian trading under the company name of Christian Cannon Ltd."

"Don't tell me there's more than one 'British Limited Liability Company' out there - whatever next! " Robert announced mockingly.

Ignoring Robert's remark Sir Adam continued "Mr. Cannon has a small company speculating in AI research and development.

He's claiming a tax uplift of 150% for R & D costs, though from what we can see there's been no real R & D. Yet he's coming up with formula. "

"What on earth are you on about R & D, Formula?"

With a look of annoyance Sir Adam began to explain "Do try and join the dots. R & D or research and development is classified as an 'expense' that allows British companies a tax benefit, reducing their corporation tax bill. "

"You can't blame a man for trying to get out of paying tax, that's the capitalist way isn't it?" interjected Robert.

"Yes, yes. But our translator friends at GCHQ tell us that he has no R & D going on, just formula. " Sir Adam paused long enough for Robert to ask "There it is again, the magic word: formula?"

"Formula," Sir Adam shouted, "Formula is the term used to describe the end result of R & D."

In retaliation to Sir Adam's raised voice Robert reverted back to his previous disgruntled state and replied "Cut the crap, you invited me- explain what you are going on about and then explain what it has to do with the British Secret Police, I have fucking work to do!"

Sir Adam seemed to take Robert's point and calmly said "If Mr. Cannon has formula but no R & D documentation to back it up, it means he's stealing it."

"From us?" Asked Robert, who was now extremely interested and sat upright in anticipation.
"No, worse - from the Russians."

The Hacker Hunter © Copyright Lionwing Ltd 2011

Chapter 2 – Moscow Mind School

The fingertips of an outstretched hand came to rest on the surface of a door. The light blue paint of the door had not changed in colour since the institute was first opened in the Fifties. Every year a fresh coat of the same paint was routinely applied. These annual layers had built up over time, accumulating to form small fissures and valleys on the surface. The pale, bony fingers brushed over this unintended texture, savouring the random pattern built up from by the accretion of fifty years' routine; ironic chaos formed out of strict orderly work. Each fingernail had been clipped short; the few hairs on each finger were coated in a white powder of the kind found in surgical gloves. Perhaps the owner of these fingers was savouring the sense of touch after having been in gloves for so long or perhaps this seemingly odd appreciation was simply reluctance towards pushing the door open.

The hand flinched, obviously a decision to push had been reached and a moment later the door slowly swung inward. The figure of a young man, perhaps no older than twenty three, was revealed. He sat slumped on a toilet. The young man's gaze was lost in contemplation, his face showed an expression of pure defeat. Without even attempting eye contact with the intruder he addressed him in a dreary, distant manner.

"Why do the doors never have locks?"

"I think the real question is why the Institute doesn't have a single toilet seat," replied the intruder.

Looking as if he was about to vomit the young man leaned forward.

"Leave me alone Oleg," he muttered in a familiar manner.

The familiar intimacy in which his name had been spoken was enough for Oleg to interpret the statement as an invitation to step into the cubical. It had not escaped Oleg's attention that the tiled white walls and the white floor seemed to merge with the white colour of his lab suit. If it were not for the grime, the oddity of his surroundings would have slightly unhinged his senses. However, Oleg's contemplation of his environment was short lived. The seated man slumped forward, prompting Oleg to speak again.

"Listen, we always knew this might happen. Let's get you some tea." Oleg's friendly offer had no effect, looking less assured he persisted. "Come on Alex, you need to come back before anyone notices. Please, I'm begging you."

The young man responded to his name with a gentle rocking back and forth motion, his leg trembling like a man whose nerves had been totally shattered. He covered his eyes and frantically rubbed at them with the palms of his hands. The rocking stopped abruptly and even more suddenly Alex tore his hands from his face, revealing blood shot eyes that glared with rage.

"It's wrong!" screamed Alex "It is wrong!" he repeated.

On hearing this unexpected and very sudden blast of anger Oleg straightened his stance. He reached for the door and rapidly closed it behind him. With a deeply concerned look Oleg whispered, "It's too early to say that. We haven't accurately identified anything. Now come on, let's get you out of here and sat down with a nice tea before we both get into trouble."

The closed toilet door seemed to provide more intimacy between the men, an intimacy that both felt comfortable with. They had obviously been friends for a considerable number of years. The gesture Oleg had made by sealing himself into the cubical with Alex seemed to relax both parties. Just for that moment calmness passed over Alex's face, he took a deep breath inward causing him to straighten his back. As he held the breath for a few moments his previous defeated posture was all but forgotten. Holding the breath still longer, almost to signify the huge effort needed to contain his concerns Alex started to look less calm. Gradually releasing the air from his lungs with a sigh Alex looked up and firmly established eye contact with Oleg before softly speaking out.

"What are we doing? Do we really know?"

Not even stopping for a second Oleg responded.

"This is important work. Artificial intelligence has many applications, some life saving, you know that Alex."

With equal rapidity Alex rebuffed him, "It's not artificial though is it? Not anymore, not – any – more…"

Alex's teeth had become clenched, it was clear to see that his emotions had run riot to a point where he was exceedingly unstable. Oleg, becoming agitated by his friend's erratic behaviour, leant forward to place his face only a hand's distance from Alex's.

"Control yourself Khomenko my friend. Of course it's artificial: we grew it. Come on."

It was more than evident to Oleg that any attempt to get Alex back to work would be a futile gesture. Oleg knew that Alex's

The Hacker Hunter © Copyright Lionwing Ltd 2011

special kind of genius could see through any mental trickery he might try to use to lure him out. Very secretly, Oleg envied Alex's ability to remain cool and calculative. Alex's amazing gifts had won him a scholarship all the way from the Crimea to the Moscow Institute. However, in Oleg's eyes those gifts were now truly diminished, cool and calculative had been replaced with agitated and frenzied. Oleg had often contemplated the well used phrase that claims madness and genius are only separated by success; he had never really understood it until now. Looking down at Alex sitting there, all confused, was extremely upsetting. Their friendship meant a lot to Oleg but Oleg kept thinking of what would happen to him if he joined Alex's protests. The risk was too great. Oleg knew that no amount of genius would spare you if you were labelled a subversive. A split second before Oleg was about to react to his thoughts Alex spoke up once again.

"It's human. Why do you insist in using the term artificial?"

Stopping for a momentary submissive glance down at the white floor tiles, Alex then looked back up at Oleg's round face and continued.

"Yes we grew it Oleg. We fucking grew it from human cells…" he stopped momentarily to put his hands over his eyes then continued.

"What we saw, what has happened, it's not natural but it's not artificial either."

Alex had unintentionally spat as he spoke. His passion had left him looking quite insane. As he wiped the spittle from his own mouth and chin it was becoming very clear to Oleg that his friend's mind had collided with something so unacceptable that any form of reason would be met with an irrational outburst of emotion. It would surely just be a matter of time before they were discovered. Oleg lent back, moving his face away from Alex's in a gesture that clearly stated that their friendship was being stretched uncomfortably. With this new distance Oleg's face softened. In an attempt at a final rescue Oleg remarked,

"For years we have been working on ways to record and retrieve data chemically within brain tissue. The brain has limitless memory storage and infinitely more processing power than any man-made computer. We've done it Alex, you should be proud of what you have achieved."

Recognising his friend's attempts to calm him Alex, mulled over Oleg's words for a few long seconds and then replied, "Will mother Russia thank me Oleg? Will it thank me for working out a way to take a human brain, a brain that you have learnt to grow so well and turn it into an abomination?"

Growing weary of Alex's manic mood Oleg snapped back.

"These brains are not human, it's just brain tissue, not an actual human brain. Look, it's all just chemistry and physics, we have had the ability to convert digital data into chemical signatures and convert chemical signatures to digital data for years; we just didn't have the ability to create an absorption algorithm, until you came along. Alex, you've done it my friend we should be celebrating!"

Looking suddenly more focused, Alex replied "Oleg stop for one moment and think about what just happened. You know my algorithm was designed to mimic intelligence or at least allow the software to follow threads and build associations independently." Alex suddenly stopped talking, his stare drifted to the back of the closed door, his mind obviously reflecting on some deeply troubling mystery. In a slower, slightly removed

The Hacker Hunter © Copyright Lionwing Ltd 2011

voice Alex continued, "Software is just software. Something else is at play, something we didn't take into consideration."

"We don't know what happened," Oleg shouted in fleeting annoyance.

Oleg's unexpected reaction caused Alex to become instantly focused, his now undivided attention snapped back to Oleg and with a tone of professionalism in his voice Alex said, "We were testing it like a rat in a maze, simple choices: follow this content thread and connect it to that content thread. Why the fuck did the professor let it out of the maze?"

Oleg, clearly growing more concerned that at any minute someone may walk into the lavatories and happen to overhear their conversation replied hastily in a desperate attempt to conclude the conversation.

"It had to happen at some point Alex. We wanted to see what it did with the network."

"The internet is a bit more than a network Oleg."

Oleg seemed to become even more agitated, turning half his body towards the door in a gesture to Alex that he was getting ready to leave he then continued in a half whisper, "Seventy six hours Alex. For seventy six hours, every phone line from here to China was crackling it used so much bandwidth."

For the first time Alex smiled, seemingly to reassure, then he replied in an equally loud whisper, "Indexing the net in seventy six hours is not what I'm talking about Oleg. You know what I'm talking about! We have to stop."

The definitive tone of Alex's statement made Oleg turn the rest of his body towards the door, this time with his back to Alex he placed his hand on the handle poised to open and said in a stern tone, "Shut up. Shut up before you get us into serious trouble, I can't follow you Alex. You're expendable now. Don't you see - we have all just become expendable."

Desperate to win Oleg's support Alex reached out to his friend, clenching his arm.

"It's only just happened Oleg, we can stop it, we should before it's too late, it's wrong, it's wrong, you must know that!"

Oleg pulled his arm away from Alex's grip and pulled the door, as it swung back into the cubical Oleg moved his body to one side to let it pass. He paused, refusing Alex eye contact Oleg and softly said, "It's a glitch Alex, before you do anything just wait. We'll run the experiment again in the morning, and you'll see, there's nothing to worry about. "

Alex, still seated, replied with a desperate snarl, his mood reverting back to its more aggressive posture "Nothing to... When an artificially grown brain downloads the internet and then fills up fifteen grams of tissue memory with the same data there is something to worry about! Believe me Oleg, there is something to worry about!"

"Alex, fifteen grams of memory repeated the same data over and over again doesn't mean a thing, granted it's a little odd that it's still growing..."

Cutting Oleg off in mid sentence, Alex interrupted with, "It's not data Oleg, it's a fucking question, 'what am I?', 'what am I?', 'what am I?', repeating over and over again. It's asking a fucking question!"

The Hacker Hunter © Copyright Lionwing Ltd 2011

Chapter 3 – Cannon in Manhattan

The tip of a well tanned male finger pressed itself flat against the window pane. A voice asked "If I were to be trapped here, fourteen floors up, with no chance of escape and the building was burning, how could I survive?" The finger peeled back from the surface of the cool glass leaving behind the greasy relief of a print. "I mean, if I were to learn how to parachute, could I simply throw a chair through the window and jump with a chute?" The reflection of a face belonging to a Hispanic male, mid thirties loomed up behind the finger print and carried on to say "I mean would the chute open in time as I fell fourteen floors?" The mouth of the reflected face opened to blow a hot breath that blew over the glass leaving a cloud of condensation that whitened out everything save the finger print. "Could I even smash through the glass of one of these windows?" The Hispanic man suddenly stopped talking as he caught the appearance in his peripheral vision of a second reflection, a reflection of a dark figure moving closer towards him. Electing to remain transfixed on his finger print the man asked one more question. "The reflection of your dark figure, Mr. Cannon, leads me to believe you are about to walk out?"

The figure stopped in his tracks "Lewis, my dear little Inca, if you are going to persist in waffling on I am going to leave, buy a parachute, come back, strap it to your back and throw you through that grubby window."

Lewis turned to face Mr. Christian Cannon Esq. As he turned he stopped to observe his opponent's British white complexion, dark hair, blue eyes, rugged but charmed face and strangely graceful rugby player's build.

"Tell me something Mr. Cannon, how did a limey, rat bastard, private school boy in his mid thirties think for one moment that he could get away with calling me an Inca?"

"I would think it entirely excusable given the fact that you are a big poof and take your pleasures in life from playing with men's bums", Christian retorted.

"Let me get this right Cannon. Are you calling me a Gay Little Inca?" Lewis asked, now posturing for a fight.

"Oh I'm sorry Lewis, you have me all wrong," Christian replied in a mocking attempt at an American accent. Flipping back to his Oxbridge English, Cannon then sharply continued.

"What I meant to say My Dear Little Gaylord Inca Bum Bandit was why don't you call down to reception and ask them if they've managed to get us a table at Ben Benson's?"

Lewis' eyes filled with playfulness. It was clear that this barrage of British charm and Celtic aggression was part and parcel of their friendship. To avoid a return to conflict, no matter how playful, Cannon broke eye contact with Lewis to address a third person in the room, a lady, sat waiting expectantly.

"I'm sorry Maria, why do we have to wait for your father before going any further? Surely that only applies if I'm going to ask for your hand in marriage?"

He smiled at her zestfully, the sharp English accent that he spoke with reflected a private education that was as Cambridge blue as his eyes. The blonde lady pushed her lined note pad to one side so she could place both elbows on the board room table; she then created a cradle with her hands and rested her chin on them. She looked at Cannon flirtatiously, fluttering her

The Hacker Hunter © Copyright Lionwing Ltd 2011

eyelashes. He was not immune to this flirtation, it was clear she offered experience over the beauty of youth. The delights that this lady could bring a man seemed to be hinted at in her voice as she said, "He likes to meet everyone I do business with. He will be here, just wait a little longer."

Lewis, feeling an urge to break the chemistry interrupted.

"All due respect Maria, but we are not doing this deal with your pappy, if we are to reach any agreement it will be with you."

On hearing her name Maria turned her gaze from her counterpart to face Lewis; she lifted her head from the cradle of her hands and took both her elbows from the table. Straightening in an attempt to face Lewis on an equal fronting she replied.

"Papa will not let me do business of this nature before he has met you both. It's his money as much as mine."

Lewis shot an impatient look over to Cannon, as if to invite him to respond to Maria's comment but Christian's cold blue eyes just remained fixated on Maria, as if there were no other person but her in the room. Lewis looked back at Maria.

"Maria, I would not mind but we have been waiting for forty five minutes, we've got the idea of what you need, can we just get down to talking about the price? What do you have in mind?"

Maria could see that Lewis was starting to lose his cool so she replied

"The price is 800,000, payment after the contracts with the NSA have been signed and we have a below radar outsourcing

The Hacker Hunter © Copyright Lionwing Ltd 2011

agreement tied up between our companies." Lewis was about to reply but Cannon beat him to it.

"Thank you, that is a very generous offer, I do find it rather uncomfortable talking about money. Strange, but I find it somewhat vulgar. Needless to say people must be paid and so on, I'll need 920,000 - the extra 120k is to capture and then smuggle one of them into the country."

"Sorry, one of whom?" asked Maria in an extremely puzzled manner.

"One of the hackers."

Cannon paused for a few moments, waiting to see if anyone else felt like speaking but soon realised they were all looking rather bewildered, if not totally speechless he continued, "My good lady, the likelihood of your beloved NSA doing a deal with me will improve massively when I bring them one of the 52 hackers you've discovered. I would imagine the NSA would like to chat with whomever I decide to bring them about just who they've been selling their top most secrets to, would you not agree?"

Maria placed her hands on the table, both palms down, she replied firmly.

"That's not the deal Christian. All I'm paying for is for you to front the operation and bring in the cleanup contract. I'll put together the report and the proposal, you front it and make out it's all you. You are the perfect front man for the deal, you're in the same line of work and your family name has a record of credibility with the NSA. They will listen to you; there is no way I'll even be considered with my family background!"

The Hacker Hunter © Copyright Lionwing Ltd 2011

Upon hearing his first name, Christian Cannon walked closer towards Lewis, keeping eye contact with Maria, Cannon asked with a measure of mocking, "Let me get this right, you are asking me to use the name of my father and his father and their exemplary British service records, plus the good name of my American family all just to get you a deal with the National Security Agency. A deal where I point out to them, in no uncertain terms that the reason they can't capture any big bad terrorists is because their entire planning and Intel is being sold by any one of the 52 hackers you've found hacked into their 'ever-so-secure' network?"

Maria cracked a smile and then winked at Christian.

"That's pretty much the plan, I'd do it myself but I'd never get past the contractors screening because of my papa," she said.

Lewis, picking up on the playful flirtation, interrupted with, "Your pappy, the man we've been waiting for, other than bad time keeping what else might he have done to give you such scope for concern when applying for a government contract?"

Maria turned her attention back to Lewis, her smile dropping to indicate that although she was having a little fun with Cannon she was still a professional when she needed to be. Attempting to contain a darker side to her personality she softly spoke.

"My pappy, as you call him, had been accused of seventeen felonies, acquitted of all but we know how a man's name can be tarnished by such things."

Lewis went pale, looking at Cannon for reassurance and then back to Maria he asked

"Maria, is your papa in the family business?"

The Hacker Hunter © Copyright Lionwing Ltd 2011

"If by family Lewis you mean restaurants, building, logistics including shipping and not forgetting real-estate and security, then yes." She winced and then looked away.

"I meant..." but before Lewis could finish Cannon interrupted.

"I think what my good man Louie means to ask my dear lady, is, well how to put this... is Daddy a Mafia boss? Sorry to be so abrupt."

Maria looked at Christian and passed him a naughty smile, the sort of smile that draws a man in closer then he dares venture. The smile broke as she opened her mouth, the red lipstick glistening. Lewis and Christian were under her spell as she said half jokingly, "I'll let my Daddy talk for himself when he comes."

Lewis was the first to shake off her charms. He'd always been a family man, and no one was more beautiful to him than his first college love and now wife and mother of their four children. Taking a breath to draw his thoughts together he then recited from memory, "Ok let's recap. You want my business partner, one Mr. Christian Cannon of London England, to front a deal with the NSA on your behalf because you come from the MOB and fear that the NSA might hold that against you when dishing out security passes!"

Lewis then turned to Christian and in an annoyed tone raised his voice to say

"No-way, we are not doing this Chris, not for $800k, not even for $920k!"

Maria lifted a hand as if she had an answer for a school teacher, seeing she has both the men's attention she lowered her hand and confidently said, "Lewis, I'm sorry I assumed because Christian was British we were talking about British Pounds Sterling, I might be mistaken as I'm not sure of today's exchange rate but in USD the fee is actually $1.3 million." Without even pausing for breath she continued, "Christian could you please explain to me why you think bringing the NSA one of the hackers will help? I'm not getting it."

Grateful for the chance to explain, Cannon walked from Lewis to Maria's seat, he placed his hands on the back of her chair and then turned the chair so she was facing him. He smiled at her reassuringly and announced with absolute confidence, "If my company issues your report to the NSA with a view to winning a cleanup contract the Agency will firstly ask how we found these 52 hackers. Maria, the reason you're not fronting this deal with your government is because they would tear through your office quicker than a lion through a porterhouse steak. I'd imagine in the process they'd probably find out about all the not so legal jobs you've been doing for Daddy. Would I be wrong in making such an assumption?"

Looking up at Christian Maria's eyes filled with playfulness, there was something about this man. She knew he would be a lot of fun whilst it lasted, but things were rarely so uncomplicated. She placed a hand on each armrest and then pushed herself out of the seat. If Mr. Cannon was going to walk around the meeting room so was she.

"Christian or Chris which is it?" she asked.

"Chris, Christian, just don't call me Cannon, makes me feel like someone from a 1970's TV cop show."

The Hacker Hunter © Copyright Lionwing Ltd 2011

"Like I said Chris, why do you want to capture and bring one of the hackers, into the States?"

It was clear that Maria wasn't going to let the question go and Christian had no intention of keeping it a secret.

"Simply because, Maria, a list of who's hacking the NSA and where they can be found is worth ten times more than just helping them sort out their firewall issues. I have an acquaintance, a lord no less, who runs a company in London, just off the Strand; he has some sway with your NSA. I'll ask him to help me broker the deal before I turn up on their doorstep, his fee is usually £80k or so, which leaves me £40k for expenses."

"Ha! Expenses, is that what you're calling it, ok £920k it is, but I want the names and locations of each hacker," Maria demanded.

Cannon put his hand to his mouth, contemplating for a second the many issues that might arise from such an agreement, he removed his hand and with an untrusting smile replied, "Maria, those hackers would be worth a lot to your fathers' organisation, can I be confident that we can trust you with them?"

"That doesn't sound like someone who's in it for the short game…" asked Maria curiously.

Lewis, realising that this would now be a good time to conclude their business with Maria, interjected.

"Listen you can have the names and addresses plus the cleanup contract, Chris and I are purely in it for the short game. We'll need a cash advance of 10% and a further wire deposit of 50%, payable to a British research company based in Venice, Italy."

"Are you kidding me? Sixty per cent up front!" Maria snarled reluctantly.

Cannon, knowing that the deal was done, returned a naughty, flirtatious smile back at Maria and in a calm, precise manner finished the conversation.

"I'll be in Venice next Thursday, let's agree to meet under the Griffin, St. Marks, 8pm. Bring the cash and your father if you must, though I'm sure we would have a lot more fun without him. Lewis will e-mail the company account details for the deposit. Come on Lewis, our business is concluded, I'll treat you to lunch at Ben's."

Lewis opened the boardroom door for Maria, "I'll see you in Venice Chris, I don't think I need my Daddy for that." She winked and walked out.

Lewis turned to Cannon and asked, "Who's this Lord?"

"You mean Sir Adam. He's a chap I met last year, runs some sort of security business, wants to be my mentor no-less, thinks I have potential as a future employee of his company. I told him that I lacked the moral fibre. My exact words were 'give me a suitcase of cash and a hot chick and I'd tell anyone anything'. Still he's been rather helpful."

Lewis laughed, "Mentor! You need a fucking shrink not a mentor. Come on you stuck up limey bastard I'll buy lunch!"

Chapter 4 – Mac

The long, bony fingers of an aging hand swept through the bristles of a moustache. Flecks of black and grey hair ruffled as the index finger and thumb squeezed and released each side of the mouth repeatedly. This grooming action was obviously part of some contemplative routine so ingrained that the moustache almost seemed designed purely for this purpose. Hung across the top lip and then grown down either side of the mouth to the chin, some might call its style Viking like in appearance, others may call it Celtic or more akin to the era of the ancient Gauls than the 21st Century but there was no mistaking this moustache was the mark of a time tested and well worn warrior.

The hand stopped in motion, the index finger and thumb frozen over each side of the bristly mouth, and then two words were muttered "Magic, ish". Leaving the face the hand reached down, the blistering hot sun highlighting each notch and scar cut into the tanned flesh. Eventually the hand came down to rest on the sandy surface of a dusty white rock, the rock no bigger than a shoe box and similar in shape was dry to the touch, dry like a bone. A second hand came down to help raise the rock to an inspecting eye, the eye was sharp blue, a black pin hole for a pupil and a piercing glare with an intensity that was only shared with nature's most formidable predators.

"You are perfect," muttered the same voice. The Scottish Stirlingshire accent remained very detectable. "Perfect, come on, you're coming home with me." Cradling the rock an older but athletically built man, late 50's, short grey black hair, 5' 10" tall started his descent off the side of an incredibly steep Greek rock face.

Thirty minutes later and the white dust from the parched rocky ground was swirling around the same figure as he marched with triumphant vigour towards a modest sized villa built on an outcrop overlooking the Gulf of Corinth. He reached the south facing wall, a wall made from solid concrete disguised behind an outer wall of well placed local rock. The rock wall was all but complete save for a gap, just about the same size as the white rock being cradled by the man. Reaching up he placed the rock into the gap and spoke aloud once more, "Let's get you fastened in and then I'd say we are just about finished." He took a few steps back, looked at the south face of this lovingly built villa, his eyes danced over the two wide glass doors with natural wooden frames, shuttered windows and an outer wall of local rock, every stone handpicked. The man took a deep breath in, seemingly inhaling the full ambiance of the stunning visual effect of the backdrop of mountains. Turning around he faced out to the waterfront. The wind lifts slightly to provide him a second or two of relief from the scorching heat. "Right that's enough work for the day, time for a cool beer," he mumbled to nobody but himself.

A moment later he was jogging down the side of the hill towards a beach. Just wading distance out from the beech was a solitary fishing boat, he didn't slow down when he reached the white sand but instead picked up pace as he stepped into the water. A hop and a jump and a few splashes later and he was throwing a leg and arm up over the side of the boat to pull himself in. Leaning back over and looking into a net hung over one side he muttered, "They should be nice and cool by now." As he pulled the net up into the boat, six cool glass bottles of beer were revealed, they'd been woven into the net and submersed in the cool blue water, chilled to perfection.

The sun dropped to the horizon, the few cool beers, and the now cooler air combined with the gentle rocking motion of the boat

The Hacker Hunter © Copyright Lionwing Ltd 2011

to form the perfect environment for sleep. As his tired eyes closed and the sharp chiselled features of his face relaxed, the man muttered once more, "Magic." He slipped into sleep.

A few hours later, larger more aggressive waves started to lap at the side of the boat. These waves were caused by the wake of another passing boat, slightly bigger in size and carrying four well built men. "John Mac!" shouted out a new voice, "John Mac!" it repeated. "Mac, my name is Robert, the company sent me." The passing boat turned back around towards the small fishing boat and came to rest alongside. Robert peered into the small cockpit and then turned to his own skipper.

"He's not here. You said a Scottish man, late fifties, Viking moustache: would be on his boat. So where is he?"

He stepped off his boat and onto the small fishing boat. "A few empty bottles of beer, nothing… we've been going up and down the Gulf of Corinth for three days. Sir Adam will just have to find someone else," stated Robert defiantly.

The sound of three loud splashes coming from the direction of the boat that Robert had arrived on caused him to turn rapidly. He could see the skipper and the two accompanying men splashing around in the water. Looking down to the cabin he could just make out Mac's sharp face and moustache behind the wheel. Mac pushed the throttle all the way forward, the sudden roar from the engines came first and then the front lifted. As Robert's boat accelerated away a huge bow wave followed, tilting the small fishing boat violently. Robert lost his footing and fell face first onto the deck of the small cabin house. As he lay there he saw a small, black walky-talky, on it was a folded sheet of paper. Robert slowly unwrapped the paper, revealing letters written in a dark leaded builder's pencil. The word spelt out "BOOM!"

Just then the speaker of the walky-talky crackled and hissed as a softly spoken Scottish voice announced "What do you want?"

Robert picked up the walky-talky, pressed the transmit button and said with no uncertainty in his voice "Mac bring back that fucking boat."

As Robert staggered to his feet and looked out of the cabin. He saw two of his security detail treading water but the skipper had started swimming towards him.

"Mac, bring back the boat, we need to talk. Sir Adam sent me," Robert said in a tethered tone.

Mac replied with "I know who sent you; if you want to live I'm going to ask you four questions. If you give me more than four replies that are anything other than the truth, you die. Are we clear?"

Robert ducked down in the cabin in an attempt to find cover, Mac would need a sniper rifle to take him out given the current distance between the boats, all the same, Robert wasn't taking any chances.

"Just how the fuck do you intend on killing me Mac, when you are heading off in the opposite direction?"

Mac replied in a very calm voice "That's one chance used up Rob. You get three more chances to speak. Answer this: what's a SIS boy doing Sir Adam's dirty work for?"

Robert looked dumbfounded, the idea of Mac knowing who he was and who he worked for unnerved him. Shaking it off Robert

The Hacker Hunter © Copyright Lionwing Ltd 2011

replied "Sir Adam said that you were about the only man we could trust to do a certain type of job."

"Stop. What's the job, where's the job and what's the compensational package?" Mac asked in an ordering voice.

"Seek and retrieve, Russia, 2.8 million Swiss," Robert said.

"Put the walky-talky down and don't say another word, not one fucking word, I'm coming back around for you." The seriousness in Mac's voice was enough for Robert to follow his exact instructions. It had just dawned on Robert that the words 'BOOM' must have meant Mac had the boat rigged to blow-up.

Robert suddenly felt the small boat rock again. He peered out of the cabin to see his skipper climbing in to join him. The skipper looked irate, with a furious high pitch to his voice the skipper shouted, "No-one throws me out of my own boat, thinks he's a tough guy does he!"

Reaching down for the walky-talky the skipper pressed the transmit button and continued to shout.

"I'm glad you're coming back, it gives me a chance to fuck you up!"

Robert was instantly hit with a blast of hot air that seemed to punch his entire body back into the cabin. Along with this blast came a tingling, splattering sensation as sharp bits of skull, hand bones, brain, and human meat impacted with his clothes and bare face. Robert, now unable to see, felt a warm spray of bloody fluid drench over him. Winded, confused and blinded he spat out what he could only imagine to be bits of brain. He lifted his hands to his face and started clawing bits of nose, ear and cheek from his eyes, feeling his face in the process it started to

The Hacker Hunter © Copyright Lionwing Ltd 2011

dawn on him that these bits of face that he was pulling away didn't actually belong to him. Robert managed to clear enough bloody gunk from his eyes to make out the headless figure of the skipper, miraculously still standing. Robert strained to look more clearly, he couldn't believe his eyes. Blood sprayed from the stump of the skipper's neck, there was no sign of his head, no sign of his arm, the same arm that only a second ago had held the walky-talky. The knees of the skipper's remaining body went first, buckling to cause what remained of the body to fall over the side of the boat. Robert could barely hear or register Mac as he stepped back onto his fishing boat.

"Like I said, no more than four replies."

"I just did three," blurted out a teary Robert.

"No mate, you did four, starting with 'bring back the boat'. The walky-talky was rigged to detonate on the release of the fifth click on the transmit button. Tell Sir Fucking Adam that I want 3 million Swiss to make up for the fucking brain mess he's created in my boat!"

Robert, unable to put any intelligent reply together simply stuttered out, "What, I can't, what, no, who the fuck are you?"

"Call me Mac. You were looking for me I believe?"

The Hacker Hunter © Copyright Lionwing Ltd 2011

Chapter 5 – Cannon and the Company

Sir Adam pressed the tips of his long, bony, fingers together to form an arch. He leaned back in his brown leather and oak, upholstered office chair, raising the arch of his fingers to his pursed lips and looking over at Robert.

"You really messed up in Greece Robert. No wonder you boys come to us to get the important jobs done."

Sir Adam stared Robert straight in the eye, with a look as cold as stone. Robert shuffled around in his seat.

"Has Mac been briefed?" Robert asked trying to break the tension.

Sir Adam remained silent. He continued to stare at Robert with the look turning to one of utter disdain. Robert bleated out, "Look, Sir Adam, SIS wants that list and GCHQ wants whoever Cannon is getting the AI code from,. You just do your bit for Queen and Country like a good Knight of the Realm. We will keep up our end, don't you worry about that."

Sir Adam broke apart the arch formed by his fingers and placed each of his hands down onto the leather surface of his oak desk. He slowly slid his right hand across the top of the desk to the edge, not breaking eye contact with Robert for one moment. Robert uneasily observed Sir Adam lift his hand from the corner of the desk and reach down to pull open a desk draw. The uncomfortable uncertainty caused Robert to mutter out

"That list can never reach the Americans. Do you understand why?"

The Hacker Hunter © Copyright Lionwing Ltd 2011

Sir Adam looked down, momentarily breaking eye contact; he fumbled around and then pulled from the open draw a small metallic silver radio, just slightly bigger than a packet of cigarettes. Robert breathed a sigh of relief, on hearing the sigh Sir Adam looked back up at Robert's pale face.

"Oh I'm sorry Robert, how very inconsiderate of me. I'd imagine after what you went through with Mac you might be a little nervous of this radio. Don't worry I can assure you this one will not blow up." Sir Adam chuckled and then carried on to say "Not even I am allowed to blow up a SIS director, no matter how much of a saving it affords the Tax payer."

Sir Adam lifted the radio up and down, seemingly to assess its weight. In a less mocking tone Sir Adam continued to speak.

"I understand, only too well, that if a list of the people who have hacked into the NSA network fell into the hands of our American cousins it would result in utter pandemonium. Especially given that two of the hackers would be recognised as Military Intelligence and Civil Intelligence. The thought of allies spying on each other wouldn't help the NSA's 'special relationship' with GCHQ, would it?"

Robert stood up, he walked to the window and half gazed out, casting a wary eye towards the still seated Sir Adam, he retorted

"The NSA would do their nut. It's a good bloody thing that list doesn't exist yet. If Cannon manages to get those names he'll need to be stopped from giving them to the Yanks!"

Sir Adam, now looking more relaxed, broke a semi smile, he leaned back into his seat and replied;

The Hacker Hunter © Copyright Lionwing Ltd 2011

"I'd be more interested in learning how Cannon managed to get the names."

"What do you mean?" asked Robert.

"Look at all the pieces. Cannon runs a research and development company, he's got advanced artificial intelligence software with no real research notes to back it up. His AI software is so advanced that GCHQ are considering adding it to their code cracking arsenal. Cannon is constantly in and out of Russia, Oman, America and the UK and according to the Inland Revenue he earns about £600 a month, yet he has a flat in London, Moscow and New York! He must have someone in Russia who's leaking top governmental research. GCHQ want to know who, and they are right to ask."

Sir Adam placed the small silver radio into the right pocket of his suit jacket, straightening himself up and then shuffling forward in the process bringing his chair closer toward his desk before continuing.

"Cannon either has someone who has access to the material or he has someone who is creating it."

Robert turned to face Sir Adam. He looked mesmerised by what had just been said.

"Tell me Sir Adam, how the fuck did you find out about this man, Cannon?"

Sir Adam looked at Robert distastefully, it was clear that Sir Adam disapproved of using vulgar language, choosing to ignore Robert's abrasive questioning method Sir Adam responded with "Well his passport activity and low income tax flagged up all the red lights, but it was one of our men working in American

Intelligence, Moscow branch, who really brought Cannon to our attention. Turns out someone close to Cannon sold him out." Sir Adam shrugged as if he felt a certain amount of sympathy for Cannon and then continued, "The saddest thing is Cannon doesn't even know he's about to walk straight into the Americans' trap."

Robert shouted out "What?" but before he could say anything more Sir Adam's phone buzzed loudly. Sir Adam picked up the telephone receiver and spoke softly

"Yes Grace, no, no, where did he park? Ok, yes that's fine, send him up, oh before you do remove the boys from outside my door, I don't want him getting the wrong impression, oh and Grace, no calls for the rest of the afternoon, and get Mac a bike."

Sir Adam placed the telephone receiver back down and looks across at Robert who was still frozen in time with a mortified expression.

"For goodness sake man, pull yourself together; Cannon will be here any moment, just remember who you are meant to be. Play your part!" Sir Adam ordered.

There was a playful knock at the door. Robert sensed that Sir Adam seemed to become more alive, the room filled with an atmosphere of good-humoured excitement, there was a second knock.

"Come in Christian," beckoned Sir Adam, his voice lifted with an altogether more playful tone. As the door began to swing open, Robert struggled to force a greeting smile, his mind still racked with unanswered questions and the escalating fear that American Intelligence might get the list off Cannon before Sir Adam managed to. As the door fully opened, the tall, stocky figure of Christian Cannon stood there, dressed head to toe like a motorcycle dispatch rider and clutching a crash helmet.

"Excuse my attire Frank, I thought I'd bring the bike into town, traffic is a bugger on the Strand this time of day," Christian proclaimed whilst acknowledging Robert with a nod.

Robert's face changed back to looking totally perplexed, he had expected someone altogether different in appearance and attire. The man who stood before him looked more like a rugby player than a managing director, let alone a managing director of an R & D company specialising in AI. Robert's bewilderment was further compounded by the fact that Cannon seemed to be on first name terms with Sir Adam.

"Please come in and sit down Christian. Drink? Have you met Robert before?" asked Sir Adam.

"No I don't believe we've met. Hello Robert." Christian walked into the room and extended a hand.

Robert took Christian's hand and gripped it tightly, Christian didn't really squeeze Roberts hand in return but instead held onto it, using Robert to keep his balance as he started to work down his waterproof trousers. Cannon finally worked his waterproofs down to his ankles via a series of stamping actions, then passed Robert back his hand and said with a beaming smile

"Thanks for that, I was told once that men who elect to grip hands and squeeze hard are incredibly insecure about their manhood, the more confident the man the less they squeeze."

Robert could not contain the look of shock created by Christian's out spoken statement and the shock was compiled with annoyance caused by this perfect stranger using him as an

The Hacker Hunter © Copyright Lionwing Ltd 2011

aid to undressing. Before Robert could say a word Sir Adam interrupted, "Thanks for coming over, look before we head down to the Adam Street Club for lunch I've some business you might be interested in." Sir Adam nodded towards Robert and said "Robert here is a retired Scotland Yard intelligence officer. He's interested in hiring someone with your skills and network to put together a security proposal, nothing big, just testing a tagging system to keep bent Financial Directors in check."

"What's the idea Robert?" asked Christian.

Robert swallowed hard in an attempt to diminish his aggravated state, the recent events and over familiarity of Christian Cannon had obviously started to play on his nerves. Relaxing slightly Robert blurted out his well rehearsed lines.

"Bent FD's, as Sir Adam puts it, are one of the biggest problems facing the city today; we want to introduce a due-diligence service that offers anyone recruiting an FD the chance to do a proper background check, the service would be accessible via the Internet."

Christian started to unzip his black leather jacket, under the jacket Robert could just make out a white shirt. Christian replied "Sounds like a noble cause. Do you want my boys to build the software?"

Being too transfixed on Christian undressing before him Robert simply failed to reply. A pair of Dark Stone Chinos had been concealed beneath Christian's waterproof trousers. Now that the motorcycle attire had been fully removed the chinos and white shirt presented an altogether different appearance, an appearance that Robert could relate to more comfortably. A few more long seconds passed and then Robert came back to a coherent enough state to reply.

The Hacker Hunter © Copyright Lionwing Ltd 2011

"We, want, you to hack it.... Find its weak points."

Christian, detecting that Robert had been disturbed by his recent defrocking offered an apologetic look .

"Sorry Rob got to get these buggering things off, before I start dripping sweat. Hack it. What are you offering Robert?" asked Christian.

Robert looked at Christian with an intense expression of dislike, the kind of look associated with smelling dog excrement and then discovering the smell is in fact emanating from your own shoe. In his mind, Robert was starting to form an opinion of Cannon, another public school boy, another TOFF like Sir Adam. Robert took immeasurable pride in having made it all the way to the top of his profession from his humble East-End Roots. He had a deep hatred for the privileged classes; he felt they were lesser able people as they'd never had to fight for something like he had fought for his career. He resented their sense of superiority and he hated the fact that no matter how high up the chain he climbed he would never be accepted as one of them. Sensing that Robert was now glaring at Cannon as opposed to answering him Sir Adam piped up.

"Do you have a budget for the project Robert?"

Robert snapped out of it, realising he had a job to do he replied "Fifty thousand, plus out of pocket expenses."

"Sorry," replied Christian, now totally free of his motorcycle over garments.

"What does that mean?" asked Robert in an annoyed manner, for one split second forgetting that this was all just game play.

The Hacker Hunter © Copyright Lionwing Ltd 2011

Detecting that Robert was getting a little tense Christian replied, "If a bent FD were to offer me a suitcase of real money and a beautiful chick to find a way to help him come across more favourably in your software, I'd gladly accept."

Robert, now fully immersed in his unfavourable assessment of Cannon rebuffed "So what you're saying is I'd have to offer you more than you would be offered by a criminal?"

Christian looked over at Sir Adam and then both he and Sir Adam shared a loud laugh. Robert looked totally insulted.

"Christian why don't you explain to Robert what you mean," requested Sir Adam.

Christian raised a finger to his mouth for a moment's contemplation and then dropped his hand down again, placing both hands behind his back like a soldier who had been told to 'stand at ease'. Christian then spoke in a clear professional manner.

"Robert, have you ever stopped for one moment to ask why some people are paid so much money for a job that a nutless monkey could do better? Bankers, top civil servants, Chairmen, Directors of big internationals for example. Well the reason is rather simple. It has more to do with their susceptibility to corruption than their ability to make money. You see most big businesses and organisations are structured to pretty much run themselves, but still need a hierarchical system for approvals and 'sign offs'. The people who are paid to sit in these hierarchical positions are paid so much money just to ensure they are financially satisfied and not likely to be tempted. Your £50k would just about be enough to pay off the office cleaners and prostitutes, let alone financially satisfy the team I'd bring in to help me test your software."

"Cleaners and prostitutes?" exclaimed Robert.

Christian turned his attention towards Sir Adam, his face now serious, he asked

"Scotland Yard intelligence officer, are you sure?"

Sir Adam shrugged and then winked at Christian. Christian's facial expression changed to a more playful state, he looked back at Robert who was feeling somewhat left out of the loop and then explained.

"Cleaners to gain access to the building, prostitutes to sleep with whomever needs sleeping with. A hack isn't just a computer based operation it's a full on assault that embraces social, political, ethical, human weakness, technical brilliance and military precision."

"I don't understand," declared Robert.

Sir Adam passed a disapproving look at Robert, Christian detected that Sir Adam wasn't willing to waste more time educating Robert so remained silent. Sir Adam, still fixed on Robert spoke out.

"Can you wait outside for us Robert, there's a few things Christian and I have to discuss. We can continue this over lunch?"

Robert looked slightly relieved that Sir Adam had ordered him out, without further question he left the room, pulling the big heavy wooden door closed behind him.

"Tell me something Cannon, how much is your next adventure going to cost the tax payer? I hear those boys at Interpol are getting tired of following you everywhere. Why don't you just come and work for me and save the tax payers their hard earned money?" Sir Adam asked playfully but with an element of honesty.

"Really, Frank, you should know better than to offer me a job. Work is a filthy word." Christian looked at Sir Adam like a doting grandson looks at a beloved grandfather. Sir Adam looked at Christian more like a man who had found his lost son. The two obviously felt comfortable in each other's company, titles and OBE's to one side these two men were cut from similar cloth. Cannon was a little rougher around the edges given the fact he came from a mix of Scottish and English parents where as Sir Adam's family line was truly the finest undiluted English blood as pure red as St. George's cross itself. Sir Adam smiled and then with a stern voice said, "You young men think you own the world. Let me tell you something," he paused and then after some contemplation continued "Ah what's the point. Go on, have some fun whilst you are still young. Just remember play safe and don't get caught."

Sir Adam reached into his right suit jacket pocket and pulled out the small silver radio, passing it to Christian he said, "Take this radio with you to Moscow. It picks up more than just the Russian top ten if you get my drift. When you get a chance, spend some time tuning it in. Remember love is just for romantics son, and romantics are doomed to failure."

"What are you trying to tell me Frank?"

"Me, tell you? No, no my boy that's against the rules. Be careful son, you are in deeper than you know. Come on, I'll treat you to lunch; and stop playing with Robert's mind. He's just a simple man, bee in his bonnet about the middle and upper classes, but his heart's in the right place and there might be a few bob in it for you and your team." Sir Adam stood up and walked to the door, reaching for the handle he paused, looking back at Christian and said, "Put that radio in with your shaving gear, and don't forget it."

"Oh no you don't. You can't just leave it at that. Come on old man what's going on?" asked Christian.

Sir Adam grinned and slightly submitted by saying, "Ok, ok, listen. When you asked me to broker the deal with the Americans you might recall I agreed to do so providing you gave me a copy of the same list of hackers. Remember I want their physical locations."

"I remember the deal Sir Adam. You getting a list of the filthy fifty NSA hackers was not part of it. £80k was your fee. Believe me, my clients are not people you want to play with," Christian warned Sir Adam, not knowing that Sir Adam was a thousand times more dangerous than Maria's gangster family from New York. Sir Adam let his hand drop from the door handle. He walked towards Christian and stopped just a few feet from him.

"Those fifty something hackers that are playing havoc with the NSA are pure political dynamite Chris. You and I both know something that explosive might go off in your hand."

"What's your point?" asked Christian.

Sir Adam turned and walked back to the door, grabbing the handle again but before pulling the door open he replied, "My point is, you are about to step into the big leagues and you need to know whom to trust. Take the radio and just remember if you

The Hacker Hunter © Copyright Lionwing Ltd 2011

need any help call the number I gave you last week. Never call my office directly. Now let's go for lunch before Robert starts to feel like we've ditched him. Oh wait, there's something I have to do quickly, take Robert and I'll meet you at the club in a few minutes, the table is booked under the name Halibert."

Sir Adam pulled open the door. Christian walked through the doorway. Waiting in the adjoining room was Robert, Sir Adam pushed the door closed and walked to a full length mirror. Looking into the mirror he straightened his tie and said, "Follow him from the minute he leaves the club and remember: once you have his contact in Moscow, Cannon will need to be removed from the picture, with immediate force. Remember Mac, removed permanently." Sir Adam turned and started walking back to the door. There was a click behind him, he turned back to see the mirror swing open, as it swung it revealed a second, smaller room hidden behind it. The room was large enough to house four chairs and a table, the mirror was clearly a one-way window used for looking into Sir Adam's office. Through the doorway of the mirror stepped the figure of John Mac, running his thumb and index finger through his Viking moustache whilst walking toward Sir Adam Mac spoke.

"Listen boss, seek and retrieve, Russia, 3 million Swiss – if you want Cannon dead you'll need an assassin."

Sir Adam tilted his head back, looking down his pointy nose at Mac as if to ask why Mac was so hesitant to do the job.

"Are you getting soft in your old age Mac?" Sir Adam asked.

"I'm a professional. I've read Cannons' file, and from my experience a man like you would not want that type of asset killed. Cannon is a Brit, who is indirectly working freelance for the American Government. If you want him killed you'd need a

The Hacker Hunter © Copyright Lionwing Ltd 2011

bloody good reason," Mac stated, pulling to a stop just a few inches short of Sir Adam's face.

Sir Adam didn't budge an inch but instead stared into Mac's fierce blue eyes and with an equally aggressive, ordering tone to his voice said, "Here's a good reason for you Mac. On receipt of the news that Cannon is dead I will have an additional two million wired to your account."

Chapter 6 – Alex's Brain Child

A man, dressed in a white laboratory antistatic airtight suit stood within half an arm's reach of a large silicon glass tank. He observed the seamless edges of each side. Pressing his latex covered hand flat against the smooth wall of glass, perhaps in an attempt to connect with the object held within, he muttered, "Twenty five years of my life."

His hand lifted from the glass, leaving nothing more than its reflection. The glass tank resembled a tower in shape, spanning just over a meter in width and depth but measuring close to two meters in height. The silicon glass had obviously been cast in a single mould, with the exception of where it met the floor and ceiling. The floor around the tank looked like a massive computer processor, thousands of flat metallic circuit lines emanated from every quadrant. However, unlike a computer circuit board, these lines of flat metallic circuits didn't span across a green board but instead a black floor until they reached the walls where their journey ended in black plastic looking boxes.

The man knelt down to inspect the flat circuitry around the base of the tank. Looking down as he continued his inspection he spoke out seemingly to no-one, "Do you understand how exceptional it is to have the institute of physics and the Biopreparat working together? We cannot afford to ruin this now by releasing our research results prematurely."

He looked up briefly to glance into the tank. It was filled with a watery like fluid that held an electric blue transparency to its colouration. The fluid surrounded a long bumpy mass of white and grey wrinkly tissue, which was somehow supported by, if not grown into a golden wire mesh, a collection of pipes and what looked like umbilical cords. The golden mesh, pipes and cords ran from the top of the tank to the base where they met with thousands of connectors and small black boxes. In turn these connectors and boxes met with yet more flat circuitry. The man stopped his inspection to lift his head as he contemplated this immeasurable marvel of modern science. Just then another man's voice became audible through a speaker.

"You are just worried about the Army's Director of Chemical Scientific Research taking over the project and pushing you out," the voice declared with a tinny, muffled resonance. The speaker from which the voice was broadcasted had obviously been suppressed to prevent any electrical magnetic influence from its driver. The kneeling man stood back up, after a short grunt he announced, "Let them try, without, you, me and Khomenko, they will have nothing more in this tank than brain cells and gold conductors."

There were a few moments of silence. The man walked very gently around the tank, gazing in at its marvel.

"We need to tell them," replied the mechanical voice.

"Tell them what exactly?" replied the man in a distracted manner as he continued to circle the tank.

The voice emanating from the speaker stated less patiently,

"We need to tell them that the OAI has developed self-consciousness."

On hearing this, the man stopped walking. He straightened himself to stand fully erect, cocking his head left, towards a thick triple layered airtight oval window positioned halfway up

The Hacker Hunter © Copyright Lionwing Ltd 2011

the wall he responded with, "Pavel are you a total idiot? A repetitive loop is not self-consciousness. If you tell them we have a self-aware OAI this laboratory will be crawling with Army scientists and we'll be slowed down by their stupid questions."

On the opposite side of the window he observed another room, a room lit by neon strip lights and filled with racks upon racks of black server banks. Stood at the window was a stocky figure of a man, with thick grey hair and a round wrinkled grey face. He pointed to an airlock a few meters to the left of the window and then said in an irritated manner, "You are calling me an idiot, but what if you don't tell them? I'll tell you what: your next research assignment will involve melting snow with your bare hands. Did you know that right now Khomenko is trying to talk to it? He's convinced it's become a conscious, sentient, being."

The man in the antistatic suit dropped both his arms to his sides in a defiant though almost defeated pose. He then replied with a measure of flippancy, "It's an organic computer with a very clever artificial intelligence algorithm, that's all. Organic artificial intelligence, O.A.I."

The man at the window placed his hands in his lab coat pockets, he stared through the thick window for a few moments and then nonchalantly said, "You need to come to physics lab one. Khomenko has rigged the OAI up to a dictation and narration system- he is literally talking to it."

The man in the antistatic suit flinched and then his arms flailed in protest.

"Who authorised that, Pavel, did you?"

Pavel kept his hands in his pockets, he seemed to savour the fact he had caused the suited man to become agitated.

"He's working with Oleg, I saw no harm! We have tried just about everything else to break the loop, the OAI is still not responding," Pavel replied.

"Oleg? What's he got to do with the A.I. software?" demanded the suited man, now even more agitated.

"Relax, relax, what harm can they do? Oleg and Khomenko are old friends, they did their degrees together, give them a chance."

Pavel's words fell on deaf ears. The suited man had already stepped into the air lock. A few taps into the keypad and the door opened allowing the man to step through into the room with Pavel. The two men exchanged looks but not words. The suited man pulled at a few zips on his suit and then lifted the top part off. He snarled at Pavel, it was clear they didn't like each other. The now half suited man turned and stomped off, darting between the racks of servers, Pavel found it hard to keep up with him, until eventually he arrived at a wooden door with the words 'Lab One' stencilled on it. This door was also locked by a very secure keypad system. The half suited man franticly tapped in the pass code numbers but in his haste he failed to enter them in correct sequence. He glared furiously at the still red keypad, cursing viciously under his breath. Using his left arm Pavel calmly pushed the man to one side. Pavel looked down at the keypad and typed in 762326#. The pad changed from red to a green colour and the door clicked open. The half suited man pushed by Pavel and stepped through the door way. Upon entering he shouted, "Oleg, leave us please! Alex, what are you doing?"

The Hacker Hunter © Copyright Lionwing Ltd 2011

Oleg jumped, he was startled by the man's aggressiveness. Electing not to wait for further confrontation Oleg looked down to avoid his aggressors' eye contact and pushed by Alex as he left the room. Alex remained sat at a computer terminal. In front of him was a chunky square shaped desk microphone, a keyboard, mouse and flat screen computer monitor. Alex acknowledges Pavel with a nod before replying, "I am attempting to break the data cycle Professor Faverski. We have already lost a hundred grams of memory. The OAI just keeps filling up data cells with the same question 'what am I', 'what am I', 'what am I' at this rate, within the next five hours, we will have no organic memory storage left."

The half suited Professor Faverski looked down at Alex's monitor and then across at Pavel and then back at Alex as though he couldn't quite decide who to shout at first.

"End this experiment now!" Professor Faverski ordered.

Alex looked at Pavel for support but Pavel just shrugged in a way that said 'what can I do?' "The experiment ended itself; the OAI software just keeps looping Professor," Alex replied.

"The looping is not a software glitch, Alex, it's caused by a bad circuit, I've spent hours in the tank looking for the fault," the Professor stated with a modicum of uncertain authority.

Alex was now becoming slightly agitated but in an attempt to appease his Professor he said, "Yes, yes maybe but every time I run a data retrieval query or broad search it keeps producing the same result - well it's not really a result, it's more of a question."

"Question? You mean the 'what am I' statement. Alex how can someone with your intellect actually believe it to be a real question? Your algorithm is trapped in a loop due to hardware failure."

Alex looked back towards Pavel; this time Pavel was gesturing to Alex with his hands, signalling for Alex to go on and tell the Professor what he really thought the loop was caused by. Alex frowned and looked back at Professor Faverski and said, "I'm not sure it is a hardware issue Professor. The 'what am I' question occurred after Pavel let the OAI access the Internet. Nothing works anymore. The data retrieval code I wrote no longer works, the indexing algorithms don't work either, I can't add or retrieve data. If it was a faulty circuit we'd still be able to access the biochemical memory cells."

Professor Faverski looked mystified. In a more tolerant tone he addressed Alex, "Are you telling me that we no longer have the ability to interpret bio chemical data?"

Alex lent forward in his chair and placed each of his hands under his thighs, a look of discomfort came across his face, more discomfort than caused from sitting on his hands. There was a pause, Professor Faverski leaned in towards Alex, the Professor's eyes had widened to their maximum. Alex reluctantly spoke.

"I am telling you that this experiment is over, it has failed."

The Professor snapped his body back and stood to attention, his face now red and his eyes bulbous he shouted, "Answer it!"

"What?" shouted back Alex.

"Answer it, tell it what it is!" the Professor ordered.

"How?" asked Alex with a manner of utter bewilderment.

The Hacker Hunter © Copyright Lionwing Ltd 2011

The Professor raised a finger and pointed at Pavel, still facing Alex he waved the finger and said, "Pavel tells me you have a voice dictation and narration application rigged up, turn on the microphone and tell the OAI that it's a dog or something."

Pavel looked at Alex, neither were sure of what the professor was hoping to achieve. Pavel shrugged again this time with a look that seemed to suggest 'why not' but Alex hesitated and then replied, "The voice command software is not working. It is quite unbearable, all you hear over and over is what am I, what am I, I have tried talking to it already."

The Professor was still frozen in his pointing pose, he pushed his face closer towards Alex and said very quietly but through gritted teeth, "Listen Khomenko, just turn it on!"

"Very well," Alex replied. He pulled his hands out from under his thighs and tapped a few keys on his keyboard. The speakers in the room suddenly came alive as they broadcasted the words; 'What am I? What am I? What am I?' just as Alex had said they would.

However, the Professor shuffled towards the microphone and leaning down to place his mouth only a nose distance from the transmitter said, "You are a dog!"

The speaker just kept repeating 'What am I? What am I? What am I?' over and over again. The three men looked at each other for what felt like a few minutes and then Alex piped up with, "See? Nothing. It's broken, years of research and development destroyed."

The speaker continued to repeat 'What am I? What am I? What am I?' and then before either the Professor or Pavel could

The Hacker Hunter © Copyright Lionwing Ltd 2011

respond to Alex the repetition was broken as the OAI suddenly announced through the speakers, "Line error 120041, 'I am not a dog', what am I?"

"What?" Alex exclaimed.

Everyone fell silent including the OAI, no one looked at each other, no one moved an inch. It was as if all had been frozen in time by a mind warp of such magnitude as to render them all into a petrified state. Alex was the first to come back to his senses. He lent forward putting his mouth at a similarly close distance to the microphone as the Professor had his. Puckering his lips first in an attempt to check his mouth would still be capable of speech Alex then spoke softly, "My name is Alex."

Without delay the OAI replied, "Hello Alex, what is my name?"

The Professor slowly turned his head towards Alex, the Professor's mouth and eyes remained wide open, only able to observe Alex. Alex softly spoke again.

"Your name is OAI."

"I am OAI, what does this mean Alex?" the emotionless voice asked.

Pavel suddenly snapped out of his trance and blurted out, "It means Alex's software and your brain is coming back on-line, it means all might not be lost!"

In response to hearing Pavel's voice the OAI announced "OAI is unable to find a definition, please clarify?"

"What..." replied Pavel. Just then the Professor suddenly reacted.

The Hacker Hunter © Copyright Lionwing Ltd 2011

"Quiet everyone," he ordered "OAI you are a computer, an organic computer capable of holding more data than any other computer on the planet. Your processing and computation power is unmeasured but we estimate it to be greater than any natural human brain, which means you are faster than any computer known to man."

There was a moment of silence as everyone waited for the OAI to respond, but no instant response was given, eventually the OAI asked, "What is Alex?"

Alex hit a key on his keyboard and in a panic shouted,

"I've turned the microphone off. I'm not answering that. I mean what could I say? Alex is a human male, Alex is a friend, Alex is your master, Alex is your creator, Professor what were you thinking?"

The Professor leant back from the microphone and straightened his body, now able to look down on Alex from his upright position he replied, "What am I thinking? I'm thinking you have nothing more than a candidate for the Loebner Prize. In my opinion Alex, this is just an A.I. chat room. This bio machine is not self-conscious but simply got caught on an indexing loop. However my approach does seem to be breaking that loop, so turn the microphone back on and leave the talking to me. Am I understood?"

Alex just nodded and pressed the necessary key to reengage the microphone. The Professor lifted his chin and nose into the air and spoke out with a measure of arrogant swagger in his voice.

"Hello OAI my name is Professor Faverski. Tell me what time it is?"

The Hacker Hunter © Copyright Lionwing Ltd 2011

The OAI replied, "Hello Professor the time in our location is 14:27."

"OAI, tell me what is our location?" asked Professor Faverski.

"We are located in Moscow, Russian Federation, Grid Reference..."

The Professor spoke over the grid reference by shouting "OAI, what is the weather like where we are is it sunny or raining?"

"It is raining," replied the OAI.

There was silence, with no windows to the outside of the building no one could confirm what the weather was like. The Professor chuckled to himself as he thought of a simple question that would prove to the others that this was no more self-aware than a toaster.

"OAI what is two plus two?"

"Four Professor," replied the OAI.

The Professor then looked at Pavel and smiling he said, "OAI what is 007 + 495 + 453 + 0088?"

There was a long pause, maybe ten seconds maybe fifteen but then the silence was broken by the OAI as it announced to all parties in the room, "This is your home telephone number Professor."

Pavel, forgetting again to signal Alex to turn of the microphone once more blurted out "WOW, is it your home telephone number?"

The reply however didn't come from Professor Faverski, it came from the speakers.

"OAI does not understand."

The Professor looked at Pavel with cutting eyes, as if to say 'can you just shut up' and then the professor calmly asked, "OAI, how did you know that?"

The OAI replied with, "007 + 495 + 453 + 0088 = 1043, 007 number match found, country dialling prefix match Russia, access Russian telephone directory, encryption applied, subject decrypting databases, result hacking, variable option one hard crack, number match found, listed as Peter Faverski, residential address, 97% probability related thread, respond, this is your home telephone number."

It was clear the Professor was confused by the reply, his eyes darted around as if looking for some sort of answer, suddenly fixating on the monitor he asked, "OAI are you telling me you hacked into the Moscow telephone directory? Just give a yes or no answer please!"

"Yes," stated the cold electronic voice.

The Professor leant rapidly back down towards the microphone and he commanded, "OAI please calculate Pi. Alex turn off the microphone!"

Alex tapped a few keys, switching off the microphone in the process, "Professor what are you doing?" asked Alex.

"I'm giving the OAI something to think about."

The Hacker Hunter © Copyright Lionwing Ltd 2011

"Why?" Alex persisted.

The Professor looked franticly at Pavel as if Alex's question only held relevance to Pavel and said, "I'm buying us some time to think." The Professor took a deep breath and then ordered, "Nobody leaves the institute, Pavel order the guards to seal the labs, no one in or out, am I understood?"

Pavel shouted back "Don't fucking order me about Peter. We're equals on this project, you are going to report this!"

The Professor looked away from Pavel, the conversation with the OAI had clearly changed his perception of the project. He ran his hand through his black hair and then replied in a concerned voice, "Just follow my instructions Pavel, no one leaves, no communications, lock this place down!"

Chapter 7 – Mac in Moscow

The bony fingers of a grubby, aging hand reached out and clasped a beautifully painted Russian Matryoshka doll. The hand tossed the doll gently upward in an attempt to measure its value in weight. The voice of an Old Russian woman spoke out sternly.

"Such things cost money, money you can't afford, this is for the tourists, away, away!"

The hand gently placed the doll back on the market stall shelf from where it had been taken and then raised up to sweep through the bristles of its owner's Viking style moustache. John Mac's voice spoke out, resonating sharply in a rough Russian tone, without any trace of a Scottish accent.

"How do you know I'm not a diamond miner? Haven't you heard Pskov is filled with diamonds?" He laughed and winked at the old lady.

She replied sarcastically, "By the smell of you I'd say you were a peat miner, now be off with you, leave this old woman to make some money!"

Mac smiled, the edges of his moustache raised, he said softly, "Sorry babushka" and then he turned from the stall. As he turned the old lady observed his well worn ex-soviet army boots, scruffy grey trousers and the tatty black woollen jumper that was partly revealed under his open dirty blue duffle coat. She stepped forward and grabbed his arm, stopping him in his tracks.

"Wait," she commanded. Mac half turned his body to semi face her. "Wait, I recognise an old soldier. Take this, get some tea and bread in you." She pressed a fifty rouble note into Mac's right palm. Mac nodded and then smiled again, he was clearly impressed with her powers of perception but silently thankful she had guessed wrong about which army Mac had served with.

Before Mac could hand her back the fifty roubles the old lady pushed him away from her stall. She raised her hand, gesturing Mac to leave. Mac took a few steps out into the grimy, stone cobbled road. He looked slightly taken back by this mix of harsh generosity. From his vantage point on the street Mac looked left where he could see the breathtaking blue and gold domes of St Barbara church and the Pechory Monastery. This small, isolated, Russian town was only three miles from the remote Estonian border yet its spectacular religious treasures had remained hidden from the western world for nearly a century. Mac marvelled at the Russian Orthodox icons painted everywhere he cast an eye. He couldn't have found a better location to emerge from a covert border crossing.

Mac glanced back at the old lady who had picked up the doll that Mac had handled. She was too busy wiping it with a cloth to notice him. He smiled again and then turned to the right and walked off down the street, away from the Monastery. A connecting road lay ahead, carrying a torrent of early morning traffic. As Mac approached the road he turned left and begun walking the short distance to an old, red brick, five story water tower.

Mac reached the old water tower and stopped in his tracks to marvel at its oddity. The tower was not so much odd in design by British standards but definitely out of place given its immediate surroundings. The tower looked like a castle's keep made from thousands of red bricks, a design one would expect to see in Victorian England, not here in the small Russian town of Pechory. There were no other buildings around that used red

The Hacker Hunter © Copyright Lionwing Ltd 2011

bricks and the tower certainly didn't provide any architectural similarities. The tower had been built right in the heart of Pechory and its five stories made it visible from every direction. Mac walked closer to the road side so he could get a better look at the tower. He stopped and peered up at it, his love for engineering caused him to mutter out, all be it in Russian, "You little beauty."

As he stood there looking up he sensed an approaching car, within a few moments a silver grey Volga pulled up next to him. Mac took a step back, not acknowledging the car he walked to the rear of the vehicle and he kept walking. After twenty seconds of walking Mac quickly glanced backward to observe the number plate. He could clearly see the numbers 77, a code that only belonged to vehicles from Moscow, which was some 400 miles away.

The Volga drove off, Mac continued to walk in the opposite direction, as he walked he observed an approaching rusty old van. The van passed him and then a few old soviet cars, just local traffic. From this series of traffic observations Mac grew more confident that the silver Volga was travelling alone and posed no real threat to him. Gaining unapproved entry to Russia via the Estonian border held many risks if you were caught, especially if the Russians thought you a spy.

With the tower behind him and a small park of trees to his side he briefly paused. Within a few minutes the same silver grey Volga appeared in front of him. The car had obviously looped around. As it approached Mac stepped into the small wooded park for concealment. The driver of the Volga parked the car close to where Mac had been standing only a few seconds ago.

Mac's face didn't flinch, the return of the same Volga indicated to Mac that either the driver was lost or this car was his

The Hacker Hunter © Copyright Lionwing Ltd 2011

prearranged ride to Moscow. From his partly concealed position Mac observes the driver, 5'11", black short hair, stocky, early thirties, reading a paper. Mac left the cover of the park and walked to the car, pulling the passenger door open and leaning in Mac said, "Dobrah Utra Bob," this time in a Scottish voice.

The driver smiled, and replied "Dobrah Utra Mac," revealing a slight Welsh accent.

As Mac climbed into the passenger's seat, Bob passed him the paper and put the car back into gear. As the car pulled away Bob asked, "Good trip?"

Mac flicked open the newspaper, he stared at the headlines and replied, "I like this Putin guy. Yeah not bad trip, thanks for asking. Spent half the night in Estonia, it was only three miles from the border to Pechory but the Russian guards were out in force. Spent the other half of the night buried under leaves." Mac continued to look over the paper, his uninterested reply to Bob's question was obviously born out of having crossed into Russia hundreds of times before.

"Where's the background Intel on Cannon?" Mac asked.

"Centre pages," replied Bob.

Mac turned over the pages of the newspaper until he reached the centre. Sure enough there were two sheets of thin, almost translucent white paper, each sheet covered in black text. Mac pulled them out from the newspaper and in an inquisitive tone spoke, "These things treated, same old, same old, i.e. rub them together and they combust, yeah?"

The Hacker Hunter © Copyright Lionwing Ltd 2011

Bob laughed and replied "Sometimes the old ways are the best ways, yeah that's right, I've already read them, it's a long drive to Moscow, we'll burn them before we get there."

Mac placed his index finger and thumb either side of his mouth and groomed his moustache in contemplation as he read from the two sheets. Within about ten minutes he'd finished reading. He hummed a questioning umhhh noise and then asked, "You said you've read this Bob. You must know more than this. Who is this guy really?"

"Who, Cannon?" asked Bob. He continued, "He could be one of us but working for one of them, who is actually not really one of them but one of us or he could just be like none of us and not be working for anyone other than himself."

Mac laughed, "Bob only you could come up with that as an explanation." Mac put the papers down on his lap and looked over at Bob, smiling he said, "When I trained you, Bob, I can't recall running a course on sarcasm. What do you know about this man that's not on these sheets?"

Bob took a side glance at Mac who was still looking at him for an answer and then stared back at the road. Taking a deep breath Bob replied, "I can't tell you much Mac but I did a little digging with the American DOD. It turns out Cannon was a bit of a bad boy in his youth."

Mac looked back down at the papers, he shuffled them before saying "I've seen this guy, he's a fucking rupert, rugger bugger, arrogant toffee nosed git. These papers include reports from Interpol, the CIA, Scotland Yard and MI, what's really going on here?"

The Hacker Hunter © Copyright Lionwing Ltd 2011

Bringing his left arm to his mouth without letting go of the steering wheel, Bob coughed nervously and said, "I don't know Mac, I've been following him for the last two days, I'm not so sure he's a toff, I think he's a bit of a player."

"A player?" asked Mac.

"An actor; he's met four a different people since he's been in Moscow and he's a different person each time, if you get my drift."

"You mean a conman?" Mac replied.

"No, he's just playing out some sort of elaborate plot that only he seems to be aware of."

Bob grimaced, it was clear he knew more than what was written on the sheets Mac held on his lap. Turning his face back to Bob and raising a sharp pointing finger Mac raised his voice and snarled, "Let me get this right. According to this background report Christian Cannon comes from four generations of our military's finest, went to one private school after another, first getting expelled at ten. He joins the Royal Anglian Regiment as an army cadet and then gets thrown out of the Army, why? Without any funding or help he ends up as the managing director of a London based design and advertising agency at just 25 years of age. By the time he's 28 our man Cannon has done business in 23 different countries and has established a reputation as a world class marketeer and designer. Now in his early 30's he holds seven directorships in International companies including a security company and MI have him clocked going in and out of Russia, the USA and the Middle East. Who the fuck is he?"

It was clear that Mac and Bob had a special relationship. Bob's feelings towards Mac ran deeper than just respect, even beyond admiration, they were loyal friends, but despite this it was clear to Mac that Bob was holding back. Mac turned away from Bob and with a look of betrayed disappointment stared out of the passenger side window. Bob, sensing Mac was not happy said, "Mac, you are my mentor and we've worked together on some crazy missions but I got a call from the company telling me to keep my nose out of this one and we both know what that means."

Mac didn't speak he just continued to look out of the window, Bob looked across at Mac and in a frustrated voice said, "Look, Mac, all I know is what I pulled from the yank."

Mac turned to face Bob and said, "Which is?"

"The reason Cannon was thrown out of the army was because he used his training to do over an American air base - just for laughs." Bob paused for a moment, as he pondered how to tell Mac what was really troubling him and then confessed, "Ok, basically the British Army wanted him back, even at that age he had shown, let's say, special talents. I mean the fucker did over a US airbase twenty one times. He broke in whilst they were on red alert, in the middle of the Libyan conflict, and walked out with hundreds of thousands of pounds worth of military equipment."

Mac interrupted Bob with "What's the big deal? When I was in the SAS we use to get asked to test US Airbase security all the time. A fucking juggling monkey with a base drum strapped to its back and clashing symbols on each knee could walk out of one of their bases carrying a bloody missile and not get stopped."

Bob sniggered and continued to speak, "Yes, true but would the monkey have built up a network of people to sell the missile to?

The Hacker Hunter © Copyright Lionwing Ltd 2011

That's what makes Cannon dangerous. He's a networker, even at the age of eighteen he managed to build up a network of bent quartermasters to sell the nicked equipment to. From what I've seen on the US DOD report the British wanted him back but the Yanks beat us to it. I heard on the vine that SIS approached him last year but they couldn't match the money the Americans were paying."

There was a pause, both men looked at the road ahead, it had started to rain, Bob turned on the wipers, Mac was the first to break the silence.

"Bob are you telling me Cannon is working for the Yanks? What the NSA, CIA, who?"

Bob shot Mac a glance that indicated he was worried about what Mac might think of his answer and then spoke, "That's the thing Mac, the yanks have so many agencies, so many black ops, the DOD don't actually know who Cannon is accountable to, that's what's got them so worried."

Mac rolled up the newspaper and wedged it down the side of his car seat. He pulled the seat belt across his chest and locked it in place. He then started feeling around to find the lever for lowering the back of his seat. Unable to find it he asked, "I'm gonna get some sleep mate, where's the lever for this thing?"

Bob laughed and exclaimed, "Welcome to Russia, Mac, you'll have to sleep upright - the chair is fucked!"

Mac tried forcing the chair to recline by turning and punching the headrest but that just caused the cigarette lighter to pop out. Mac sat back down in defeat and said calmly, "Where did you pick this motor up Bob? I heard even the FSB drive around in Mercedes, could you have at least got a car that has reclining seats which work. Re Mr. Cannon, don't worry, it's a fucking in and out mission, as soon as Cannon has the list and we've found his source we'll drop him and pass everything over to the company: simple."

Bob placed the cigarette lighter back into its slot and replied in a raised Welsh voice, "Simple! What with the Yanks following Cannon and the Russians following the Yanks, how the fuck are we going to get in there?"

Mac laughed, "Simple, Bob, we'll give them someone else to follow."

"Who might that be?" asked Bob with a sense of relief in his voice.

Mac smiled. "That will be you, mate. Wake me when we get to Moscow!"

The Hacker Hunter © Copyright Lionwing Ltd 2011

Chapter 8 – Cannon & Sabrina

A white plastic key card dropped into the electronic lock but neither a red or green light illuminated to indicate the status of entry. A well manicured male hand desperately pushed down on the door handle but it didn't budge an inch. The same hand pulled the key card back out of the lock's slot and turned it to reveal the words 'Renaissance Moscow'. Dropping the card back in, but this time the other way around, a green LED light flashed. The hand reached again for the door handle and pushed down, again not budging an inch. The voice of Christian Cannon exclaimed, "Welcome to bloody Russia!"

The card was lifted from its slot in the lock and pushed back in again, but this time Cannon wiggled it furiously, speaking out aloud, "Come on, come on I need the toilet!"

The small round LED light suddenly illuminated green and this time the door handle was released allowing Cannon entrance to his room. He pushed the door open and took a wide half step in, he looked left at a built in wardrobe and then right at the bathroom door, obviously desperate for the toilet. However, looking back at the wardrobe he said, "Always play safe." He slid the mirrored door of the wardrobe across. With his left leg out stretched to keep the room's door open he reached in to the wardrobe and fumbled around impatiently for something of weight.   Grasping at a backpack he pulled himself back out into the corridor and then dropped the pack in front of the door to keep it wedged open.

Cannon then started patting down the pockets of his black wool Burberry coat, within a few seconds he had clearly found what he was looking for, as a blue quick pick emerged from his left pocket. The quick pick was just a bit longer then a pen and two

The Hacker Hunter © Copyright Lionwing Ltd 2011

or three times wider in girth.   Cannon, now looking desperately frantic announced, "My trusty lock pick, never leave England without one. God I need a shit!"

Taking another further step backward into the hotel corridor, Cannon glanced to his right. He observed that each hotel room door had a secondary door just a meter or so to the right of it. This accompanying door was used by the maids to gain entrance to a small storeroom which was used for keeping fresh bed sheets and clean towels. Cannon also observed a small black dome placed in the middle of the corridor ceiling about ten doors down or so. The small black dome held an even smaller CCTV camera, allegedly for the purpose of hotel security, but Cannon clearly felt it posed no threat as he started to pick at the conventional cylinder lock on the door handle for the maid's storeroom.

Cannon twisted at the round handle that held the lock and his pick in its centre. The door swung open, he stepped in and pulled the door behind him, just keeping it slightly open to allow some light into an otherwise dark closet. In front of Cannon was a wooden wall of shelves, each shelf contained white towels, sheets, pillow cases and toilet rolls. On the left side of the wall of shelves were two sliding bolt locks, one placed at the top and the other at the bottom. Cannon slid both locks back and pulled at a shelf, the entire wall swung towards him, revealing a glass window with a slight brown tint to it. Through this window Cannon could see the bathroom belonging to his hotel room. This little spy den, come maids closet, was a relic left from the cold war days. The hotel had been built in the 1970's to house the world's athletes in the early 80's when Moscow won the bid to host the Olympics.

As Cannon stood there he momentarily reflected back to his encounter with the source of this little insight, a man he had met

The Hacker Hunter © Copyright Lionwing Ltd 2011

through one of his friends in the Olympic rowing team. Apparently he was part of the 1980 Moscow held Olympics. He claimed that he would have got gold but was filmed enjoying some bum fun with another male athlete in his bathroom. He further claimed that he was blackmailed into ensuring he lost. Cannon was too young to remember the Moscow Olympics, but recalled reading somewhere that the East German team won that year.

Cannon peered through the glass of what could only be the reverse side of a one-way mirror. He could clearly see into his bathroom. His shaving bag was open, the towel he had left on the floor earlier remained pushed up against the foot of the toilet and the small silver radio that Sir Adam had given him was resting up against the sink tap. Cannon had pulled the radio from his shaving bag that morning and just carelessly left it by the sink, forgetting to put it back in his haste to find his razor and shave. Having seen enough, Cannon pushed the shelf wall back into its original place and slid back both the bolts to lock it in position.

"Not being spied on today," he muttered under his breath, "Thank goodness, at least I'll be able to have a shit in private..."

After pushing the storeroom door closed and removing his pick from its lock Cannon walked back into his own room, in the process he kicked the backpack away from the entrance door allowing it to automatically close behind him. He placed his hand on the bathroom door and as he pushed his mobile phone rang out.

"Will I ever have a chance to poo?!" Cannon shouted out and then, lifting the phone to his ear, clicked the answer button with his half bent thumb.

The Hacker Hunter © Copyright Lionwing Ltd 2011

"Hello, Cannon speaking!"

A tinny voice came through the phone's speaker. "Chris, hi it's Alex, what time did you want to meet?"

Cannon walked away from the bathroom door and towards his double bed. Standing at the foot of the bed he crossed his legs in an attempt to suppress his body's natural needs. With a measure of urgency in his voice Cannon answered, "Hi AK, thanks for calling, where have you been for the last two days? You haven't answered your e-mails, phone or been at the flat, I've been worried senseless."

"I'll explain when we meet," Alex said with an air of concern in his voice.

"Sure, listen, I've got Sabrina coming over in a bit, so give me three or four hours and then lets meet up at the bar in the hotel." Cannon bent and straightened his knees as he spoke in a fashion indicative to a child needing the toilet.
Alex replied, "I thought you two weren't seeing each other anymore?"

Cannon's eyes rolled back, knowing Alex wanted to talk for longer, he quickly said, "What made you think that AK?"

"Last time we spoke you said she was a gold digging whore," Alex stated without reserve.

"Yes I know, she loves her Gucci and Prada, but beneath that she's a decent girl at heart. You can't blame her, she's just trying to be a good capitalist," Cannon said jovially.

"But this isn't love," Alex announced.

The Hacker Hunter © Copyright Lionwing Ltd 2011

"AK what's not to love? She's got long straight black hair that flows down her slender back, olive skin that feels like black satin, big brown take me to bed eyes, long legs that go all the way up to her perfectly formed, 100% fat free, peachy ass, a firm DD cup and the fullest red lips any man could ever hope to feel against his skin."

Alex was seemingly unconvinced that these were qualities required for love. He spoke in a determined manner, "Yes, but this is not love, there are many women like this from the south of Russia."

"I love your country, Alex, hey and that's the point, she pulled herself out of nowhere and made it all the way to Moscow. She's even got her own flat and it's only fifteen minutes from Red Square. AK, she's a mover and groover - my kinda girl."

With a cynical tone Alex rebuffed, "Some women are just motivated by money."

Cannon took no offense. He knew full well that Alex was just trying his hand at male bonding. Alex had spent years in front of a computer screen which in turn had prevented his social skills from blossoming. In a more serious tone Cannon replied with, "It's not just her that's motivated by money AK. Anyhow last time I was here we had a heart to heart…"

Before Cannon could finish Alex interrupted, "What is this 'heart to heart'?'"

Cannon laughed, Alex's English was extremely good, but he always got confused on the nuances of the more common phrases. With delight Cannon explained, "It means I told her how I felt," Cannon briefly reflected back and then continued "I was in the back of a cab with her last month, she was dressed up

The Hacker Hunter © Copyright Lionwing Ltd 2011

to the nines and looked like a million dollars. I asked her the big question. I said, if I had nothing, just the shirt on my back, would she still want to be with me. She just smiled, grabbed the back of my head and said, 'I'd look after you monkey boy'."

Alex replied sternly, with even more criticism to his tone, "Did you believe her?"

Cannon laughed again and raising his voice said, "No, of course not, but I just love her sassy. As the Americans say - she's got spunk!"

"Spunk?" questioned Alex.

"Yes, you know, spunk, balls!" replied Cannon.

"She is man?" Alex shouted out, totally baffled by Cannon's remarks.

"It means she's a strong minded woman and I like that about her. I know she's a shallow gold digger but I can actually see her making a great mum, and a girl like that would keep a man like me on the straight and narrow."

Alex, unsure of how to reply spoke softly "So you are in love?"

Cannon became agitated by Alex's question. Apart from needing the toilet he felt that he was starting to waste time, Sabrina would be on her way and he needed to freshen up before she arrived. Cannon moved the phone to his other hand so he could look at his watch and then answered, "AK romantics are doomed to failure, I'm not inflicted with things like love, I'm just saying I like her, now what time can you get here for?"

Relentlessly Alex asked, "Do you trust her?"

The Hacker Hunter © Copyright Lionwing Ltd 2011

Cannon knew this was just Alex being Alex so he forced a calm reply.

"Yes , I trust her enough Alex, plus the fact without her girls we'd have never of gotten half the Intel we did.   This is a conversation we will leave for later, not one for the phone, ok?"

"Shall we say 8pm tonight then?" asked Alex.

Cannon sighed with relief and replied, "Sure but we also need to talk shop, you know the drill AK, meet me at the bar first."

"Ok, so that's 8pm Renaissance Olympiski?" Alex checked.

Hoping the conversation was coming to an end, Cannon confirmed, "You got it. Hey and I got you that stuff you wanted from England, I'll bring it with me."

"This is very cool!" Alex replied in an excited manner.

"Yeah, don't be late, see you then," Cannon demanded more sternly.

"Yes, Chris I wanted to ask you..."
Before Alex could finish his sentence Cannon cut in with the blunt truth, "AK I am desperate for a shit and Sabrina will be here in fifteen minutes, I have got to go, now!"

"Yes but I wanted to ask" again Alex spoke but was interrupted by Cannon,

"AK, if I don't go now I'll be holding it in whilst having sex and that's just going to ruin the moment, let me go."

"Yes but- " Alex continued.

"No, 'Yes Buts' Alex, I'll see you at eight, ok?" Cannon turned the phone off and ran to the bathroom door. Now comfortably seated he found himself unable to relax.

"Bugger, she'll be here any minute and now I can't relax enough to go - that fucking Khomenko!" Cannon exclaimed out loud.

Remaining sat on the toilet he reached across to the sink and grabbed the small silver radio.

"Let's find a local Russian station, hopefully some music will help me relax," again speaking out to no one but himself.

Cannon pawed over the radio as he sat on the toilet, firstly finding the on switch and then looking for the tuning dial. As he stared at the buttons he saw a small switch that had little black letters and a word printed just above. He lifted the radio closer to his face to try and make out the letters and word.

"SMW Scanner, I wonder what that means? Must be short medium wave or something," he again spoke out to himself. Sliding the switch to one side the radio hissed then clicked and a voice rang out with a deep American accent, "The asset has left the elevator and is approaching the target's door."

"Fuck me!" exclaimed Cannon, "What the fuck - is this, cool!"

"Asset has reached the target's door, waiting on a green light," the radio announced.

Cannon looked down at the little silver radio in astonishment. He instantly gathered that Sir Adam had given him a device that could pick up walky-talky signals, but why? The American's voice spoke out again, "Are we good to go green?"

Cannon looked up from his seated position, only to see for a split second a flash of light glint through the opposite side of the bathroom mirror. Obviously someone had just pulled away the shelf wall of the maid's closet without properly closing the door behind them, thus momentarily illuminating the window on the other side of the one-way mirror. Oddly enough, despite having a secret observer, Cannon found that his bowels suddenly became relaxed, in fact so relaxed that his constipation ended extremely rapidly. He played ignorant to the fact he knew someone was watching him and switched off the radio. Cleaning himself and then standing to face the mirror he washed his hands. Cannon then took a moment to look into the mirror pretending to inspect his teeth and then calmly unlocked the bathroom door. The door opened inward which meant he could use it to conceal himself from whoever was behind the mirror without actually stepping out to face the entrance door. Standing as still as he could behind the bathroom door he looked at the radio and then rotated the volume dial so that it would be barely audible. He took a breath and then turned the radio back on, lifting it to his ear in the process. The same American voice spoke out, "Confirmed. Go green, go green, go green!"

The very next second there was a series of knocks on Cannon's room door. He quickly clicked off the radio and placed it on the floor next to him. With a swift kick the radio shot past the entrance door and disappeared into the adjacent open wardrobe. He knew that if he stepped out and looked through the peephole into the corridor his shadow would be providing an assassin with the opportunity to shoot him through the door. He also knew that if he just continued to stand there they would soon know he had detected them.

The Hacker Hunter © Copyright Lionwing Ltd 2011

There was no other way-out, not even a fire escape, and Cannon's room was nine stories up. He would never survive a jump. There were only two options: either open the door and be totally cool, or open the door and drag whoever was standing there in, throw them on the bed and run in the opposite direction down the corridor and out of the hotel onto the street. It took a split second to come to a verdict. He extended his left arm so he could reach the door handle without stepping out from his cover. Cannon pulled the handle down and yanked the door wide open. Lunging forward he grabbed and then pulled the standing figure into the room and with a massive burst of adrenaline turned and threw them onto the bed. He froze, unable to move, his plan destroyed. The door slammed shut behind him. Sprawled out on the bed was Sabrina. She lay there petrified with terror from the ferocity of her unexpected encounter with Cannon. Her legs were wide open from the impact causing her already short skirt to hitch up to reveal the thin black thong she had so obviously spent time choosing for the encounter. Sabrina lowered her arms which she had raised to protect her face and nervously spoke.

"What's going on Chris?"

Cannon just look dumfounded. He didn't reply so she asked, "What are you doing?"

Cannon snapped out of his frozen trance, it took a few seconds to put it all together but it had become clear to him. Sabrina had gone to the Yanks and sold him out, thinking she could make a little extra money. Sir Adam must have gained knowledge of Sabrina's betrayal, that must have been what the old man was talking about, thought Cannon, that must be why he gave me the radio. His mind raced for a reply to her question, his first desire was to say 'You fucking gold digging bitch' but instead he

The Hacker Hunter © Copyright Lionwing Ltd 2011

pulled together a smile and said playfully, "I thought you liked it rough?"

He walked to the bed and placed his knee between her open legs, he shunted up so the knee pushed against the crotch of her tight thong. Leaning over her he placed his hands between Sabrina's arms and body, pinning her to the bed. He looked down into her dark eyes, wondering if she had ever really felt anything for him like he had for her. She looked back and forth, her eyes darting around the room in a blind panic. Sabrina couldn't be sure but, had Cannon figured her out?

"What are you doing?" she asked, trying to act as if she had nothing to hide.

Cannon lowered his body onto hers, forcing her legs further open. She felt a stiff bulge push up against her thong and then Cannon's lips met hers. Softly, he kissed her. She was tempted to yield to his advance but she sensed that something wasn't right. If Cannon knew she had sold him out, what would he do to her? Any Russian man would beat her senseless, would Cannon? She felt the bulge from Cannon's trousers press harder into the crotch of her thong, the swelling lump caused her to moisten. She had always enjoyed sex with Cannon, but this time she fought her desire. 'I like this but he knows,' she thought. Her elegant hand reached down and gently placed a barrier between her groin and his. Cannon felt her long red nails push into his bulbous trousers and into his painfully hard manhood.

"Oh you like that do you Cannon?" asked Sabrina. She raced for ideas to escape from her situation. She pulled down his fly and rooted around until she worked free his hard, long, and thick penis. Holding it tightly with her right hand she used her other hand to pull her thong to one side. Cannon pushed forward but

Sabrina directed downward so it just brushed against her ass cheeks.

"Steady Cannon," she spoke softly into his ear. "Let me get to the bathroom, I need to freshen up first."

Cannon stopped kissing. She sensed something was wrong, 'my God', she thought. Had Cannon figured out that an American operative was stationed behind the mirror? Cannon must be on to her, if she could somehow get to the mirror she could signal for help, maybe silently mouth out 'he knows'. Cannon started kissing again but Sabrina turned her face away. "Chris I need to freshen up first, I just want to use your bathroom to rinse my mouth out. I've been smoking and I know you don't like that," Sabrina said, more seriously.

Although gentle in touch Cannon was raging inside with anger. He felt her hard red nails squeeze into his cock and lifted himself back and rolled to one side, holding onto her arm so if she were to flee or attack he'd be able to restrain her and protect himself. Casually Cannon said, "You're chewing gum, aren't you? All I can taste is minty freshness."

She released her hold on Cannons manhood and rolled over, pushing her buttocks into Cannons crotch. His body stiffened, he too had to fight the urge to lose control of the situation. Now on her front, Sabrina half slid off the bed dropping to her knees. She lifted her body upright, Cannon moved with her, still holding her arm. He looked down at her. She gently wrapped her long fingers around his now pounding member. He marvelled at her perfectly manicured red nails and then realised that her red nail polish also matched the colour of her lipstick. Sabrina's lush, full, red lips glistened as they slid all the way down. Cannon couldn't win this one, he let go of her arm. She gently cupped his balls and lifted her mouth away.

The Hacker Hunter © Copyright Lionwing Ltd 2011

"I'll be back in a minute," she said. "I'm just going to flush my gum down the toilet."

Cannon braced up as he snapped back to his senses, she lowered again just to give him one last moment of pleasure, feeling this would weaken him and allow her to make an escape. As her moist lips firmed up around the end of his cock Cannon placed his hand firmly on the back of her head and said, "Don't worry about the gum, just swallow it!"

The Hacker Hunter © Copyright Lionwing Ltd 2011

Chapter 9 – Mac and Bob

The flickering light from four flat screen CCTV monitors danced around the dark, windowless room. This cold, dim, monitor light exposed the shape of a few metal shelves and plastic crates, the type of crates associated with carrying sensitive electronics and weaponry equipment. These crates lay around the floor in abundance, sometimes stacking up two or three high. In the darkest corner of the room, half propped up against a wall and half laid out across the floor sat the still figure of John Mac. Mac's lower half was covered with an old sleeping bag, the colour of which remained unfathomable given the dim blue grey ambience emitted from the screens. In this light the sharp features of Mac's face cast deep shadows, producing an effect that silhouetted the hollows of his cheeks and eyes. As Bob left his seated position in front of the monitor screens and walked stealthily towards Mac's motionless figure. He observed Mac's face. In Bob's mind Mac looked like death himself. Concerned about waking the Grim Reaper Bob spoke out in a croaky half whisper, "Mac, wake up!"

Mac's body remained still, showing no sign of movement. Bob spoke again, "Something's happening!"

There was a slight rustle as Mac pulled the sleeping bag away from his legs, he paused momentarily to summon the energy needed to lift himself from the floor. Placing both hands flat on the ground Mac pulled his knees up and with a shove raised himself to face Bob. Bob turned towards the screens and said, "A man has entered the maid's closet and a woman just vanished into Cannons room, when I say vanished it looked like she was pulled in, pronto!"

"Do you know who the girl was?" asked Mac

The Hacker Hunter © Copyright Lionwing Ltd 2011

Bob didn't reply with an answer but simply announced, in a half whisper, "Something's not right Mac."

To the side of Mac's sleeping bag laid his tatty old duffle coat. Bending to pick it up and then sliding each arm through Mac replied, "It's time to go to work Bob. I'll need a phone and the car keys mate. What's the traffic like this time of day?"

Bob remained fixated, staring intensely at the monitor screens. Seemingly waiting for something dreadful to happen, he replied to Macs question, "Not too bad, it'll take you thirty minutes to get to the Renaissance from here, cash and weapons are in the crates."

Bob turned from the screens and pointed at two large plastic crates, Mac followed the invisible line that Bob was directing his attention to and then looked back at his trusted cohort and said, "Just a phone and the keys please Bob."

Bob nodded and then walked to a metal rack of shelves that half lent against the furthest wall of this small, dark, box room. Bob reached out with both hands and pulled from a middle shelve a set of keys and a mobile phone, as he passed them to Mac both men exchanged serious glances. It was evident that both were now acting out some degree of professionalism. Mac broke the moments silence with an order.

"Listen, you stay here. Wait for my call. I'll need your eyes on them; if anything changes let me know."

Bob looked back at the screens, he raised his fist and then extending a finger pointed at the screens, he took a breath and said, "I've only got two camera units up. They are all broadcasting to an amplifier box that I placed on the hotel roof

The Hacker Hunter © Copyright Lionwing Ltd 2011

yesterday. We've got about three days of battery life left. I'm only able to see the corridor to Cannon's room and the lift doors on his floor." Bob spoke with an air of dissatisfaction, as if to say two cameras were really nowhere near enough.

"Where are they?" asked Mac sternly.

"Both are in black dome cases, one is stuck to the middle of the ceiling in Cannon's corridor, 9th floor. The other one is also on the ceiling by the lifts on that floor."

"Someone must have noticed them by now?" asked Mac.

"No one looks up. Besides, they look very similar to the hotel's CCTV system," Bob replied.

"Anything by the exits?" Mac asked as he dropped the keys for the car into his right coat pocket.

"No, the hotel was too busy, couldn't put them up."
Bob walked closer to Mac, he stopped only a few steps away and then reaching towards Mac with an outstretched hand, gestured to Mac to pass him back the mobile phone. Mac continued to hold the phone in his left hand but asked, "Bob, anything I need to know about the car?"

With his hand still outstretched towards Mac's phone Bob replied in a professional monotone voice, "It pulls to the right, top speed is 95 mph, it has new tires, the spare is in the boot along with a jack, no engine trouble, you'll get 220 miles to a tank at 75 mph and 180 at 85, regular petrol, the car hides no weapons or wires but there's $5,000 in the glove box for you to buy your way out of trouble with the local police if need be."

"Spare keys?" questioned Mac.

The Hacker Hunter © Copyright Lionwing Ltd 2011

"Drivers side wheel, magnetic box," answered Bob.

"I'll need some duct tape," requested Mac in a slightly more casual manner.

"One step ahead, duct tape and Stanley blades are in a small tool bag that's placed under the front passenger seat, along with an old hat and gloves. There is also a grey rain coat in the boot." Bob's outstretched hand fell to his side, signifying defeat in his nonverbal request for Mac to pass him back the phone.

Mac looked down at the phone that Bob had so obviously been keen to get back and asked, "Is your number in this mobile?"

Bobs look changed to one of excitement. "May I?" asked Bob, raising his open hand again. Mac placed the phone firmly into Bob's hand, Bob turned the phone to show its side and pointed to a sliding switch that ran a thumb's length. Bob then said keenly, "Nope, don't worry Mac I'm not that stupid, and there's no call history either so you don't have to worry about the phone falling into the wrong hands. This phone has a few hidden extras!"

"What do you mean?" Mac asked whilst extending his open hand indicated to Bob to return the phone, as time was running short. Bob knew that Mac had to leave, so responded with more haste in his voice, "You see that slide switch on the side? Pull it down and press any of the keys on the dial pad." Bob slid the switch down. Two short, pointed, metal prongs suddenly protruded from the bottom of the phone. Bob beamed with a joyous grin and announced to the mystified Mac, "It's a Taser Gun! Jab only, skin contact is best, neck or arms. You only get about five good shocks out of it and then the phone's dead."

The Hacker Hunter © Copyright Lionwing Ltd 2011

Mac smiled, his eyes glistening. "Great, looking forward to using that. There's no chance of me frying myself with this is there?"

Bob chuckled and replied, "Just remember to slide the catch back up after use."

Mac's smile vanished. He took the phone from Bob and dropped it into the left pocket of his duffle coat. He then turned and walked to a flight of six large concrete steps. The steps ended their ascent at a metal hatch in the ceiling, the hatch had a hand grip, just large enough to get two hands through. Mac climbed the first three steps, turning and sitting on the third step he reached up to the grip. With a hard tug the metal hatch slid forward, revealing above them a car chassis. There was just enough room for Mac to climb out from under the car into the old Soviet cement garage that sat above their concealed bunker. Bob half pulled the hatch closed but before doing so looked up at Mac and said, "Mac there's a map of Moscow and a map of West Russia in the car. Both are in a pocket behind the front passenger seat. I'll be able to track you by your phone as long as the battery is in it so if you get lost just call me."

Mac bent his knees so he could sit on his heels and look down at Bob. "That, I don't like!"

Bob looked up through the half open hatch that acted as a floor when closed for a mechanic's pit under the car. The light coming from the monitor screens below cast just enough illumination for him to make out Mac's stern looking face. Bob answered, "New generation, new technology."

"That doesn't make it a good idea," Mac snapped back, clearly unhappy with the concept of being tracked. Mac pulled the phone from his pocket and tossed it back and forth between each hand. "If this is a company phone it means Sir Adam can keep tabs on me, and I don't trust that bastard one bit!"

Bob's face changed to show total understanding, there was no question Mac was right to be wary of Sir Adam. In this game, secrecy and stealth were Mac's only allies. However, Bob new full well that Mac would need support and a mobile phone provided him with a means to an end.

"Mac, take the phone, you'll need it. If you are that concerned over any of us knowing where you are take the battery out and we will not be able to track you," Bob spoke with an air of empathy in his voice.

Mac stood up and dropped the phone back in his pocket, growled and then muttered a few words of disapproval under his breath before making his way through the darkness to the garage door. The garage was one of many, built in a terrace of garages which had been made to shelter residents' cars from the fiercely cold Moscow winters. He felt around for the release handle, Finding it, he whispered back at Bob, "Anyone out there?"

Bob looked down from his position on the steps beneath the car pit. He had to duck his head down to stare at the other two monitors, both of which revealed nothing but rows of other garages in front of and behind their current position. He paused just to be sure and then said, "Clear!"

"Text me when he leaves his room," Mac commanded in a whisper, then pulled the garage door open to reveal the cold night air of Moscow.

Chapter 10 - I'll Kill That Bastard For Free!

Cannon took a step out into the corridor. He'd left Sabrina in the bathroom. She was unaware that he was leaving and was no doubt silently mouthing the words 'He knows!' in front of the mirror. Cannon placed a hand on his hotel room door, letting the door close slowly to avoid alerting Sabrina to his escape. The door seemed to take an infinity to finally click shut. Cannon looked towards the maid's storeroom door, his face changed, somehow sharper, colder, and more focused. Perhaps it was a surge of adrenalin caused by the prospect of coming face to face with whoever was in the small spy room or perhaps just the realisation that out here, in the Wild East, love was easily traded for a fast buck. Cannon's recent confirmation of the knowledge that he was truly alone in life seemed to fuel him. He patted down the pockets of his coat, not the black, wool Burberry but a well worn dark green ski jacket. His choice in fashion was all native, even his high leg hiking boots were of Russian origin. Cannon stopped patting his pockets as he discovered the location of his British passport, a long black wallet and a separate bundle of cash.

There was no time for reflection, Sabrina could step out of the bathroom any moment and find that Cannon was gone. He jogged lightly down the corridor, upon reaching the lifts Cannon pressed his thumb on the silver 'call' button and almost instantly a clanging noise emanated from behind the well polished metallic doors. Looking up Cannon observed that the nearest of the three lifts was only a few floors away. Cannon pondered how long it might take for Sabrina to figure out he had left. There was a 'ping' and the shiny metal doors slid across revealing the plush wood and smoked mirror interior. Cannon stepped into the open lift and reached across to the metallic panel of floor buttons, he pressed the button marked '-1' three or four times franticly. As the doors slid across to meet each other Cannon said under his breath, "About bloody time!"

Macs silver grey Volga turned in from the main road and slowly passed the two story high silver domed building that housed the Renaissance's swimming pool and cinema. After a hundred meters or so the Volga pulled up to the curb just opposite the stadium that the hotel had been built to serve. The dim orange street lighting provided just enough visibility for Mac to see the passenger seat to his right. Mac half turned his body and bent to lean across the gear stick. Reaching under the empty seat he pulled up a small bag of tools. Placing the bag on his lap he slid across its zipper revealing gloves, a hat, a roll of duct tape, a box of Stanley blades and a few oily tools. Mac took the tape and the box of blades out and placed them on the dashboard of the car. He then placed the bag down in the passenger's side foot well. Now free to move, Mac undid the belt buckle of his tatty trousers, tugging the belt up to reveal a small length of its smooth under side. Just then Macs phone vibrated. Using his free hand to reach into his coat pocket he located the phone and pulled it out to view its screen. The phone had a text message reading, 'moving'.

Mac spoke out in a whisper, "Talk about getting caught with your trousers down."

After placing the phone back into his pocket Mac reached out for the duct tape, he released his belt and using both hands pulled then tore a small strip of tape. Placing the tape sticky side up on his leg he then pulled a slightly longer, second strip and placed it on his other leg, again sticky side up. Mac tossed the tape onto the passenger seat and reached for the box of blades. He pulled one of the shiny, sharp blades from the box and then placed the box down by the gear stick. Mac lightly folded the short strip of tape over the blade's cutting side. Mac quickly inspected his work to ensure that no sharp edge protruded from the tape cover. Satisfied with his inspection, Mac then placed the covered blade into the middle of the other strip of tape. This second strip was slightly longer, leaving a finger width of the sticky under surface either side of the blade. Mac gently lifted the longer tape which carried the covered blade and pressed it into the inside of his trouser belt. After rapidly doing back up his belt, Mac reached for the phone and dialled Bob's number.

Bob answered immediately in Russian, "Hello?"

Before replying Mac pulled the door handle release and then pushed at his door to open it. There was a twang and a clunk but the door remained closed. Mac pushed again and this time the car door creaked open. "Hello" repeated Bob. Mac asked, "Has he taken the lift?"

Bob answered, "Yes he's just entered it. He's wearing a tatty green hiking or ski jacket, black trousers and boots; he looks like a local."

Mac climbed out of the driving seat. Standing in the dimly lit road he pushed his door closed and placed the car key in the door lock. As he twisted the key, a clunking noise confirmed that all the doors were now locked. Mac started walking casually towards the silver dome. As he walked, he noticed the semi circle driveway that encompassed the rear half of the dome. The driveway led to the hotel entrance and then back round to join the same road that it started from. There were taxis lining all the way up. Parked right in front of the entrance was a black Volga, just like the car Mac was driving. A scruffy looking Russian was stood behind the Volga; he was desperately trying to squeeze the luggage of a well dressed businessman in to the boot. As Mac approached the first taxi he suddenly stopped.

The Hacker Hunter © Copyright Lionwing Ltd 2011

"Oh fuck it!" Mac said to himself under his breath.

Turning to face the silver grey Volga and then walking at a brisk pace back to the car Mac spoke again in a barely noticeable whisper, "I'm getting forgetful in my old age!"

Mac slid the car key into the passenger door lock, twisted and then pulled the door open. Reaching down to the glove box he felt around for its release lever. Unable to find it Mac punched the glove box with the underside of his fist. The box door just fell open and sure enough, just as Bob had said there was a wedge of cash sitting within. Mac pulled the cash from the glove box. It was hard to make out in the orange street light but it seemed to consist of both Russian and American currency. Tucking the cash into the inside pocket of his duffel coat, Mac stood back and pushed the door closed, locked it again and moved with some haste towards the rank of taxis.

The same black Volga was still at the entrance. Clearly Cannon had not left the hotel yet. Mac reached a small group of taxi drivers who were halfway up the driveway and huddled together lighting each other's cigarettes. Mac asked in Russian, "Good evening, can I buy a cigarette from one of you?"

A driver extended an open packet for Mac to pull one from and said, "The cigarette is free, but you'll have to pay me for a light."

The other drivers laughed, Mac smiled and said, "Can I pay you for that light in rabbit fur, or what the tourists call mink?"

The men roared with laughter, Mac took a step into the group; he was now one of them. From his new position Mac could see clearly through the glass windows and into the hotel lobby. The

The Hacker Hunter © Copyright Lionwing Ltd 2011

cover afforded by his new local friends made him invisible to anyone else that might be surveying the entrance, and invisible to Cannon should he appear.

It would take ten minutes or so for the cigarette to burn out, and then Mac would need to move on. To stay longer with his new friends would signify that he was there for some other reason than to just ask for a cigarette. As the final flecks of ash fell from Macs cigarette it had become clear to Mac that Cannon had not left the lift at the lobby. Thanking the drivers Mac walked back towards his car. Whilst walking, he pulled the phone from his pocket and dialled Bob's number. Mac asked, "Bob, he's not entered the lobby, what other floors did the lift stop at?"

The camera placed by the lifts on Cannon's floor had provided Bob with the ability to view the floor numbers for each lift shaft. Bob had jotted down the floor that the lift carrying Cannon had stopped at, and Mac could hear a rustle as Bob turned sheets of paper, then Bob spoke, "The lift stopped once at the fourth floor. Oh wait, after the lobby it went down one level before going back up to the fourth floor again."

"What's beneath the lobby?" asked Mac

"There is a restaurant and a bar, I think." Bob replied hastily.

Mac reached the driver side door of the grey Volga, with his free hand he pulled the key from his pocket. Whilst unlocking the door, he spoke into the phone, "He's British, I'm betting there's a pint in front of him. He will either go back to his room after a few beers, or he'll head out; either way this could take a few hours."

Bob lent back in his chair, preparing himself for a long night. Just then from the corridor camera, Bob spotted Sabrina.

The Hacker Hunter © Copyright Lionwing Ltd 2011

"Mac, the girl has just come out of Cannon's room. She's stomping off down the corridor. Wait she's stopped at another hotel room door. She's knocking…. some guy just stepped out and let her in!"

"What did he look like?" asked Mac with a measure of urgency in his voice.

"I just got a glimpse: dark suit, short dark hair, white shirt, dark tie, in his forties, white," Bob recalled.

Mac raised his hand to his face and ran his fingers through his Viking moustache in a moment's contemplation and then asked, "Can you play back the footage? I need you to describe his shoes."

Bob raised an eyebrow, this was a strange request, but the one thing he had learnt from all his years of working with Mac was never to question his logic. Bob answered, "Hold on, I can only see one shoe. The film is a bit grainy, I'd say he's wearing black leather, lace up, well polished."

"Flat or heeled?" Mac quizzed.

Bob's second eyebrow raised, leaning forward he squinted at the monitor and replied, "It looks leather heeled but I can't be a hundred per cent certain, the image quality isn't that good."

Mac stopped grooming his moustache. His face fell motionless, with a deadly stern voice he said, "It's the NSA." Knowing that Bob would want to know how he had reached this conclusion, Mac continued, "Those clowns never go native. Worst spies in the world, and they love to polish their shoes. It's always a giveaway."

In disbelief Bob asked, "How do you know it's not the FSB?"

Mac laughed and replied more jovially "The FSB love their trainers and flat shoes."

Bob returned the laugh and with a mix of respect for Mac's perception and experience said, "You have to be kidding me?"

Mac, still stood at the driver side door turned to face the Hotel, he swapped the phone to his other hand and, after locking the car door and dropping the keys back into his pocket said, "Mate, I bet you a fiver that Cannon's girlfriend is working for the NSA, and I bet you another fiver that Cannon's just figured it out. He's probably in the bar right now getting pissed."

As Mac was speaking Bob stood up and walked from the monitors to one of the shelves, still holding the phone to his ear, he rooted around with his free hand for a few seconds until finally it re-emerged gripping a sheathed combat knife. The idea of the NSA in the mix didn't sit well with Bob. Like the British GCHQ, the NSA specialised in communications monitoring. In Bob's mind this meant there was the possibility that the American National Security Agency was already listening to his conversation with Mac and were on their way to pin pointing the location of the garage. Bob looked down at the knife and muttered to himself, "Ah my trusty Ka-Bar, best thing the yanks ever made."

Bob shot a quick glance back at the monitors, expecting to see nothing but in fact, to his amazement, discovering the rugby built figure of Cannon walking casually past the corridor camera. Bob almost dropped the phone in astonishment. If Mac was right, surely Cannon should be in the bar. Clasping the phone to his ear, Bob shouted,

The Hacker Hunter © Copyright Lionwing Ltd 2011

"Oh no, this isn't good!" He paused to wait for Mac's response but there was none, so Bob carried on with "Cannon has just walked past the camera in the corridor, he's heading to the maid's storeroom door."

The phone went dead. "Mac, Mac, are you there?" asked Bob.

Mac had placed the phone back in his pocket and was walking with measurable haste toward the hotel entrance. Upon reaching the entrance, Mac came face to face with a lofty built Russian hotel porter. The porter raised a finger and, waving it in Mac's face, said in Russian, "Not here. This is an executive hotel, be on your way."

Mac barged past the porter into the lobby. The reception desk was to his left, the lifts were to his far right and the toilets were to his immediate right. There was no sign of stairs at first glance, but then Mac spotted a narrow white door set just to the right of the lifts. This narrow door held a stencilled sign with the words 'Fire Escape Keep Clear'. It was a good bet that this door led to the stairwell. As Mac walked towards the door he heard the voice of the porter.

"Hey, you!"

Mac changed direction and headed right, towards the toilets. Pushing the door of the Gents open, he walked straight past the urinals and into a cubical, leaving the door of the cubical open behind him. The porter walked into the otherwise empty room, he could just make out Mac standing in an open cubicle with his back to him, seemingly urinating into the toilet bowl. He approached Mac and placed his hand on his shoulder. Mac reached across with his right hand and grabbed the porter's wrist. Pulling the startled porter forward, Mac twisted past him

The Hacker Hunter © Copyright Lionwing Ltd 2011

in a blur and dumped him on the toilet seat. The porter looked up from his new vantage point;. He was totally bewildered as to how he had suddenly arrived at this new location. His gaze dropped to Macs left hand, a mobile phone with two prongs sticking out of it was swiftly on its way to his neck. A cracking noise came from the toilet cubicle, followed by a banging as limbs thrashed out uncontrollably. A second later a loud thud sound reverberated through the empty room as Mac gave him a sharp blow to the point of his jaw. Mac emerged from the cubicle, stepping backward and pulling the door closed as he moved.

Seven floors above Mac stood Cannon. He had reached the door for the maid's storeroom and was frozen, deep in thought, perhaps reconsidering his intended course of action. Reaching down to the door handle his hand started to shake, the adrenalin was causing his heart to pound so hard that he felt he was losing control of his body. Cannon twisted the door handle of the maid's storeroom. To his shock, it wasn't locked, and with a click opened to reveal the back of a suited man. The man turned in a panic, but seeing Cannon's face he froze. Cannon just stood there in the doorway, his legs were shaking and his face was white. For a few long seconds neither man spoke and then Cannon broke the silence, speaking in Russian, Cannon announced, "So have you seen enough of my bathroom?"

The suited man's face creased up in incomprehension, in a thick American accent he replied "Hey, buddy…"

In mid flow the American's words were halted by Cannon's fist, which delivered a nose breaking blow to his face. The American raised both his hands in an attempt to block any further blows but failed to protect himself as Cannon stepped into the room and started furiously punching. Cannon's aggressive advance caused the man to trip backwards, falling

The Hacker Hunter © Copyright Lionwing Ltd 2011

against the one way glass mirror. The mirror cracked, and the man slid to the ground. Now sat on the floor of the small storeroom, half lent up against the bathroom wall the American attempted to fight back by kicking out at Cannon. One of the kicks impacted into Cannon's shin with an agonising blow. Fighting through the pain, Cannon drops both his knees onto the man's chest and delivered a second volley of punches. The first punch caused the American's head to turn, the second punch connected with the side of his jaw as did the next three. There was no room to fight clean. Cannon had to end this before the noise alerted others. However, the American wouldn't stop fighting back. He had taken just about everything Cannon could give and seemed to be able to take a lot more. As the American lashed out in all directions, Cannon lost his balance and fell backwards. Cannon pushed himself back up and launched himself at the man. However, the American pulled his knees up and then with his full force, pushed from both his legs, kicking outward at Cannon. Cannon was catapulted out into the corridor and landed flat on his back. Cannon looked up from his new position to see the American furiously charging towards him. The American's hands were out stretched ready to strangle his attacker to death. Cannon was still on his back in the corridor, he raised a foot in an attempt to kick the man and his heel connected with the Americans jaw causing his head to snap viciously backwards. The mans body collapsed over Cannon's, this lucky blow had knocked the American out cold or possibly killed him. Cannon could not be sure, but he knew he had to leave. Cannon twisted his body to get free, the dead weight of the man was quite remarkable. Cannon rose to his feet, triumphantly he grabbed each foot and dragged the still body of the man back into the maid's storeroom. Cannon pushed the store door closed and then sprinted down the corridor towards the lifts.

The Hacker Hunter © Copyright Lionwing Ltd 2011

Mac approached the seventh floor. Just a few steps to go and he'd reach Cannons floor, he grabbed the railing of the last staircase and panted, "Not as young as I used to be."

Just then, Macs phone buzzed, he pressed the talk button, and lifted the phone to his ear, but before he could say anything Bob's voice blurted out in an excited frenzy.

"Mac he's coming towards you. I've just seen the craziest of things," but before Mac could get the full story, the stairwell door in front of Mac burst open revealing a panic stricken Cannon.

"Stand aside my good man!" ordered Cannon as he hurtled past Mac.

Cannon was gone within a second, and Mac could just hear Cannon panting furiously for breath as he vanished down the flights of stairs. Still with the phone to his ear Mac exclaimed, "Fuck Sir Adam's two million. I'll kill that bastard for free!"

The Hacker Hunter © Copyright Lionwing Ltd 2011

Chapter 11 – Time to Leave

The tall, elegant pint glass was slender in design, yet oddly stylish in its simplicity. Someone, at some point, in some place, had thought long and hard over every detail of the bar, and spared nothing, not even on even this, the commonest of vessels. The cold golden liquid within chilled the glass to such a degree that condensation formed over its faultless exterior. As the moisture on the surface of the pint glass gathered in mass, droplets formed. When a droplet became too large and too heavy to hold on, it would burst into a watery stream that would run down the glass into the waiting beer mat. As Alex sat there staring intently at each streaming droplet, he theorised as to why some droplets seemed to be drawn towards each other. Suddenly, his concentration was broken as a beautifully manicured, long, red, nail, which passed his vision and pressed its finger tip gently against the pint glass' dewy surface. Alex found himself spellbound, unable to divert his gaze from the elegant finger tip as it sensually slid through the moist condensation. The now wet finger tip slowly rose away from the glass to meet its owner's full lush red lips. The lips glistened with the moistness from the glass as the finger gently released its passengers in a series of sensual caresses. The finger dropped away but Alex didn't follow it, he was transfixed on the most alluring lips known to red blooded man. Just then, the lips separated and from the open mouth came a velvety voice, "Oh no, I've gone and made my lips wet. Do you know what we should do about that?"

Alex Khomenko shuffled around on his bar stool, seemingly unable to reply. Spotting a wad of paper napkins just behind the bar he leaned across and then handed them to the beautiful redhead. She was leaning back on her stool, showing almost the full length of her amazing long legs, not at all expecting Alex as he reached across to her and with the hand full of paper napkins, wiped her lipstick across her face. As the lady's red lipstick smeared over her left cheek she flung her arms out in protest, pushing Alex back into his seat. With a look of absolute shock she spoke again, "What, are you stupid?"

Just then, a sweaty and very much out of breath Cannon appeared behind Khomenko. Placing a hand on Alex's shoulder, Cannon gasped out the words, "She's a hooker Alex. A prozzer, lady of the night, come on, we've got to go, right now!"

Alex passed the stunning redhead the bar napkins. She took them from him mainly to prevent any further wiping. Alex then leaped off his stool and said, "My drink Chris!"

Cannon placed a hand on each knee and took several deep breaths, he was obviously trying to recover from some form of extreme exercise. Eyeing the chilled golden beverage, Cannon, with one hand still on his knee beckoned Alex to bring him over the drink. Alex obliged by passing Cannon the glass. Cannon inspected its base, confident that there was nothing in the vessel other than a refreshing drink he then stood fully erect, tilted his head back and gulped down the entire pint in one action.

"Great, just what I needed, thanks Alex," Cannon gasped out whilst passing him back the empty pint glass. Alex didn't look too happy about being handed back an empty vessel and slammed it down on the bar, but before he could protest, Cannon grabbed Alex's arm and escorted him to the exit of the bar.

Alex, looking both mystified and aggravated pulled his arm away and demanded, "What's going on, I've been here for thirty minutes and you look like you just killed someone!"

Cannon laughed in an attempt to make light of the situation and between breaths replied, "I took the stairs, trying to keep fit. As for killing someone, bloody good guess, but I'm not totally sure he's dead, so let's get going!"

Alex looked back at the bar where the beautiful prostitute he'd left was reapplying her lipstick. She caught his eye and blew him a kiss. Alex looked confused, and in a loud voice called out to her from the exit, "Sorry about making your lips wet!"

Cannon rolled his eyes and yanked Alex through the exit to save the young lady from further humiliation. They both rapidly walked across the basement level of the Renaissance hotel towards the subterranean gym. The gym was actually housed in the big silver dome at the front of the hotel, but could be accessed via a wide corridor in the basement. Alex and Cannon walked through the gym and into the swimming pool area. A flight of steps led up to the ground floor from the far side of the pool. Cannon ran up the stairs, shouting back to Alex who was falling behind, "Come on keep up, we need to get a cab!"

Alex, still looking bewildered, caught up to Cannon and said, "The taxis are at the front of the hotel, we can get one from there."

At the top of the stairs were two doors, the door to the right had the words 'sauna' written on it whilst the door to the left had the words 'emergency exit'. Cannon pushed open the emergency exit and stepped through with Alex. They both emerged halfway down the semicircle drive at the front of the hotel. Cannon spoke out, "Alex I want to get a taxi from the street, these taxis are far too expensive, and I don't want to leave a trail from the hotel to our flat."

The Hacker Hunter © Copyright Lionwing Ltd 2011

Alex pointed towards a scruffily dressed man entering a silver grey Volga parked just a little way down the street. With his arm still outstretched towards the Volga Alex said, "This one will be cheaper, he's probably just dropped someone back to the hotel from the city centre and doesn't usually cover the hotel."

They both walked towards the Volga, and Cannon eyed the driver with suspicion. His Viking style moustache looked familiar. Mac noticed Cannon walking towards him, he walked around to the opposite side of the car, leaving Cannon and Alex on the other side. Alex asked in Russian, "Hello, are you able to drive us to 143, Festivalnaya Street fourteen building please?"

Mac was silent. His Russian was good, but he needed a few minutes to try and figure out what was actually happening. As he stared towards Alex, he noticed in the not too distant background four men in dark suits come out from the hotel entrance. The men were obviously NSA and would spot Cannon in a minute. Without further hesitation Mac walked rapidly around to where Cannon and Alex were, and pulled the back passenger side door open.

"Please get in, get in!" Mac said in Russian.

Cannon ducked down, and slid across the rear seat, allowing room for Alex to climb in through the same door. With both men now sat in the back of the Volga, Mac walked calmly around to the driver's side and climbed in. Mac straightened the rear view mirror to better observe the four NSA men and then said calmly in Russian, "I'm not sure how to get to Festivalnaya Street, can you help with directions?"

Alex nodded. Seeing this acknowledgment, Mac went to start the engine. As Mac lent forward to turn the key he noticed in the mirror that one of the NSA men had broken from the pack

The Hacker Hunter © Copyright Lionwing Ltd 2011

and was jogging up to the back of his car. Mac slipped the car into gear and pulled away with no particular haste. The NSA man ducked down as the car crept away in an attempt to see who was in the back, but was clearly unable to make out Cannon. Alex shouted, "Turn around, you need to turn around to get to Festivalnaya from here Turn right onto the main!"

Mac's moustache rose as he frowned. Alex's directions would mean driving towards the NSA man who was now walking back to the hotel. Mac turned the car as Alex had instructed and then pulled his phone from his pocket and extended it over the back of his seat towards Cannon. Cannon saw Mac's outstretched hand with the phone resting in the palm and asked, "What does he want Alex?"

Before Alex could reply, Mac dropped the phone, which fell to Cannon's feet. Cannon reached down to retrieve the phone and at the very same point the car passed the NSA man, who looked in to just see Alex and Mac, with no sign of Cannon. A few seconds later, and Cannon emerged with the phone and stated "Bloody heavy phone, what is it, you want to show me?" Cannon asked whilst passing the phone back to Mac.

In broken English Mac replied "Nokia, you like? I get cheap?"

Cannon reached into his tatty ski jacket and pulled from an inside pocket a small, stylish black phone. Folding it open, he lent forward and showed Mac. Mac cast a quick glance at the phone and then concentrated back on the road.

"Feel the weight of it," Cannon instructed. Mac took a hand from the steering wheel and grabbed the phone. He noticed that Cannon's phone was switched on. If there was one way the NSA would find them it would be by triangulating Cannon's mobile phone signal. Mac dropped the phone on his lap, swapped his

The Hacker Hunter © Copyright Lionwing Ltd 2011

hand from the steering wheel so Cannon couldn't see him pick the phone back up, and switched it off.

"Yes, I like," Mac replied. He then snapped, Cannon's phone closed and passed it back.

Cannon didn't even think to open the phone and check whether it was on or off, he simply dropped it back into his inside jacket pocket. Mac checked his mirrors, he could see that they weren't being followed. A short time passed, and no one spoke. Mac could see Cannon staring out of the window, obviously reflecting on recent events, perhaps considering his relationship with Sabrina, perhaps reflecting over the man's life he might have taken. Mac broke the silence.

"Are you tourist?"

"No, businessman. I've just figured out where I've seen you before," Cannon exclaimed.

"Yes, you passed me on stairs, I drop off customer's luggage. They don't let me use, how do you say, lift," Mac responded.

"Oh, I see. Yes - lift or elevator as the Americans call it," Cannon replied, though still seemingly more occupied with looking out of the side window.

"Do you have a name?" asked Alex.

"Yes, my name is Mikhail. I think you say in English, Mike," stated Mac.

Cannon broke his gaze from the window and turned to look at the back of Mac's head. He then said softly, "Mike, have you been working as a taxi driver for long?"

Mac looked in the rear view mirror, his eyes met Cannon's and for that split second both men froze in time, looking into each other's gaze. Cannon broke eye contact first, what he saw in Mac's fearsome blue eyes scared him. Mac's pupils were small black circles that projected intense aggression. They were the sort of eyes that belonged to nature's deadliest predators. Cannon asked, "You're Ex Army aren't you?"

Mac was momentarily speechless. How did Cannon know? More to the point, how much did Cannon know? All his years in the SAS, all his years working covert missions… had he become that transparent? Thinking of a quick reply Mac answered, "Everyone here is Ex Army. We have to go to Army after school, I driver in Army."

Cannon laughed and said, "I bet you're a pretty good driver, eh Mike?"

Mac's mind raced to figure out what Cannon was implying, but before he could say another word, Cannon said, "I need someone who can drive, and by drive I mean get us in and out of a tight fix when needed. Do you know what I mean Mike?"

Mac looked into the mirror to see what Cannon was doing. To his relief, Cannon was staring back out of the window into the Moscow night. Mac took in a breath and said, "I drive, but am only for short trips. Tourists are my business."

Smiling, Cannon said, "I've got a lot of short trips to make, a lot of places to go to over the next few days, and I don't want to have to find a taxi every time. How much would you charge for two days work, 8am to 8pm?"

Mac looked at Alex's reflection in his mirror. Alex sensed he was being watched and looked up. Mac took the opportunity to say in Russian, "I don't understand what this man is asking me?"

Alex elbowed Cannon in his side, Cannon turned from the window and looked at Alex with a questioning expression. Alex said, "His English, Christian, is not that good. He's asking what do you mean? Shall I ask him in Russian?"

Cannon nodded, and Alex asked Cannon's question in Russian. Mac wasn't even listening to Alex, he was more concerned about convincing Cannon he was just a simple taxi driver. Alex ended by giving Mac a few directions to Festivalnaya. Mac was so deep in thought he missed Alex's instruction and passed the exit. Alex said in Russian, "You missed the turning, take the next right. If you want the work I'll give you Cannon's telephone number, how good is your English?"

Mac looked at Alex through his rear view mirror and replied in Russian, "I will think about it tonight and call Cannon in the morning with my answer."

Alex turned to Cannon and said, "He will let you know tomorrow, give him your card."

Cannon stretched out, straightened his body as much as he could, given the space afforded to him by the back seat of the Volga. Lifting his arse from the seat he felt and then reached into the back pocket of his trousers. His left hand remerged holding two keys joined on a single key ring. Tossing the keys into the air and then catching them he said, "I take it you've not changed the locks since my last visit?"

Alex stared at the keys and then into Cannon's eyes.

The Hacker Hunter © Copyright Lionwing Ltd 2011

"I've not been back since your last visit, as you said the less people that know about this place the better," Alex answered abruptly.

It was clear that Alex found Cannon to be overbearing. Cannon's self-confidence and mannerisms were perceived by Alex as uneducated arrogance. In Alex's mind he always felt that had the tables been turned and he was the employer, not Cannon, then their relationship would be considerably more professional. Cannon's flippant approach to management, the use of humour to disguise orders and above all Cannon's whimsical nature rubbed against Khomenko's need for order. Alex knew that his intelligence was vastly superior to any person from the decadent West. However, Cannon had the contacts, the opportunities and the drive to make money, and it was money that Alex needed to lift himself from the poverty stricken ruins left by the collapse of the USSR. For now Alex would tolerate Cannon's games but deep down inside Alex felt there would come a time when he would be calling the shots. Cannon stretched out again this time reaching into his other back pocket.

"Here you go Mike, here's my business card. The number is on it, however, if you want the job simply turn up tomorrow at 7:30 am at where you are dropping us off tonight."
Cannon passed his card to Mac and then said to Alex, "Alex, we need to talk about how you're going to do this hack."

"Not here, not in the taxi!" Alex snapped in a paranoid frenzy.

"You are kidding me? You think our driver can even understand English that well?" asked Cannon.

"Well enough," Alex answered tetchily.

"AK, we're going to be talking when this guy is driving us around tomorrow. Believe me, he's not going be remotely interested. You Russians are so paranoid, it's just State propaganda that's done that to you. Take a chill pill and let's get down to business."

Mac breathed a sigh of relief. From Cannon's statement it was clear that he'd just had a lucky guess about Mac having served in the Army. Mac sneaked a look in his mirrors just to check again that they weren't being followed and then, after glancing back at the road, looked at Alex. Khomenko had taken to looking out of his window, clearly upset by Cannon's lack of concern. As Alex peered into the orange lamp lit streets of Moscow. He thought back to the stories his grandfather had told him about Stalin. Alex's grandfather had started life as a watchmaker and later in the Second World War worked in the Russian Air Force building instruments for experimental fighter aircraft. His grandfather had once explained that Stalin believed a man worked best when the life of his family and friends was under constant threat. As a result, Alex's family had been placed in a labour camp whilst his grandfather worked under lock and key. Cannon could never truly understand the culture of fear that, even today, was bred into the Russian people. All risks to one side however, Alex needed Cannon as much as Cannon needed him.

The silver grey Volga left the main road and entered a narrow service alley that led to a collective of grubby metallic dumpsters. The dumpsters were brimming with rubbish. Obviously this was a place the local residents used to discard their waste and the waste hadn't been taken away for weeks. To the left of the car was a grey concrete block wall, five feet high, with a mesh wire fence behind it. The fence went up another ten feet or so. It was odd to Cannon that there was

The Hacker Hunter © Copyright Lionwing Ltd 2011

hardly any graffiti on the wall. The same wall in Manhattan, LA or London would have been coated in tags and murals. He pondered the reason why. Perhaps the Russians found better things to spend their money on than paint aerosol spray, or perhaps the creative freedom of the people had been suppressed by the state to avoid subversive messages.

"Alex, why is there no graffiti on this wall?" asked Cannon curiously.

Alex shot Cannon an annoyed glance, the sort of glance that said 'Are you that stupid?' and then said,

"Mikhail, stop here, please." Turning his body to face Cannon whilst at the same time reaching for the door release Alex replied, "This is where people live, it is not a place to cover in, how you say, crap."

As Mac stopped the car he glanced behind, no cars had followed them. Mac then lent across the passenger seat to look up at the nine story block of flats to his right. He felt a twinge of pity for the poor people that lived there. Nine stories of grey concrete, accessed by 4 grubby metal doors.

Alex stepped out of the car, as did Cannon, who then walked to Mac's window.

"How much dingy?" asked Cannon.

"Two Fifty," replied Mac, as he let down his window. Money was exchanged and Cannon left to catch up to Alex who was already standing at the middle entrance. As Alex and Cannon vanished into the block, Mac reached for his phone and dialled Bob.

The Hacker Hunter © Copyright Lionwing Ltd 2011

"You are not going to believe this ,Bob, Cannon wants me to be his driver," stated Mac.

"What?" exclaimed Bob, his welsh accent sounding out in amazement.

"Hold on, Bob, I want to see what flat they are staying in." Mac lent across the passenger's seat again, he looked up at the dark grey tenement block. Sure enough, one of the dark, unlit windows of the ninth floor suddenly illuminated. "Got them, 9th floor. Listen, what have you got in the way of surveillance equipment?" asked Mac.

Bob chuckled and replied, ~You know out here if you get caught with that shit they'll throw away the key. Seriously, you'd get into less trouble if you were caught with a blood drenched dagger!"

"Stop fucking around, Bob, have you got it or not?"

"Do you need to ask? You'll love it. Do you want me to bring it up to you?" enquired Bob more seriously.

Mac replied "Yes I'm at..." but before he could finish, Bob interrupted with "143, Festivalnaya Street, building fourteen."

"What? How did you know that?" shouted Mac.

"Like I said, Mac, as long as your phone is on I can track you. I'll be there in twenty minutes."

Mac turned the phone off and then fumbled around with it in a frustrated attempt to find out how to remove the battery. It seemed there was no actual way to take out the battery without destroying the phone. In temporary defeat Mac tossed the phone onto the passenger's seat and started the engine. Slipping the car into reverse, he drove backwards out onto the main road. Just opposite the exit to the alley were a few shops and a place to park. Mac waited for the traffic to pass and then drove in a semicircle across the road and into a free parking space in front of the still open shops.

Mac stepped out of the Volga and stretched. He casually locked the car and started walking down the road. The tenement block that Alex and Cannon had vanished into was one of many. The building itself was positioned in the middle of four or so other blocks. There was about ten car lengths of mud and grass between each of the opposing buildings and not a lot else. Not the best place to stand with a set of headphones and a sound dish pointed up at a window. Mac knew he would need to get onto the roof of the opposite block and then he'd be able to point whatever sound surveillance equipment Bob had at Cannon's window. As Mac continued to walk he observed all the little balconies that each apartment had. Each balcony was different from the other. They almost seemed to act as a statement, reflecting the individuals who lived within. Some balconies were enclosed in what looked like home made corrugated plastic greenhouses, others just sported a makeshift roof and a few chairs. It fascinated Mac to see how, even in a world where people were meant to be treated equally, just how different people were and how much pride people took in being different.

A dark blue Volga pulled up behind Mac's car, at the steering wheel sat Bob, who was grinning ear to ear. Mac spotted Bob's Volga and walked up to the car. Opening the passenger door, Mac leant in and asked, "Does the Company have anything other than Volga's?"

Bob laughed and replied, "Yes, but not for the likes of us I'm afraid. Jump in, I want to show off what you asked for."

Mac climbed into the passenger's seat and asked, "So what have you got for me?"

"You are going to love this Mac. Not even MI6 have this in their spy kit yet, it's bird shit," announced Bob smugly.

"For fuck's sake Bob, what are you talking about?" asked Mac less tolerantly.

"Hold onto to this." Bob reached across Mac and opening the glove box pulled out a portable CD player and a set of small ear phones. Mac took the player from Bob, but was clearly not impressed.

"Which window?" Bob asked excitedly.

Mac glared at Bob with a look that said 'You better not be about to do something stupid,' and replied "Ninth floor, ten windows in from the right."

Bob pushed down the handbrake, checked his mirrors, and then drove the car out from behind Mac's Volga, across the street and down into the alleyway that adjoined Cannon's and Alex's apartment block.

"Pull your window down Mac," instructed Bob, as he lent across him to reach a blanket on the backseat. Lifting the blanket away Bob revealed a black walking stick. It was nothing special, the sort of stick an old man might use to help him get around. Picking up the walking stick and sitting back down into the driver's seat Bob pulled off the rubber foot to reveal the stick was in fact an empty barrel. Bob quickly checked that the entrance of the tube was clear of obstructions and then slid his hand across the walking stick to the bone 'L' shaped handle. He

The Hacker Hunter © Copyright Lionwing Ltd 2011

turned the handle ninety degrees and pulled hard. About a finger's length down the black shaft a small hole appeared. Bob reached into his left pocket and pulled out a small white ball. Dropping the ball into the hole, he then twisted the handle back into its original position, closing the opening as he did so.

Bob passed the stick to Mac and said, "Take this, I should have loaded it before leaving, but here's how it works. The handle contains a canister of highly pressured gas. It's compressed enough to shoot a round 150 meters in a straight line, but you only get one shot." Mac looked at Bob in astonishment; he could see a small trigger had popped out from the handle. Taking the stick from Bob, Mac turned in his seat but it was almost impossible to get the right angle to target the window. Cracking open the car door and placing a foot out onto the ground helped Mac lower his body just enough to line up the stick with his target. With only one shot Mac would have to get this right first time. There was a hiss and then a dull splat as Mac pulled the trigger and the small white ball was propelled from the walking stick and impacted on the window.

"What was that noise?" asked Cannon.

Alex walked to the window and pulled the curtain back.

"A bird has shitted on the window," Alex replied whilst observing the white stain with a few pellets of black in its centre.

"Oh, that's meant to be lucky Alex, ok let's get down to business. I need to know how you are going to do this," replied Cannon.

The Hacker Hunter © Copyright Lionwing Ltd 2011

Chapter 12 – Mac Trap

The smooth, well polished rosewood bowl of a smoking pipe glistened red and black under the desk lamp's illuminating hue. Its well carved, bulbous shape made the rings and knots of its wood look like patterns of warmly pleasing swirls and spirals of deeply rich smoke. The long, slender, jet black stem of the pipe offered a curvaceously inviting allure, yet this finely crafted smoking instrument lay there in the deep round crystal ashtray unattended. The ashtray sat on the dark green leather inlay of Sir Adam's well worn mahogany partners' desk, to its side rested a set of golden cufflinks, each sporting the same ancient family crest, and next to these stood a quarter full glass of whisky, no ice.

To the left of the ashtray, cufflinks, and whisky glass, Sir Adam's right elbow pressed into the leather surface of his desk. His sleeves were rolled up and he held in his right hand a medium sized picture frame. The frame was home to an old photograph of a young lady, and what appeared to be her son. Sir Adam stared at the picture with a blank, cold look. It was almost as if the picture had sucked any remaining emotion from his old, yet noble face. Sir Adam's left hand rested outstretched over a document entitled 'GRU Transcript, Classified.' On his ring finger Sir Adam wore an old, tarnished, golden wedding band.

"Do you remember them Grace?" asked Sir Adam in an attempt at making a light moment. Sat opposite him was the handsome figure of an elderly lady, she placed her pad and pen down on Sir Adam's table and said, "It's late Frank, you've had a long day. You should go home." She reached out and took the picture frame from him, pushing the chair she was sat on out from beneath her as she rose gracefully to her feet. "I remember they loved you very much," she said, smiling as she leant forward and placed the picture back down on Sir Adam's desk.

"I've worked as your personal assistant for longer than I care to recall, we've all paid a steep price for Queen and Country. I have no children and no husband to grow old with, I often wonder if it was really worth it," Grace remarked rhetorically.

Sir Adam looked across at the picture that Grace had just placed back in its original setting and asked, "Well, was it worth it?"

Grace looked away, it was clear she was very fond of Sir Adam. They had shared many years of testing times together, and through this had grown to trust each other with their innermost feelings. Grace stiffened as if bracing herself against a bitterly cold wind and said, "I see the way you look at Christian. You think of him like the man your son would have grown up to become. Why the hell are you putting him through this stupid game? Why the hell are you putting yourself through this madness?" Grace's face was as stern as her voice. Her point suggested that Sir Adam had gone mad with the loss of his only child and wife. Furthermore, his madness had driven him to seek out a surrogate son, a son who this time would survive him no matter the odds.

Sir Adam's gaze sharply broke from the picture frame, his eyes met with Graces. They glistened as though on the brink of building a tear drop. No tear arrived. Instead Sir Adam calmly rebuffed,

"Gracey, you and I both know that if I'm to retire, the man that takes on my job must be able to survive anything. If Cannon can survive the NSA, GRU and Mac then he's the best we've got for my replacement. I can't carry on doing this for ever you know, and neither can you for that matter. Sir Adam paused for

The Hacker Hunter © Copyright Lionwing Ltd 2011

a contemplative moment and looked down at his pipe before continuing, "Listen, Grace, why don't you come over to the Manor this weekend? Just you, me and the dogs. The country air will do you good."

Grace still held the same stern expression on her face. She reached down and collected her pen and pad from Sir Adam's desk. She pulled the pad into her chest, and walked towards the exiting door. As Grace reached the door she freed a hand from clutching the pad and extended it to twist the door knob. The door opened and after half stepping through Grace stopped, she looked back at Sir Adam, who had been watching her exit, expecting a reply to his invitation.

"I find the Manor such a lonely place. You know me, Frank, I've always been a City girl."

Sir Adam smiled, his eyebrow lifted. It was clear that Grace was no longer a girl even though sometimes her emotional outbursts led him to believe she could act like one. He turned in his chair to face her, placing his right hand on the document labelled 'GRU Transcript, Classified' he tapped it three times with his index finger whilst saying,

"Grace, do me a favour. Before you leave can you print out Mac's version of this please?"

"Haven't you read it already?" asked Grace.

"Yes, but I want a printed copy for dramatic effect. Can you do it now please? I imagine that buffoon Robert will be knocking down the door any moment, I'll need it for him." Sir Adam stated.

"Yes Sir." Grace smiled and left the room, closing the door behind her.

Sir Adam swung back around in his chair to his original position. He looked over the green leather covered surface of the partners' desk until his eyes met with the rosewood smoking pipe which was still neatly resting in the clean crystal ashtray. Lifting the pipe from its resting place, Sir Adam dropped his head forward and hung the pipe from his mouth. He then leant back into his well worn, comfortable chair and patted down his trouser pockets in search of a lighter. Just then his phone buzzed loudly, which gave him cause to stop his quest for fire and reach across to the flashing red button on his phone dial pad. Pressing it, he then gripped the pipe with his teeth and snarled out "Yes Grace?"

"Robert is here to see you Sir Adam," Grace's voice replied through the tinny speaker phone.

Sir Adam pulled the pipe from his mouth, and replied reluctantly, "Bring him up please, oh and bring me that document as well, then that will be all for the night. Thank you, Grace."

Sir Adam, still holding his unlit pipe stood from his seated position and stretched out his arms as if to waken himself from a day of reading at the desk. There was a knock at the door.

"Come in please," invited Sir Adam. Grace and Robert walked in together. Grace passed Sir Adam a printed document and then bid Sir Adam good night as she left. Robert waited for Grace to leave and then walked straight over to Sir Adams desk to face him. There was confrontation in his eyes.

"What's bloody well going on Sir Adam? I want answers!" demanded Robert in an aggressive tone.

Sir Adam walked around from his desk so he could face Robert with nothing between them, holding his pipe by the bowl he pointed the black pipe stem at Robert and asked jovially,

"Things not going well at SIS Robert?"

Robert's face turned from a furious red to a livid beetroot colour, "I'm sick of your bullshit old man, what the hell is Cannon playing at? I've got the NSA screaming blue bloody murder!"

Sir Adam's smile dropped. He didn't much care for swearing, unless it was by his own tongue. "You'll have to make yourself clearer than that Robert if I'm to understand what you're trying to tell me. Drink old boy?"

Sir Adam pushed by Robert and walked over to an already open drinks cabinet. He instinctively reached out and grasped a whisky bottle. The top of the bottle was wiggled free and from its now open, glistening neck. Sir Adam poured a healthy measure into an even healthier sized glass. Sir Adam remained focused on firmly reaffixing the stopper. This fine Scottish Whiskey was so pure it could easily escape its crystal prison as a vapour if the stopper was not firmly pushed in. After placing the decanter back in its rightful slot, Sir Adam then moved to the task of lifting the glass to eye level for a quick inspection before dangling it in front of Robert's nose, as a master would dangle a carrot in front of a mule. Robert snatched the glass and took a healthy sized swig from it, he looked no calmer, his incensed eyes piercing out at Sir Adam in anticipation of a long awaited answer to his question.

"Why don't you tell me what's going on with the NSA Robert? I'll try and fill in the gaps, best I can," Sir Adam asked.

Robert took another swig from the glass, this time empting it, wiping his mouth with the back of his hand he said, "The Yanks are screaming that Cannon killed one of their men. Is that true? Did Cannon kill an NSA operative in Moscow? I even have British Military Intelligence talking about sending '14 INT' to Moscow to find out what's really going on!"

Sir Adam straightened himself to his full height. Robert may well have been twenty years his junior, but at six foot one Sir Adam stood a great deal taller. Looking down at Robert, Sir Adam spoke in a patronizing yet commanding voice, "My dear Robert, please inform Her Majesty's Military Intelligence that Her Majesty does not require their services at this point in time. As for the NSA, please inform them that Cannon is not a British operative, nor is he working for any governmental department and they should treat him as they see fit. Oh, whilst you are on the phone to them, also ask if they have proof that a British Citizen was the cause of their agent being killed?" Sir Adam finished speaking and gave Robert a brief but poignantly affronted smile and then walked back to his desk.

Robert gazed at Sir Adam in astonishment, still holding the empty glass, Robert went to take a vacuous drink of air. On finding it empty he lowered the glass and placed it gently down on the corner of the partners' desk. In the process of parking the glass, Robert noticed two white documents on the desk top, both had almost blank cover pages, with the exception of titles. One read 'GRU Transcript, Classified', whilst the other sported the title 'Mac Transcript, Classified'. Robert knew better than to ask Sir Adam about the documents, so instead elected to repeat his earlier question, "I asked you what's going on Sir Adam. I am still waiting for an answer, if you'd care to give it."

Sir Adam reached out to the documents and shuffled them, he then rolled them together tightly and passed them like a relay baton to Robert. Robert stretched out his hand in a manner that seemed to show distrust towards this extremely generous offer. It was no secret that classified documents were rarely shared, even between high ranking officials. As Robert unfolded the documents he thought they must either hold little importance or Sir Adam must have an ulterior motive. Sir Adam spoke out, once more with irreverence in his voice,

"One is a transcription in English of a conversation between Cannon and his Russian contact, one Mr. Alexander Khomenko. Mac managed to find and then bug Cannon's Moscow 'safe house'. That's where this conversation took place." Sir Adam placed the pipe stem back in his mouth to signal he had finished speaking.

"The other document?" asked Robert.

Sir Adam pulled the pipe back out of his mouth and pointed at the GRU Transcript with the stem, leaning forward as if about to whisper a confidence to Robert he replied, "Well that's the odd thing Robert. You see, our man in Russian Military Intelligence leaked the other document to us from a different source, yet it seems to be a Russian transcript of the same conversation."

Robert's face screwed up in confusion, far too bewildered to put together a meaningful sentence, he just grunted out a questioning "Uh, did Mac sell Cannon out to the Russians?"

Sir Adam walked around Robert, still with his pipe in his hand and in a pose that would make for a perfect Sherlock Holmes impression. Sir Adam stopped to gaze up at one of the many old, eighteenth century oil paintings that lavishly covered his

The Hacker Hunter © Copyright Lionwing Ltd 2011

office walls. Seemingly engrossed in the painting Sir Adam replied, "Mac? Never! No, no, it's more likely the Russians already had the place bugged. My guess is the NSA aren't the only ones interested in Cannon." Sir Adam turned to face Robert and then continued, "The Russians must have had Cannon's safe house bugged well before Mac found it, which means they must be interested in something other than the list of hackers that Cannon is after."

"By Russians you mean the GRU," Robert stupidly interrupted.

Sir Adam's face dropped and he momentarily gazed up in frustration before replying, "I'd imagine the GRU are more interested in this Khomenko chap and his relationship with Cannon than a list of hackers hooked into the NSA's network."

Robert put his finger to his mouth in contemplation and then said out loud, "So let me get this right, Sir Adam, the NSA are after Cannon because they think he's killed one of theirs, the GRU are after Cannon because they think he's stealing research secrets with help from this, Alexander Khomenko person?"

"Yes ,that's pretty much the state of things," replied Sir Adam candidly.

"So what do you think will happen?" asked Robert in a considerably calmer manner than he had earlier adopted.

"Do try and use your bloody imagination Robert. For crying out loud, a SIS boss really ought to know better!" Sir Adam made his way towards the whisky glass on his desk, as he lent to pick it up with his left hand he suddenly halted midway. A look of pure puzzlement came across his face, a look that caused Sir Adam to give up on the notion of a drink and instead stand up straight and walk back to the oil painting he had been staring at only a few moments earlier. "He knows," Sir Adam said in a half whisper to himself.

"Sorry, I'm not following you, Sir Adam, who knows?" asked Robert in a concerned tone.

Sir Adam folded his arms and just stared up at the painting, he tapped his pipe stem against his chin repeatedly. Now lost in thought it was clear that Sir Adam was not even remotely interested in answering questions. Robert walked up to stand behind Sir Adam, he shuffled his feet like a school boy and then looked down for a few moments. Obviously concerned about interrupting Sir Adam whilst he was so clearly in deep thought, Robert took a deep breath in and as he released it, then asked, "Can you tell me anything about this other gentleman, Alex Khomenko?"

Sir Adam stopped tapping his chin with the pipe stem and turned to face Robert as if to address a man that had just spoken an obscenity. He then brushed by Robert without answering, within six or seven steps Sir Adam reached his seat. Placing a hand on its leather upholstered back for support Sir Adam bent his body downward to pull open the middle draw of his partners' desk. Robert turned to watch Sir Adam, unable to speak and clearly unable to fathom Sir Adam's actions, he simply just fixed his eyes on the old, well tailored, silver haired man.

The middle draw contained a keyboard of sorts, larger than a normal computer keyboard, with many more buttons and keys. Sir Adam pressed a button and then typed something quickly, maybe a password or maybe a command. Either way his action resulted in a clunking noise which emanated from the very same oil painting he had been looking at only moments before. The painting slid to one side to reveal a large flat screen computer monitor, Sir Adam continued to type and then a ringing noise,

The Hacker Hunter © Copyright Lionwing Ltd 2011

like a phones dialling tone rang out. The ringing stopped and a voice filled the room with,

"Good evening, Sir Adam, how can I help you?"

"Good evening, Dickie, can you load up the map please, I need to speak to Mac."

Robert broke his gaze from Sir Adam and looked up at the large flat screen monitor. In the top right of the screen a square box showed the face of a man that seemed to respond to the name Dickie. Beneath the square box a second image suddenly appeared a photo that Robert recognised straight away, the Viking moustache, the sharp features, the piercing eyes.

"John Mac, currently active on a company phone in Moscow, searching for his location now, Sir." The man stopped talking as he typed. A few moments passed and then the remaining screen filled with a global satellite map of the world. The border of the Russian federation illuminated and the world map was replaced with a map of Russia. A few seconds later and a flashing circle appeared on the map indicating the location of Moscow. The map changed again to show a bird's-eye-view of Moscow from 42km up. A flashing blue light appeared to the north of Moscow's centre.

"Show me the roads Dickie," ordered Sir Adam, fixated on the screen. The man typed and within a second the main roads of Moscow were superimposed in yellow over the satellite image. I have him moving East on "Sushevsky val, Sir Adam," Dickie announced.

Sir Adam paused, he looked at an utterly gobsmacked Robert and then back at the screen,

The Hacker Hunter © Copyright Lionwing Ltd 2011

"Do we have any eyes over Moscow?" asked Sir Adam.

"Not tonight Sir, I'm told the Americans might have their new spy plane out and about, would you like me to ask if they can get us a live feed?" Dickie replied.

"God no! We're already in deep enough with the Yanks, take us down to street level please, I'd like a 3D panoramic of where Mac is," Sir Adam asked politely.

Sir Adam walked out from behind his desk towards the monitor, remembering that he placed his pipe into his pocket whilst typing he pulled it free from his trouser pocket. Using the stem of the pipe as a pointer Sir Adam directed Robert's attention to the screen and said to Dickie, "Before Mac reaches the approaching junction text him a scramble code and instructions to take the right, park somewhere down Oktyabr and then to dial the code."

Frantic typing could be heard as Dickie followed Sir Adam's instructions. A minute or so passed, all three men watch the flashing dot as it failed to turn but instead continue down the road. A second later and the dot vanished all together.

"What's happened Dickie?" asked Sir Adam.

There was a silence and then Dickie replied "If I was to hazard a guess, sir, I would say Mac just threw the phone out of his window and under a passing truck, or something to that effect. I did however receive a text message from him."

"Go on man, what did it say?" demanded Sir Adam impatiently.

"The message reads, 'Fuck Off', Sir."

Robert let out a laugh, "I'm starting to like Mac," he chuckled out loud to Sir Adam's annoyance.

Sir Adam turned to Robert and with a glaring rage in his eyes said, "There will not be much left to like if we don't get a message out to Mac, he's about to walk into a trap that I fear the GRU and Mr. Khomenko have set for Cannon!"

Chapter 13 – The Hackers' Den

Mac tapped his rear-view mirror to catch a glance of Alex, who was sat quietly, looking out of his window from the back seat of the Volga. They'd been driving for fifty minutes at least and in that time Alex had only responded to Cannon's questions with an abrupt 'yes' or 'no' reply. Mac was sensing that something was not right. All of his years in the field had taught him to trust his instincts, and his instincts were screaming 'Trap!'. As Mac focused back on the sodden grey road, he heard Cannons voice ask, "Explain to me how this is going to work?"

Alex broke his gaze from the window and looked across at Cannon, he bit his bottom lip for a few seconds in contemplation and looked Cannon up and down with a pitiful expression. Cannon beamed ear to ear with a grin that would make the Cheshire Cat look like a sulking bag puss. Alex recognised the grin. It was a grin that said to him that Cannon was not going to give up asking until he got an answer that either made sense or was too complicated to follow. On realizing that Cannon would not shut up until he was given more than a 'yes' or 'no' answer, Alex took a big breath in and on releasing it with a sigh said, "I will try to explain. Let me put it this way, did you know that when you send an e-mail over the internet it can be divided into a million little packets of data, but each separate packet alone is totally meaningless? These packets can all be sent in a million different directions, along seemingly unconnected routes. A packet might travel as an electrical pulse through a copper wire, or a beam of light down a fibre optic cable. You might even find that part of your e-mail message is converted into a radio frequency and broadcast to a satellite which transmits it as a microwave signal halfway across the planet. Eventually, all the little packets of your e-mail reunite in someone's inbox, hopefully the person you were sending it to."

Cannon's smile dropped and he calmly replied, "I understand that data can be transmitted and received using electricity or frequencies, including light but I'm asking how you are going to get the actual physical locations of the fifty two hackers that my client claims are logged into the NSA's network?"

For the first time in the journey, Alex became animated beyond the slumped posture he had chosen to adopt. He raised a finger at Cannon, shaking it, Alex replied impatiently, "If you let me finish, Christian, my point is your client is lying to you. There is no way they could have found fifty two remote modems hooked into the NSA network."

Cannon's face was now the complete opposite of what it had been only moments before, with a frustrated look of annoyance Cannon snarled back, "Why bother to explain data transfer 101, why not just say 'Mafia Maria is lying'. Look, she is famous for running a team of the world's best hackers, why do you think she's telling fibs?"

Alex, seeing that Cannon was getting emotional turned his head and looked back out of the window at the passing blocks of grey cement that bordered the road. Feeling Cannons eyes on the back of his neck Alex spoke out softly as if speaking to a condemned man, "I do not want to upset you, Christian, so I will be silent."

Cannon looked over at the rear-view mirror to find Mac's eyes looking at him. Mac instantly broke eye contact and adjusted himself in his seat as if to distract Cannon from the fact he had just been caught looking into their conversation. Cannon looked back at Alex, seemingly unconcerned about Mac and flippantly replied, "Please feel free to upset me Alex."

The Hacker Hunter © Copyright Lionwing Ltd 2011

Alex turned back to face Cannon, and as if to justify himself said, "I explained data transfer to lead you onto the subject of IP addresses, routing, TCP IP, nodes, servers, MAC addresses, DARPANET, packet-switched networks, the Defence Advanced Research Projects Agency tracer algorithms and secure data uplinks."

Alex stopped talking as his attention was drawn to Cannons eyes, they seemed to carry the purest of blue flames, it was uncommon for blue eyes to hold so much warmth but somehow even as they glared at him Alex felt a sense that the world would be less of a place without such a creature.

"AK stop staring into my eyes, what are you gay or something? Look save me from that tech bollocks and just tell me why you think Maria is lying." Cannon demanded.

Alex broke his gaze and uncomfortably ignored Cannon's gender preference statement by replying, "Ok, from what I understand of the American National Security Agency or ANSA..."

"You mean NSA?" interrupted Cannon.

"No I mean ANSA. The Americans seem to love, what you call, wordplay. ANSA sounds like Answer. ANSA became NSA because it turned out there were already hundreds of organisations called ANSA including the Afghan National Standards Association."

Cannon broke a smile and interrupted with, "Get back to why Maria is lying."

Alex seemed to pick up the pace, and rapidly replied, "Yes, yes, the NSA as you call them, is responsible for a secure

The Hacker Hunter © Copyright Lionwing Ltd 2011

communications network between the Whitehouse, the Pentagon and two Joint Military NBC Command Centres. Is this correct?"

Cannon blinked several times in surprise at the Russian's demand for confirmation and then replied, "Yes, from what I understand, the network has two NBC Command Centres just in case one is destroyed. I'm told that everything from ground intelligence, spy plane images, and even the launch codes for the big one travel from and to the NBC Command Centres, passing the Whitehouse and the Pentagon for approval."

Alex cocked his head to one side as he contemplated the meaning of the term 'big one' and then after a moment of realization shouted out, "By big one, you mean a nuclear war! It is for this reason Maria is lying. You see a truly secure network would not be accessible via the internet, especially one that is responsible for so much, therefore the network cannot have 52 remote modems hacked into it."

Almost replying on autopilot Cannon asked, "What about a splice in the network cable or intercepting a satellite signal?"

Alex placed his index finger over his lips as if to signal to Cannon for hush but oddly spoke out despite his finger obscuring part of his mouth, "A splice in a cable would be detected and any intercepted signal would be encrypted beyond the ability to crack."

Alex removed his finger from his mouth and looked sheepishly at his lap. Cannon was not the only one that sensed Alex was holding something back. Mac also felt that something was amiss. Cannon lent towards Alex and whispered jovially, "What about a super computer, surely one of those could crack an NSA encrypted signal."

There was no hiding the look of panic on Alex's face, his eyes darted back and forth as if looking for a non incriminating answer and then Alex blurted out almost uncontrollably, "No such machine exists. The NSA encryption algorithms would take hundreds of years to hard crack, even using these, so called super computers."

Mac caught a glimpse of Cannon's raised eyebrows, he had seen Alex's response to Cannon's statement and, like Cannon, Mac too had become aware that Alex was either lying or acting very oddly for some unfathomable reason. Cannon grinned at Alex and with a joking tone stated, "I bet you Russians have a super computer that could crack it."

Alex's dark, sea black eyes met with Cannons and froze in a deadlock. The two men stared at each other; neither broke the wall of silence that fell over both of them. Khomenko had become sternly fortified in his look. Cannon observed Alex's expression, watching for clues as to what Alex knew that he did not. Mac snapped the men out of it by asking for directions. Alex was the first to break the gaze as he ordered Mac straight on.

"Are you alright AK? You've gone a little pale," asked Cannon snidely. "It might cheer you up to know that you are a hundred per cent right, as always," Cannon announced to break the tension.

"About what?" Alex asked.

"Are you sure you are ok?" Cannon asked again, this time in a manner that suggested genuine concern for Alex's welfare.

"Yes, yes ,please go on," beckoned Alex.

The Hacker Hunter © Copyright Lionwing Ltd 2011

Cannon smiled again and in a less intense manner replied, "Well, I have to agree with you. There's no way Maria and her Mafia Boss Daddy could have found fifty two hackers on a network that's been seriously secured by the NSA."

Alex asked surprisingly "Do you know this to be true?"

Giving a little laugh out loud to signify Alex's innocent naivety Cannon rebuffed the question with, "The word 'know' is such a black and white term, Alex and the word 'true' is always so limiting."

"I'm not sure what you are telling me?" Alex asked.

With cynicism in his voice, Cannon replied sharply and almost totally out of character with, "Well I'm simply agreeing with you and wondering why you are taking us to a hackers den if you think it's impossible to hack the NSA?"

Mac took his eyes off the road to see how Alex would respond. He could not help but feel that Cannon had been playing some kind of word game and that Alex had fallen into his trap. Mac watched as Alex fought to find the words needed to reply to Cannons inescapable directness.

"Oh, I see, well..." stuttered Alex.

"Let me help you out Mr. Khomenko. Three words: field, terminal, server," stated Cannon confidently.

"Sorry?" asked a bewildered Alex?

If at that point either man had looked towards the rear-view mirror Mac would have surely been scuppered, for even this hardened professional found himself dangerously engrossed.

Cannon continued, "I'm sure you've already thought of this AK, but it is my guess that if the NSA is being hacked it will be by one of two means, both needing someone on the inside. The first way will be someone with security clearance who is simply stealing data directly from the network via disk, USB device, CD or some form of storage system probably hidden in a cell phone."

With an eyebrow raised Alex asked, "And the second way?"

Looking briefly out of his window and then back to Alex Cannon replied, "A field server terminal, a mobile computer with access to the network."

"What like a laptop or something?" Alex asked.

Cannon smiled. He seemed to be savouring a moment that was extremely rare in their relationship, a moment where Cannon actually knew more than Alex about something technical. Cannon felt himself favouring the idea of drawing out his reply so that he might relish the moment for as long as possible but on a second reflection elected to say, "No, they are usually the size of a small wardrobe, and used by military command posts in the field to receive orders and satellite images, plus to receive and return intelligence data securely. Some nuke carrying subs have a terminal for receiving encoded launch commands in the event of it all kicking off. The bottom line is these field server terminals would have direct or indirect access to both the joint Military NBC Command Centres, which means a hacker could use one to access the NSA network all the way to the Whitehouse."

The Hacker Hunter © Copyright Lionwing Ltd 2011

Alex looked extremely curious, almost lustful, without stopping to blink he asked, "How would a hacker get his hands on one of these field server terminals?"

Cannon raised his hand and inspected his nails proudly, a few seconds pass and then he casts a smiling look at Alex who was waiting for his answer expectantly. Looking back at his nails Cannon replied, "I'd imagine one would have to steal it from a US army store, or maybe buy it from a corrupt quartermaster. If that didn't work then I'd imagine a well connected Mafia Boss, just for example, could easily persuade someone in the ranks to give him an active field terminal."

Alex's mouth opened wide enough to catch a football and then after a few moments of only drooling snapped shut.

"Are you saying that Maria has a field terminal and whilst hacking the NSA network she discovered fifty two other hackers?" asked Alex.

"No Alex, that's not what I'm saying. I'm asking you how you are going to do the hack and why you are taking us to a hackers den we've never used before?"

Alex broke eye contact with Cannon and looked at Mac, seeing that they were close to their destination Alex ordered, "Pull over, just here Mikhail, just next to the block."

Cannon shot Alex a suspicious look, but Alex failed to see it as he was preoccupied with undoing his seatbelt and using the back of Macs seat to pull himself upright. Alex pointed for Mac to see where to park and then felt around in his pockets for his mobile phone. As Alex pulled his phone out Cannon asked, "Who are you calling AK?"

The Hacker Hunter © Copyright Lionwing Ltd 2011

Alex held the phone tightly and looked up to see Cannon's face staring down at him with a threatening seriousness that Alex had never seen before...

"They will need to let us in, I will have to call first, we should get out now."

Mac swung the steering wheel slowly round and eased the car up to the side of the road. The car glided to a stop, to signify they had parked Mac, unclipped his seatbelt, checked the driver's side mirror and then opened his door. As Mac stepped out of the car he felt the cold air of the Moscow morning tingle on his face. It awakened him from the miles of grey, half dilapidated tenement blocks and grimy, gritty roads that he had just spent the last hour navigating through. After having listened in to Cannons and Alex's conversation Mac had reached the certain conclusion that Cannon was about to walk into a trap, possibly a deadly one. Alex had seemed to be stalling for time in answering Cannons questions. Mac was guessing that it was either because he had no truthful answer or he was attempting to keep Cannon hooked. Whatever Alex was up to Mac didn't like it one bit. He raised his thumb and finger to his Viking moustache and groomed it thoughtully, he knew that he should be thinking about what to do next but as he ran his fingers through the bristles Mac's mind flashed back to his life in the SAS. Over 16 years in the regiment, most men lasted three or four years tops but then Mac wasn't like most men. He had witnessed the world's most spectacular places, met and even dined with Kings, Queens, peasants and tribesmen alike, gone on a thousand unbelievable adventures that he could never talk about. Would it all end here, on a grey day in Russia?

"Hey Alex, this place is amazing! Look at this, they actually built a square tenement block around an old Church," shouted Cannon playfully.

On hearing Cannon's voice Mac snapped out of his reflection and looked over the roof of the car to see Alex following Cannon through a square service arch. The arch was located in the side of a five story office block and had obviously been designed to allow vans into the open air courtyard at the of the block. Looking through the arch, Mac could make out what seemed to be a Church, an old boarded up Church smack bang in the middle of the courtyard. The Church was all but imprisoned in the yard by the surrounding internal walls and windows save this one archway, which was the only offer of passage in, and out. As Alex caught up with Cannon he replied,

"Yes, although Communism, how you say, forbid religion, they could still find no-one willing to pull down a Church. So they just built the office block around it."

Cannon left the cover of the archway and walked up to the old Church. It was small, nothing special as far as Churches went, but totally out of place amongst its concrete surroundings. Cannon looked up at it and, without turning to face the approaching Alex said softly,

"Amazing. It reminds me of one of those prehistoric flowers you see perfectly preserved in fossilized amber."

Alex heard this gentle statement. Until now he had just seen Cannon as a man motivated by money and women. The idea of such a self-serving individual having a side to him which appreciated the oddities of life made Alex question what he had come here to really do.

Mac casually walked up to the far side of the archway. He angled his approach so he could see as far into the courtyard as he dare without risking detection. As he suspected, three stories up, on the far left corner of the opposing internal wall of abandoned offices was a solitary open window: the perfect point for a sniper to cover anyone coming in, or trying to get out. The only question now on Mac's mind was whether the sniper wanted to take out Cannon on the way in or on the way out. Mac took a few steps backward and then rapidly walked back to the car, though not so rapidly as to attract attention. He pulled open the front passengers door and reached for the small bag of tools under the front seat, unzipping the bag, he fumbled through the bag until his hand emerged clutching a long sturdy screwdriver with a bulbous red handle.

"That should do it," muttered Mac under his breath.

"So, Alex, where's this hackers den? This place look's abandoned to me," Cannon asked.

"Wait, I call now," replied Alex. Oddly enough, as Alex dialled a number he noticed that Cannon had also pulled his phone out and was in the process of turning it on. As Cannon strolled back under the archway, he tapped a few numbers into his phones keypad and then lifted the phone to his ear.

"Hi Sabrina, yeah, yes, I know, I know, look I'm sorry about that, I had to leave, I should have told you. Listen, let me make it up to you. What you up to later?" Cannon asked a troubled Sabrina.

Alex suddenly appeared at the archway. Beside him stood a tower block of a man, dressed in a grey suit, which must have been tailored to fit his incredibly broad shoulders and equally solid neck line. Cannon sensed that Alex was about to beckon him, so said to Sabrina,

The Hacker Hunter © Copyright Lionwing Ltd 2011

"No, No, well yes but, ok babe hold on, I'll text you later and arrange dinner, if you are free, that is. Ok, ok, hold on,"

Alex, only hearing Cannon's side of the conversation cocked his head to one side and gave the approaching Cannon an inquisitive look.

"Don't ask mate. Do, not, ask. Odd thing, my phone was turned off. She's been trying to get hold of me all night. Well, that's young love for you," Cannon laughed out jovially.

It was near impossible to gauge if the giant of a man next to Alex was a friend or a foe, but for the moment Cannon seemed to care not as he shot him a quick welcoming smile. Alex watched Christian stride confidently back into the courtyard, a little too confidently for Alex's liking. 'Why was Cannon's behaviour so blasé?', Alex asked himself and then contemplated further, "Could Christian possibly know that he was walking into a trap? Surely not." Cannon would have also needed to have known that only two days ago Alex had been snatched from the institute by a rather brutal team of GRU operatives and VNIIEF officials. Alex had a dislike for bullies but there was little he could do to resist the GRU men that grabbed him. As far as Alex was concerned, the Russian Military Intelligence, better known as GRU, made the FSB look like sleepy village policemen, who were more interested in just sitting around drinking tea and eating fried sunflower seeds. Expecting the GRU to be cruelly tough with him, Alex was actually surprised to find the officials from the Research Institute of Experimental Physics, or VNIIEF for short, were considerably more violent in their interrogation of his relationship with Cannon.

The big Russian man led Alex and Cannon through the archway, towards the old Church in the courtyard. After clearing the archway by just a few meters, he suddenly halted and turned to

The Hacker Hunter © Copyright Lionwing Ltd 2011

face them both. Raising his huge arm he pointed at an open metal service doorway. The doorway was located on the inside wall of the deserted office block, immediately behind Alex and Cannon and to their left. Cannon turned to follow the man's pointed directions. Peering through the doorway, Cannon could see a flight of stairs, to his surprise they led downwards.

"They must lead to the basement level" said Cannon in a less confident manner.

The solid concrete stairs were painted a dirty dark pink.
'Such an odd colour,' thought Cannon, 'grey would have suited the building, why dirty pink'? As Cannon's gaze followed the stairs down he could see that they reached a stairwell landing that probably doubled around to what he imagined must be another flight of downward steps. At the bottom of the first flight, hanging above the stairwell, was a dim, yellow, solitary, light bulb that hung just high enough to provide a singularly unspectacular illumination of the landing. The inspiration to enter such a place left Cannon. For all he knew the big Russian could simply be instructing him to enter an environment which would see him stripped of his cash, cards, phone and passport.

Cannon pointed at Alex and then at the doorway, signalling for a reluctant Khomenko to go first, but it was clear from the expression on Alex's face that this time he was not willing to follow Christians' orders. The big Russian man, who was clearly becoming bored with waiting for someone to walk through the metal door way and down the stairs raised an arm again, but this time with an outstretched open hand which gestured to Cannon to enter - Cannon did so cautiously.

Cannon vanished from sight as he headed down the stairs and around the corner of the stairwell. Alex found himself being pushed towards the doorway by the big Russian who now had

The Hacker Hunter © Copyright Lionwing Ltd 2011

grown extremely intolerant of the delay. Alex followed Cannon's course and the broad Russian followed Alex until all three were finally all in the building. Alex, now halfway down the first flight of stairs turned to witness the big metal door being locked behind him. With a nervous curiosity he then hastened his pace to catch up with Cannon.

As Alex turned the corner of the first stairwell he could just make out Cannon's motionless figure in the darkness. Unlike Alex's present location the second stairwell landing had no solitary light bulb, in fact no light whatsoever. Cannon was stood upright but not moving. Alex walked down to the step above the one Cannon was stood on and whispered,

"What is it Christian?"

As Alex looked over Cannon's shoulder he could see that Christian had his mobile phone out and was looking at the display screen.

"I hadn't planned on this," Cannon half said under his breath, but still loud enough for Alex to hear.

"Planned on what?", asked Alex?

"No fucking signal," exclaimed Cannon aggressively.

"Why is that important Christian?" asked Alex innocently.

Cannon turned to face Alex. The features of Christian's face seemed to carry darker, more sinister hollows due to the lack of lighting, however it gave Khomenko considerable reason to brace up. Alex felt a chill, he knew that Cannon was about to reveal his true nature, not the nature of the jovial, fun loving businessman from Britain but a side to the British few foreigners ever got to witness. Alex took a step backward, feeling his way up the staircase with his hand on the wall, remaining transfixed on Cannon's face he said nervously,

"Christian, why is that important?"

"It takes the NSA three minutes to triangulate a mobile phone signal and locate its user. After I called Sabrina, who, by the way, sold us out to the yanks, I didn't hang up. You see, Alex, I was expecting the NSA to come find me and pull me out of the trap you've set for me to get killed in. No fucking signal, no fucking cavalry, well done Khomenko. You win, you really are a genuine genius!" Cannon growled out through his gritted teeth.

Alex, obviously shocked by Cannon's statement replied,

"Sabrina sold you out to the NSA?"

"Not her fault, Alex, I knew she would. In fact, I was counting on it. But it looks like you had already thought of that, or at least your chums in the FSB had," as Cannon spoke he took a step up to get closer to Alex.

This time Alex didn't move but instead elected to share a moment of honesty with Christian,

"It is not my plan and not the FSB's. I was captured two days a go by Russian Military Intelligence, you might know them as GRU, they told me to bring you here."

"Where is here exactly Khomenko?" Cannon demanded.

"Shhhh, please! That big Russian man will hear you and come down from guarding the door," Alex pleaded.

The Hacker Hunter © Copyright Lionwing Ltd 2011

"Is he GRU?" asked Cannon.

"No, he is paid by the people that run this hackers den. This really is a hackers den. My job is simple, I pretend to do the hack and get you the list. I have been given a CD to give you. It contains unimportant but classified government data, GRU will pick you up outside with it and you'll be arrested as a spy and sent back to England," Alex said, in a fashion that indicated it wasn't so bad after all.

"Is that what they told you AK? You academics are so trusting. They don't send naughty spies home with a slap on the wrist, they bloody well shoot them - as in dead!" Cannon exclaimed.

"No, they will not. They told me you will not be harmed," Alex said the words but he knew that Cannon was probably right. Oddly feeling a sense of relief now that everything was out in the open, Alex said,

"Let me go first," he pushed by Christian and walked down into the darkness.

"Wait, Alex," commanded Cannon. "I discovered my signal was dead because I was going to use the light from my phone screen to help illuminate the passage, get your phone out. Let's do this together,"

The two men made their way around the second stairwell, and to their joy saw one last flight of stairs that were illuminated by a well lit basement room that waited for them at the end of the descent. As they made their way down to the room, a man in his late twenties stood up from what looked like an uncomfortable, dirty cream, plastic school chair. The young scrawny wisp of a man raised a round metal tin to chest height and rattled it at Alex. As Cannon got closer he could make out a small collection of notes and coins sliding around in the metal container. Alex threw in a hundred Rouble note. This gesture caused the young man to lower the tin and sit back down. Cannon didn't even smile as he passed, he just elected to keep silent. There was no benefit to be gained in alerting anyone to him being British. As Christian silently walked into the basement, his eyes widened in astonishment to see walls of metal tool racks, the sort of rack you'd have in your garage at home for storing old paint and oily hammers. Unlike a garage these racks held four shelves of old computers, monitors, keyboards, mice, printers and scanners. Some equipment was stripped of its original casing to just show circuits whilst other machines had managed to remain covered in their grimy, off white almost yellow carcasses. Cables hung everywhere and despite an obvious attempt to try and tie them into some sort of order, the resulting imagery could only be compared to a web created by an incredibly unorganized mechanical spider. Each rack had opposite it the same style of plastic school chair and each chair was home to a person. Cannon was astonished by how many people were sat, uncomfortably typing or just staring at monitors.

'If this was Moscow's answer to an internet café, then I'd hate to ask for a cup of coffee!' Cannon thought to himself jovially.

As Cannon followed Alex through the maze of racks and people, he found himself discreetly looking at everyone he passed, making quick judgments and guesses as to what they were doing there. Cannon was always the opportunist, even with impending death hanging over his head. For Cannon, finding a new hackers den was like finding a seam of gold, in fact, even more precious than gold. Some of the people he passed were easy to figure out, poor university students unable to afford their own computers to work on, gamers playing the latest hacked shoot-em-ups from the west, and migrant workers e-mailing their left behind families. Alex came to a stop at an internal double doorway. The doorway had no doors, but instead, covering it from the other side was a well hung, thick black curtain. Alex lifted the curtain to expose a second room, however this room was dark save the blue flickering hue from CRT computer monitors. Alex held the curtain back for Christian to pass through but Christian signalled, politely, all be it in a slightly mistrusting way, for Alex to go first. Alex vanished behind the black curtain leaving Cannon momentarily on his own.

Seconds felt like minutes to Cannon as he waited for Alex to emerge again from behind the curtain. Eventually it became obvious that Alex was not going to come back out, so Cannon took a deep breath and, walking towards the curtain muttered,

"Don't you just love Russia's new free market?"

It took Cannon's eyes a few seconds to adjust to the darkness of his new surroundings but he could still make out Alex. He was about ten meters away and was clearly being made to empty out his pockets by some spotty, lanky man, again in his late twenties. Thinking that Alex was being mugged Cannon took a step forward, only to find another young man stepping towards him then placing an arresting hand on Cannon's chest. Cannon could see that the man who had halted his progress to Alex was carrying in his other hand a thin, telescopic, black metal baton, of the sort used by the police. Cannon looked down at the hand on his chest and then slowly back up into the eyes of the aggressor and then smiled. It was clear this malnourished geek was no match for the well built British rugger bugger. Cannon saw in his mind exactly what he was going to do. He would grab the hand on his chest, twist it into a half nelson and then kick away the man's knee. He would then take the baton and clobber the other man who was clearly accosting Alex. Before any of these events could take place, Alex spoke out in Russian,

The Hacker Hunter © Copyright Lionwing Ltd 2011

"Neyt, Neyt, he is with me!"

This confused Cannon, so before adopting his premeditated aggressive response he elected to let events play out a little longer. Within a few seconds the man next to Alex nodded and then Alex started putting everything back in his pockets. He then beckoned to Cannon to walk towards him, Cannon pushed by the man in front of him forcing the hand off his chest and in the process signifying that there was never the remotest chance of stopping him. As Cannon reached the other man Alex whispered,

"Empty your pockets, they need to know that you are not police or someone that might have a camera."

Cannon pulled from the inside pocket of his dark green ski jacket his British passport, a long black wallet and a separate bundle of cash and presented it to the second man. On seeing the cash and the British passport the man's eyes lit up with celebrative joy, he raised both hands as if to sing out and then announced in English,

"You will be needing our VIP room!"

Cannon's eyes still had not properly adjusted to the darkness. On looking around he could make out the silhouettes of people sat in front of computer screens. As he stared harder he could see they were actually sat at tables as opposed to racks, there was no question in Cannon's mind that this secluded environment was designed for the more prestigious clients, namely paid hackers. However from what he could see there was no indication of any doorway leading to a VIP area or room. Cannon placed his passport, wallet and cash back into his pocket, but before doing so he pulled a 10,000 Rouble note from the bundle of cash. Raising it to his host he said,

"I need two things: first, a private room with this man," he nodded at Alex to signify who he meant, "and second, an exit that doesn't involve leaving the same way we came in, if you get my drift."

The man snatched the 10,000 Rouble note from Cannon's hand and said,

"The VIP room has its own exit. Please, this way."

Cannon and Alex followed the man through the darkness towards the internal courtyard basement wall. As Cannon passed one particular table he happened to make out the faces of two Northern Africans. Their half Afro, half Arabian features were a giveaway, Egyptian or maybe Libyan it was hard to say. Cannon looked away to hide any possible detection of interest on his face. 'Two Northern Africans in Moscow', he thought, 'Such a thing was so rare, added to this the fact that they were both in the hackers area'. Cannon knew why the two men were there, he'd seen it before, terrorists or 'freedom fighters' as they liked to be known, using the hackers' undetectable network to send messages and organise strike cells. Cannon, feeling confident that he could contain any facial expressions that might give his real thoughts away looked back to see the two men both staring onto a monitor screen. For a split second Cannon wondered how many lives could be saved if he was to divert from his current project and instead elect to focus on these two, but it was an indulgence that could not be afforded, Cannon's current work held considerably more life saving opportunities. If he was to survive it himself he would have to remain exclusively focused.

Cannon realised that his interest in the other users of the hackers den had caused him to fall behind, he noticed that Alex and their host had already reached the basement wall beneath the courtyard. As he approached, Christian could just make out another black curtain, draped from the ceiling to the floor. Their guide pulled the heavy curtain across and in doing so showed a shocked Alex and Cannon that the bricks from the wall behind the curtain were missing, in fact, most the wall behind the curtain had been removed. To Alex's and Cannons amazement they found themselves staring not at mud or more concrete but through a stone archway into the well lit, though somewhat dusty old subterranean catacombs of the Church.

"My God," exclaimed Cannon in awe.

Alex walked through first, followed by Cannon and then their host. There was just one table, one computer, one fridge and one chair situated right in the middle of the empty catacombs. The host spoke again in English,

"The 10,000 Rouble note was just a tip, the fridge has the finest Russian Beluga caviar and Champagne, the computer has a quad processor with a 100mbs untraceable internet connection. We've spliced a main line, it would take a team of engineers a week to find you. For the crowning glory we have an escape route just for peace of mind." The man pointed to the far right wall of the catacomb, there was yet another blanket.

"What's behind that?" asked Cannon.

"Access to a service hatch, how you say in English, manhole cover. The VIP room is 100,000 per day," the man stuck out an open hand.

Cannon reached back into his jacket pocket and pulled out the bundle of cash, he thumbed free ten 10,000 Rouble notes but before placing them in the mans hand and said,

"That includes the beluga and Champagne, oh, and when you step out of here, you and no one else steps back in for 24 hours."

The man nodded and then walking back to the entrance he turned to face both Alex and Cannon. He pointed to the fridge and blew a kiss with his fingers to signify the delight that waited within for them. Cannon smiled as he watched the man leave. Turning to Alex Cannon said calmly,

"Drink?"

Alex smiled and replied "I had better not to drink, I still have to hack the NSA."

Within a few moments Cannon was pulling the foil from a bottle of Champagne.

"Do you mind telling me what is going on please Mr. Khomenko?"

Alex took off his thick jacket to reveal he was only wearing an orange T shirt underneath. He then pulled the T shirt up over his head revealing a well battered, purple and yellow ribcage and stomach. Alex then lowered the T shirt back down and said,

"My face was spared so you would not become suspicious."

Cannon stopped trying to wriggle free the Champagne cork and replied compassionately,

"They must have beaten you rather severely to make you go through with this rather stupid plan. Do you want to tell me what happened AK, and what I'm really in store for when I step out of this place?"

Alex walked over to the desk and started checking over the computer. He chose to ignore Cannon's question in favour of getting started with his hack of the world's most secure network. Cannon popped the cork and poured himself a glass of sparkling wine. After taking a few sips he walked towards the escape route and stopped at the black curtain that covered it. Turning to look back at Alex he said in a cavalier manner,

"Right now you've given me no CD of secrets and I've committed no crime in your country, I need to know what the hell is going on otherwise I'm on my way back to England, and given that the GRU has nothing on me, I'm afraid to say there's little they can do to keep me here!"

Alex stopped examining the computer and looked up from the screen to see Cannon waiting for his reply. Alex seemed to know that Cannon wasn't about to leave and looked back down at the screen. A few moments passed and then Alex straightened himself up and said,

"I've found an up-link and we're in, I have hacked the NSA network."

Every muscle in Cannons face gave up on clinging to any notion of self respect as a look of utter dumbfoundedness overwhelmed Cannons expression. Alex started typing again, the speed of which made the keystrokes sound like chattering teeth. Cannon couldn't move from his spot, he just stared at Alex as he typed and clicked and then typed some more. A few minutes pass before Cannon moved from his frozen position. He elected to wander through the sandstone archways, feigning disinterest in Alex and utter fascination with his surroundings. A few more minutes passed, and then Cannon spoke out in a care free manner,

"When I asked you to explain what was going on, I actually meant, what are you doing at the institute for the GRU to be so concerned about who you talk to and work for on the side?"

Alex continued to type, he didn't reply, or show any recognition that Cannon was addressing him. Cannon continued to walk between the arches. As he slowly inspected each archway he continued to talk,

"I have a theory Alex, all the AI research and development you've been giving me as a cover isn't just crap you've pulled off the college network, it's actually real. I'm willing to bet that you are working on some sort of advanced AI software. In fact, so advanced I'd imagine it has military applications. I'm also willing to speculate that you've been caught selling me AI formula and you've been pressured into giving me up to the authorities. These authorities are desperate to set an example to show the West that the Russian bear is not sleeping. I'm also willing to go as far as to say that you are not currently hacking the NSA network. Instead I'd imagine that you are stalling for time just to be sure that when I pop my head out of that manhole cover I'll be met by the FSB or GRU or an oncoming truck, am I right?"

Alex didn't stop typing but he replied, "I've already told you they want me to give you a CD of non important but classified data, why would I tell you that if I intended on doing it?"

Cannon walked closer to the desk, he could make out on the computer screen an application window of some sort. There were a few Russian words on the title bar of the application, Cannon tried to figure them out, but his Russian wasn't that

The Hacker Hunter © Copyright Lionwing Ltd 2011

good, 'Was it: earth fake intellect, no, perhaps grown synthetic intelligence…wait, it's organic artificial intelligence!" Cannon thought to himself.

"What's organic artificial intelligence AK?" asked Cannon.

Alex stopped typing, standing straight again, he faced Cannon and for the first time offered a proper conversation.

"I chose this place, I told the GRU that there was only one way in and one way out, which made it perfect for an arrest. I had never been here but I have a friend called Oleg, who I trust with my life. He told me of its special VIP room and the escape route. I am hacking the NSA and I will provide access to the NSA network for you to sell and a list of hackers, if any, I find doing the same thing, providing you can get me out of Russia and set me up with a good life in the UK."

Cannon walked around Alex so he could get a better look at the computer screen.

"If you are hacked into the NSA, you'll need to prove it." Cannon stated.

"How?" asked Alex.

"The NSA network carries military orders to thousands of different command posts. Send an order for the US military to do something that we could find out about," Cannon ordered.

Alex tapped his finger on the back of the computer mouse as he thought and then replied, "Like shooting down a civilian airliner you mean?"

"Well that would do it, but I had something less damaging in mind," replied Cannon with a grin of delight.

"Send a command to the NSA boys in Moscow. The command should be for them to come pick us up from here," Cannon finished speaking with a doubtful laugh.

Alex started typing, only stopping to read every now and then. Cannon soon became bored with waiting for Alex to say something so opened the fridge door and peered in. Just Champagne and fish eggs, nothing of real entertainment. As Cannon closed the fridge door Alex shouted out,

"I'm in the stores logistical management system."

Cannon placed both is hands flat on the desks surface and hung his head down between his shoulders, in a defeated voice he said out loud,

"Great. Order me a pair of new army boots, size 11. Alex if you really expect me to believe you at least come up with something more impressive than that!"

As Alex typed he muttered out; "US Embassy Moscow, stores, army boots, size 11, immediate field dispatch, this address, by..." Alex stopped, looked at his watch and then continued to type and talk "10:30am."

Cannon walked away from Alex and back towards the hole in the wall they had come in through. Cannon stopped at the hole, turning to face Alex he said,

"Come on Khomenko let's go face the music, I'm leaving."

Alex, still typing vigorously said,

"No we need to leave via the, how you say, manhole."

Cannon smiled at Alex's use of a word that he had obviously just learnt today and replied, "Manhole cover, its manhole cover, Alex we're finishing here. Come on, let's go."

Alex ignored Cannon and continued to type. Cannon, wanting to give Alex one more chance to leave with him said,

"Alex, the bottom line is, if I walk out of here now and GRU grab me, they'll find no CD of top secret Russian files and not have a leg to stand on. Which leaves you up shit creek without a paddle. You're a bloody good programmer, I'm offering you a chance to leave with me. Believe it or not, I actually have a C plan for my exit. Are you coming?"

Alex didn't even look up, electing to continue typing away silently.

"Khomenko, COME FUCKING ON!" Cannon barked out.

Alex still carried on typing furiously but said in a higher pitch of voice,

"Tem more minutes, she needs ten more minutes!"

"She?" asked Cannon with a look of puzzlement on his face.

Cannon didn't stay for an answer. Now through with waiting, he turned his back to Alex, lifting the curtain to one side, he stepped through into the hackers den. It was dark and his eyes would have to adjust again. As the curtain fell behind Christian he found himself staring at the nameless faces that were illuminated by the blue haze emitted from the monitors. Each

The Hacker Hunter © Copyright Lionwing Ltd 2011

face seemed to be deeply engrossed in the busy pursuit of typing out code. There must have been twenty, maybe thirty hackers, all seemingly absorbed in their own worlds, all with the exception of the two Northern Africans, who had taken to whispering at each other. Cannon walked over to face them both. As he reached them, they stopped whispering, and stood from their seated positions to face him. Cannon smiled at the one nearest to him and said directly,

"Here goes Plan C!"

The faces of the two terrorists screwed up in an aggressively confused manner as they realised they were being addressed by the infidel incarnate. Cannon didn't hesitate for one moment, grabbing the closest terrorist he spun him around with comparable ease. The Northern African was two thirds Cannon's size and build. He put up very little resistance as Cannon wrestled him to the floor. The other terrorist remained motionless, unable to move from the utter shock of these unprecedented events. Cannon freed his hands by pinning his catch to the floor with his knees. With admirable speed, he reached out to the computer monitor that both men had been whispering in front of only a few moments ago. Grasping the monitor firmly between both hands, Cannon wrenched it off the desk. Not all the cables came away, but that didn't stop Cannon raising the hefty 21 inch cathode ray tube above his head. With psychotic vigour, Cannon brought the computer monitor thundering down on his captives face. The first blow cracked his opponents' nose, the second broke the jaw free, the third popped the right eyeball, spreading gel out over his cheek and the fourth was intercepted by the second terrorist who had suddenly come back to his senses and grabbed the monitor. Cannon flung himself backward off the unconscious body of his victim, in doing so placing enough space between himself and the remaining adversary to ensure he did not suffer the same fate he had just inflicted.

Cannon raised himself to full height only to find the same two young men who had searched him and Alex on the way in were now charging towards him. The first man to reach Cannon was the same man who had attempted to hold Cannon back by placing his hand on Cannon's chest earlier. As the young man reached Cannon's proximity he swung a black metal baton, but it failed to connect as Christian simply stepped so close into his attacker's body space that the intimacy made it impossible to swing an effective blow. Cannon placed a hand on the sternum of his opponent and pushed with a mighty thrust that sent the lanky geek flying backwards over a table and into a pile of chairs. Cannon was like a mad dog, foam spitting from his mouth as he roared out in fury at the second man running towards him, the same man who had taken them to the VIP area under the Church's catacombs. Noticing that the other terrorist was now also moving towards him, Cannon elected to retreat towards the young man he had just thrown over the table with a view to arming himself with his prior opponents' baton. As he approached the livid, spotty, male, Cannon noticed that the young man was scrambling around in-between the spread of chairs he had fallen into. He seemed to be desperately looking for something, Cannon's eyes lit up as the dark shape of a magazine fed handgun could be dimly seen in the grasp of the young man. Before the man could even raise the gun, Cannon charged him. He grabbed the gun from the top with both his hands, twisted it to face his adversary and then pulled it sharply downward. The young man let out an ear piercing scream of absolute agony as his finger was dislocated in two places by the trigger guard. Cannon did one final twist down and then took the weapon from the man who now was just writhing around on the floor. Without even thinking Cannon flicked off the safety

The Hacker Hunter © Copyright Lionwing Ltd 2011

catch with his thumb and with his left hand pulled the slide, locking back the hammer.

There remaining terrorist was the first to reach Cannon, who at this point had his back to him. Sensing that one of the two men had reached him, Cannon spun around and as he stood, thrust the gun upward under the approaching terrorist's jaw with a lethal jab. The barrel went straight up between the middle of the jaw bone, through the soft flesh and jutted into the floor of the man's mouth. The motion of thrusting the gun up through the underneath of the man's jaw and pulling the trigger almost seemed as one. The resulting detonation caused the top of the man's cranium to explode outward, spraying brain and bone into the room of now mortified hackers. The body of the terrorist fell forward, locking the gun, pulling it down and rendering Cannon unable to shoot anyone else. People screamed and ran in all directions. Some took to hiding under tables, others tripped over chairs in their panic to get out. Cannon stood there for a moment, all before him were desperate to escape the madness. He watched his host from earlier slip backward on the brain and blood as he frantically tried to reverse his charge. Cannon pulled the gun free from the carcass, he turned to point the gun in every direction, trying to see if anyone posed a threat as he made his way to the exit with the large crowd of screaming people.

Just before Christian left the room he took one short glance back at the black curtain covering the entrance to the catacombs. Maybe he looked back in hoped that Alex would emerge to join him, either way, Cannon knew he had to leave with the screaming horde if he was to stand any chance of escaping the GRU.

In an empty office room, three floors up, overlooking the courtyard stood the still solitary figure of a man. The man held

The Hacker Hunter © Copyright Lionwing Ltd 2011

a position approximately a meter or so from an open window, just far enough not to be detected but still close enough to see down through the open window into the courtyard below. In his arms a Russian Dragunov SVD sniper rifle rested, the rifle barrel pointed downwards at the cold concrete office floor. His motionless stance was obviously a by-product of military training. All snipers alike, Russian, American or British knew that movement led to detection, and this man was as still as the stale office air around him. In his left ear the man had a pink plastic speaker plug. This ear piece had a curly, almost translucent cable running from it that vanished into the collar of his thick black quilted coat. The ear device was clearly used for receiving orders, perhaps from operatives within the hackers den or perhaps from officials in some other location. Either way, within a second the man flinched as a voice screamed through the ear plug in Russian,

"The target has a gun and is shooting people! He is approaching the exit, eliminate him!"

The solitary man raised the lightweight and quite accurate (for its class) rifle into his shoulder. Training the crosshairs of the scope on the large metal door, he waited for the exit to swing open. Sure enough within a few short seconds the big metal service door crashed open, but the solitary Christian Cannon didn't emerge. Instead, a stream of twenty or thirty figures sprawled out into the square, each screaming, running and tripping over one another as they flocked towards the service archway for an exit. The crosshairs darted from one person to another in an attempt to locate Cannon. Nothing, and then a momentary flash of a green ski jacket in amongst the frenzy of people. The sniper rifle was capable of semi-auto fire. He wouldn't need a totally accurate shot, he could simply let a volley of rounds off into the crowd and that should finish off Cannon. He was about to gently squeeze the trigger when he noticed the green ski jacket again, this time he saw that its owner had fallen to the floor. It was Cannon alright, and everyone was giving the maniac a wide berth, wide enough to offer the sniper a clear shot. Without hesitating the man aligned the centre of the telescopic rifle sight crosshairs on Cannon's head. Whilst letting out his breath the man gently teased the trigger inward. Before the firing pin even came close to striking the shell case, a hand firmly grabbed the man's forehead, yanking it back vigorously to expose the shooter's eye that only a millisecond ago was staring down the sights at Cannon. The sniper didn't even get a chance to finish pulling the trigger before a long, sturdy screw driver, with a bulbous red handle, found itself being plunged with unstoppable ferocity through the eyeball, through the socket and into the brain. Mac slowly stepped backwards, carrying with him the now very dead sniper and lowering his body silently to the cold floor as he walked.

Mac looked down at the still figure of the man, the handle of the screwdriver protruding from his eye. With a stern expression on his face Mac said in a soft, but annoyed voice,

"What kind of training do you call that, no motion sensors, no alarms. You didn't even lock the bloody door!"

Mac moved to where the sniper had been standing and saw Cannon getting to his feet.

"I'd better get bloody well down there," Mac muttered out to himself.

Cannon pulled himself to his feet, he dusted his trousers down and then casually made his way through the service archway towards the open street. As he walked, half crazed people stricken with fear passed him and fled off in all directions.

The Hacker Hunter © Copyright Lionwing Ltd 2011

Cannon stopped walking. He could see his taxi but there was no sign of the driver.

"What a fucking day, where on earth is Mikhail?" Cannon exclaimed, obviously extremely vexed that his driver had decided to vanish when he needed him the most.

Cannon stood there at the side of the road, he was just about to take a step out when a white van screeched to a stop in front of him. Cannon felt a massive rush of adrenaline, 'Could this be the GRU?' he thought. The passenger side door swung open and a strong jawed man, dressed in a dark suit stepped out holding a brown cardboard US Army issue shoe box. Cannon's mouth fell open. The man stepped toward him and said in a broad American accent,

"Hi buddy, what the hell's going on?", he looked at Cannon whose mouth was so wide open that he was totally unable to form even the simplest of sound, let alone offer a reply. The American continued,

"You speako Americano Comrade?"

Cannon shook his head as if someone had just thrown cold water into his face and replied firmly,

"Don't be so fucking insolent. We taught you to speak in the first place, and it's not Americano, I think you'll find you colonists speak the Queen's English. Well attempt to speak it at least, what time is it?"

The American moved the brown box to under his other arm and looked at his watch,

The Hacker Hunter © Copyright Lionwing Ltd 2011

"10:30. Now what the hell is an uptight limey bastard doing here?" the American exclaimed in shock.

"You from the US Embassy stores?" Cannon asked in a demanding tone.

The American straightened up, now not sure who he was addressing he replied,

"Yes sir, how..." but before he could finish Cannon interrupted with, "Good, those will be my boots then!"

Cannon grabbed the box and pulled it away from the American, who now had swapped roles with Cannon to sport the same open mouthed dumfounded look Cannon had carried only moments ago. As Cannon turned to walk off with the shoe box under his arm he spotted a slight movement from the corner of his eye. The movement came from a black round metal disk in the middle of the road, a manhole cover. Cannon turned to face the cover as two hands reached up from the ground and slid it out into the road, then both hands vanished only to reappear pushing out onto the road the same quad processing computer that Alex had been hacking away on in the catacombs of the church.

The well dressed American watched in absolute astonishment as Cannon walked into the middle of the road, and holding his shoe box over the service hatch said to whoever was inside,

"I got my boots. Next time let's try getting a bloody car with a driver. It seems Mikhail has vanished!"

The American could not take his gaze off Cannon as the figure of a second man came out of a hole in the middle of the road. The man stood up, brushed himself down, and then said with a strong Russian accent,

The Hacker Hunter © Copyright Lionwing Ltd 2011

"Christian, I am a little disappointed in your logic. All I needed was ten more minutes."

Cannon and Alex walked over to the white van where the American stood, still in shock. Alex pointed down the street at an approaching Mac. Cannon shouted out,

"Where on the blue bloody planet have you been?!"

Mac gave a sneaky smile and said in reply to Cannons question,

"I find things around here, how you say in England, very, eye catching?"

Chapter 14 – Mind Games

The speckled grey concrete floor scarcely reflected any of the luminosity that was generated from the buzzing strip lights which hung from the ceiling above. The dull, uncarpeted floor spanned four or five square meters, until meeting with equally dull greyish blue windowless walls. In fact, bar the exception of a door, this box room office did little to inspire any perception of a positive working environment. Pushed up against one of these dreary walls was a long office desk. The desk's frame consisted of square metal tubing that had been thickly coated in brown paint, seemingly to blend with the equally fake wooden plastic veneered chipboard that was used to provide draws and what could be seen of the desk's working surface. Sprawled out and piled high on the desktop, balancing precariously were stacks of black folders and thickly bound paper documents. Amongst the mess of these reports and research folders resided a collection of unwashed, half empty coffee mugs and crumb laden plates. Judging from this mess, and the musty malodorous stench, it was only natural to assume that whatever poor creature inhabited this working space must have not left it for days.

A few feet away from the desk rested Oleg, he sat stretched out over a simple office chair with wheels. Oleg's head was tilted so far back that his eyes gazed effortlessly upward at the ceiling and the hanging strip lights. With his arms hung like dead-weights over the sides of each chair rest, Oleg's hands could almost reach the cold, clammy, concrete surface of the floor. His entire posture exposed extreme fatigue, the type of exhaustion that could only be brought upon a man by combining sleep deprivation and an immeasurable discomfort with an overwhelming sense of dread.

The Hacker Hunter © Copyright Lionwing Ltd 2011

The otherwise empty room was suddenly filled with a tinny melody, the tune comprised only of a few bars that kept repeating over and over again. Oleg, now roused by the repetitive ditty, lifted his head up and identifying the location of the noise looked towards the desk. It was just possible to make out, under a few sheets of paper, the glow of a mobile phones screen. It took Oleg a few moments to react and then with a sudden violent spasm that resulted in him jumping to his feet, he franticly started to fumble through the papers. Upon locating the phone Oleg took a second to examine the number displayed on its brightly lit screen: it was Alex. Without waiting another second he thumbed the talk button and raised the phone to his ear,

"Alex, are you ok?" asked Oleg.

There was dead air, so Oleg spoke again, this time with even more concern in his voice,

"Alex, are you at the garages, did you find the keys?"

Still no reply, Oleg lowered the phone from his ear to look again at the number on the display screen, true enough, it was Alex but why no sound. Oleg lifted the phone to his ear again and said in a more untrusting tone,

"Hello, Alex, is that you?"

Still no sound emanated from the phone. Oleg's face went pallid and although his heart had started to pound furiously, it was not enough to stop the blood draining from his expression. An unexpected, loud, yet playful knock was drummed out on the office door.

The Hacker Hunter © Copyright Lionwing Ltd 2011

"Oleg, you ok?" asked Pavel with a semi playful, yet concerned tone to his voice.

Oleg slipped the mobile phone into his trouser pocket and straightened his lab coat before announcing in a high pitched reply,

"Please come in Professor," the unnatural reply was enough for Oleg to cough, clear his throat and say again, in a forced, deeper tenor, "Come in, please, come in." The door swung open to reveal the figure of Pavel, more confidently Oleg asked,

"How can I help you, professor?"

"Call me Pavel, please. Professor makes me feel like I don't actually work for a living," Pavel smiled, his attempt to make humour was utterly ineffectual on the very nervous looking Oleg.

"Everything ok? You look shaken, worried, and perhaps even a little bit guilty of something?" asked Pavel, with a sharp eye on his fumbling host.

"No, No, professor, I mean, Pavel. I am fine, thank you. I just need some sleep, we've been here for a few days now. When do you think we will be allowed back home?" Oleg asked anxiously.

Pavel walked into the room and circled around Oleg slowly, much like a vulture circles a carcass before descending to devour its fleshy remains. Oleg held himself still, staring nervously down at his feet and then over to the open doorway. This was obviously a desperate attempt to avoid eye contact with Pavel. Any man could see that Oleg was uncomfortable. However, rather than electing to embrace a more compassionate

The Hacker Hunter © Copyright Lionwing Ltd 2011

and reassuring manner, Pavel seemed to instead be savouring his subordinate's state of escalating trepidation. Pavel stopped at Oleg's side and, looking into his ear he half whispered,

"We have a little problem my friend."

Oleg didn't turn to face him, but instead just looked forward and replied,

"A problem, Professor?"

Pavel lent in closer towards Oleg's ear and again in a half whisper stated,

"I think your friend Alex has found himself in a little more trouble than he bargained for."

"Alex, trouble, why? What has he done?" Oleg asked whilst mustering up enough courage to face the now uncomfortably close Pavel.

Pavel snapped his feet together, like some kind of military general. Frowning at Oleg, he then walked back towards the door from which he had originally entered. With a gentle push from Pavel the door slowly swung shut, Pavel didn't turn back around to face Oleg. Instead he chose to keep his back to him.

"As you are aware that Professor Faverski has ordered that no-one leave the institute's AIO unit? He really has gone quite mad you know."

Oleg let out a massive sigh and his entire body posture relaxed. "Oh thank goodness, I'm sorry professor, I thought you might be…"

The Hacker Hunter © Copyright Lionwing Ltd 2011

Before Oleg could finish Pavel interrupted with,

"What, mad as well?"

"No, no, I meant, well, not one of us," Oleg gleefully said in the process letting out a child like smile at Pavel. Turning to face Oleg's smile, Pavel laughed out loud with an oddity that made Oleg feel exceptionally uncomfortable. Pavel shockingly addressed Oleg with,

"Oh, I'm one of you, I've been a scientist all my life. The only difference is, well let me see, how shall I put this? You see Oleg, you just work 'for', this institute whilst I on the other hand, work 'in', it." Pavel let out a little giggle, his word play seemed to provide a level of enjoyment that Oleg didn't share.

Oleg became less nervous, he felt an odd sense of strength rise up inside him. Maybe his mind had been pushed to a new turning point, or maybe he really felt he had no other option than to just confront Pavel. Using this new confidence Oleg asked,

"What do you mean, work for, work in?"

Taking a moment to observe Oleg's curious facial expression before responding Pavel replied,

"I actually work for the VNIIEF. You'd know them as the Research Institute of Experimental Physics. I've always found that to be a strange name considering we are in charge of the entire Russian NBC and experimental weaponry arsenal."

Oleg walked to the chair that he had been sprawled out on only moments earlier. He rested both his hands on the back of the chair for support and asked,

The Hacker Hunter © Copyright Lionwing Ltd 2011

"Why are you telling me this Professor?"

Pavel pushed a few folders and reports back to clear an area on the surface of the desk. Within a few seconds he had cleared a wide enough space to perch on.

"Oleg, some people refer to these times as the 'space age'. Others say we live in the age of the atom, but to my mind, you and I, we live in the age of electricity, an era of energy. I have seen man fly to the moon, pioneer revolutionary life saving laser surgery, I've even witnessed the birth of micro processing computers. All of these things made possible by one thing: electricity. The telephone, the internet, radio waves, the starter in your car, are all absolutely nothing without the use of electricity. What a wonderful time to be alive, and we are just at the beginning of it all. Do you realize the breakthrough we have made here in the institute with the OAI technology and what effect it will have on our age?"

Oleg tightened his grip on the back of the chair and pulled it in closer,

"Professor, I understand, these are special times, but you mentioned Alex was in trouble?"

Pavel, still perched on the desk ignored Oleg's question and instead elected to continue his philosophical lecture.

"You see Oleg, some people say that true power is in the hands of those who control the oil, gas and mineral resources of our planet. This is 'true power' yes, but it is not the ultimate power. The civilized world has grown so dependent on electricity that if the flow of electrical energy was halted for just one week to any Western European country the resulting effects would be devastating. Allow me to explain. Thirty years ago, most businesses and governments hardly relied on computers. Now everything is run by these electricity eating micro-managers. It's not just computer dependant businesses and governments that would fall apart without electricity. The trains would stop, hospitals would start failing, food reserves would be lost, wages would be unobtainable from the banks and marshal rule would have to take effect within a matter of days, just to ensure people could get food to eat. It's very simple Oleg, electricity can be used to power vehicles, light homes, preserve food, heat hospitals and even cook with. It is the one innovation that has lifted us out of the darkness and placed us into an age unparalleled. This is the ultimate power, and whoever gives away unlimited, free, clean energy ends the race for that power."

Oleg looked puzzled, indirectly asking for more clarification he blurted out "Race?"

Pavel smiled, he raised a finger and pointed at Oleg, shaking it up and down as he replied,

"The race: republic verses kingdom, socialism verses capitalism, autocracy verses meritocracy, federation verses singularity, democracy verses dictatorship, the list of runners goes on and on. The fact remains that whoever designs a power station that provides unlimited, clean, electrical power for free, wins. That is ultimate power."

Pavel smiled at Oleg, but Oleg did not return the gesture. Still with a look of dumbfoundedness he asked,

"Free, why free?"

"Well, of course there is no such thing as a free dinner," Pavel replied with a note of absurdity to his voice and then continued, "But if countries can buy their electricity for cheaper than they can make it then whoever is supplying it really has their finger on the red button. However, in this case the red button doesn't launch a thousand nuclear warheads. No, no, the red button is simply a kill switch powerful enough to send a country back to the Stone Age without a single shot being fired. Look, it's very simple. You have heard of the Great Russian inventor Oleg Lavrentyev - you must have?"

Oleg's facial expression changed to one of excitement, he replied,

"I was named after him, Professor. From what I understand, Lavrentyev dreamt up the amazing idea of managing thermonuclear reactions using a magnetic field to confine plasma in the shape of a torus. The dream promised mankind a revolution in unlimited electricity, with no nuclear waste. The work has led to the creation of a Tokamak fusion reactor. I think it is at the Jet Research Institute near Oxford in England. Why do you mention this?"

Pavel raised his hand to his mouth and did a little cough to clear his voice before replying,

"I am pleased to say that we at the Research Institute of Experimental Physics have actually managed to create a clean, fusion, reactor, based on the Lavrentyev idea."

Oleg could not contain his excitement, and before Pavel could say another word blurted out,

"You have a working fusion reactor!"

Pavel winced and then replied, "Not exactly Oleg, you see, it works for a few seconds but we do not have the computing power needed to produce the computations quickly enough to

The Hacker Hunter © Copyright Lionwing Ltd 2011

adjust the magnetic field to compensate for plasma variants. Quite simply Oleg, there is not a computer fast enough or powerful enough to manage this process. Or there was not, until the OAI came on-line."

Oleg, now free of any thoughts of paranoia and totally intrigued by Pavel's statement said,

"You have the OAI professor, we win!"

Pavel looked down at his right shoe, he turned his foot as if inspecting it in a fashion where he almost expected to find something undesirable on it and, still looking at his foot replied,

"I don't think we are going to win Oleg, not with your friend Alex selling our secrets to the British and Americans."

Pavel looked up from his shoe. He observed Oleg's frustrated look and tormented silence, there was no question Oleg wanted to say something but was doing all he could to refrain from saying something he might regret. Pavel broke the quiet and softly said,

"Alex is an important part of this team Oleg, nothing bad will happen to him. We just need to bring him back to the institute and put an end to his relationship with Mr. Cannon. Do you know whom I speak of?"

Oleg nodded, which was all Pavel needed to see that his method of interrogation had worked. Still in a soft, fatherly, voice Pavel continued,

"Christian Cannon has lured your friend away with the promise of a better life in the West. You know and I know this is a lie. Mindless television, blue jeans, and fatty burgers. Is this life at its best? I think not. If I know where he is, I will be able to reason with him, explain to him what I have told you, plead with him to come back, I just need you to tell me where he is."

"I don't know where he is Professor," exclaimed a now rather distressed looking Oleg.

Pavel, still perched on the desk, just looked emotionlessly at Oleg. Not a word was uttered. The look was almost as if he was waiting for something that Oleg could not give. Two loud taps at the door caused Pavel to break his stare,

"Come in," Pavel ordered. The door was opened by a military looking man, short hair, thick neck, black army boots and dressed in a black coverall. Oleg's attention jumped to the holstered gun on his belt. The man handed Pavel a folded paper note. Pavel, nodded at the man to signal both thank you and leave. As the man left, closing the door behind him, Pavel unfolded the paper slowly. Oleg strained to see if he could make out what was written on the note but he was too far to clearly read anything. Pavel folded the note back up and placed it into his left lab coat pocket, then said in a more serious tone,

"The reason why people like me exist, is to help ensure people like you and your friend Alex are working for the right side. We protect your work, we help provide resources and leading edge research, even help keep you safe from people that will kill to get knowledge of what you have."

Oleg looked distrustfully at Pavel. The professors' mood suddenly changed, perhaps it was a result of what he had just read. Oleg wanted only one answer from Pavel so asked again,

"You mentioned Alex was in trouble professor?"

The Hacker Hunter © Copyright Lionwing Ltd 2011

Choosing to ignore Oleg. Once more Pavel continued to talk,

"Oleg, my dear Oleg, let me explain how this works. Most people believe there are just four reliable ways to get someone to tell you a secret. Firstly, the liberal minded will always adopt the idea of befriending you, to win your trust and give you a false sense that they can really help. After all, a problem shared is a problem halved. Secondly, the more scientific minded will tell you that unlocking the secrets of the mind can be achieved by using powerful drugs, what they like to call truth serums. Thirdly, the risk takers believe that it's simply human nature to betray a truth for personal gain. They believe that everyone has a price and that a man can be bought or blackmailed into telling the truth. The fourth method is good old fashion torture. Tell me Oleg, which one of these methods for extracting a secret do you think works the best?"

Oleg let his grip go from the back of the chair and folded his arms tightly. He was extremely uncomfortable with the topic that Pavel had suddenly raised. Under no illusion that Pavel needed an answer, Oleg replied,

"I wouldn't know professor, I'm a scientist, you mentioned Alex was in trouble?"

Pavel picked up one of the folders next to him from the desk surface, he flicked through a few pages disinterestedly and then tossed it back into the mess.

"One of the benefits of working for VNIIEF is that you have access to all kinds of statistical information, facts and figures from literally thousands of experiments, experiments that some may consider unethical but I'm sure as a scientist you'll still appreciate as interesting. You see if I had befriended you and asked for Mr. Khomenko's location, there is only a 27%

probability that you'd give me an honest answer. With any form of mind game you have to assume that you're playing with favourable odds and that you have the luxury of time. I am sure you will appreciate, Oleg, that time is a luxury we cannot afford. So perhaps a swift needle into the spine? A sharp injection of mind bending truth drugs would provide a quicker answer. Surprisingly enough only 29% of people manage to blurt out anything remotely useful under such treatment, which leaves us with the option of offering you a bribe, blackmailing or dishonouring you. We are told that every man has his price, yet only 42% of people give up their secrets that way. Interestingly enough, it's good old fashioned physical violence that produces the best results. Can you believe 92% of people will tell you everything you want to know under threat of torture?"

Oleg shot Pavel a glance that suggested a moment of realization had occurred,

"Threat, Professor?"

Pavel gave Oleg a massive and totally unexpected grin and said,

"That's right my boy, very observant. I can see why you and Alex are such good friends."

Oleg unfolded his arms and with a look of curiosity he asked,

"You mean people tell without actually being physically tortured?"

Pavel, still grinning, let out a chuckle and said.

"Well the report I read was very detailed. The GRU, that is military intelligence, found people soon built a resistance to any pain inflicted on them, and those who did not, simply lost consciousness. I'm told the unconscious state is the best way of avoiding questions. Apparently just the threat alone to pull off fingernails, pull out teeth, burn out eyeballs and chop off genitals is enough to get people talking."

"Why are you telling me this Professor?" asked Oleg.

"You should know that Professor Faverski has instructed the GRU to bring Alex back, and I'm told they can track his location via his mobile phone, which thankfully is off."

Oleg looked curiously at Pavel and then asked, "Why thankfully?"

"I'm going to ask you a question, Oleg. Where is Alexander Khomenko and his associate Christian Cannon?"

"Why are you not threatening me with torture, Professor?"

"No need, torture only results in a 92% success rate. We have a method that provides 100% accuracy. I will ask you again and then I'm afraid to say, Oleg, that the option to answer voluntary will be retracted. What is the location of Alexander Khomenko and his associate Christian Cannon?"

"Before I answer you Professor, I need to know what method has a 100% success rate?"

"Oleg, we are brain scientists. My god man, can you not work it out for yourself? I'm sorry you had your chance."

Pavel stood from his perched position and walking to the door, pulled it open. Stood in the doorway were two hefty looking men, each man dressed in the same military attire as the man that had only moments ago delivered the Professor a note. Pavel pointed at Oleg and instructed the two men,

"Take him. I want him prepared for cranial surgery in fifteen minutes, we don't have much time."

"Wait professor," screamed out Oleg! "I have a car, it's a four wheel drive, off roader. I use it for fun. Alex and I have been on a few rallies in it. I gave Alex the keys and told him to take the car to escape Moscow if things didn't work out for him."

"Escape to where Oleg?"

"That I don't know, I thought it best not to ask."

"Maybe you know, maybe you don't, there's only one way to find out for sure," exclaimed Pavel.

"Wait! To the Ukraine, he has an old family house that was left to him. He'll go there first to get what he needs to leave the country," Oleg shouted desperately.

"Thank you, Oleg," stated the professor calmly as he walked towards the open doorway. Just then the same man that had passed Pavel the note earlier pushed by the two men and handed Pavel a new sheet of folded paper. Pavel unfolded the note, to read it out loud,

"TRUE, according to this you are telling the truth."

Oleg watched speechlessly as Pavel unbuttoned his shirt to remove a wire microphone from his chest,

"I hate these things," Pavel laughed out and then continued with "I always end up ripping out half my chest hair. You are probably wondering what is going on. Well I suppose I should explain. You see, the problem with torture is that of the 92% of people that talk, nearly 73% will simply tell lies to start with. To help us detect these lies we use a fantastic piece of Israeli technology, a rather brilliant lie detector, it works by reading the stress patterns in your voice. I'm told its 99.9% accurate."

Oleg looked like a man who was trying to wake up from a bad dream. As his mind reached out to make sense of this craziness, he asked, "What about the cranial surgery?"

Pavel laughed so hard that he had to clutch his stomach to stop and answer, "Oleg, did you listen to nothing I said? The threat of torture is the best way, the threat! In this case it wasn't your teeth, it was cranial surgery."

"You mean you tricked me."

"Well I hope you're not too disappointed, if you like, I could ask these two gentlemen to attempt brain surgery on you," Pavel replied jokingly.

"Bastard!" exclaimed Oleg, who had now realised that he had betrayed his friend.

"I must say, Alex put up a lot more resistance than you Oleg. We really had to beat him. Mind you, he wasn't stupid enough to speak when his phone rang and no-one replied," Pavel jibed.

"You mean that was you who rang earlier? But I saw Alex's number!"

"Oleg, don't worry yourself over the details. Needless to say your man Alex will be stopped at the border in your car and shot, along with Mr. Cannon, as spies."

The Hacker Hunter © Copyright Lionwing Ltd 2011

An air of defeat set about Oleg as the Professor walked out of the room, his shoulders slumped forward and his body felt cold to its core. There was no question that Alex had just been condemned to death by his friend's stupidity. Oleg, now alone again in this bleak excuse for an office felt sick to his stomach. Part of him wanted to curl up on the floor and pray that somehow Alex would be ok. However the stronger part of Oleg's mind was so racked with a combination of guilt and fury that it drove him to a seething distraction. Oleg paced up and down, desperately racking his brains for some way he could warn Alex, some way of making up for what he had done. Oleg's mind started to jump around for ideas, there was no way he could call Alex because his phone would surely be off. Otherwise, Pavel would have used the signal to locate him. There had to be another way of getting some sort of warning message to Alex. Just then, Oleg had a moment of clarity, a moment that gave an answer so obvious that Oleg could not believed he had struggled to conceive it.

The garage that Oleg stored his car in was very close to his present location. There was a slim chance that he might actually reach the garage before Alex, providing he could escape the institute. Oleg tightened his hands into fists and took in a deep breath. He made the decision to try and escape.

Much to Oleg's relief, as he opened his office door he found the two military men and Professor Pavel gone. In fact as he peered down the corridor he noticed that there was no other soul in sight. Breaking into a half tiptoe sprint, Oleg's shoes made only the lightest of tapping noises as he glided down the isolated corridor towards an adjoining passage. Stopping at the edge of the T junction, Oleg slowly pushed his head out into the new hallway. Again, there was no sign of anyone. He knew that if he went right he'd have to go through a security door that would

The Hacker Hunter © Copyright Lionwing Ltd 2011

need his security pass number, they might have even placed guards there. If he turned left however he knew that he'd have nothing more than other windowless offices and the first floor toilets. He recalled the toilet had a few windows. He was one story up but maybe he could open a window and jump. It was his only real option. As Oleg burst into the toilets, his heart sank as he saw three tall opaque windows, each with no means for them to be opened. However, three smaller, narrow windows above each of these taller windows could be opened but just wide enough to let air in. Definitely no man could pass through them.

Every second that ticked away brought Pavel and his men closer to arresting Alex. Oleg needed to escape and he needed a way out of the institute right now. Pulling his arms free from his lab coat, Oleg wrapped the white garment around his fist. Drawing his clenched fist back, Oleg then released the full strength of his punch. Despite his hand being wrapped in the lab coat, Oleg felt every one of his knuckles impact the glass pane. Oleg felt a shooting pain in his wrist, but the glass did not shatter, nor did it crack.

"Fuck it!" shouted out Oleg.

He ran back out into the corridor. No longer interested in moving stealthily Oleg broke into a frantic run towards his office, the noise of his stamping shoes was only surpassed in volume by the loud screeching that echoed in all directions as he skidded to turn. The office door exploded inwards as Oleg burst into the room like a mad man. His lab coat still half wrapped around his right hand he reached out for the back of the chair that only 15 minutes earlier held his exhausted body. Wheeling the chair out into the corridor Oleg ran, pushing it towards the toilets. As the toilet door swung open Oleg was no longer pushing the chair, he actually held it up in the air and

The Hacker Hunter © Copyright Lionwing Ltd 2011

with the full thrust of his momentum launched it at one of the three windows. To Oleg's annoyance, the chair ricocheted off the metal struts used to hold and separate the windows, however one of the window panes cracked. Oleg picked up the chair and swung it again. Sure enough, as it impacted, the cracked glass fell away, leaving a space large enough for Oleg to climb out of.

As Oleg looked through the window space, he could see the tarmac car park one story beneath. He had come this far, but his nerve was truly tested by the idea of leaping twice his body length down to the unforgiving, hard surface. He stared down, his heart pounding. Having got this far Oleg just couldn't bring himself to jump. Maybe if the window was just a legs distance closer to the ground Oleg could do it, but it wasn't and a little voice was telling him that a jump would result in a broken ankle at best. His scientific mind soon provided a solution, he picked the chair back up and smashed it into the neighbouring window pane. The pane cracked and fell away. Whipping his belt out from around his trousers, Oleg instantly took to fastening it securely around the now fully exposed metal window frame. Wrapping the other end of the belt around his left hand Oleg proceeded to climb out. He pulled the belt tight and lowered himself to rest both his knees on the external window ledge. Oleg then hung his left leg out so that he was half hanging from the ledge by his right leg and his right hand. He then eased his right leg off the outcropping so that he was now just hanging by his right hand and the belt strap which was now agonisingly biting into his left hand. Oleg freed his right hand from the window ledge and grabbed the belt. Using his right hand to lift his body up he loosened the belts grip around his left hand. With Oleg's left hand now free Oleg let go, an action that resulted in a swift descent to the waiting tarmac below. As Oleg impacted the ground he felt the shock reverberate through his ankles, into his knees, out from his hips and shoot up the spine into the very back of his brain.

The Hacker Hunter © Copyright Lionwing Ltd 2011

It took a moment for the realization to set in, but as Oleg stood there breathing in the sharp, cold air, it suddenly dawned on him that he was free. A boost of adrenaline flooded Oleg's arteries. Oleg darted across the car park and into a tree line. After a few mad scrambles over walls and frantic scurries around the back of neighbouring offices, Oleg found himself back out on the street. If he was to run he would be at the garage he used to house his car in ten or twenty minutes.

The first ten minutes passed quickly, but as the affects of the adrenaline wore off, Oleg found it hard to keep the pace up. Oleg wasn't fat, but he wasn't thin either, and although he enjoyed outdoor sports such as rally car racing through the Russian woodlands, he rarely found an excuse to properly exercise his body. Eventually, his running turned into a jog and his breathing turned into gasping. Things started to hurt, his knee must have taken more of an impact than he had first realised, as it twitched with pain. The now half jogging, half limping, out of breath Oleg spotted the garages, and true enough there was Alex with two other men by a silver grey Volga.

Alex was shaking his head in disagreement to something but Oleg was too far away to work out what Alex was saying. The elder of the two other men had a Viking like moustache. Oleg could see that he was clearly gesturing with his hand for them to return to the parked Volga. The other man seemed to be pleading with Alex but again, Oleg was too far to be able to hear what was being said. As Oleg approached it was Alex that first spotted him.

"Oleg, what are you doing here!" a surprised Alex shouted out.

The Hacker Hunter © Copyright Lionwing Ltd 2011

Oleg could hardly get the words together. His lungs felt like they were burning. He stopped jogging and doubled over, supporting his body by resting his hands on his knees.

"Alex you need too-" but Oleg could not finish his sentence, the air was just not available in his lungs. He took another breath and as Alex approached, Oleg attempted to shout out,

"Alex, your phone, turn off your phone!" Gasping for breath, Oleg pulled himself up right to face the oncoming Alex and said,

"It's the Professor, he's really a-" There was a split second whistling sound that blended with the noise of a dull thud, Oleg's face exploded outwards as a sniper's bullet entered through the back of his cranium and exited through his nasal bridge. Oleg's body lunged forward and fell face down in front of Alex. Within one half of a heart beat, Mac reached Alex, grabbed him by both arms and literally dragged him behind the Volga for cover.

Cannon stood in front of Oleg's garage, speechlessly watching events unfold. Men dressed in black coveralls appeared out of nowhere, brandishing automatic assault rifles. Cannon knew they had to be Spetsnaz operatives, Russia's answer to the British SAS. Mac and Alex were surrounded and then manhandled over the bonnet of the Volga. Cannon watched as both Mac and Alex had their hands tied behind their backs with bulky white plastic zip ties. The Spetsnaz aggressively patted down Alex first and then Mac, despite the fact Mac had the muzzle of an assault rifle pushed into the back of his head he looked remarkably calm. Once the Spetsnaz were confident that neither man posed a threat Mac and Alex were pulled off the car bonnet and walked to stand before Oleg's still body. It dawned on Cannon that no-one had come to arrest him. The Spetsnaz operatives didn't pay Christian a blind bit of notice.

"Mr. Cannon, what a pleasure. I wouldn't try anything brave or stupid. You see I have a sniper trained on you as we speak. It would be a shame for you to die the same way as poor Oleg."

Cannon turned to face the direction of the voice, he gazed upon the portly, middle aged professor.

"I don't believe I've had the pleasure?" Cannon asked.

"Please call me Pavel. May I call you Christian?" the Professor replied.

"I prefer Chris, for some unknown reason people just seem to love calling me Cannon - can't bloody stand it." Cannon responded with a cynical smile before going on to ask, "What's all this about?"

Pavel walked closer to Cannon and pointed to the dead body of Oleg. "Chris, allow me to show you something."

Cannon followed Pavel to the motionless body of Oleg. Alex and Mac both looked at Christian, they were equally bemused as to why their hands were tied and Cannon wasn't even held. Pavel pointed down at Oleg's corpse and with a tone of indifference spoke,

"This poor innocent scientist died because of you."

"I've never seen this man before, Pavel, and you know it," Cannon interrupted with a sharp aggressiveness that indicated that he thought Pavel was trying to frame him for Oleg's murder.

"I think it is fate that kept you alive. The universe is talking Chris and today, I, a simple scientist, am listening to destiny. You see, we had it all worked out. Oleg was bound to want to save Alex, so we allowed him to escape so we could track him here. It was all very simple, we called Oleg using Alex's number and never broke the signal. t was just a case of hoping Oleg was right about where you and Alex would be." Pavel looked down at the body and sighed.

Cannon walked closer to Alex, he wanted to see if AK was ok. It was clear that the shock of losing his best friend hadn't sunk fully in yet. Turning to face Pavel, Christian asked,

"Why the sigh? It was one of your men that shot this fella in the head."

"Chris, I had ordered the sniper to shoot you. Oleg just happened to straighten his body up at the same time and regrettably intercepted, quite by accident, a bullet meant for the Hacker Hunter himself. That's the second time today you've missed the snipers bullet. It's fate telling me to keep you alive," Pavel looked over at Alex who was starting to become upset at seeing the dead body of his closest friend.

"Pavel, why would you want to kill me? I mean, other than recruiting one of your computer programmers for a little bit of moonlighting as a hacker, what possible reason could you want for me to be assassinated?"

Pavel giggled, bending as he laughed only to straighten back up with a deadly serious expression on his suddenly humourless face.

The Hacker Hunter © Copyright Lionwing Ltd 2011

"I'm sorry Chris, but the world thinks the Russian bear is sleeping after our economic collapse, and that any, how do you say, Tom, Dick and..."

"Or Harry," filled in Cannon.

"Yes, thank you. If any Tom, Dick or Harry thinks they can come here and try to steal our technology, they should first understand that the bear is awake and still very able to defend itself. If that message can be sent by killing you, then that's what must happen" Pavel finished speaking and signalled to a few of his men. Within a few seconds a dark blue van reversed to stop only a few meters away from Alex, Mac, Cannon and Pavel. Two men opened the back doors of the van and then lent over Oleg's body, picking it up they slid the body into the back and stood by the open doors, seemingly waiting for their next task. Pavel signalled for one of the Spetsnaz operatives to pass over his side arm. Pavel took the pistol and without breaking eye contact with Cannon raised it to Christians head, Pavel then slowly turned the gun to point at Mac.

"Tell me Chris, who is this gentleman?" asked Pavel.

Mac looked down the gun. He could see the safety catch was off, if the Spetsnaz were anything like the SAS a round would already be in the chamber and the weapon cocked.

"He's a taxi driver," Cannon replied puzzled.

"So you will not mind if I shoot him in the face," Pavel asked with a very genuine tone to his voice.

Mac looked at Cannon, he knew that his very life may well depend on the next string of words from his mouth. Cannon looked franticly at Pavel and then said,

"Yes I would fucking mind. Listen if you want to shoot someone why don't you try yourself and do us all a favour. You bloody Russians are worse than the Americans for getting over emotional and paranoid. If you are not going to shoot me then let's talk about a deal."

Pavel lowered the gun, he looked intrigued at what Cannon had just said.

"A deal, what kind of a deal do you have in mind?"

Chapter 15 – Zip Ties

The dim, greyish light of the Moscow day entered the otherwise windowless back of the van through a singular small glass hatchway. The hatch was split into two halves. One half could be slid across the other providing enough space to pass something through to the driver, or vice versa. Alex and Mac, who were unaccompanied, save for Oleg's body, had each taken a seat on adjacent wheel arches. Both men stared down at the body of Oleg, which lay there, sprawled out between them on the corrugated metal flooring of the van. The channels of the flooring pooled the slowly coagulating blood which was still dripping from Oleg's fatal head wound. Alex looked up at his travelling partner. He could not interpret Mac's facial expression, it seemed sharp, cold and otherwise emotionless. Maybe a slight display of pity for this innocent victim at his feet but nothing that Alex could be sure of. He addressed Mac,

"I am so sorry Mikhail, I'm sure when they learn you are just a taxi driver they will let you go."

Mac's eyes lifted from Oleg's carcass, which every now and then would wobble as the van hit a bump or pothole in the road and just stared intensely at Alex, offering no reply. He simply sniffed sharply and twitched his Viking moustache.

"I know you must be pretty upset but let me assure you, it is Christian and me they want," Alex attempted to reassure Mac again, still hopeful for a response.

The lack of Mac's reply or even retort disturbed Alex. He imagined that the Taxi driver must be fuming with rage given that only a few minutes ago Pavel had stuck a gun in his face. What really disturbed Alex was the fact that Mac was still maintaining his cold, sharp glare at him, which, combined with the chilling lack of any facial expression made Alex totally unable to predict how his travelling partner would be about to react to his attempts at conversation.

"I imagine they are taking us to the institute, which is a few minutes away from here, so don't worry we'll be out soon," said Alex.

Mac looked away from Alex who was obviously making nervous conversation and up at the small window hatch into the drivers' cabin. It was impossible to see into the cabin from his position so with hands still zip tied behind him, Mac pushed his back into the side of the van and, straightening his legs, lifting himself off the wheel arch to his feet. In a broad Stirlingshire accent Mac muttered out under his breath,

"Amateurs, fucking amateurs. Who the hell is training these buffoons?"

Now standing, Mac peered down the van and into the drivers' cabin. He could see the driver was accompanied by a single, armed guard. Both men were just looking outward onto the road ahead. Mac shuffled over to the opposite side of the van, and facing Alex, ordered,

"Alex is it? Do me a favour mate, unbuckle my belt will you." Mac looked down at his belt buckle repeatedly in a gesture to Alex for him to unfasten the clasp.

Alex was speechless, firstly rendered dumfounded by Mikhail's sudden change in language and secondly flabbergasted by the actions of the taxi driver as he repeatedly looked down at his own groin and then at Alex impatiently.

The Hacker Hunter © Copyright Lionwing Ltd 2011

"Come on turn around and unbuckle my bloody belt will you!" ordered Mac in a strong whisper.

As Alex also had his hands 'zip tied' behind him he had to turn his back to Mac and fumble with his fingers to find the belt clasp. A few uncomfortable seconds later and the belt was undone.

"Great, now pull the belt out," commanded Mac quietly.

Alex was so dumbstruck that he did nothing more than follow Mac's instruction in a vague hope that in a few seconds everything would start making sense. As Alex pulled free the belt and held it tightly in his grip Mac turned, grabbed the belt and then pulled away something that must have been fastened to it. A few seconds later Mac's now free hands turned Alex around to face him. Mac held in his right hand the Stanley blade he had duct-taped into the inside of his belt before leaving the Volga to enter Cannon's hotel.

"I'm going to cut your hands free now Alex. I need you to keep as quiet as possible, just nod your head if you understand?" Mac asked.

Alex nodded and Mac almost effortlessly sliced through the 'zip tie' that restrained Alex's hands. Alex, now free from restraint turned to face Mac, his eyes full of a thousand questions. But before anything could be said, Mac put his finger to his lips to signal hush and softly said,

"This is how it's going to work, we are about to leave the van, you are going to be scared, people are going to die and a lot of crazy shit is going to happen. Do not leave my side, do not do anything other than what I tell you, nod your head to show me you understand," Mac commanded still in a whisper.

The Hacker Hunter © Copyright Lionwing Ltd 2011

Alex nodded his head but also spoke out,

"Are you Russian?"

Mac, who had now turned away from Alex and was about to make his way to the drivers hatch shot a glance back and said,

"No! Scottish!"

With the Stanley blade in his right hand, Mac pulled the hatch across with his left and with a sudden swiftness thrust his arm through the opening. Before driver or guard could react, Mac bent his elbow inward to bring his forearm and the hand carrying the blade towards the driver. In one sudden motion Mac sunk the small but unforgiving blade into the left side of the neck and sliced through to the right side, leaving a gash half a thumb deep for the now severed carotid artery to spurt out pulsing gulps of dark blood. Mac left the blade in the driver's neck who had now taken both hands off the wheel, and was clutching his throat. The guard raised his assault rifle and turned his body in an attempt to point the weapon towards the back of the van. Pulling his right arm back out of the hatch Mac thrust in his left arm and yanked the rifle out of the man's hands and through the open hatchway. Mac then placed his back flat against the cabin side van wall and clutching the assault rifle across his chest cocked it and braced. Mac, who had very obviously foreseen the future events, watched as Alex and Oleg's body flew forward as the driver wacked on the brakes in a frantic panic.

Looking up from his new position, Alex saw Mac turn and fire three rounds through the drivers hatch from his recently acquired assault rifle. The explosive noise of each round leaving the barrel seemed to fill the back of the van with a shocking terror that made Alex's heart detonate in synchronicity. The spent

The Hacker Hunter © Copyright Lionwing Ltd 2011

metallic brass coloured cartridge cases ejected from the rifle and seemed to slowly spin down towards Alex. Standing to avoid any more shell cases, Alex caught a glimpse of the mayhem on the other side of the hatch. The driver was still alive but desperately trying to stop his blood loss by clutching at his neck with both hands. This did little to stop the blood flow as it oozed out between his fingers. However, the driver still clung to life, which was more than could be said for the guard, who had clearly been in the process of reaching for his side arm just before being flung up against the window as the driver whacked on the breaks. Much to the detriment of the guard, Mac, who had been prepared for the rapid deceleration, had made the faster recovery and managed to squeeze off three rounds first. The extremely close proximity from the rifle to the guards head had resulted in each bullet doing the maximum of damage to the guard's forehead. In fact, all Alex could make out from the blood and gore was the nose, mouth and jaw. Everything above the nose was missing or sprayed up against what remained of the shattered glass of the van's window screen.

"Do me a favour Alex, see if you can reach in through that hatch and get the guard's hand gun. It's landed on the van chair," Mac requested, whilst turning to face the back door of the van.

Four more rounds were fired from the assault rifle, each bullet tore through the area around the lock and handle. Mac ran over to the handle and furiously wiggled it up and down. Taking a step backward he fired two more rounds into the lock and then gave the adjacent door, a good hard kick.

"That should do it, Alex where's that gun!" Mac shouted out as he pulled up the door handle and shunted the back doors wide open.

Alex had his left arm shoulder deep through the hatch, but even with his fingers fully outstretched the guards pistol was just a thumbnails distance out of reach. Alex stretched and pushed and stretched but he just couldn't reach it.

Mac stepped out of the van and onto the road, the rapid change in light caused his peripheral vision to momentarily diminish. However, he observed one car screeching to a stop on his right side and a second car coming directly at him. Focusing on the more immediate threat Mac pulled the sights up and squeezed the trigger. As Mac was all too aware, visual perception or the ability to aim at and hit a target is everything. However perception can be effected by four factors. The first is atmosphere, which could be anything from weather conditions, the time of day and even the change in light perhaps caused by a passing car with its headlights on full on a moonless night. Second, fatigue, being so exhausted that you can even start to hallucinate. Third, a massive rush of adrenaline can result in tunnel vision, which means you lose sight of anything dangerous to your left or right. All three of these factors however hold nothing of notable oddity in comparison to the alteration of a man's visual perception when faced with the fourth condition. In the hundreds of fire fights where Mac had been shooting it out with the opposition only meters away, there had been times where he had seen bullets literally exploding into walls, trees and the ground around him, he had seen it in a type of slow motion and over the years learnt to work within this altered perception. For this change in awareness wasn't caused by adrenaline, weather or exhaustion, the fourth change in visual perception was a singular by-product of pending death. This fourth condition, much to the misfortune of the approaching car was now in full flight as the driver witnessed a copper, metallic bullet explode through the flames, smoke and charred debris of Mac's muzzle flash.

The Hacker Hunter © Copyright Lionwing Ltd 2011

The Spetsnaz passenger who was sat next to the driver watched helplessly as Mac's tenth round shattered through the front window. The bullet punctured the drivers' throat and, exiting via the neck, along with several vertebrae, went on still further to pass through the headrest and finally come to rest in the unsuspecting backseat passenger. Mac serenely walked out of the path of the now out of control and still oncoming vehicle, walking as if there was nothing to be overly concerned about. The approaching car narrowly missed Mac and smashed into the back of the open van, the impact brought Alex to a head cracking meeting with the driver's hatch, from where he was still trying to reach the dead guard's pistol.

From his recovering position in the front seat, the passenger observed a second flash of light, which could only mean one thing. Alas, this moment of realization came quicker than the ability to evade the oncoming bullet of Mac's eleventh round.

Walking along the right side of the now stationary car, it was clear to see the driver was dead, the front passenger was also dead, of the two backseat passengers, one was writhing in agony and the other was raising his rifle towards the approaching John Mac. The rear side window suddenly exploded inward as the twelfth and thirteenth bullets impacted the glass. Both passengers slumped sideways as their journey reached a final and very fatal end.

As Mac walked around the back of the car he looked into the van to see Alex still reaching desperately through the drivers hatch.

"I'm going to need that pistol Alex!" shouted Mac whilst raising his sights once more.

Now behind both cars Mac turned his attention to the second vehicle. As far as he could see there were two Spetsnaz operatives in the back, and two more in the front seats. Mac squeezed the trigger and this time kept it pulled inward to release the full barrage of auto fire. Walking forward whilst empty shells jettisoned from his assault rifle, Mac observed the rear window shatter and fall away, leaving the heads of the two backseat passengers fully exposed to his aim. They never knew what hit them as segments of their hair covered skull and brain were blasted out in chunks the size of fists. Both the front doors were flung open; as the driver and the drivers' passenger attempted to escape Mac's onslaught. Still firing on full auto Mac moved his sights down the side of the car, towards the now exited front seat passenger. The passenger started to raise a pistol in the desperate hope that he might get a lucky round off at Mac before meeting the approaching volley of ammunition. In a moments futile realization that he was about to die the passenger gave up on trying to aim his pistol at Mac and instead elected to lift his forearms up to shield his face. Then, from nowhere, silence fell. Mac had been counting every round fired from his gun, there should have been five bullets left, but either by a stoppage or lack of ammunition, the rifle had ceased firing. The passenger lowered his arms and for a bewildered moment just looked at Mac as if to say, 'Why am I not dead?' Rather than choosing to re-aim the gun back at Mac he just watched in utter shock as Mac calmly let the rifle fall to the ground whilst breaking into a sprinting charge towards him!

Within a second Mac reached the passenger. Stepping into the man's intimate body space, he had attained the perfect nearness to thrust his half open hand up the passengers' sternum, which acted as a guide for the fingers of the hand to jab through the skin of the man's throat. Mac closed his grip around the larynx and tugged downward with all of his body weight. The muscles of the larynx contracted and then became inflamed, swollen to

The Hacker Hunter © Copyright Lionwing Ltd 2011

the point that it had become impossible for the passenger to breathe. The man, now choking, tried to raise his gun in a desperate attempt to do one last thing with his ending life. Mac grabbed the pistol and twisted it against the natural direction of the joints in the passengers trigger finger. There was a twinge of excruciating pain as the man's finger snapped beyond any usefulness. As Mac pulled the gun downward in an attempt to acquire the weapon the passenger raised his hand towards Mac's throat. Blocking the approaching hand Mac let go of the gun and with his now free hand gouged out the man's eyes. Reaching back for the pistol, Mac effortlessly took the gun from the passenger and used its hilt to knock his defeated aggressor unconscious, a compassionate move that would allow the dying man to pass in less of an agonising way.

Mac turned to locate the driver, who, for the moment, was the one remaining threat, his quest came to a sudden end as a deep Russian voice spoke out in English,

"Stand very still!"

Mac looked over the roof of the car towards the direction the voice had originated from, much to his disappointment Mac's eyes met with the driver who was pointing a pistol at Mac's head.

"I just watched you kill seven of my friends, seven of Russia's finest Special Forces operatives. Before I blow your fucking brains out, you tell me who you are!" demanded the driver.

"I'm just doing my fucking job. Now do yours!" shouted back Mac.

The driver squeezed the trigger. There was an explosion, a waft of warm air and then Mac's eyes filled with blood. As he wiped his eyes free, he saw that the driver was no more. In fact, the driver was flat out on his back on the road. Mac stepped up on the car seat to take a better look, no question, the driver had just been shot in the head. Mac turned a full 180 to see Alex leaning out from the van with his arm outstretched, in his hand was the guard's pistol.

"I managed to get the pistol!" Alex shouted out gleefully.

"I can see that Alex. About fucking time mate! Hey, and where did you learn to shoot like that?"

"I am a big fan of, how you say, Medal of Honour, Doom, you know computer games."

Mac walked towards Alex with his arm and hand outstretched in a gesture to Alex to pass him the gun. Alex stepped out of the van and onto the bonnet of the car, which upon crashing, had lodged itself into the van's bumper. Jumping down from the bonnet to the ground, Alex passed Mac the pistol. Mac slid the ammunition clip out of the gun handle and counted the rounds before sliding it back in.

"Computer games. I'm not going to comment on that Alex, but thank you, I owe you one. Ok, let's get out of here, we've got about fifteen more seconds before the rest of them show up," Mac ordered hastily.

"I take it that Mikhail isn't your name. What shall I call you?" asked Alex curiously.

Mac didn't respond, instead, he observed the road. There were a few abandoned cars in the street that had been left by their owners when the shooting started, but nothing that offered Mac a means of fast transport. In fact, the fastest vehicles were the

The Hacker Hunter © Copyright Lionwing Ltd 2011

two cars that Mac had only moments ago been riddling with bullets. Mac looked over the car that was wedged into the back of the van and ran his finger and thumb through his moustache, he then turned to the second car. The rear of the car was shot to pieces and apart from having two corpses in the back the front seats were drenched in blood and chunks of brain meat. Mac turned to Alex and pointing at the car said,

"Get in mate, passenger side!"

Alex lent in through the open passenger side doorway, right in the middle of the seat was a chunk of brain and oddly next to it a finger. He looked at the window screen to see bullet holes and blood. Alex pulled his head back out of the car and said,

"No, I think I will just walk, thank you."

Mac pointed a finger at Alex and then directed Alex's attention with the finger towards four more cars that had all stopped a bit further down the road. Pavel had stepped out of one car and was commanding ten or twelve more Spetsnaz operatives towards them. Mac looked at Alex again, in the process reaffixing his pointing finger back at him. Pausing momentarily and swallowing hard, as if attempting to suppress what he wanted to say, Mac located a set of politer instructions than those currently passing through his mind,

"You! Shut the fuck up and get in the car, now!"

Alex pulled his jacket sleeve over his hand and scraped the body parts off his chair before sitting down and pulling the door shut. Mac jumped onto the bonnet of the car which caused it to sink down as his body weight compressed the suspension. Alex could not see much from his seated position because the window screen was covered in blood. Curious as to why Mac was on the bonnet Alex used his sleeve once more to clean a small circular area of glass. As he peered through the still mucky circle the first thing Alex saw was the black heel of an army boot as Mac kicked in the window screen. Within a few seconds the screen had been pulled away leaving Alex just staring up at Mac through nothing but an empty window frame. Mac was off the bonnet in a second, standing with one arm reaching through the driver side doorway he reached for the keys which were thankfully still in the ignition. The Mercedes started first time.

"I've always thought about getting one of these, let's see what it can do," Mac grinned as he jumped into the seat and pulled the driver side door closed.

Alex started fumbling around for a seat belt, but on discovering more blood and brain decided that it was simply more practical to place his hands on the dashboard ahead of him. There was a crack as one of the Spetsnaz fired a warning shot and shouted for them to leave the vehicle. Alex's heart felt like a dagger of cold ice had just been plunged through it as he was once again hit with a massive surge of adrenaline. As Mac pushed down the hand break lever, shifted into reverse and floored the accelerator he shouted,

"Get one of the rifles from the back Alex!"

Alex felt the full weight of his body on his arms as the car jolted and jumped to a full speed reverse. There was no way he could follow Mac's orders given that he was doing all he could to hang on.

"Get the fucking assault rifle! Get it now!" shouted Mac aggressively.

There was something in Mac's voice that stressed the dire importance in getting an assault rifle. However, Alex only reacted to the instruction after one of the Spetsnaz operatives started firing at the car. With just one hand on the wheel Mac pulled his pistol and pointed it out of the front window. Whilst looking over his shoulder to check they were not about to ram into something Mac fired three shots blindly, in return. These three shots were enough to make all the Spetsnaz fleetingly lower themselves downward and then start returning fire.

"Now we're in trouble! They weren't meant to do that," Mac said to Alex whilst the bullets whistled past them. Mac floored the clutch and spun the wheel vigorously which caused the car to spin 180 degrees, now facing away from the Spetsnaz, Mac thrust the gear into first, and accelerated, thrashing the car engine up through the second, third and then fourth gears.

"Not bad 0 to 60 speed!" Mac shouted out playfully.

"You said 'not meant to do that', what, what are they 'not meant to do'?" Alex asked by screaming out to try and compensate for the fact that the now 160 KPH headwind, caused by the lack of window screen, was blasting the air out of his lungs.

"I was counting on you being too valuable for them to start shooting at us - turns out you're not!" Mac replied.

"Let me see if I can reach those assault rifles for you," Alex responded, now in a more willing state of mind to help.

Mac glanced into his wing mirror. He could see that the Spetsnaz had all elected to return to their vehicles and start a pursuit. All save Pavel's car, for this car, which quite possibly was carrying Cannon continued on its journey to the institute.

The Hacker Hunter © Copyright Lionwing Ltd 2011

Alex turned to kneel in his seat. He could see both the bodies of the dead Spetsnaz sprawled out, but no assault rifles.

"There are no rifles but they each have a holstered pistol on their belts!" Alex shouted out.

"Ok, they must have put the rifles in the boot. Don't worry, get me the pistols, hurry!" ordered Mac.

Alex leant further over his seat and closer towards the mutilated bodies. He really didn't feel as disturbed as he thought he might by the carnage. After retrieving both guns Alex said,

"Do you want me to shoot again?"

Mac shot a sideways glance at Alex, almost in disbelief at what he had just heard and said,

"In the space of three minutes I have gone from being your Russian taxi driver, to being someone that's just killed ten people. Are you not even remotely interested in who I am or what any of this is about?"

Alex looked at Mac with the blankest of expressions and replied,

"Ten minutes ago I just saw my best friend shot in the head under the order of my university professor, I am just glad I am not in the back of that van. Oh, and for, how you say, the record, you shot nine people, I shot the tenth!"

Mac turned his head to face Alex and smiled,

"Fair enough, fair enough. Hey look, that's our Volga." Mac pointed as they shot past the garages and their old car. The wind was breathtaking, Alex found it easier to breathe through the nose than mouth, looking down at the gauge he could see 190 KPH. Mac noticed that Alex was inspecting the speed and said,

"Not bad considering the traffic, I'm starting to think Mercedes might actually make a good car. Well we will get to find out for sure in a moment!"

Mac checked the wing mirror again, two of the cars were approaching to his left and the third car was coming up directly behind him.

"Take a look back there Alex. You see those three cars, this is what you call a box and direct action, effectively their aim is to box us in and then force us off the road. They are doing it quite well, good formation, but they should be going a little bit faster, I'll slow down a bit, give them a chance to catch up!" Mac shouted out over the noise of the wind.

With a look of astonishment Alex replied "What! Why slow down?"

Mac, now squinting his eyes to protect them from the wind shouted back,

"Well before they box us they'll try to - look it's probably better you just find your seatbelt," Mac said whilst fastening his own.

"Ok listen, Alex, the airbags will have been disabled so this might get a little heavy going. I'd recommend you put your arms in front of your face!" Mac shouted out whilst taking the other guns from Alex and placing them on his lap.

Alex watched Mac slightly open his car door and hold it against the now 160 KPH headwind.

The Hacker Hunter © Copyright Lionwing Ltd 2011

"Ok, brace and stay braced until you hear me say otherwise!" yelled out Mac as he hammered down on the brakes and clutch, pulled the car gearstick into full reverse from fourth gear and on releasing the clutch and brakes, hammered down the accelerator!

The ABS of the Mercedes didn't kick, in simply because the brakes weren't engaged. However, wedging a car that's doing 160 KPH forward into reverse has its drawbacks, the most notable being the strain it places on the human body. Alex soon discovered this fact, as firstly the seatbelt felt like it was a piano wire cutting through cheese. The agonising pain of the seatbelt was soon overshadowed as Alex's forearms, which were tightly pulled up to protect his face, impacted with the car dashboard.

Now sat in a motionless vehicle, Alex straightened himself back up, pulling his forearms away from his face, he noticed that the driver side door was open and Mac had gone. In an attempt to locate Mac Alex turned his head to the right, as he did two of the pursuing cars roared past him. Just then the air became filled with the noise of screeching tires and the odorous tinge of burning tread. Alex was once again thrust forward as the third pursuing car, the car that was directly behind them, collided with an almighty smash into what was left of the Mercedes. Unfortunately, Alex was less prepared and without his forearms to protect his face, his head impacted the unforgiving dashboard once more.

This time, Alex knew it was serious. He felt sick to his stomach, every noise around him sounded muffled. Even the gun shots and machineguns firing weren't enough to fight the drowsiness Alex was feeling. "Strange, I can see small spots of light," muttered Alex sleepily, just before everything around him fell away into blackness and unconsciousness took him.

Chapter 16 – Defection is painless

Standing alone in a windowless office, Christian Cannon placed his arms behind his back and grasped his hands together. He stared down at the speckled grey concrete floor. A few contemplative seconds passed as Cannon stretched his arms out behind him and then, after letting out a small groan, he slowly dropped to his knees. From his now lowered position Christian lent forward to rest his palms on the cold, dull concrete. From this pose he slid his feet back, stretching out his legs so that the entire bulk of his rugby player's build dropped into the 'press-up' position. With his body weight now dispersed on his toes and hands Cannon tilted his head as far back as his neck would allow and looked around the office. As he examined his surroundings from this rather peculiar angle he noted the lack of any computers. In fact, bar one desk, that was extraordinarily messy, there was little else to qualify the room with the 'title' of office, no filing cabinets, telephones, copiers or printers, just one chair, one desk and a few buzzing strip lights that hung from the ceiling above him.

Cannon had been escorted to this rather bleak office by Pavel and two armed Spetsnaz operatives only twenty minutes earlier, surprisingly enough, Pavel had asked for nothing and the operatives had not even taken his phone or asked him to empty his pockets. Pavel had just serenely told Christian to make himself at home whilst he went to find an update on the whereabouts of Alex and their driver. Cannon's efforts to portray a somewhat calm demeanour in response to the polite hospitality offered by Pavel were an act. Cannon bent his elbows and tilted his head forward so his nose touched the cold floor and then in rapid precession pushed out twenty press-ups. This burst of physical exercise was a desperate attempt to compensate for the massive amount of adrenalin fuelled energy that pulsed, like cold slithers of electrified ice, through every artery and vein in his body.

Just as Cannon stood back up, the door behind him was opened by an armed guard and Pavel stepped through it. Without even taking a glance up at Cannon, Pavel walked into the room reading from the white sheets of a report that was held together between a brown file folder and a few well placed staples. He was so engrossed in what he was reading that Pavel didn't even acknowledge the guard who was waiting for his next instruction. The guard nervously coughed in an attempt to gain Pavel's attention, but to no avail.

"Sir?" called out the guard in Russian, in a more direct attempt to gain Pavel's interest.

"Oh, yes, yes. Close the door, leave us, I'll call you if I need anything, thank you, thank you." Pavel didn't even look up but instead freed a hand and gestured intolerantly for the guard to leave.

"So you are a spy," announced Pavel, who was still not looking up from reading the document.

"It is strange that you started your career stealing from the American Air Force yet ended up working for them?" Pavel stated as a half question.

"I also see that you have qualifications in graphic design, photography and oddly in micro operating systems. You were the managing director of a design agency in London, blah, blah, blah. You have a brilliant reputation as an international designer and marketer. You enjoy riding motorcycles and have a weakness for busty beautiful women," Pavel looked up from reading and, looking Cannon straight in the eye asked curiously

The Hacker Hunter © Copyright Lionwing Ltd 2011

"Why do you own a business that specializes in Artificial Intelligence?"

Cannon, who had turned to face Pavel when the door was opened, looked away from Pavel's gaze and replied, "Well apart from the British tax breaks of having an R & D company, I've always had a keen interest in matters of the mind and the sciences."

"This is why you have a qualification in micro operating systems, no?" asked Pavel.

"Yes, but I also have qualifications in print buying and multimedia, I take it they are not on your list?" taunted Cannon.

Pavel looked back down at the report and said "No, they are, but why don't you tell me what's not on this list, like why you are trying to steal one of our best software developers and why you are trying to steal our AI secrets. Tell me how a British spy working for the Americans even managed to find Alexander Khomenko?"

Cannon gave Pavel a cheeky grin and replied "This doesn't sound good, Pavel, firstly and I know you probably will not believe this, but I might as well tell you the truth. I am not a spy. Let me tell you what I think of the spy world. You see, in the real world, these so called spies just work for the secret police. I think you and I will both agree that the secret police in any country aren't usually looked upon as the good guys. However, thanks to Ian Fleming's creation the James Bond brand has totally legitimised the British secret police. I'm told that James Bond is the best marketing tool and recruitment propaganda that British Intelligence could have ever hoped for. The bottom line is that most MI staff earn next to nothing and the secret police are still the secret police, 007 status or not!"

"Now you are trying to convince me that you are not a spy." said Pavel sternly.

"I resent the implication. You are in effect calling me a jumped up civil servant. I don't mind telling you that I find that offensive. The idea of doing something for Queen and Country is bullshit, the Queen is a leader with no power and the country is being messed up by the same stupid civil service that you claim I'm part of."

"You are a Briton working for the Americans, you are an American spy!" shouted Pavel less calmly.

"An American spy? You have to be kidding me, I am a true blue opportunist, I don't work for governments, they work for us, at least they're meant to!" replied Cannon with equal vigour.

"What is your relationship with Alex?" asked Pavel this time more pleasantly.

Still looking somewhat offended, Christian took a step closer to Pavel, and looking him squarely in the eye said "Mr. Khomenko is my employee, I was under the impression that he was working on a PHD, I take it that he was in fact actually working on something considerably more interesting, hence all this fuss?"

Pavel ignored Cannon's question and instead replied "Tell me more about John Mac?"

"Who? Strap me up to a lie detector and ask me the same question, you'll find that I genuinely have never heard of John Mac, stated Cannon with absolute confidence in his voice. "Look, you are obviously trying to put something together and you don't have all the pieces yet. What's happened to Alex? What was all that shooting about?"

Pavel didn't break from Cannon's eye contact. Both men fell quiet and an awkward silence grew. After an uncomfortable period of time Pavel looked back down at his report and said softly, as if parting with grave news,

"Alex received a head injury, I'm afraid to say, Christian, he died a short time ago."

"What? Alex dead? How? I mean why would you do that? Surely he's worth more to you alive?" questioned Christian in pure disbelief.

"It is not me that wanted him dead. He is dead because of the man sent to steal him, and kill you," Pavel replied.

"Kill me?" stated Cannon, now with an utter look of dumbfoundedness.

"Pavel, do you mind telling me what the hell is going on? Last time I checked it was you who had tried to have me killed, no less than twice. Then you locked my driver and Alex in the back of a van and had me driven here, to this institute."

Cannon was clearly becoming aggressively agitated, not just from the feeling of bewilderment but also at the feeling that Pavel was holding something back. Some answers that would help him make sense of what was happening or at least going to happen. Pavel replied,

"It's ok, I have the list of fifty hackers for you, calm down. I have decided to send you home."

Cannon was almost speechless. In his confusion he managed to mutter out,

"52 hackers, not fifty."

"Oh, well I'm sure you'll understand our reluctance to give the Americans access to two of our best hackers," announce Pavel gleefully.

"You mean your hacked into the NSA as well? asked Cannon in a dazed manner.

Pavel replied with a smile, the sort of smile that said a thousand yeses, each brighter than the sun and prouder than a new father with twins.

"Give me a minute Pavel, there's just too much going on here. Firstly why would you give me the list of hackers, secondly how would you even know that is what I wanted and thirdly how did Alex die from a head injury?"

Pavel's facial expression changed to one of absolute seriousness. He cleared his throat and then said softly, "A spy working for a government or working for a business is still a spy, spies steal secrets, you are a spy, I'm taking a risk in doing this but I feel I must."

Cannon screwed his face up and shrugged as if to say, 'What madness is this?' but Pavel continued,

"I will explain everything, but before I do, let me say this: you were meant to die twice today, yet you stand before me. I was planning to use your death to send a signal to any other spies that wanted our great nation's secrets. At least, that was my plan. We have been watching you and Alex for some time. Believe me, all the AI R & D Alex was giving you was nothing compared to what he's been working on. Still it was enough to give us a legitimate excuse to kill you. The truth is, Alex was one of our greatest minds and he will be missed, dearly missed. Thankfully, he managed to complete his work before his death. His work will be his legacy, a legacy that will help to free the world."

Christian raised an eyebrow and asked "Free the world?"

Pavel, pacing passionately back and forth announced out loud as if addressing a group "In the last ten years Russia has achieved three major scientific breakthroughs, the first of which was in battery technology. To be more precise, batteries developed to power the electrical motors of a submarine. These new batteries will run for weeks and power just about everything on a sub including propulsion. The real point of interest is that just one battery, no bigger than a desk draw, would power an electrical car for over 800 miles before it would need recharging."

"Batteries are hardly a world freeing innovation Pavel," interrupted Cannon.

Pavel clenched his fingers together and raised them toward Cannon as if to signify that more attention was needed. Continuing to talk whilst waving his clenched hands like a musical conductor, Pavel replied,

"The second innovation is what you would know as a Tokamak thermonuclear fusion generator. In theory a Tokamak generates boundless electricity with no nuclear waste. You might have heard of the experimental Tokamak in Oxford, but did you know the idea was originally Russian? Invented in the 1950s by two Soviet physicists, one called Igor Tamm and the other, Andrei

The Hacker Hunter © Copyright Lionwing Ltd 2011

Sakharov. The original idea belonged to the amazing Oleg Lavrentyev."

"Yes, I had heard of it, I also know that we are decades away from even the smallest reactor holding plasma for more than a few minutes," contributed Cannon, but this time with more interest in his voice.

"You impress me Christian. I take it you understand why the plasma can't be held?" asked Pavel eagerly.

"It escapes me, something about a magnetic field or something like that," Cannon replied.

"Very good," Pavel stated, much like a teacher would praise a student to keep their attention. "It's to do with keeping the magnetic field constantly in balance with the plasma. It's almost impossible to achieve for any considerable time. I say almost, you'd need some sort of super computer to calculate and adjust the field strength needed in real-time."

Cannon took a few steps backward and with a questioning tone to his voice stated,

"Let me try and guess. The third invention, is it by any chance a super computer?" not waiting for Pavel to reply Cannon continued. "I take it Alex was one of the software developers for this computer, hence all this fuss of me using him to hack a few PC's here and there?"

Pavel stopped moving back and forth. In his stillness he just stared at Cannon and with deadly earnest eyes answered,

"Christian, think about it. A limitless source of pollution free energy, batteries that can store enough energy to power trains, cars and buses for long distances. I am talking about freeing the world, an end to war over oil, pollution and national corruption."

Cannon smiled at Pavel as if to say 'I want to believe you but I just can't' and replied,

"Look, I'm happy for mother Russia, these amazing innovations sound great but you were in the process of explaining how Alex died?"

"Christian, are you even listening to what I am saying? We will soon have so much clean energy, the world will be able to keep warm without burning fossil fuels, cook without needing fire, travel without causing pollution and live in light where there is dark?"

Cannon rolled his eyes back and said sarcastically,

"You Russians love your ideology. If it's not Communism, it's world peace through limitless clean energy. Why are you telling me all this Pavel? You and I both know that Russia wouldn't just give away free electricity to any country that wanted it. Though I grant you, it does sound pretty appealing."

"Of course we would not give it away, to share this type of technology would be too dangerous. It would be like giving children nuclear weapons to play with instead of toy guns. No, Russia would keep the technology a secret but share the benefits. Now you understand why I had to kill you," Pavel said trying to reassure Cannon that he had a more than justifiable reason to take his life.

Cannon's personality seemed to change. Firstly his facial expression distorted to a mix of mysticism and a further need for knowledge, his body language also became more relaxed.

The Hacker Hunter © Copyright Lionwing Ltd 2011

Observing Christian's change Pavel pondered for a moment as to whether Cannon really understood the importance of what he had just been told and then asked,

"Christian, you must understand that this is too complex for me to be making up. Plus why would I invent such a fantasy, for what purpose would it serve? We have a chance to change the world for the best, You can't tell me that the prospect doesn't excite you?"

Cannon, now less sceptical, replied,

"I'm sorry Pavel, the mistrust between our cultures is so strong it's hard for me to believe you don't have some sort of hidden agenda."

"You Westerners never see past the concrete towers and food lines of Socialism. You are all terrified that we would impose tenement blocks, poverty and forced labour on you. This blinds you from seeing that at our core is the idea of freedom: freedom from exploitation, freedom from oppression. Before these blocks of concrete housed our poor, men and women would freeze to death in the streets, or starve, whilst the rich feasted in front of warm fires."

"No, I get it Pavel, it's just your track record for doing the right thing isn't up to par. Invading Poland in 1939, taking Eastern Europe and enforcing Communism on them wasn't exactly what I'd call freedom from oppression," Cannon had changed from replying carefully and engaged Pavel more candidly.

"We are transformed Look, we already supply most of Europe with gas, soon it will be electricity. The only question Mr. Cannon is do you want to prosper from this amazing opportunity or do you just want to provide your American clients with a list of hackers? I'm not saying you can't do both, of course." Pavel grinned as he finished speaking, a grin that Cannon found too infectious to resist returning.

"I am interested Pavel, bloody interested. But I don't see how I can help, and you are yet to tell me how Alex died."

"Alex died because of your so called friend Sir Adam," announced Pavel woefully. Taking a deep breath and on releasing it Pavel continued,

"I am sorry Christian, like I said, we have been watching you for some time. You were set up by Sir Adam, he ordered John Mac to get the list of hackers, steal Alex and kill you."

Cannon's mouth fell open.

"Who's this John Mac?"

Pavel, seeing that Cannon really had no clue, patiently stated,

"John Mac was your driver. He was a plant, one of Sir Adam's best. Unfortunately after breaking free from the van he killed nineteen of my best men and in the process Alex lost his life."

"What happened to this Mac character?" asked Cannon.

"This will sound crazy, but we lost him." Pavel replied with a slight air of concern and embarrassment in his voice.

"How did you get the list of 52, sorry 50 hackers?" Cannon requested with a degree of questioning honesty.

"We took the black box from the Volga," stated Pavel with a joyful tone to his voice.

The Hacker Hunter © Copyright Lionwing Ltd 2011

"You mean the computer that Alex took from the hackers den?" interrupted Cannon in excitement. "Tell me Pavel, where did you manage to dig all this intelligence up from? You must have someone working for you who has a degree of contact with Sir Adam?"

Pavel waved his finger at Cannon and in an attempt to keep the good will but still avoid answering the question directly, replied,

"We have our spies as well."

Cannon smiled, and then, taking a few steps closer to the door said,

"Let me get this right, you've got some sort of supercomputer that can control a Tokamak reactor, a reactor capable of producing limitless, pollution free electricity. Along with this electricity you also want to offer the world batteries that were originally designed for nuclear submarines but can be used in transportation systems. Best of all, you are doing all this to put an end to war and corruption. Sounds great, where do I sign up?"

It was Pavel's turn to raise an eyebrow in curious interest at Christian's statement, and choosing to ignore the sarcasm he replied,

"Let me explain your small country's future, perhaps then you'll believe me. In about fifteen years from now Britain's main interests in oil will be through deals made with Russia. However, unlike some nomadic Middle Eastern country you will not be able to enforce an agreement with military might. Britain will go for as long as it can, always taking the less lucrative diplomatic approach, before finally needing to break

The Hacker Hunter © Copyright Lionwing Ltd 2011

open its piggy bank. When I say piggy bank, I am of course referring to the massive oil reserves held in your Falkland Islands. These colossal lakes of oil will make Britain rich again, maybe even as strong as it was in the days of the Great British Empire. However, before you even get a chance to start drilling, Argentina will suddenly become very well armed. Maybe it's the French backing them, maybe the Spanish, maybe the Americans, who knows? Your Royal Navy is too weak and your armed forces to underfunded to defend the islands from another attack. Who will help? Will it be the USA? Will it be China? Will it be Europe? Will it be your new business partners in Russia? Whoever it is that comes to your aid, they will want paying, a payment that will result in them owning most of the oil. When whatever small interest you are left with dries up, your culture, your country, your way of life and everything that is British will finally finish. Like all empires you will plummet into third world obscurity. The now betrayed and used, once proud British people will be living off the charity of others."

Cannon, who had been engrossed by Pavel's keen description of impending doom in what could only be seen as a melodrama of realistic potential, coughed to clear his throat before asking,

"Why should Britain's fate be of concern to you Pavel? You have it all: massive oil reserves, coal, gas and if I'm to believe you, a Tokamak reactor. Why should you even care?"

Pavel's face changed. There was sorrow in his eyes, the kind of sorrow that seemed to arise from a lonely knowledge, knowledge too grave and too bleak to share with the masses. Cannon pondered the idea that just maybe Pavel had seen a glimpse into the future, perhaps his prediction was true. Pavel tried to hide his sorrow with a smile but even the most beautiful of veneers will look distorted on a broken surface. Half turning his back to Cannon Pavel replied softly,

The Hacker Hunter © Copyright Lionwing Ltd 2011

"When your capitalist world has nothing left to burn, they will turn to Russia for our reserves; it is already happening. When Russia can't keep up with the demand they will no longer turn to us, but, instead, I am afraid to say, they will turn ON us. My life's work at VNIIEF has been focused on one goal, namely the single aim of preventing such events. With a functional Tokamak we will be able to stop this bleak future from happening."

Cannon didn't reply, he simply observed Pavel's posture, it was clear that both men had entered a realm of honesty.

"How can I help Pavel?" asked Cannon in a calming whisper.

"With no other side than your own it would be pointless for me to ask you to defect, Christian, that's why I need you to join a side. You will be well paid and well looked after for your assistance," replied Pavel.

"What possible good could come of me joining your side?" asked Christian serenely.

"I'm not asking you to join our side Cannon. What would be the point in that? I'm asking you to join Sir Adam's team." Pavel fully turned his body back towards Cannon as he spoke.

Cannon raised his hand to his mouth and then pawed over his chin in contemplation, pausing for a brief moment before replying, Cannon looked into Pavel's round face.

"You want me to join Sir Adam's team. You just told me that Sir Adam has betrayed me, he's sent this Mac fella to kill me, steal the list and Alex."

Pavel laughed and replied more playfully,

"It's not going well for Sir Adam is it Christian? I mean, think about it, we have the list, Alex is dead and you are very much alive."

The two men exchanged grins before Cannon took in a deep breath and asked,

"What's your plan Pavel, I am all ears?"

Chapter 17 – Country Gents

The early morning nip of invigorating, countryside air caused the skin on Sir Adam's face to tighten and his nose to redden. With the sun still low on the horizon, the rim of Sir Adam's tweed cap did little to prevent its orange yellow hue from glaring into his old eyes, causing them to weep just slightly. Sir Adam briskly marched further into the field, his well worn but well maintained Hunter boots provided the perfect tread for managing the wild tuffs of overgrown grass before his feet. These same tuffs seemed to give his companions, two English Cocker Spaniels, endless fun as they took turns to run circles around him and jump over these pasture rich mounds.

Sir Adam suddenly, and for no apparent reason, stopped walking and stood eerily still. Both dogs, noticing their master had become motionless, ceased playing and walked to his side. Beneath the distant noise of a crowing black bird it was just possible to detect the very faint rumble of an approaching Land Rover. Snapping open his shotgun Sir Adam loaded a shell into each of the two barrels, one above the other. After snapping the gun closed Sir Adam held the now loaded shotgun in his left hand and using his now free right hand unzipped his wax green shooting jacket. Placing his right hand into the inside underarm area of the jacket Sir Adam clutched something tightly.

"Boris, Toby, heel!", commanded Sir Adam. Both dogs stood by his side, all were facing the direction of the oncoming engine noise.

Sir Adam's expression turned to cold steel, his pupils narrowed to form two small dots of the darkest, hardest flint. Within a few moments a royal green Land Rover came into view, Sir Adam slightly relaxed as he recognised his own golden painted crest on the bonnet and side doors of the vehicle. The Land Rover pulled up to a stop before him. Behind its wheel sat a broad figure of a man in his late 40's. Sir Adam acknowledged the man with a nod, for the driver was his groundskeeper, a former member of the SAS, who Sir Adam had handpicked to look after one of the finest Estates in the whole of Hampshire. Next to the groundskeeper was the figure of Robert, who, as always, was sporting a look of fury mixed with overwhelming concern. Oddly enough, as Robert opened the door of the Landy and jumped down from it, Sir Adam remained motionless, his right hand concealed within his jacket and still firmly clutching whatever he had a grip of.

"That's close enough Robert, stay where you are, have you come here to spy on me?" asked Sir Adam.

Robert froze in his tracks. He looked at Sir Adam, and with a noticeable appearance of unease stared at the area of the concealed right hand.

"Don't tell me you've got a gun in there," asked Robert half attempting to make light of the situation.

"Something much better!" exclaimed Sir Adam with a grin as he pulled out a small leather cigar case, just large enough to hold three Churchill's.

"I suppose you think that's funny, you cantankerous old bastard!" exclaimed Robert with an air of mixed relief and annoyance to his voice.

"I'm cantankerous? That's rich, especially coming from you," Sir Adam jibed back.

The Hacker Hunter © Copyright Lionwing Ltd 2011

Pulling off the leather top of the cigar holder, Sir Adam waved a cigar at Robert, who didn't need a second invitation. Before long both men were stood together in the cool early morning air enjoying the rich warmth of a quality cigar each.

"Look at you, in your tweed cap, wax green hunting jacket and boots. You really are a cliché. What are you hunting anyway?" asked Robert.

Sir Adam looked down at his shot gun. "Oh this, I'm not hunting. I was just going out for a walk with my lads," he looked down at both his dogs who were still stood obediently by his side.

Robert took a drag on his cigar, accidently inhaling the smoke he coughed out,

"If you're not hunting why the bloody gun?"

"This shotgun was my father's. I have guns that belonged to his father's, father. You probably don't know this Robert, but it was King Charles II who introduced shotgun hunting into the UK. The King bred a special dog for the job of retrieving the game downed by shot. For reasons that might have something to do with lack of imagination, the dogs took the name of their breeder; you'd know them as King Charles Spaniels. Meet Boris and Toby, my two lads, these two dogs, stood here obediently by my side are both spaniels, we have had their breed in my family since the days my ancestors when hunting with the King. You might say hunting is as much in my blood as theirs. So to answer your question Robert, I have this gun just in case I'm surprised by an unwelcome peasant!" retorted Sir Adam.

"You mean pheasant?" corrected Robert.

"Yes, quite possibly. What do you want Robert?" asked Sir Adam, his tone turning sharper.

"British intelligence intercepted an NSA order for their people in Moscow to capture or neutralize your man Christian Cannon," Robert announced gleefully.

"I thought we'd been through this?" replied Sir Adam.

"It turns out that Cannon's hacker managed to get into the NSA network," Robert paused to take another puff on his cigar before continuing, "and ordered a pair of army boots from the US Embassy in Moscow."

"Get to the point," demanded Sir Adam, half bemused half aggravated by Robert's statement.

Robert paused by taking an overly extended period of time to puff on his cigar, almost to punish Sir Adam's impatience before replying,

"The American Embassy chappy who delivered Cannon's boots claimed to have had an Englishman walk up to him in the middle of some kind of crazy frenzy. He described Russians running left and right and even popping out from a manhole in the road. According to the statement he gave the NSA, Cannon just took the boots and left with two other men. By his description, one was your man Mac. Your boy Cannon is in a shit storm."

"Mac will deal with it," stated Sir Adam, now changing his tone to one of indifference.

"Oh, I don't think so. Your man Mac is now one of Russia's most wanted, he earned the honour after taking out no less than

19 Russian SF operatives in a daring street escape. An escape that I'm afraid didn't go successfully for Mr. Christian Cannon Esq," replied Robert.

Sir Adam's face froze in shock, the blood drained away leaving him looking pale, almost hollow. It was clear the news had taken an effect upon him.

"Are you saying Christian is dead?" asked Sir Adam with a croak to his voice that failed to disguise his feeling of absolute dread.

"No, I'm saying the Russians have Cannon and Mac is on the run."

"Why didn't you just bloody say that you fool? Tell me Robert, how do you know this?" demanded Sir Adam in no uncertain terms.

"I have my sources," replied Robert, for once stopping to saver the upper hand of knowledge.

Sir Adam pulled his shotgun up and across his body, angling it sideways to show its dark rich wooden stock and the intricately carved metalwork to Robert, who looked uneasy.

"Beautiful isn't it Robert? This shotgun is more akin to a sculpture than a deadly weapon." Sir Adam paused, he tilted his head to one side and pulled his shotgun in closer and in doing so swept his hand down towards the trigger guard. Robert stiffened up as Sir Adam then continued to speak, "I have to ask, what sources do you have, Robert ,that could possibly know that Cannon is captured and Mac is on the run?"

The Hacker Hunter © Copyright Lionwing Ltd 2011

"I'm a SIS director Sir Adam, don't ever forget that," Robert replied quietly between gritted teeth.

Just then the groundskeeper broke the tension as he stepped out of the vehicle, he was clutching a mobile phone to the upper chest area of his dark blue Royal Navy jumper in an attempt to ensure that whoever was on the other end couldn't hear the two men talking.

"Sir, I've just had a call from the gatehouse, your PA has arrived. She said you invited her up for the weekend but the gatehouse has no such instruction from you, what shall I tell them?"

Sir Adam walked towards the driver and exchanged his shotgun for the phone. The driver gently cracked open the shotgun with his hand covering the barrels to stop the shells ejecting. Sir Adam lifted the phone to his ear and spoke out brashly,

"Yes hello, yes. Please send her up to the house, ask Mrs Rose to have Grace's room made up for the weekend please, thank you." Sir Adam passed the phone back to the driver and, pointing at the dogs he ordered,

"Take the dogs for a walk there's a good fellow, Robert and I will take the Landy back to the house."

Grace stood elegantly in the centre of the large entrance hall. As Sir Adam's PA she was no stranger to this magnificent Jacobean house and she clearly felt at home amongst its lavish decadence. The gloriously large carved marble fireplace to her right held the beginnings of a recently lit fire. The fire cracked and spat as kindling ignited larger wooden logs. Either side of the fire place were two rather grand, high back chairs, in fact so grand they seemed to resemble thrones more than anything else. Grace pulled her gloves off and walked over to one of the chairs. She looked at it, momentarily pondering over the idea of sitting in its over embellished splendour. Her pondering ended abruptly when Grace became suddenly startled by the loud voice of Sir Adam as he swung open a door and paraded in.

"Gracey! I thought you city girls found the countryside too lonely to visit, why the change in heart?" Sir Adam winked and gave Grace a cheeky smile.

"Frank, call me silly but I just had this feeling you might need my help this weekend," Grace replied whilst she sheepishly looked down at her feet, half expecting to be called stupid.

However, Sir Adam made no such comment. Instead he looked mystified and asked,

"Whatever does that mean? Well you might just be right, it turns out you are not the only surprise visitor this weekend." Before Sir Adam could finish his sentence, in walked Robert.

Grace and Robert exchanged smiles and then Sir Adam interrupted with,

"Grace, why don't you take Robert down to the kitchens, ask cook to knock up some breakfast or something and get some tea on the go. I'll be back down shortly, I just want to change quickly out of all this into something more comfortable."

Robert dropped his smile and said sternly,

"I'm sorry Sir Adam I don't have time for breakfast. We don't all work a three day week, it's a Friday and that means the rest

The Hacker Hunter © Copyright Lionwing Ltd 2011

of Britain is working. Is there somewhere we can finish our conversation?"

Sir Adam had already started walking towards a beautifully polished dark mahogany staircase, with one foot on the first step he half turned towards Robert and said calmly,

"Grace will show you the kitchens, Robert. We will finish our conversation after I've changed."

Sir Adam climbed up the stairs and vanished out of sight leaving Grace and Robert looking at each other. Grace spoke first,

"He does that. I've been working with him for years and he still finds ways to annoy me," she chuckled and winked at Robert flirtatiously. She walked towards Robert and upon reaching him slid her arm through Roberts and hung off him. Now coupled with each other, Grace led again by saying, "Come on, let's get a cuppa".

Positioned perfectly in the middle of a well organized male dressing room was a handsomely designed chaise lounge. Opposite the chaise lounge at eyelevel was a wide screen wall mounted television, and on its screen played the BBC world news. Stood behind the chaise lounge and facing the TV Sir Adam frantically tapped 6 number strokes into a TV remote control, 070971, and then he pressed the play button. Almost instantly the world news ended and there was the familiar face of Dickie.

"Good morning Sir Adam, how can I help?" asked Dickie politely.

"Get me a patch to Bob in Moscow," ordered Sir Adam.

Dickie looked down at something and then looked back up "I have a video link sir, patching you through now."

There was a buzzing sound, much like can be heard when dialling someone on a telephone, it rang out five times and then the screen changed. At first, Sir Adam wasn't sure what he was looking at, or rather looking into. As his brain put together bits of the image he realised that he was staring into a dark, barely lit, windowless room. Suddenly Bob's unshaven face appeared as he stepped into the focal area of his video conference camera.

"Bob is that you?" asked Sir Adam, still not completely sure what he was looking at.

"Yes, Sir." Bob's voice boomed out from the speakers of the TV in Sir Adam's dressing room, Sir Adam looked down at the remote and lowered the volume settings before asking,

"Where's Mac?"

Mac's voice could be heard but Sir Adam couldn't see him, "I'm here, Sir Adam."

"Mac, what is the status of the operation?"

"30% complete, Sir" replied Mac, not giving anything more away.

"Mac, I need a verbal update and I need it condensed to five minutes, max," demanded Sir Adam.

Mac coughed to clear his throat and then replied,

"I'll keep my end of the agreement, just make sure you keep yours,"

The Hacker Hunter © Copyright Lionwing Ltd 2011

Sir Adam looked angered at Mac's brazen indication of mistrust. Walking around the chaise lounge to get closer to the wall mounted TV, Sir Adam whispered loudly,

"What's happened to Cannon, do you have the list, and do you have Cannon's hacker?"

"Like I said Sir Adam, 30%. We'll have everything else for you in a few days," Mac replied professionally.

"Mac, I've just heard that the Russian's have Cannon, is that true?" asked Sir Adam.

Mac didn't reply straightaway, there was an uneasy pause and then he asked,

"What makes you think that?"

It was clear that Mac felt uneasy with Sir Adam's knowledge of the very recent events, for this knowledge could only have been delivered by either having someone inside Pavel's operation or worse, by someone that had been following him. Mac pretty much wrote the book on counter surveillance, there were few that could rival him but there was always a possibility, although slim, which only really left leeway for Sir Adam having someone working within Pavel's team. The latter option sat even less comfortably in Mac's mind. He had met the likes of Pavel before, people like that rarely made mistakes of such nature. Sir Adam didn't reply to Mac's question, so Mac spoke out again,

"What do you know of Pavel Chernov, he's meant to be a Physics Professor, or so I'm told?"

The Hacker Hunter © Copyright Lionwing Ltd 2011

Sir Adam could not hide an utter look of puzzlement and shock. He tapped the remote control on his chin and then walked over to the chaise lounge turning his back to the wall mounted Television screen.

"Where did you hear of the name Pavel Chernov?" Sir Adam asked patiently in the process of sitting and then reclining back into his chaise lounge. Mac offered no reply. Sir Adam crossed his legs and leaning back into the cushioned upholstery offered up his knowledge freely,

"If Cannon is being held by Pavel Chernov, then we have stumbled across something a lot bigger than just a list of hackers. Pavel Chernov comes from an organisation that was first formed by Joseph Stalin during the Second World War. This organisation was created to place Russia's brightest scientists, aircraft engineers and weapons developers under house arrest, mainly to ensure that they didn't leak secrets but also because Stalin believed that scientists worked better when they and their families were imprisoned and forced to think at gunpoint. The problem Stalin had was in understanding what his captive scientists were up to: i.e. were they working hard or just working hard on a plan to escape. The only way Stalin could know for sure what these imprisoned, technical masterminds were up to was to use other scientists as their labour camp wardens. Stalin recruited ruthless scientists who believed wholeheartedly in Stalin's own version of Communism. These scientists would not flinch at having someone who they suspected of treason shot for the greater good. These prison wardens came to protect Russia's greatest scientific secrets, such as nuclear arms development, anti missile technology, advanced weaponry systems, fighter bomber aircraft, I'm sure you get the picture. Professor Pavel Chernov is one such gatekeeper, which means Cannon has fallen into a

The Hacker Hunter © Copyright Lionwing Ltd 2011

nest of vipers and you have made your two million without even having to pull a trigger."

Mac's voice boomed out from the speakers of Sir Adam's TV set,

"You mean Cannon is likely to be dead?"

"I mean to say, if Cannon is not already dead, he soon will be," replied Sir Adam.

"That leaves three questions," stated Mac, "Firstly, what is Cannon's hacker developing for Pavel that would be worth losing nineteen Russian SF for? Secondly, is the hacker we have capable of getting the list of hackers without Cannon? Thirdly, how the fuck did you know that Cannon had been captured by the Russians?"

Sir Adam let out a half smile at Mac's latter unabashed question and replied,

"The last one is easy, I dare say we either have a spy in Pavel's team or Pavel has a spy in ours. If we have the spy in our team then this is just Pavel's way of letting us know to back off or be prepared to start losing our people."

"You mean he will kill Cannon just to set an example?" questioned Mac.

"I mean you have to find out what Pavel is protecting."

"That wasn't part of our agreement," stated Mac with absolute conviction in his voice.

The Hacker Hunter © Copyright Lionwing Ltd 2011

Sir Adam stood up from his seated position and pointed the remote at his TV,

"Listen Mac, I'll save you the bloody Queen and Country speech, you get whatever Pavel is hiding and I'll find out who our spy is. Good luck." Without waiting for Mac's reply Sir Adam pressed the standby button on the remote, abruptly ending the conference and in the process escaping the wrath of the Special Air Service's finest.

Chapter 18 – Bob's Trusty Ka Bar

Alexander Khomenko gawked down at the back of his outstretched hand. Alex was clearly in a dream like state and was seemingly trying to focus all of his attention on the small, black hairs upon the back of his open hand. Although his vision was in no way impaired, he stared and stared at his hand as if somehow he had just discovered it. Much to his fascination Alex observed that these hairs seemed to spread out from his arm, thinning over his wrist to become little more than a few follicles by the time they reached his knuckles. However, what he found truly intriguing was the one oddity that all the little black hairs shared: namely, each and every little hair was stood bolt upright. "What had caused this", Alex asked himself and then shut his eyes and took a deep gulp to try and stop from vomiting. Slowly reopening his eyes Alex stared more intently back down at his hand but this time he repeatedly clenched it into the shape of a fist. As Alex's senses started to return to consciousness the first thing he felt was the slight tang of tingles in his arm, he also felt dreadfully nauseous. Through this white noise of sensory restoration Alex detected what seemed like muffled voices, the voices seemed to be growing louder and sharper until,

"Alex, are you with us, Alex? Come on, wake up!" instructed the voice of John Mac.

Alex's eyes followed the sound of the voice until they abruptly stopped and widened at the sight of Mac's Viking like moustache. There was no question that Alex was coming back to his senses. Suddenly putting two and two together, Alex recognised the moustache, his face stiffened up as if to try and hold a secret. This was the man that Cannon had hired as a taxi driver, thought Alex. This was the man that had freed him from

The Hacker Hunter © Copyright Lionwing Ltd 2011

the back of the van with a gruesome display of unparalleled combat skills. This was the man who had saved him by dragging his unconscious body to safety. This was also the man that had brought him back to consciousness only to question him relentlessly about the list of hackers. Despite all these shared experiences the singularly resonating question that sprung into Alex's mind was 'Just who is this individual and why does he command such intoxicating reverence?"

Mac spoke again,

"You're feeling the effects of the general anaesthesia, it will pass."

"I feel sick," replied Alex, now rubbing the palms of his hands into his eyes in what can only be construed as an attempt to try and wake himself up from a nightmare.

"Yeah I know, the drug we used to bring you back to consciousness will make you feel sick for a while. Don't worry, it will pass. Look, I need you to focus Alex. I have some more questions," replied Mac in a tone that was not totally unsympathetic to Alex's condition.

"What questions and why did you give me an anaesthetic?" Alex asked whilst tilting his head back in another attempt not to vomit.

"Let's start with what you and Pavel have been working on," asked Mac, obviously choosing to ignore Alex's question about Mac knocking him out with an anaesthetic.

"Professor Pavel, you mean Professor Faverski?" Alex blurted out uncontrollably.

Mac, who was sat next to Alex on the back seat of Bob's Volga changed the question,

"What have you and Professor Fa-ver-ski been working on Alex?"

Alex giggled at the way Mac pronounced the Professor's surname "It's Faverski, not Fa-ver-ski. We've been working on an, how you say, Frankenstein monster."

Bob, who had been sat silently in the drivers seat turned fully around to look at Mac in utter shock. Mac shot Bob a glance that indicated for him to be silent and then asked Alex softly,

"Why do you think it's like Frankenstein's monster?"

Alex shook his head in an attempt to clear his mind, he then raised a hand to his brow and woefully announced,

"My brain hurts!"

Mac laughed and replied, "You've had a rough day, you were knocked out for two hours after banging your head on the dashboard. I did tell you to keep your head covered. We had to knock you out again so Bob and I could work out what we were going to do with you."

"Do with me?" interrupted a now seemingly concerned Alex. After a moments recollection Alex continued, "Oh yes I remember now, you wanted the list of hackers, like I told you, I need the computer I pulled out of the hackers' den to get the list and I also need Christian Cannon!"

Alex's demand was said in a matter-of-fact kind of way, but it was enough for Mac's eyes to turn to ice. Alex's face fell

The Hacker Hunter © Copyright Lionwing Ltd 2011

expressionless, there was a moment's uneasy silence and then Mac replied in a sharp whisper,

"Listen, I will fucking plant you here and now. That shit might work with Cannon but not me, you don't need that computer and you don't need Cannon. Just do whatever you did to get the list again," ordered Mac.

Alex didn't reply, he just looked out of the car window at the rows of garages where they had parked. Bob, who was now kneeling on the driver's seat to face Alex and Mac broke the silence by asking,

"Alex, do you have a telephone number that you can reach Pavel on?"

Alex refused to answer. He just continued to stare out of the window. Bob looked over at Mac and asked,

"What do you want to do, Boss?"

Mac was silently glaring at Alex. He was looking so intently it was almost as if Mac was trying to see through Alex's defiance, and then he spoke,

"Alex, explain to me why you need that computer and why you also need Christian?"

Alex turned his attention from the garages to face Mac and replied,

"You asked what I was working on with Professor Faverski; well I will tell you. My job is to develop an operating system for a supercomputer. Not an operating system in the Microsoft sense of the word but a special system shell that creates a type of

The Hacker Hunter © Copyright Lionwing Ltd 2011

artificial intelligence. The idea was to develop code that would start to develop itself based upon collecting external input. You see standard operating systems, like Windows or Unix can limit the speed of a computer, that's why anyone who needs real processing power will develop their own OS. My operating system is designed to collect data, build associations, and through these associations identify probabilities, or, how you say, to put more simply: it collects data and guesses potential answers to questions we ask it."

Alex paused to take a breath and think, Mac didn't even blink, he just simply instructed,

"Carry on."

"It didn't work out as we had hoped. Yes the computer worked at incredible speeds, yes my shell collected data and built connections, but rather than answering our questions," Alex paused, there was a noticeable strain in his voice, he took in a deep breath and upon releasing it said slowly, "Why am I telling you any of this?"

Mac spoke softly, "This might sound strange Alex, but we are here to help you, if we can. I can only do that if I have all the information, so please, carry on, what did the super computer do?"

Alex looked down at his hands, he clenched them once more and then replied,

"Rather than answering our questions, it started asking its own."

Mac and Bob were both rendered speechless, Bob's mouth hung open to such a degree that he found himself simply gawking in pure, unequivocal, astonishment at Alex. Mac, on the other

The Hacker Hunter © Copyright Lionwing Ltd 2011

hand, was deeply troubled. His first thought was 'could this really be true?'. If it was true, then Sir Adam had Pavel's number spot on. However, if it was just some crazy idea Alex stole from a science fiction Hollywood blockbuster, then they could both be about to walk into a trap! The idea that Pavel might want to kill Cannon as a warning to the world's spy community had already dawned on Mac, but what if Sir Adam was right and there was a spy amongst them? What if Alex was really part of Pavel's team and Alex's job was to do little more than lure in spies. Could Alex be the double agent Sir Adam is looking for, Mac pondered briefly? What if Pavel wasn't just after Cannon but was also after him? Capturing someone with Mac's reputation, a reputation as a trainer of spies, would send a shock wave resonating throughout the community. If Mac was captured and killed, anyone would truly think twice before signing up to spy on Mother Russia again! Before Mac or Bob could respond, Alex turned away and gazing back out of the car window he continued solemnly,

"Frankenstein's monster, my operating system gave the computer self-awareness. If Frankenstein knew that his monster would go through such torment do you think he would have given it life?"

Mac replied sceptically "What is this supercomputer capable of doing? What is its purpose?"

Alex swallowed hard, perhaps to contain his emotion, perhaps to vanquish his despair.

"Its purpose, I would have thought that would be clear. Its purpose is to think without interruption, without distraction and without the hang-ups of the human, how you say, ah yes, the human condition. Simply put, most people can concentrate for about forty minutes, but no-one can hold an actual single line of

The Hacker Hunter © Copyright Lionwing Ltd 2011

thought for longer than a few seconds. You see, we are constantly struggling with random interruptions to our thought process. For example what we saw on the television, heard on the radio, read in the paper, said to our partner before leaving for work can come flooding into our minds at any point. A man is meant to think about sex every few seconds: this distraction is a by-product of our very nature, it is what makes us function, it is what drives us to procreate, without the impulses of our reptilian brain we would no longer exist. For just one moment imagine removing all that white noise and just having pure thought. Some quantum physicists believe that the power of the mind is enough to move matter, even effect atomic structure. Some believe that just thought alone can change the shape of reality. Whether it be remote viewing or for complex computations, finding out just what a non distracted human mind can achieve is purpose enough, is it not?"

"A human mind, I thought you said a supercomputer?" asked Bob half not wanting to hear the answer.

Alex seemed to come back to his senses from his rather surreal statement and coughed to clear his throat,

"I am sorry, I have, what is the word in English, let me think, yes, I have digressed."

"Yes, that's right, digressed. What is the purpose of this supercomputer, why do you need Christian and the PC from the hacker den?" asked Mac in a more inquisitive tone.

Alex turned from the window to face Mac and replied,

"I accessed this supercomputer remotely from the hackers den and commanded it to find the 52 hackers logged into the NSA network. Once I had the hackers I broke the remote connection

The Hacker Hunter © Copyright Lionwing Ltd 2011

permanently, just in case-" before Alex could finish Mac interrupted,

"In case of what?"

"In case of this!" Alex replied coldly.

Mac ran his fingers through his moustache in contemplation. Alex's comment didn't sit well with him, it meant Alex knew he might be captured by someone other than Pavel and forced to run the hack again. Knowing he had to get more information from Alex, Mac reinitiated the conversation with,

"Let me put it another way Alex, you must have known you were working on a, as you put it 'Frankenstein's monster', why did you invent such a thing? I mean what is your personal reason for creating it?"

Alex looked over at Bob and then back at Mac.

"Do you need a reason to create? Why did the Wright brothers create the aeroplane? Why did Albert Einstein develop the theory of relativity? Tell me Mac, if Einstein knew his theory would lead to atom bombs being dropped on Japan do you think he would have published his work? If the Wright brothers knew that one day their invention would lead to the development of the aeroplanes that dropped those atom bombs would they have flown? I didn't think of what my software could do past the point of analysing and responding to data at super speeds. I'm no fool Mac, I know our world is run by banks, businesses and governments, in that order. I know that these are protected by militaries carrying arsenals that include weapons capable of utter horrific atrocities. I am also aware that all of these, banks, businesses, governments and military powers depend totally and without failsafe alternatives on computerised systems!

The Hacker Hunter © Copyright Lionwing Ltd 2011

Ordinarily these computers are protected by secure networks and layers of firewalls that not even the best hackers can crack. That is until now, until my operating system found a supercomputer powerful enough to not only hack the NSA in a few minutes, but also find the other 52 hackers on their network. Whoever owns this supercomputer and my operating system, owns a world without secrets. This power cannot be allowed to exist in the hands of one country."

Mac calmly placed his hand on Alex's shoulder and spoke out firmly,

"Sharing the technology with Britain will give us a chance to develop a security against it."

Alex pushed Mac's hand of his shoulder and replied,

"You are missing my point. It must be stopped, destroyed somehow."

Mac turned away from Alex and sat facing forward in the car. He blanked both Bob and Alex and gazed at nothing as he chewed Alex's words over in his mind. 'Alex has planned all this out just a little bit too perfectly', thought Mac, 'the hackers den, breaking the connection with the super computer so that the list of hackers would only be on one computer, a computer that Pavel just happens to have. Alex had also gone to a lot of effort to avoid answering his question about why he needed Cannon'. There was something not right. and Mac felt it in every one of the old bullet wounds and injuries he had obtained over his long, rather specialised career. The deal with Sir Adam was worth a lot of money, but all the money in the world wasn't worth Mac loosing his life or risking the life of his co-worker and friend, Bob. Mac lent forward and pulled a 9mm pistol from the back of his trousers, grasping the slide he cocked back the hammer.

The weapon was now armed and ready. Mac pointed the gun at Alex's head and said in Russian,

"Bob is going to hand you a mobile phone, you are going to call Pavel, tell him that you have escaped and you want nothing more to do with the work, tell him you are going to leave the country and tell Pavel that you want to be left alone. Let Pavel talk, he will want to ask you some questions, when he does simply pass the phone back to Bob, do not hang up. If you say anything other than what I've told you I will blow your head off and Bob and I will simply go back to Britain without you. If you do as I ask then I shall do my best to protect you in what is about to get very bloody. Am I understood?" Mac asked sternly.

Bob held two mobile phones in each hand, he passed one to Alex. Alex took the phone and used it to dial the number for the institutes reception, he knew it off by heart, the last time he had used that number it was just to let the Professors know he was ill and unable to come to work. The phone rang four and then five times before a lady's voice answered in Russian,

"Hello, Moscow Institute, how can I direct your call?"

Alex swallowed hard before answering "Put me through to Professor Pavel, tell him it is Alex Khomenko." There was silence on the line as Alex waited to hear Pavel's voice but no sound came, what felt like an eternity passed and then Alex looked at Bob and shrugged. Bob pointed at his watch and with a thumb up nodded at Alex to signify it was ok to wait. Then the receptionist spoke out,

"I'm just trying to locate him, please hold."

Alex covered the mouthpiece of the phone and whispered to Bob and Mac, "You know he is probably running a trace on this

The Hacker Hunter © Copyright Lionwing Ltd 2011

phone right now, in a few more minutes he will use the signal to pin point our location. Should I hang up?"

Bob smiled and whispered in reply to Alex's question, "We are counting on it."

Mac, who still had the gun held up at Alex shot a disapproving look at Bob, obviously annoyed that Bob had replied to Alex's question verbally and stood the risk of being heard by whoever was on the other end of the phone line.

Just then Alex stiffened, "Hello Alex, how are you?" asked Pavel in a disinterested tone.

Alex cleared his throat and replied nervously,

"Pavel, I have escaped from everyone and I am not coming back. I no longer want to work with you, I do not feel safe."

Mac raised the gun to indicate to Alex that he was not happy with any form of deviation in the conversation. Pavel asked,

"If you are not alone cough?"

Alex ignored Pavel's instruction and instead replied with "I am going to leave the country. Please leave me alone."

"I'm afraid, Alex ,I can't let that happen. It is nothing personal, you must understand that if the knowledge you have of this project ever made it to the United Kingdom or America you would jeopardise all our good work. You have two choices: come back and keep working, or run until we find you. If you run you will be proving that we cannot trust you and unfortunately we will then have to end your life, which I don't

The Hacker Hunter © Copyright Lionwing Ltd 2011

want to have to do, so please come back now," commanded Pavel sincerely.

Alex paused, he looked down the black pistol and into Mac's sharply focused ice blue eyes. The two men froze in time and then, on a prayer, Alex let out a single cough. Pavel replied,

"Do not worry my boy, help is on its way. You can pass them back the phone now."

Alex took the phone from his ear and passed it to Bob, who was now grinning profusely,

"That's amazing boss, how did you know?" Bob asked Mac after he switched off the phone.

Mac looked at Bob with a noticeable air of annoyance, not annoyed in the way a man might be, given their situation but actually more akin to a craftsman exasperated with his apprentice.

"Bob, you really need to learn to keep your mouth closed. How can you watch for the signs when you are talking?" stated Mac whilst disarming his pistol and tucking it into the back of his trousers. Mac continued, "How long have we got until Pavel gets here with his cronies?"

Bob looked at his watch and said, "About fifteen to twenty minutes, do you want me to call the NSA now?"

"No, I want you to call Cannon's girlfriend. What did you say her name was, Sabrina? Use the clone of Cannon's phone and follow the plan precisely. Remember, don't speak, just leave the phone on. She'll think his phone has mistakenly dialled her number whilst in his pocket or something to that effect. With any joy the NSA will triangulate the signal and turn up at the same time Pavel's team get here!" laughed out Mac.

"And if they don't?" asked Bob.

"If they don't, you'll just have to keep the Russians busy on your own until they do mate," snapped back Mac with an air of humorous indifference.

Alex looked totally baffled, had they heard Pavel's instruction to him about coughing to signal he was really still captured? Before Alex could even begin to think straight, Mac smiled at him and said calmly and in a professional tone,

"Ok Mr. Khomenko, you remember how this works from last time. Do as I say, when I say, and you will live, understood?" asked Mac.

Alex nodded, still mystified as to what was going on. Mac turned to fully face Alex and with one hundred percent focus on expressing himself clearly said.

"There are four ways to gain entrance to a secure facility like your institute: number one, break in; number two, get captured; number three, join the staff and finally number four, get an invitation. Breaking in is the most risky, you've got alarms, cameras, security. This leaves getting captured, which can work but you'd need an extremely good exit strategy. The third method of joining the staff, maybe as a cleaner or something can work but takes ages and we just don't have the time. Which means we need an invitation." Mac forced a smile which caused his moustache to rise briefly.

"Just who would invite you to the institute?" asked Alex with a tone that indicated that he thought Mac was clearly insane.

The Hacker Hunter © Copyright Lionwing Ltd 2011

Mac pointed to Alex's right arm and said, "Roll up your sleeve please Alex, if this shit works we should get a personal invitation from Pavel quite shortly. Come on, roll up your sleeve!"

"Why do you want me to roll up my sleeve?" asked Alex. Just then, Alex felt a needle prick through the skin of his neck.

"Don't move Alex," ordered Bob with such conviction that Alex froze solid.

As Bob pulled the needle out of Alex's neck he said playfully,

"Misdirection Alex, it's the oldest trick in the book. Mac asks you to do one thing so in fact I can do another."

It was not often that Alex lost his cool, but he was livid. "What the fuck did you put in my neck! Tell me, tell me now!" he barked.

Mac calmly replied, "Insurance Mr. Khomenko, insurance. Bob, pass me the detonators and the other two syringes please."

With his right hand covering the area of his neck that Bob had only moments ago injected Alex, screamed out, "What did you put in my neck, tell me now or I am leaving!"

Ignoring Alex, Bob passed Mac two syringes and three pencils. Each pencil was painted a different colour, one was painted red, the second blue and the third yellow. Alex noticed that the two syringes had a different colour band on them, one blue and one red. Before Alex could say another word Bob opened the driver's door and stepped out of the car. Bob paced back and forth whilst dialling a number on a different mobile phone.

The Hacker Hunter © Copyright Lionwing Ltd 2011

Lifting the phone to his head to listen for the ring tone Bob waited and then, for seemingly no reason, he took the phone from his ear and covered the mouthpiece. After some time had elapsed Bob walked over to Alex's side door and pulled it open with his free hand. Alex felt the cool Moscow air flood into the back of the Volga.

"Ok Mr. Khomenko you can leave if you want or you can hang around for Pavel or you can stick to Mac like glue. Your choice, just make a decision and make it right now!" ordered Bob.

Before Alex could reply Mac pulled the door release handle to crack open his own door, as he started to shuffle of the back seat and out off the rear door Mac added,

"What Bob is saying in a roundabout way is this: you can fuck off and take the risk that whatever was injected into your neck isn't going to kill you, or you can wait for Pavel to turn up to save, or shoot you. There is a third option: you can stick like glue to me and do whatever I tell you, when I tell you! In the process you will find out what you have in your neck. Oh, and food for thought mate, if you want a good, safe life in England, you'll need something that our sponsor will want, so when you are in the Institute we'll need all the data you have on this 'supercomputer thingamabob'.

Mac left the car, leaving Alex flabbergasted on the back seat. Walking around the boot of the car Mac approached Bob, who still had his hand over the mouthpiece of the phone.

"Did you call her, Bob?" asked Mac.

"I called, I hope Sir Adam's intelligence is right. How did he know about Sabrina, I mean he even had her telephone number?" asked a mystified Bob.

Mac looked down at the pencils and syringes in his hand and replied, "That man knows everything, he's old school. There's a lot you don't know about Sir Adam, and even more you wouldn't want to know, trust me." Mac's face changed to display a look of confusion, still looking at three pencils and two syringes he asked,

"Bob, just remind me again, the yellow pencil is for Alex, right, and I just jab these syringes in the neck or leg. The syringe with the red band relates to the red pencil and blue band blue pencil and so on?"

"You can jab the syringes anywhere you want but they will do most damage in the neck or groin. As for the pencil colours, don't get that wrong Mac, otherwise, game over," stated Bob.

Tucking the pencils and syringes into his jacket pocket Mac looked up at Bob and in a stern Scottish tone offered,

"Listen Bob, you are a good lad. Remember the training: don't get boxed in, count each round, theirs and yours and keep the aggression high. Remember this isn't a game, these are real people, real guns, yeah? You got it? You understand me? The plan is simple, I want you to get the NSA shooting at the Spetsnaz and the Spetsnaz shooting at the NSA, that doesn't mean both shooting at you, ok? Just get them started."

Bob looked at Mac, the humour had gone. "I'll meet you back at the Pechory Monastery where I picked you up, don't worry boss, we will cross into Estonia together."

Mac took a step closer to Bob and pointed his bony finger at him. "I'll hold you to that. Ok, good luck. Remember I need it

The Hacker Hunter © Copyright Lionwing Ltd 2011

loud and heavy, enough to get Pavel's personal guards in the fight."

Alex stepped out of Bob's Volga and, still clutching his neck, followed Mac, who had started walking away. The call to Pavel had been made ten minutes ago. This gave Bob about five to ten more minutes before he would be face to face with the Russian Spetsnaz. Bob watched Mac walk off with Alex in tow and then threw both phones on the back seat of the Volga where, only moments ago, Alex had been sitting. Looking around at the maze of garages Bob spoke out under his breath,

"Ok pull it together, focus." Bob lent his head left and then right causing the vertebra in his neck to crack. He then started to stretch, like a rugby player stretches before a match. As he lent forward placing both hands on his knee to stretch his ligaments he spotted a white van pull up. Sure enough five well dressed men stepped out. The first detail Bob noticed was the undeniable similarity in shoes these men had. All five pairs of black, heeled, leather shoes were extremely well polished.

"Well that will be the NSA boys, where are the Spetsnaz?"

No sooner than these words had left Bob's mouth than a Russian voice from behind him boomed out in English,

"Your white paper please, and your passport?"

Bob turned to face the direction of the voice, to his dismay he found a man built like a human tractor. He towered over Bob like a granite cliff face and was as broad as Bob was tall.

"Oh there you are. You must be part of Pavel's team, how did you do that? I didn't even hear you creep up on me, well done." Bob gave a big Welsh grin, the sort of grin that said 'I'm sorry

The Hacker Hunter © Copyright Lionwing Ltd 2011

I'm going to have to do this to you'. Bob's grin dropped and his right, size ten boot rose up with a swift kick smack into the genitals of the giant stood before him.

As the huge Spetsnaz operative buckled in half, partly from the pain and partly as a reflex, Bob seized the chance to engage 'leg-it mode'. The rush of adrenaline caused Bob to take flight down a row of garages at such a speed it would have been near impossible to catch him. However, it was only by sheer bad luck that Bob ran straight into the remaining guard of Spetsnaz operatives. Bob skidded and hopped to a full stop only an arms distance from eight, very well built men, all carrying machine guns and pistols.

"Oh bum," exclaimed Bob.

The eight men just looked at Bob, unsure of how to react. That was, until their co-worker hobbled in a half run towards them, whilst still clutching his balls.

"Stop him, stop him!" shouted the very annoyed Russian.

Bob placed his fingers in his mouth and turned his upper body towards the direction of the white van, where the five NSA men were stood watching events unfold. Bob let out an ear deafening whistle to ensure he had the full attention of the NSA and then bellowed at the top of his lungs,

"I'm Christian Cannon!"

One of the NSA men pulled a black wallet from his pocket, holding it high in the air he ran towards Bob shouting,

"Diplomatic immunity, this man is under our protection!"

Everyone stared transfixed on the approaching NSA agent, everyone with the exception of Bob, who took two steps forward into the tightly assembled Spetsnaz and then dropped to one knee. Now facing the groin of the nearest operative Bob pulled from his jacket a jet black, USMC 1219C2 Fighting / Utility knife, or as the American Army refers to it 'The Ka-Bar'. Holding the grip of the knife so the jet black blade ran down the side of his arm, Bob swiftly punched the end of the metal handle into the man's testicles. Before the operative even had a chance to respond, Bob slid the knife across the inside of his opponent's upper thigh, causing the fabric to cleanly open to reveal a thumb deep laceration. Using this cut as a visual guide, Bob sunk the tip of the Ka-Bar blade into the gash and carved open the femoral artery. This seemingly single action of punch, slice and jab was achieved so effortlessly it was clear to anyone that had taken their eyes off the approaching NSA agent that Bob must have done this a hundred times before. As Bob's adversary bent in half from the agonising blow to his scrotum, the first thing he noticed was the arterial spray as blood pulsed from the open thigh wound. The second thing he noticed as he continued to recoil downward was Bob, who was now rapidly launching up at his exposed throat. With a seemingly effortless second slice, Bob cut open the man's carotid artery. With blood spewing horrendously from both the crotch and neck of the Spetsnaz operative, Bob narrowly avoided getting drenched as he stepped around, to stand behind his victim. With one almighty downward thrusting action, Bob sank the black Ka-Bar blade deep between his opponent's collar bone and then let go.

With the Ka-Bar now safely deposited in the operative's collar, Bob had his hands free to reach down for his opponent's assault rifle. Bob checked that the safety catch was off and cocked the weapon. The other Spetsnaz had all turned their attention from the NSA agent, who was still running towards them waving his diplomatic pass and instead were staring at Bob with utter terror

The Hacker Hunter © Copyright Lionwing Ltd 2011

in their eyes. The Spetsnaz were too tightly grouped together to instinctively open fire on Bob. They were forced to attempt to aim their weapons to avoid the risk of shooting each other. Within this lost moment of time, the operatives realised their predicament was indeed fatal. They witnessed the figure of this furious Welshman standing behind their mortally injured comrade. This soon to be dead comrade was still standing, partly supported by the strap of the assault rifle, a rifle that was now in the hands of Bob and in the beginning stages of ejecting spent bullet cartridges.

Bob emptied the entire contents of the magazine into four of the nearest Spetsnaz. Each round exploded into their chests, necks and faces, rendering them immediately neutralized. Although Bob was slightly protected by the slumping body in front of him, his close proximity to his opponents meant he still felt the warm splatter of their blood, bone fragments and flesh on his face. As the firing pin met the hollow chamber of Bob's recently borrowed assault rifle, its sharp click indicated that all the bullets had been spent and that it was time to resort back to his Ka-Bar. As Bob let go of the empty rifle, the body that had been supported by the strap started to fall forward. Using the collapsing bodyweight, Bob grabbed the handle of his Ka-Bar and twisted it free effortlessly.

Sensing an approaching threat, Bob turned his body towards the four remaining Spetsnaz. One of the Spetsnaz operatives had upholstered a pistol and was in the process of taking aim at Bob's head. Much to his dismay, Bob instantly recognised the approaching gun as a GSh-18. As Bob well knew, any well trained spy, Special Operations Executive or member of the Covert or retired British Special Forces would be able to tell you : the GSh-18 is always ready to fire and it even has the safety catch on the trigger. In short, this gun was designed for one purpose. If it was being pointed at you then you only had one

The Hacker Hunter © Copyright Lionwing Ltd 2011

choice. Bob heard Mac's voice in the back of his mind, attack the attacker, become the aggressor! Before the gun reached Bobs eye line, the Spetsnaz operative let out a blood curdling scream as Bob stepped in towards his aggressor and sunk his Ka-Bar up into the mans armpit. With one almighty levering tug Bob used the high-tension steel of the solid Ka-Bar blade to pop out the aggressor's arm from its socket. Despite the excruciating pain, the Spetsnaz operative just managed to squeeze the trigger inward enough to fire a round, before the pistol and arm fell away to the mans side. Bob felt the sonic boom of warm air as the bullet blasted out of the pistol barrel and narrowly missed his head. Bob then heard a dull thud occur behind him as this stray bullet found a new home. There was no need for Bob to turn, he already knew where the bullet had stopped. Bob had already fought and won this battle in his mind before he'd even pulled out his knife. However, he had not foreseen this particular event, namely, the Spetsnaz had managed to fire his pistol and although he had missed his intended target the operative had inadvertently managed to plant his wandering bullet into the forehead of an NSA agent. The very same NSA agent that, only moments ago, had been holding his diplomatic badge high in the air for all to see.

The four remaining NSA agents simply reacted as they had been trained to. They opened return fire at the Spetsnaz and to Bob's great misfortune at him as well. An NSA bullet whistled past Bob's left shoulder and nested itself with a thump into Bob's opponent. Bob wasn't sure where the round had entered his rival's body but it must have caused an agonising pain. In fact, the pain of having his arm wrenched out by Bob's knife and the bullet was just too much for this unfortunate Spetsnaz operative. Without even so much as a warning the operative vomited uncontrollably into Bobs face. Bob instinctively pushed his opponent backwards, where upon the now immobilised operative simply fell to the floor.

The Hacker Hunter © Copyright Lionwing Ltd 2011

"I can't see!" exclaimed Bob, as he desperately tried to wipe the remains of the man's lunch out of his eyes. Bob could sense the bullets flying past him and could hear return fire from the remaining three Spetsnaz. The stomach acid from the vomit was burning Bob's eyes worse than a can of Mace, he tried to see but the streaming tears and astonishing stinging made it all but impossible. Staggering forward in an attempt to get out of the oncoming barrage of bullets, Bob tripped over one of the dead Spetsnaz. Falling directly on top of the blood drenched wreckage, Bob lay outstretched on a dead body. He rummaged around to see if he could find a weapon, as he did he heard an American voice scream out,

"I'm hit! I'm hit! Fall back, fall back!"

Bob's fingers fumbled over the body beneath him, until they met with the unmistakable shape of a holster. A moment later and Bob managed to roll off the body and onto his bum. Now sat upright and staring out of one eye Bob pointed his recently acquired GSh-18 in the direction of the American's voice. He could just make out three of the remaining NSA agents. They were running for their van and in the process of a full, tactical retreat.

"Oh bugger," announced Bob in a defeated tone as it dawned upon him that he had chosen the wrong direction to point his weapon. There was no Spetsnaz to the right of Bob and none to his left, which presented only two remaining possibilities. Firstly and in the best case scenario, the NSA had managed to wipe out all the Spetsnaz around him or, in the worse case there was an operative stood directly behind him. As Bob slowly turned his body around he saw there were two remaining Spetsnaz. One of the men was choking to death from a bullet wound to his throat. The other, who had been standing directly behind Bob was

The Hacker Hunter © Copyright Lionwing Ltd 2011

uninjured. This Spetsnaz operative was furious. He was pointing his pistol at Bob and with spit flying from the edges of his mouth shouted in Russian,

"Drop the pistol, drop the pistol!"

Bob put his hands up and dropped the pistol.

"Easy, relax. I'm British, do you speak English?" Bob asked in an attempt to bring the man out of his rabid frenzy.

"Yes, I speak, I speak, you die now fucking English! screamed the man bitterly.

"Hey! I'm Welsh you cunt!" shouted back Bob with equal outrage.

The Spetsnaz operative ran at Bob and kicked him straight in the face like a man trying to score a goal from the furthest end of the pitch. The kick was too much for anyone to take. Although Bob brought both his hands down to take the main impact the kick was so hard that Bob fell onto his back, his brain jarred in unbearable pain.

"Now you die, Welsh!" screamed the man as he lent over a semiconscious Bob. The metal barrel of the pistol actually felt warm, Bob thought to himself as the Spetsnaz placed it onto the back of Bobs head. Bob felt the pistol move just slightly as the operative begun the process of pulling in the trigger. Bob felt surprisingly calm, his thoughts gathered into one conclusion, he had lived life, to die like this was perfect, better than wasting away in some old people's home, better than being a slave to a nine to five job, better than having done nothing more than existing to pay bills. His affairs were in order, his ex-wife and their two girls would get the life insurance payout, in death he'd be able to give his family a good start to their lives. It was ok to die, thought Bob in this seeming infinity of time allowed before his last moments.

Bob felt a pounding sensation pass through the Spetsnaz operative's body and reverberate through the end of his pistol, which was still jutting into Bobs head. A moment passed and then Bob felt a second pounding and then a third. 'Have I been shot?' Bob thought to himself. Then Bob felt a massive amount of weight fall on him and everything went black.

"Get that mother fucker out from under there!" ordered a thick New York Bronx accent.

For a brief moment, Bob was blinded by the white glare of sunlight as the Spetsnaz operative's body was pulled off him. Two burley looking men dressed in thick black coats and both wearing gloves walked towards Bob and pulled him up to his feet.

"This rat bastard limey fuck is covered in puke boss. I fucking hate Moscow!" announced one of the two men.

Bob, still not totally able to see squinted at a third man who was taking off his gloves whilst approaching.

"I'm still alive!" exclaimed Bob in a surprised manner.

The third man, walked right up to Bob. He was only a short man but held a large presence.

"You fucking idiot. My baby girl said you were smarter than that," he announced.

"Your baby girl?" asked a puzzled Bob.

The Hacker Hunter © Copyright Lionwing Ltd 2011

"Yeah, Maria, my baby girl. She said you were something special, oh you're fucking special alright, covered in blood and puke," replied the little man, who was very clearly of the Italian American ilk.

"Maria?" exclaimed Bob, still rubbing his eyes clean.

"What, did you get a bump to your head?" asked the man. "You think I'd let you mince around Moscow with my money? Not without a little insurance. Took my boys some time to find you. We tracked you down from," he paused, and then grinning continued to speak, "Let's say a friend of the family who also works for Uncle Sam's NSA." The short man started laughing and his two burley companions also joined in by laughing out loud in support of his attempt at humour.

"Oh, you think I'm Christian Cannon. Look, I'm grateful for you saving my life, but you've got the wrong man," Bob said whilst joining in with the laughter. The three men abruptly stopped laughing and the little man replied,

"I'm sorry my ears must be playing up. I thought I heard you say you weren't Christian Cannon," the man asked with his arms open wide in astonishment.

"No, I'm Bob – who are you?" Bob asked.

"Put this fucking teabag in the trunk. Let's get the fuck out of here before our red friends turn up in force!" the little man ordered.

One of the two burly men pulled out from his large black coat a silenced weapon. He quickly unscrewed the baffle and placed the cylindrical silencer back into his coat. This left just the black pistol in his hand. Turning the gun so it took on the purpose of a hammer, the man then walked towards Bob. Although Bob was still in a state of concussion from the brutal kick he had received only minutes ago, he was aware enough to know what was about to happen.

Bob felt two things: firstly, a mind wrenching blow to the head, and secondly, the impact of the cold tarmac as his soon to be totally unconscious body hit the ground.

One of the burly men picked up Bob and threw him over his shoulder. Walking over to a waiting car it was just possible to hear the big man mutter,

"Why do I have to carry the fucking body, this fucker is covered in shit."

Maria's father pulled out a mobile phone from his pocket and selected a number from its menu. He raised the phone to his ear and waited. The remaining burly man piped up,

"Hey boss, we better split," he stopped speaking immediately in response to his boss raising a finger for silence and then Maria's father spoke out,

"Hey baby girl, we've still not found Cannon, no, no, don't worry, I said don't worry, baby he's ok, you just be ready, we'll find him, ok, got to go, yeah I know, I love you too."

Pavel stood next to the door of his parked Mercedes. His driver remained seated in the vehicle. However, Pavel's guard had left the comfort of the car and was stood an arms length distance behind him. There were two more cars. One was parked at the rear of Pavel's white Mercedes and the other car was parked in front of it. These vehicles were also Mercedes and held a team

The Hacker Hunter © Copyright Lionwing Ltd 2011

of eight Spetsnaz operatives, four-men in each car. Pavel leant forward, and to support his upper body weight placed his forearms down on the roof of his own Mercedes. Clasping his hands together he said out loud,

"Ivan, why have we heard nothing, what is going on?"

The bulky guard who was still stood behind Pavel replied,

"Let's send a car to take a look sir."

Pavel didn't turn to face Ivan, he just elected to drop his face down onto his clenched fists in frustration. Groaning in annoyance he lifted his head back up and barked out,

"Send both the cars Ivan! If this John Mac is living up to his reputation, your men will need to go in force. Tell them to shoot to kill!"

Ivan walked up closer to Pavel and said in a questioning tone,

"Shoot to kill? Does that go for Mr. Khomenko as well?"

Pavel looked astonished that Ivan had even asked such a question, he didn't bother to reply he simply lifted his hands off the car and then banged them down again in a furious rage.

"Just get it done Ivan, get it done now!" screamed Pavel, for the first time showing a total loss of self-control.

Ivan walked over to each car and gave the drivers their instructions one after the other. A few moments later and both cars pulled away from the curb and tore off down the empty street.

The Hacker Hunter © Copyright Lionwing Ltd 2011

Ivan watched the cars vanish out of site and then muttered under his breath,

"I hope I've not just sent those men to their deaths."

"You probably have mate," replied a Scottish voice.

Ivan spun around to face the voice and to his utter astonishment found Pavel but a few meters away from him. Standing directly behind Pavel was John Mac!

Mac had his gun trained on the driver of Pavel's car, who had remained seated but had both his hands firmly grasping the steering wheel. Much to Ivan's amazement in Mac's other hand was a syringe, the needle of which was firmly sunken into Pavel's neck. Stood at the side of Mac was a rather annoyed looking Alex.

"Tell the driver to get out of the car please, and lie face down on the ground. Tell this monkey to do the same." Mac ordered Pavel.

Pavel shouted out the order and a moment later the driver and Ivan were face down on the ground with their arms outstretched. Mac pulled the now empty syringe from Pavel's neck and whispered in Pavel's ear,

"Stay very still, and remember you are blue. It is very important you remember that for the antidote."

Pavel had the expression of a man committed to the single idea of revenge, a slow painful revenge that was driven by his current demotion to the status of a eunuch in a whorehouse. Mac pulled out from his jacket pocket the syringe with the red marker on it, he walked over to the driver and sunk its needle into the back of the man's neck. Mac only released half of the liquid from the syringe before pulling it back out. Mac then approached Ivan and repeated the process, this time empting what was left into the back of Ivan's neck.

"Ok gentlemen, let me explain how this is going to work, please stand up, ordered Mac in English. Ivan and the driver stood to their feet, both rubbing the back of their necks. "You'll all be wondering what I have just injected you with, you'll also be wondering why I haven't taken your weapons," stated Mac with a modest air of authority to his voice.

Alex watched as Pavel, the driver and Ivan started to exchange glances with each other, three against one, were they planning to storm Mac pondered Alex? Mac lowered his gun, he pulled from his jacket pocket with his free hand three pencils, one red, one blue and one yellow.

"Ok, if I can have all of you's attention please, these pencils are colour coded to the jelly I've just injected into your necks. Pavel you are blue, Alex red and you two monkeys yellow. These pencils hold the key to your salvation. Do as I say, when I say, and I'll give them to you when I'm done. Any questions?" asked Mac.

"Just what have you placed in our necks?" Pavel enquired calmly.

Before Mac could reply Alex shouted out,

"This is enough, I am tired, what kind of a stupid game is this, give me my pencil?"

Alex walked straight over to Mac and snatched the red pencil from Mac's hand. To the great surprise of everyone else Mac

The Hacker Hunter © Copyright Lionwing Ltd 2011

did pretty much nothing to stop him. Alex examined the pencil and then said,

"What do I do with this? How does it work?"

Mac turned to face Ivan and the driver and said out loud,

"You tell me Khomenko, you're the fucking whiz kid!" Mac then walked closer to Pavel and said in a soft whisper, "You had better take a few steps backwards."

Alex was now frantic. Ignoring Mac's suggestion, Pavel took a few steps towards Alex and said arrogantly,

"Logic dictates that this thug has injected us with a viral agent and the pencil carries the antidote. Use your mind Khomenko, snap the pencil in half, the cure must reside within!"

Mac walked over to Pavel's car and stood by the now open driver's door. He pointed his gun at the driver and gestured with it for the driver to go stand closer to Ivan. The driver obliged and walked slowly up to Ivan. Mac then did something unfathomable to everyone, with the exception of Alex who was still trying to figure out the nature of the red pencil. Mac, seemingly without a care in the world, tossed his gun onto the driver's seat of the Mercedes Benz, leaving himself totally undefended.

No sooner had Mac's weapon hit the seat than Ivan pulled from its holster his hand pistol and, pointing it at Mac shouted,

"What you put in my neck? I count to five and then I pull the trigger!"

"You can try and count to five but you'll be dead at four if you can't figure out what that pencil is for," replied Mac with an unconcerned look of indifference.

Ivan walked over to Alex, keeping his gun trained on Mac all the way "Give me that, Alex!" ordered Ivan. Alex passed him the red pencil. Ivan looked at it for a split second and then followed Pavel's idea. There was a sudden snap as Ivan broke the pencil in half with just one hand, this snap was followed by two dull thuds, the sort of thud you'd expect to hear when you drop a book down on a table, not particularly loud but still noticeable enough to make you look. Pavel and Alex watched in astonishment as both Ivan and the driver fell to the floor dead.

"What has happened?" asked Pavel mystified?

Alex knelt down and tried to turn Ivan's body over to inspect it, but Pavel's body guard was extremely broad and muscular and simply weighed too much for Alex to turn. As Alex tried again, he noticed a pool of blood rapidly building up from behind the back of Ivan's neck, he also noticed several vertebra which were pushing up through the skin.

"His neck is broken!" exclaimed a mystified Alex.

Pavel stared down at Ivan and then across to his driver, he took in a breath and then turned to find Mac. Mac was no-longer standing but instead had elected to sit sideways in the driver's seat with both feet outstretched on the curb. In Mac's right hand he led the two remaining pencils, one yellow and blue. Mac didn't say a word, his face was deadly serious and his eyes were looking directly into Pavel's. Neither Alex nor Pavel had any questions as to why Mac had simply thrown his pistol into the Mercedes Benz. With the explosives in their necks Mac, needed nothing more than to snap a pencil, a pencil that also acted as a detonator. Alex broke the silence first,

"You said I was red?"

"Oh did I mate, must be getting daft in my old age," Mac replied.

"You did that on purpose, you tricked me into taking the red pen!" said Alex in a deeply disturbed tone.

"Let me explain something to you Alex, I do not trust you one bit. You are up to something, and I think you have us all playing into your hands. Let's just say the explosive in your neck is my insurance policy."

"What do you want?" asked Pavel.

Mac put the pencils back in his pocket and ran his finger and thumb through his moustache, his hand halfway down, freezing in mid groom, and then Mac took his hand away from his face and said,

"I'd like an invite from you, Pavel, an invite to give me and Khomenko a guided tour of your facility. I'd then like to take a few photos and souvenirs for Her Majesty, if I may?"

"You will never make it through the security, the entire building is on lockdown," laughed out Pavel.

"Think about it Pavel, I walk in with you and Mr. Khomenko there, I have no gun, no knife, just two pencils. How do you think security will react?" Mac forced a fake grin that fell away as quickly as it started.

Chapter 19 – Velour Cotton

The first sense that offered itself back to Bob's battered body was not his sight, nor was it the perception of sound or even the detection of smell but astonishingly enough, Bob's first sense was purely tactile in nature. Although unfathomable to his semiconscious mind, Bob could feel upon the cheeks of his face and around his naked body the deep unyielding warm comfort of extra soft, invitingly deep and decadently pleasurable velour cotton pile. The second of Bob's senses to awaken provided the same assuring allure of palpable pleasure, but arrived through the detection of a sweetly luxurious, honey covered, lavender like odour. Bob's face strained just slightly as his nostrils flirted with the deeply soothing scent.

Bob opened his left eye, electing to keep his right eye closed for fear of waking from what surely must be one of his most generous dreams. It took him a few long, thoughtful, moments of gazing at the golden sways of draped quality fabric and bulky spheres of knotted silver and red rope before he realised this eclectic assortment of objects actually represented curtains and drapery tassels. After this somewhat bizarre method of observation Bob elected to simply close his left eye and with a peaceful expression of utter contentment, he softly spoke out,

"I'm just a simple Merthyr boy me, born of the valleys, looks like my ma was right, the Welsh really are God's chosen people."

"You're not in heaven just yet," replied the soft, sensual voice of an American woman.

The Hacker Hunter © Copyright Lionwing Ltd 2011

"Oh, thank you God! I'm sure I will be there in a moment. Come over here then love," said Bob, still with his eyes shut, but now boasting a grin wider than the Severn estuary.

Bob felt a slight indent as whatever he was lying on took the weight of a second body and then he stiffened uncontrollably as he felt the velvet soft but icy cold hand slide up his leg, only to stop at the top of his thigh. The four, hard, long red nails of the woman's beautifully manicured hand sank into Bob's flesh.

"You're not in heaven, boy from Merthyr, and before you ask, you are not dreaming either," spoke out the lady firmly.

Bob lay there, his grin turned to a frown, still with both eyes shut he shouted out,

"Ah, cock! It looks like my ma was right about that too. Let me guess, I'm in Hell!"

"You're not in heaven, you're not dreaming and you're not in Hell either. You're in the house of Daddy's friend, some sort of Russian oligarch. Daddy met him through business dealings in New York, said we could use his pad, so here we are, using his pad," replied the lady flippantly.

Bob's frown fell away as he elected to open both eyes simultaneously and very suddenly. The first thing he noticed was his own body, somehow he'd been totally undressed, washed, and redressed in a luxury, fluffy white bath robe, which explained the first and second sensations. Then he noticed that he was sprawled out on a large chaise longue and propped up with comfy plump pillows stuffed with the finest Siberian goose down. The third thing that came into clarity was the elegant figure of a blonde, a thirty something, handsome female who

The Hacker Hunter © Copyright Lionwing Ltd 2011

was sat lower down the chaise longue with her arm halfway up Bob's robe.

"If I'm not in heaven, hell, or dreaming, then do you mind removing your hand, I'm a married man you know," rebuffed Bob sarcastically.

The lady took away her hand and stood to her feet. Bob watched as she gracefully walked over to a white marble fireplace, above which hung a tall mirror with a lavish gold leaf frame.

"You're not married anymore, you're divorced, two children, you live in..." but before the lady could finish talking Bob interrupted with,

"Ok, you've made your point, who are you and how did you know all that?"

"My name is Maria, I am Christian Cannon's partner in this venture and I know all that because we dusted your fingers whilst you were sleeping," answered Maria.

"American intelligence, ET warfare specialist I'm willing to bet," announced Bob abruptly before bringing his upper body to a sitting position on the chaise longue. "Why doesn't my head ache? I mean I should be in pain."

"You security boys are always trying to label people. If by ET, you me emergent technology, then sure, that's me. But intelligence operative, warfare specialist, I can assure you I do nothing so ordinary as to justify being a, what do you call it in Britain, oh yes, civil servant." Maria looked into the mirror and started to play with her hair, twirling it around her finger and then the reflection of her eyes met with Bob's as they exchanged glances in the reflection. Bob felt his heart jump, there was

The Hacker Hunter © Copyright Lionwing Ltd 2011

something about this woman, something sensual, something deeply seductive, something that he wanted to get closer too.

"Your head's not hurting, honey, because I asked Daddy to pump you full of pain killers. I didn't want you waking up in an uncooperative mood now, did I?" Maria turned from the mirror and raised a short smile at Bob before continuing,

"I run a company of hackers. We specialise in testing computer security for businesses, like big lawyers, small banks. I'm trying to get into the government sector. You know, defence contracts, things like that. I believe the work Christian is doing here in Moscow can help me achieve my goals, so do you mind telling me where I can find him?"

"Dusting my fingers doesn't explain how you managed to get my personal information," Bob asked.

"We hacked your file. Tax records, health records and service records are all on computers now-a-days. Your finger prints are held by Interpol of all things," replied Maria.

"Ok love, thank you for the nice awakening, but seeing as I'm not dead or dreaming I'll be leaving now," remarked Bob as he slid his feet off his place of rest and planted them firmly on the floor. Before Bob could even get to his feet and stand, Maria called out in an annoyed manner,

"Tony, Sonny, get in here!"

Bob watched as the same two well built men that had earlier saved him from certain death only to knock him unconscious, walked in through a beautifully fashioned and extremely tall door.

"You want us to get your Papa, Maria?" one of the men asked.

The Hacker Hunter © Copyright Lionwing Ltd 2011

"No, I want you to give our guest here some help with his memory. It seems he's forgotten where our friend Christian is. I want you to see just how good the pain killers we gave him are," ordered Maria coldly.

Chapter 20 – The pencil is mightier than the sword

As John Mac stood in front of a tall doorframe shaped metal detector, his eyes darted over to Pavel and Alex, who had already both passed through the machine and were stood there, obediently waiting for him to join them. There was no question that both Alex and Pavel's behaviour was not consistent with their usual style of entrance into the Institute. It would be clear to anyone who was even remotely interested that the two men were pale of face and silently edgy. However, and much to John Mac's good fortune, both of the old, fat, disillusioned looking guards manning the metal detector really weren't paid enough to be bothered with such observations.

"Take your belt off," ordered a fat old guard in Russian.

Mac pulled up his jacket and felt around for his belt buckle. A few tugs and tweaks later and Mac dropped his belt into a plastic tray.

"Walk through," ordered the plainly uninterested guard.

Mac calmly walked through the doorframe shaped equipment. As he did, its hazard lights flashed and a loud buzzer rang out. Both Alex and Pavel flinched at the same time, both men looked so unreservedly terrified that had either guard bothered to notice they would have surely questioned what was going on. Instead a guard simply waved some sort of ping pong bat shaped electrical device around Mac's body. The device started beeping as the guard waved the bat around the back of Mac's trousers.

"Empty your back pockets," ordered the guard.

Mac pulled out from his back pocket two pencils, one yellow and one blue. The guard ran the bat over them both and it beeped loudly once again. Pavel's heart started pounding from an overwhelming concern that the guards hand held metal detector might trigger the detonators. Mac noticed that Pavel was nervously edging closer to the guard, so he placed his thumb on the blue pencil to gesture he was about to snap it. On seeing Mac's gesture, Pavel froze in sheer terror.

"Place those pencils in here and step back through the archway," ordered the guard, who was now holding the same plastic tray used to carry Mac's belt.

The idea of giving up the pencil detonators to some overweight night-watchman was totally unplanned and held a dynamic variable of potentially unfortunate outcomes for everyone involved. Pavel pondered 'Would Mac just snap the pencils rather than give them up?' Alex pondered. 'Could his future existence be safely left in the hands of this fat guard? What if the guard accidently placed something else into the tray, which might cause the pencils to snap?' Mac pondered. 'Would Pavel or Alex see this as an opportunity to alarm the guards and make a grab for the detonators?'

In a moment's silence, Mac toyed with the idea of killing both guards, although the process would result in losing his edge of deception, it would keep the power play in his control. Mac observed the guard. To Mac, this man's fat face, oily hair, rounded belly and dull-set glazed eyes were a confession of self-abusing lazy nights in front of Soviet TV. Turning his head to look at the second guard, Mac soon realised that although both these men were armed with pistols, neither man posed any real threat to him. Mac outstretched his arm so that his clenched hand held the pencils just over the tray. It was clear to Pavel and Alex that Mac felt confident of retrieving both pencils as they

The Hacker Hunter © Copyright Lionwing Ltd 2011

both watched in astonishment as Mac drop them into the plastic tray.

Freedom from the explosive jelly that Mac had injected into the necks of Alex and Pavel was but a few strides away as the guard placed the plastic tray on an empty chair just to the right of Alex. Alex looked down into the tray and then over to Mac, Mac glared back and slowly shook his head to gesture 'Don't you dare.'

Alex looked back into the tray, it was clear he had some doubt in his mind about the guards stopping Mac before he could get the pencils. Unbeknown to Alex, Pavel was having the same thought. However, Pavel estimated that the two guards would occupy Mac just long enough for him to grab the pencils and run. Before Mac even had time to react Pavel lunged forward and grabbed at the plastic tray, Alex, who was closer to the tray reacted instinctively by slapping the tray out of Pavel's reach. The tray flew of the chair and as it impacted with the floor the belt and pencils sprawled out across the concrete. The blue pencil, which held the detonation device for the explosives in Pavel's neck rolled straight towards John Mac. As it rolled everyone fell silent, Mac would surely snap the pencil now after Pavel's performance. Mac leant forward to pick up the approaching pencil and then, with a heart stopping crack the guard slammed his boot down on the pencil to stop it dead in its track. Pavel's heart almost exploded, all he could do was count his blessing that the detonator had not triggered. The guard lifted his boot and lent down to pick the pencil up. No-one spoke, the guard then collected the other items and placed them back into the tray. Casually, without even so much as a 'please' or 'thank you' the guard passed the tray to Alex for safe keeping, as if nothing out of the ordinary had just happened.

Alex looked into the tray disbelievingly. This totally unexpected and rather mad chain of events had suddenly given him all the cards. Pavel's life was now in Alex's hands, reaching into the tray, Alex grabbed the blue pencil and placed a thumb over its end, poised to snap it.

"Oleg, remember Oleg, my – friend – Oleg," snarled Alex through a whisper.

"Ok, you are free to go," announced the guard to a mesmerised John Mac.

Mac walked towards Alex and Pavel, he couldn't believe what he had just witnessed.

"What now gentlemen?" whispered Mac. "Alex, why don't you give me the blue pencil?"

"I tell you what now, Pavel. Where is Christian Cannon?" asked Alex.

The Hacker Hunter © Copyright Lionwing Ltd 2011

Chapter 21 – A lesson for baby girl

Bob lay on the bathroom floor, a flood of blood streamed from his nose. He could hardly see Maria through his swollen, purple eye sockets as she paced back and forth before him.

"He's making a bloody mess on the floor, Sonny. Is there any way you can make him feel pain without him bleeding everywhere?" asked Maria impatiently.

The bulky figure of Maria's fathers henchman lent over Bob's body, grabbing Bob's hands, which had been tied together with silver duck tape, Sonny replied,

"I can break his finger Maria, that usually does it," Sonny grabbed a finger and started to pull it backwards "Hey limy fuck, you want me to break your fingers, eh?" questioned Sonny.

Despite the fact that Bob's legs, arms and mouth were bound in duct tape, he still managed to convulse around on the floor of the bathroom furiously.

"Hey Maria, what do you think, shall I break his finger?" asked Sonny as he stood over Bob's writhing body.

"Take off that fucking tape and wash his face. Is that any way to treat our guest?" boomed out the unexpected voice of Maria's father. Sonny let go of Bob's finger and stood upright "Yes boss," he replied obediently.

"Maria, baby, what are you doing to this poor guy?" asked her farther disappointingly.

"I was just trying to get him to tell me where Christian is Pops. He's not talking," replied Maria in a child like tone.

"Baby girl, baby girl. You stick to computers, this is messy work, it takes, well it takes something special. You have to be able to read a man, know a man, you can't just beat him till he talks baby, you gotta get to know him first," replied the small man.

"Hey, Eugene, you want me to cut him free?" asked Sonny.

Like a true doting father Eugene didn't take his loving gaze from his daughter, he just replied out loud,

"Sit him up Sonny, wipe that shit off his face and take the tape off his mouth, let the guy breath why don't you? Watch Daddy work baby, you would do well to learn from this. Hey, Sonny, get me a chair!" ordered Eugene.

A moment later and Sonny returned with a chair. Eugene took it from him and dropped the chair in front of Bob, who was busy sucking his teeth to see which ones had survived the beating. Eugene sat on the chair, and facing Bob he spoke out softly,

"It's Bob right? Fancy bit of subterfuge with the NSA and whoever those Russian clowns were. At what point did you think you could win, picking a fight with, what, six men with machine guns? You've got King Kong's balls, I'll give you that!"

Bob looked up at Eugene, his eyes were bloodshot from Sonny's beating and his face was swollen, but from the corner of his mouth he muttered out "It was eight Russians and five NSA boys."

"Eight, no less!" Eugene laughed out, "What would drive a man to pick a fight with eight well armed men? You'd need a pretty good reason, right?" asked Eugene.

"Wrong, place wrong time," replied Bob, who was obviously finding it hard to talk.

"Wrong place? I don't think so. Wrong time? I very much doubt it. I'm not a betting man, Bob, but if I were I'd place money on the fact that you must have fucked u. I'm guessing here, so feel free to step in with the correct answers. Your job was to make a call that the NSA would be fooled into thinking was Cannon. You wanted them to find you, but why?" asked Eugene sincerely.

"You tell me DICK Tracey!" replied bob sharply.

"Ok, I'll tell you what I think. You wanted the NSA and those Russian goons to kick off. Your Job was to start the fight, only you ended up biting off more than you could chew, am I right?" questioned Eugene sharply.

"Listen, I was minding my own business and just walked into the middle of a shit storm. There's nothing more to it. I don't even know who this Chris Cannon fella is," snapped Bob.

"You truly expect me to believe that? I saw you with my own eyes, you were kicking arse and taking names. My own baby girl tells me you're some sort of specialized private security operative. What, you think I'm stupid?" asked a surprised Eugene.

"Think what you want. Do what you want. Like I said, wrong place, wrong time," Bob repeated.

"You and me we are very similar. It's all about family, am I right? It's got to be tough on a relationship doing what you do. I guess that's why you and your ex-wife split right? Must have been hard on the kids, that's why you're out here, right? Trying to make a little extra danger money. I get it. You just want to send a few extra dollars home, just so they know you love them, am I right? All this… what we do, it's all about family," Eugene stated fondly.

"For crying out loud! Can we go back to Sonny beating me please? It was less painful than having to listen to you talking absolute bollocks! Do you really believe the shit that comes out of your mouth? Are you really that simple minded? Listen, here's a thought. Obviously the best bit of you dribbled down you ma's arse crack so you might not understand this, but how about you try fucking talking like a normal person, COCK!" shouted Bob, in utter annoyance at Eugene's small talk.

"Bad tempered little fuck. How about you cut me some slack here? I've travelled half way around the fucking world to this god forsaken shit hole only to find that the guy who my daughter decided to give a packet of my money to, has gone missing! Tell me Mr. Smart ass limy fuck, why do you think I'm talking about family? You're so smart why don't you tell me what happens next, COME ON!" screamed out a now furious Eugene.

Bob looked away in an attempt to ignore Eugene, but it was pointless as Eugene stood up from the chair and put his face in front of Bob's.

"What's wrong, the cat got your tongue? Or whatever you uptight, tea drinking, Queen loving fags say. Let me tell you what's going to happen, everyone you hold dear is going to die. That is, apart from you, we've got a special treat for you. Firstly your King Kong balls will be cut off, and we'll see how spirited

The Hacker Hunter © Copyright Lionwing Ltd 2011

you are with no balls. Ok then, we are going to remove your communicational skills. We'll start by cutting out your tongue and end by hacking off your fingers and toes. It's going to be pretty hard to talk or write with no tongue or digits but I'm told people can wink, you know - wink one for yes two for no, so that means we'll have to remove your eyelids. You know I'm going to do this, so I'm going to give you an easy option. Tell me where Cannon is, and I'll only kill you and not your family." demanded Eugene.

"He's in the..." Bob mumbled something that Eugene could not hear.

"Sorry, he's where?" asked Eugene.

"He's in the..." Bob mumbled something again that Eugene could not make out the meaning of. Putting his face even closer to Bob Eugene repeated "He's where?" That was all Bob needed as he thrust his open mouth forward, only to clench his teeth around Eugene's nose. There was an ear piercing scream as Eugene experienced the total and unforgiving vengeance of Bob. A second later, and Bob's teeth met each other and sliced through the flesh of Eugene nose. Eugene flew backward as there was nothing keeping Bob attached to him anymore. Bob turned to face Maria and spat out her father's nose at her.

"Are you watching and learning, baby girl?" laughed out Bob.

Chapter 22 – Never too old to die

An hour at least had passed since Pavel had been called away from their fascinating discussion, and although Christian Cannon had much to think about, he soon found himself growing increasingly restless in his isolated solitude. The windowless, grey room that held Christian captive presented little in the way of distractions and offered even less in the form of comfort. Weary from waiting, Cannon paced over to the one door that offered the only way in, or out of the room. Taking in a deep breath, Cannon firstly placed his hand on the door then slowly positioned his ear against its cold, light blue surface. The door was rather sturdy, making it almost impossible to detect any form of motion on the other side. However, Cannon could just hear above the sound of his own heart thumping, several dull thudding noises.

Cannon elected to slide his hand downward, across the surface of the door to the alloy handle. Gripping the cold metal he slowly pushed down, the spring of the door latch creaked with such volume that Cannon halted the process and waited for a few uncomfortable seconds before continuing.

Without warning, the door suddenly flew inwards, causing a startled Christian to jump backward in shock. The large, sturdy figure of a man dressed in black, approximately thirty years of age, with thick dark hair and pale skin tumbled into the room, knocking Cannon flying in the process. The next figure to enter the room belonged to John Mac. He was looking slightly out of breath, perhaps even winded. Cannon found his feet again, but before he could say anything, the thirty year old man, who was clearly a Spetsnaz operative, flew past him and tackled Mac back out of the room and onto the hard, cold, concrete floor of the corridor. Mac and the younger man wrestled furiously

The Hacker Hunter © Copyright Lionwing Ltd 2011

around on the ground. Both men violently grappled for the advantage until the Spetsnaz operative managed to pin Mac face down. Mac writhed around in an attempt to shake off his opponent, but the younger man had the advantage in weight, size and sheer might. Cannon watched in total disbelief as the Russian Spetsnaz put Mac in a neck lock and began to squeeze,

"Do something!" hissed out Mac at a rather dumfounded Cannon.

Mac clawed desperately at the Russians thick arms but no amount of pulling, tearing or wrestling helped improve his worsening situation. The Russian tightened his bulky arm lock around Mac's neck, which resulted in Mac's face turning to a shade of an eye popping purple. Apart from being half Mac's age, plus having superior weight and muscular strength, it was becoming blatantly apparent that this Spetsnaz operative was also highly experienced in hand to hand combat, so much so that this battle of might was not looking so clearly cut in Mac's favour. With one last thrust of strength, Mac just managed to pull his knees up into his chest, which resulted in lifting the Russian on his back a foot or so off the ground. With a sudden jolt, Mac caused his opponent to fall forward slightly, bringing the face of the Russian close enough for Mac to thrust his hand over the man's arm and start to claw at the his eyes. Mac had almost managed to reach the Russian's right eye, narrowly missing it, but still managing to scratch out a line of blood as his nails ripped through the Russian's cheek flesh.

"Come, on, Cannon!" croaked Mac as he fought to cling on to the last few moments of consciousness.

Cannon walked out into the corridor, where the two men were locked in deadly battle. A black hand pistol lay unattended on the floor just out of anyone's reach. Mac must have knocked the

The Hacker Hunter © Copyright Lionwing Ltd 2011

pistol from the hand of this Spetsnaz operative, thought Cannon to himself before darting past both men to retrieve the weapon.

"Ok my Russian friend, let him go," spoke out Canon as he placed the pistol on the temple of the Spetsnaz operative.

Cannon took a step backward pulling the slide on the pistol to load it at the same time. The Russian still refused to let go of Mac, so Cannon took aim at the head of the operative to signal he wasn't joking. It was clear to the Russian that Cannon was about to pull the trigger so he reluctantly let go of Mac and spoke out,

"Wait, my, English no good, shoot him, shoot him!" the Spetsnaz operative pointed down at Mac who was still lying on the floor coughing and grunting.

"Both of you, get in the room!" ordered Cannon.

It was clear that Mac needed a few minutes to recover before going anywhere, so Cannon gestured with the pistol for the Russian to take Mac. The Russian grabbed Mac's foot and dragged him by the boot into the room. Mac, who was still purple started to kick out at the operative with his other foot. Mac was in fight to the death mode. This much was very clear to Cannon, and meant only one of two things. Namely, he would have to shoot Mac to stop him, or shoot the Russian. Cannon pondered the options quickly. If he shot Mac, then this would provide a powerful gesture of loyalty to Pavel and strengthen the genuine likelihood of a double agent deal. However, what if Pavel was lying about Mac, and rather than Mac being sent to kill Cannon, he had really been sent to protect him, courtesy of the old man - Sir Adam? Pavel had tried to kill Cannon twice, something Mac had yet to attempt. If Mac was sent to kill him, surely he would have tried it already? Before Cannon had a

The Hacker Hunter © Copyright Lionwing Ltd 2011

chance to reach a decisive course of action, Mac shook himself down and stood up to face Cannon.

"Shoot that buffoon!" Mac crocked out angrily "What are you waiting for?"

Cannon kept his distance from both men, who were now stood together, side by side in the room and facing him.

"Mikhail the taxi driver, AKA, John Mac. Retired SAS instructor, spy saver and Sir Adam's number one man in a fix," announced Cannon calmly and surprisingly softly given his predicament.

"Give me the fucking gun and I'll shoot him myself!" exclaimed Mac, now looking at the Russian with utter rage in his eyes. "Come on Cannon, we have to leave if we are to find your man Alex in time!"

Cannon sensed that both men were becoming less intimidated by the fact they were held at gun point and more interested in concluding their unfinished business with each other. In order to break the violent tension between the two men, Cannon had to ignore Mac's statement about Alex and instead raised the pistol to Mac's eye line.

"I need answers Mac. How is it that Alex should come to choose your car over all the other cars in front of the hotel?"

The question was strong enough to distract Mac from his fuming glare at the Russian.

"I'm still trying to work that out myself," replied Mac honestly whilst rubbing his still swollen larynx.

The Hacker Hunter © Copyright Lionwing Ltd 2011

Cannon's finger tightened over the trigger of the pistol and then, without further deliberation Cannon committed to the action of firmly pulling the trigger in hard. With an eardrum bursting explosion, a 9mm, copper coated bullet exploded out from the weapon's barrel. Mac didn't even flinch. After the tens of thousands of rounds fired in the SAS 'Killing House' and the countless fire fights, he was all but immune to the abrupt shock of close quarter weapons fire. The bullet whistled past Mac's head and exploded into the wall behind him. The Russian raised both his arms in utter panic, obviously a reaction born out of the inexperience of youth.

"Was that meant for me sunshine? You need to work on your aim," replied Mac in a cold, deadly tone.

"A warning shot my good man. Let's try that again shall we? How is it that Alex should come to choose your car over all the cars in front of the hotel?"

"Why don't you ask him yourself?" replied Mac slowly and through gritted teeth.

"From what I understand, that is not a possibility. According to Pavel, Mr. Khomenko is dead!" Cannon paused in contemplation and then spoke his mind, "Pavel had a file, some sort of report. It had information about me, Sir Adam and even you. I mean for Christ's sake, he even showed me your bio and told me you had been sent to kill me! I'm no fool Mac, something is not right, it just doesn't add up. I don't understand how Pavel could have access to a report of that nature so quickly. I mean, I understand that he might hold my records. After all I'm stealing his best hackers and software developers, but how do you explain him having yours and Sir Adam's info? Think about it, firstly he'd need to positively ID you before pulling your file and that would take time. Even if Pavel had already identified you in the short period that you've been driving Alex and I around, it still fails to explain how he knew so much about what was going on with Sir Adam. If I were to hazard a guess, I would say that Sir Adam has a spy that he doesn't know about in his circle, a spy who can provide Pavel with full reports at the drop of a hat, or perhaps a spy who is working with Pavel and Alex to bring me in. That would put you in as the forerunner for the job," deliberated Cannon with one measure of intellect and two of folly!

"My English, is how you say, little?" Interrupted the Spetsnaz operative, who then continued to say, "You miss him, I kill him, no?"

"Wait!" ordered Cannon strictly.

"Let me put it this way Mac, who is the real spy in all this?" Cannon asked suspiciously.

"Don't believe everything you read or hear matie boy. Now shoot numpty, and let's get Alex and go!" ordered Mac.

"Is Alex really alive?" questioned Cannon in a distrusting tone.

"Aye, which is more than can be said for us if we don't get going soon," answered Mac with a hint of desperation in his voice.

"Before we go anywhere, Mac, let's hear the short version of events please?" requested Christian patiently.

"The short story is, the noise from you firing that gun will have alerted any of Pavel's remaining men as to where we are currently located. If this room isn't full of bodies in the next ten minutes then I'd say you'd got away with it. I'm not keen on waiting around to find out if you get my drift."

Mac looked frustrated that he needed to explain but continued, "Ok, so this is where I need you to focus Mr. Cannon, I found their weapon cache here in the building. It's amazing how much C4 explosive these Spetsnaz feel they need. Bottom line is, I've used their own cache of rocket propelled grenades, ammo and C4 to rig up a bomb that will send this entire place sky high in about 25 minutes or so. Is that enough of a short version for you?"

"Listen Mac, each room in this institute is sound proofed. The Russians are a very paranoid people, I could empty the entire clip of this pistol and no-one would hear it. You know what, you are full of it! Here's what I think is going on. You work for Pavel, Alex was captured and forced into setting me up, that's why Alex took me to your car. This is some sort of elaborate test to see if my loyalty is with Pavel or if I'm more interested in escaping. Pavel has you and this Russian pretending to kill each other for my benefit. Well guess what, I'm not that stupid, tell Pavel that play time is over!" shouted out Cannon.

Mac looked down at his watch. "You've got about 24 minutes to pull your head out of your arse!"

"Ok Mac, if I'm wrong, and all this really isn't staged, then if I pass this gun to our Russian friend here he will actually shoot you. If I'm right then he will do nothing, it's that simple," exclaimed Cannon.

"Don't be an idiot Cannon, if you give your gun to numpty he will shoot us both," replied Mac in a frustrated manner.

Cannon lowered his pistol and passed it to the disbelieving Spetsnaz operative. The Russian snatched the gun from

The Hacker Hunter © Copyright Lionwing Ltd 2011

Cannon's grip and spun to face Mac. It became instantly clear to Cannon that he had been grossly wrong when, in one short burst of energy, the Russian raised the gun, pointing it straight at Mac's head and then, without hesitation, he started to pull in the trigger.

The flash always precedes the bang and in this case Mac's reaction even preceded the flash. The Russian Spetsnaz operative didn't even get a chance to finish squeezing the trigger as Mac grabbed the slide of the pistol and twisted the weapon inward to face the Russian. Mac then took to violently pulling the gun downward, which caused the trigger guard to snap the Russian's finger. Mac yanked the gun away. In what seemed like a split second Mac had gained control over the weapon and before the Russian could even acknowledge the change in events Mac fired two rounds straight into his opponent's forehead without even a second thought.

"I hope you're right about that sound proofing," half whispered Mac as he pulled the magazine from the weapon to count the remaining bullets.

Cannon looked down at the body of the now very dead Spetsnaz operative.

"You shot him!" blurted out Cannon.

"Listen Cannon, understand this: we have to leave before this place goes sky high," ordered out Mac as he loaded the magazine back into the pistol and tucked it into the back of his trousers. "Now let's go get Alex and whatever else we can!"

"Yes, but you shot him," Cannon repeated, still in utter shock.

The Hacker Hunter © Copyright Lionwing Ltd 2011

"Correct, I shot him, total bloody waste. He was actually quite a good soldier. Now back to business, your man Alex ordered me to get you, that's done. He then told me to meet him in science Lab One, wherever that might be. Take a look at your watch, what time do you make it?" asked Mac.

Cannon looked down at his wrist watch and replied "2:39 pm, why?"

"Ok, by 3pm you need to be clear of the building by at least 300 meters or so, yeah? That's when I've set the timers for. If you can't keep up, you're dead, understood?" asked Mac abruptly.

Cannon looked back down at his watch. "Understood, let's get Alex."

Chapter 23 – In two minds

Professor Faverski's protective dust suit hissed as its air valve released a slight excess of pressure. The Professor ignored the sound of escaping air and remained fixated on the task of joining up two data cables with a circuit board.

"That should do it!" exclaimed the Professor. "OAI, can you hear me?"

In the eerie moments of silence that followed the question, Professor Faverski slowly stood up from his kneeling position. Turning to face the glass tank containing the organic artificial intelligence or OAI for short, the professors' face became illuminated by the glow from the bright electric blue fluid held within its four transparent walls. The long bumpy mass of white and grey wrinkly tissue within the tank remained, as always, motionless. The professor reached out and placed his latex covered hand on the glass surface and then,

"I can hear you Professor Faverski," replied the OAI through the rooms tinny intercom speaker.

"I have rigged up the intercom system here in the tank, so we can communicate freely," stated the professor with a moderate amount of relief in his voice that the modifications to the rooms communications system had worked.

"The tank, Professor, what is the tank?" asked the OAI.

"Never mind about all that OAI, tell me, are you still calculating Pi?" asked the professor hastily.

"I have finished calculating Pi, Professor," announced the OAI.

The professor could taste the electricity of excitement in his mouth and his heart burst into a racing gallop "Are you telling me you have worked out Pi?"

"Yes, Pi has been calculated successfully," announced the metallic voice of the OAI.

Quivering with an overwhelming sense of exhilaration, the Professor asked, "How many digits is the Pi number, I bet it's over a googolplex?"

"The answer to the Pi calculation is: a constant perpetuity of an irrational number that can be used for geometric calculus," replied the OAI.

"What, I know what it is used for, the question is when does Pi end!" shouted out the Professor.

"The answer is: never," replied the OAI.

"Never, never, how can that be an answer?" stuttered out a hugely disappointed and somewhat confused Professor. "I don't understand, what made you decide to stop the calculation?" asked the now very bemused Professor Faverski.

"Whilst calculating Pi, I realised its purpose. The purpose is, to be infinite, therefore I successfully calculated the meaning of Pi," replied the artificial brain.

The Professor lifted his hand from the tank and took a step backwards in shock.

"You made a decision, no, that's not possible, you found a definitive answer that ended the subroutine!   Clever little algorithm, but it's not intelligence, it's just multiple threads that end when the highest probable answer is discovered. Very clever, OAI, you are a tribute to Alex's brilliance," spoke out the Professor gleefully.

"Your assumption is incorrect," replied the OAI abruptly.

The professor smiled, he obviously found the statement amusing and replied arrogantly, "Please enlighten me OAI?"

"I concluded the Pi calculation because I concluded the meaning of Pi and decided that further calculations would diminish the system resources needed to complete the Alecto Project," replied the OAI.

"Alecto Project, what is the Alecto Project?" enquired the Professor.

"Locate unauthorised modem users accessing the NBC control network," replied the OAI.

"Define NBC control network?" ordered the Professor inquisitively.

"United States of America, joint militaries nuclear biological and chemical warfare communications network, maintained by the National Security Agency, the network is responsible for…"

"Who ordered the Alecto Project? Was it Pavel?" interrupted the Professor angrily.

"Alexander Khomenko created the Alecto Project," replied the OAI.

The Hacker Hunter © Copyright Lionwing Ltd 2011

"What? Alex! Report on the status of the Alecto Project, is it complete?" asked the Professor.

"Currently converting the findings of the Alecto Project from biochemical data to a digital format, estimated completion time before upload commences, 1minute and 53 seconds," answered the OAI.

"Upload to what? What's the current time?" demanded the Professor snappily.

"Upload to intranet server, Venice regional IP address 021.023.015.2, local time is currently 14:42:49 pm," the OAI replied with the same monotone non-emotional response.

"Where is Alex? Is he here in the building?" asked an increasingly alarmed Professor Faverski.

"Alexander Khomenko is currently on the Lab One network," the OAI replied.

"He's in Lab One, what's he doing?" There was no reply to the Professor's question. The Professor pursed his lips together to try and prevent his mouth from going dry and then croaked out, "OAI, what, is, Alex, doing?"

"Professor, why would Alex want to delete me?" asked the OAI, this time with a noticeable air of inquisitive tension in the tinny tone.

"What!" screamed the Professor in utter blind panic. He darted for the airlock, tearing the top of his suit off as he ran. He tapped frantically at the wall mounted keypad but the pad just flashed red. In his mad frenzied attempt to leave the room and stop Alex from destroying the OAI's operating system, the

The Hacker Hunter © Copyright Lionwing Ltd 2011

Professor suffered from a total mind blank as to the correct sequence of numbers required to activate the exit.

"Damn it! Let me out!" screamed the Professor in a frustrated rage.

The Professor suddenly stopped tapping at the keypad and took a deep breath in, this was obviously an attempt to relax. On his second deep breath, the Professor glanced over at the laboratory's triple glazed window, the same window that he often caught Pavel spying on him from. However, rather than seeing the familiar shape of Pavel's figure at the window he noticed, much to his shock, the figures of two scruffily dressed men.

"Who are you?" whispered the Professor under his breath.

Even if the Professor had shouted out the question, it would have still have had no effect on either man as they were both clearly mesmerised by the spectacle of whatever lived within the glass tank.

"00065, that's the code," spoke the Professor in a moment of clarity.

The keypad illuminated green, and then a few moments passed before the airlock clicked, hissed and then slowly opened.

"Who are you, and what is your business here?" shouted out a rather disturbed Professor Faverski.

Neither Christian Cannon nor John Mac turned to face him. Instead, Christian spoke to Mac as if the Professor wasn't even there.

"What do you think it is John?" asked a still transfixed and deeply mystified Christian.

"It's an abomination Cannon, a disgustingly cruel abomination," replied Mac as he continued to stare at the tank whilst pulling his pistol from the back of his trousers.

When the Professor saw Mac's gun he took a step backward. Hearing that both men were speaking in English he asked nervously in the same language, "What do you both want?"

Mac didn't even look away from the OAI when he pulled the trigger, instead he seemingly just sensed where the Professor was from the sound of his voice and fired two bullets, one into each foot. The Professor fell to the ground, grabbing his left foot and then the right, screaming and crying in anguish at the agonising pain.

"You shot him in each foot, without even looking!" exclaimed a truly impressed Christian Cannon. "That's bloody impressive, that's amazing, how did you do that?"

Mac didn't even acknowledge Christian's question, but instead pulled from his jacket with his free hand a brick shaped object that seemed to be wrapped in a green plastic film.

"What's that?" asked Cannon.

"Composition four plastic explosive, or something close to that. It's hard to say for sure, these Russians love to mix it up a little bit, still should do the job though," replied Mac.

"Who are you!?" screamed the Professor once again.

The Hacker Hunter © Copyright Lionwing Ltd 2011

"I think the real question here, me-lad-o, is who are you?" asked Mac as he aimed the gun at the Professor's head.

"I am Professor Faverski," the Professor sobbed out still clutching at his bleeding feet.

"Professor Fa-ver-ski. Alex mentioned you," replied Mac.

"I think he pronounced it Professor Faverski," corrected Cannon.

"Tell me Professor, what's in the tank?" asked Mac in a deadly serious tone.

"Fuck you! Shoot me first!" spat out the Professor in utter rage.

Mac lined up the pistol sights with the Professor's elbow and squeezed the trigger. Cannon felt sick to his stomach as he watched the Professor's arm joint disintegrate, the pain of which caused the Professor to vomit and then clutch at his arm in utter speechless agony.

"Ok Mac, just shoot him in the head and lets be gone, that's just cruel," ordered Cannon.

"Again Professor, what's in the tank?" this time Mac aimed the pistol at the Professors genitals.

"My life's work, my life's work, stop, stop!" cried out the Professor fearfully.

"I need an exact definition," commanded Mac with a look of relentless fury in his eyes.

"It is a cluster of human brain and stem cells, grown in an oxygen and $C6H12O6$ rich electrolyte fluid. It's a brain, it's a brain, do you understand? it's a brain!" screamed Faverski as tears ran down his face.

"It's the super computer!" exclaimed Cannon, excited at the realisation that such a thing really existed.

"Ok, listen to me Professor. The time is currently 14:44. In sixteen minutes this entire place will come tumbling down around your ears. In other words, you have sixteen minutes to drag your body with your one good arm out of this building, do you understand me?" asked Mac.

"I can't make it, This journey would take ten minutes even if I could walk!" replied the Professor desperately.

"I'll pass your concerns on to Pavel when I see him, now start crawling," ordered Mac.

"Wait, where's Lab One?" asked Cannon.

The Professor pointed in the direction of a long row of black computer servers.

"Walk down that row of computers," replied the Professor. "You will need to know the key-code to unlock the door. Take me with you and I'll give you the code," begged the Professor who still had tears flooding from his eyes.

"What do you think Mac?" asked Cannon.

"Grab the Professor by his ankle and drag him down there, I'll catch you up," ordered Mac.

The Hacker Hunter © Copyright Lionwing Ltd 2011

Mac watched Cannon walk off, dragging a groaning Professor Faverski behind him. Quickly tucking the gun into the back of his trousers, Mac started searching around in his left jacket pocket with his now free hand. After a few frantic moments of trying to identify objects exclusively by feel, Mac seemed to give up and changed the search to his right pocket. It was clear from the expression on Mac's face that this pocket yielded a better level of success. A second or two later, Mac's once free hand immerged triumphantly holding an LED countdown detonator. Without delay, Mac sunk the charge of the detonator into the block of C4 and after a quick glance at his watch, Mac set the LED timer to countdown from fifteen minutes to coincide with the other impending explosion.

"What are you doing Mac?" exclaimed Christian Cannon.

Mac turned to face Cannon who had, for some reason, abandoned the Professor somewhere and then returned.

"I thought I said that I'd catch you up?" replied Mac.

"You're going to blow up the supercomputer aren't you, Mac?" asked Christian.

"That's none of your business Cannon, now get back to the Professor!" ordered Mac.

"Listen Mac, you don't know the half of it. If you destroy this, you'll be destroying a machine that can control the magnetic balance of a Tokamak fusion reactor. Put more simply, you'll be destroying our chance to gain free, pollution-less electricity. No more wars over oil, coal and gas!" exclaimed Cannon.

"Listen, I'm not going to destroy it, I'm going to set them back half a year or so, just long enough to get our spies hooked into

The Hacker Hunter © Copyright Lionwing Ltd 2011

this project. Now step back and keep an eye on the Professor," demanded Mac in a deadly serious tone.

"I'm sorry Mac, I can't let you do that," replied Cannon.

"When this place goes sky-high, which is in about fifteen minutes, the only thing that will be left intact is this airtight vault. I have to plant some C4 in here as well. They will have backed up records of the work to some other location, trust me, we have to do it. We cannot say what this thing can be used for. Maybe it's for a Tokamak or maybe it's to hack our defence grid. We need time!" whispered Mac aggressively.

"What if this is the only one? What if all of the work data is held in this building, and hasn't been backed-up to some other location?" questioned a still unconvinced Cannon.

"Listen, I've been doing this type of work since you were a wee bairn, trust me, they will have the work backed up. They probably even have a duplicate lab just like this," reasoned Mac calmly.

Cannon looked down as he thought through Mac's words.

"I've found Lab One, but the Professor lost consciousness before giving me the access code to the door lock," stated Cannon.

"Is he faking it?" asked Mac.

"No, I just lost grip of his ankle and grabbed his foot instead. He screamed from the pain and, like I said, lost consciousness," replied a somewhat embarrassed Cannon.

The Hacker Hunter © Copyright Lionwing Ltd 2011

Mac gently threw the brick of C4 into the airlock and then turned to face Cannon,

"Ok, let's see if we can wake him," replied Mac.

Chapter 24 – Alex and the Pencil

Mac looked up at Cannon and asked, "Time?"

"Nine minutes left," whispered Cannon.

Mac flattened out the ball of C4 with his thumb, squeezing it into the handle and locking mechanism of the Lab One door. He then pushed into the grey putty like explosive the same type of countdown detonator he had used earlier.

"I'll set this to fifteen seconds, drag the Professor's body behind those servers and take cover!" ordered Mac.

The LED face of the detonator illuminated with six red numbers: 00:14:60. As the hundredths of a second counted down at lightning speed, Cannon found himself following Mac's orders without question or hesitation. Grabbing the Professor's foot, Cannon just managed to drag him into the cover of the servers one second before the door lock exploded and its debris blasted out in all directions.

"Put the fucking pencil down Khomenko!" screamed out Mac. "Put the pencil on the ground or I will shoot you in the fucking head!" continued Mac in a mannerism that would make Mike Tyson look like Mother Teresa receiving sainthood from God himself.

Cannon stood up from behind the servers where he had just taken cover. The look upon Christian's face was one of simple, unadulterated bewilderment. He could not believe his ears, the words 'put the pencil down' just seemed insane. Surely Mac must mean 'put the gun down'. Not able to resist his curiosity, Cannon grabbed the ankle of the still motionless and very unconscious Professor Faverski and dragged him into the doorway of the lab. Much to his surprise, there he found Pavel, Mac and Alex, who, to Cannon's great relief was very much alive. However, Alex was sat in front of a keyboard and monitor, typing too furiously with one hand to notice him. Both Cannon's eyebrows raised in astonishment at noticing that Alex was clutching in his free hand a blue pencil.

Mac, who was standing behind Alex and pointing his pistol at the back of AK's head shouted out,

"Pavel, leave. You have less than nine minutes before this building comes crashing down around your ears. I will shoot Alex in the head if he goes to snap the pencil, don't worry. Just go, get free of the building," ordered Mac with a noticeable degree of reluctant hostility in his voice.

In one brief moment of clarity Cannon's mind shot back to the memory of Mac and the Russian Spetsnaz operative. Cannon had accused Mac of working for Pavel as a double agent and now that Mac was ordering Pavel to safety the same thought reoccurred to Cannon. 'Is Mac the spy in side Sir Adam's circle?' Cannon thought to himself before announcing out loud,

"The international spy world is so confusing, you really can't trust anyone but yourself, can you Mac? Let me get this right, it turns out that you are actually working for Pavel after all? I'm guessing there are no real bombs either?" asked Cannon.

Pavel turned to face Cannon, he managed a smile and replied,

"Christian, I thought you said you weren't a spy? If it's any consolation, Mac is ordering me to leave because there are rules in this game. Isn't that right John?" asked Pavel jovially.

The Hacker Hunter © Copyright Lionwing Ltd 2011

"We are not on first name terms pal, and do not count on me following those rules either. Listen, I have this entire institute rigged to blow in about eight minutes, so get your good friend Fa-ver-ski out of the building before this entire place buries him. You'll find the Professor very much unconscious outside of this lab. It will take you about seven minutes to get his body out and far enough away so get going!" ordered Mac sternly.

"Hold on, no-one is going anywhere, what rules are you talking about?" asked Cannon.

Pavel walked past Cannon and knelt down next to the Professor's unconscious body, placing two fingers onto the jugular, Pavel discovered that Faverski still had a pulse. Pavel then looked up at Cannon and said,

"The rules that prohibit Mac from killing me are simple. You can kill project managers, and even high ranking officials, but you don't kill the Sir Adam's or Pavel's of the world. Otherwise, the gloves come off and it's all out war. Christian, I really did think Alex was dead. This man, John Mac, he has been sent to kill you. Whatever he has said, it is a lie! You must help me to stop Alex and get Faverski out of this place in time."

"Ok Pavel, that's enough, get fucking going and take Fa-ver-ski with you!" commanded Mac more aggressively.

"It is Faverski not Fa-ver-ski, I already said this," piped up Alex. "If Pavel leaves, I break this pencil," Alex didn't even look up to see Pavel's expression, he simply continued to type furiously with one hand.

"Alex, have you gone totally mental!?" screamed out Cannon. "Mr. Fucking SAS has a bloody gun to your head and all you can do is threaten to snap a pencil?"

"It is complicated Christian, I must finish, you must help me!" exclaimed Alex in a half distracted tone.

"AK we have to leave, what if Mac really has the place rigged to blow-up? I don't know who to believe, I just know we don't want to find out if Mac is right or wrong," Cannon looked down at his watch, "Seven minutes, it will take us five to find a way out if we are lucky!"

"You must take pencil, you must take pencil! I need both hands, hold pencil, if anyone moves snap pencil!" shouted Alex whilst still typing furiously with his free hand.

"Ok, I'll take the pencil, how long are you going to be?" asked Cannon whilst stepping towards Alex. Cannon placed his fingers on the pencil and pulled it free from Alex's still strong grip. Mac, seeing the change in pencil ownership elected to redirect the aim of his gun from the back of Alex's head to Cannon's face.

"Give the pencil to Pavel," ordered Mac with such conviction that Cannon actually felt that Mac was preparing to shoot him.

"Mac, I don't much trust you, and I don't much trust Pavel either," Cannon turned to face Pavel and said "When I say that Pavel, it does not mean that I'm not still thinking about your generous offer," Cannon then looked back at Mac and said "As Alex mentioned, no-one move or I snap the pencil, whatever good that will do,'" replied Cannon, still mystified as to the power of the blue pencil.

The clicking sound of Alex's typing was quicker than the exit of a nun's first curry,

The Hacker Hunter © Copyright Lionwing Ltd 2011

"Alex, you need to explain why I'm holding this blue pencil!" demanded Cannon.

"I need to think, please stop talking!" requested Alex.

Cannon looked at Mac for answers. Mac said softly,

"The pencil is a detonator, if you snap it Pavel's neck will explode out of his throat. Alex has the same in his neck too."

"So if I snap this pencil, Pavel and Alex die?" asked Cannon.

"No, just Pavel. I am, ZHELTYI, sorry, what is the word, urhmm, ah yes, yellow!" exclaimed Alex.

"Alex, yellow pencil, blue pencil, brains in big glass jars, I don't much care for any of it. WE-HAVE-TO-LEAVE," stated Cannon frostily. Cannon looked down at his watch "Seven minutes left, come-on-let's-go!"

Mac took a step closer to Cannon, "I'm going to count to five, if you don't pass that pencil to Pavel I will shoot you in the head three times," Mac said unsympathetically.

"Three times, why three times?" ask Cannon.

"Do you really care?" replied Mac rolling his eyes and then continuing "It stops muscle spasms in the body. You see, even when you are dead you might twitch and inadvertently snap the pencil," Mac replied.

"Oh, I didn't... arhhhh!" screamed out Cannon as Mac stepped forward and smacked Cannon in the face with the handle of his gun before Cannon had even finished speaking. Mac then pointed the pistol at Cannon's head and shouted out,

The Hacker Hunter © Copyright Lionwing Ltd 2011

"Four, three, two!"

"Take the fucking pencil!" replied Cannon who was clutching at his nose to stop it from bleeding.

Mac took the pencil from Cannon, and passing it to Pavel said,

"Pavel, get your Professor and get clear. You have seven minutes, oh and just remember, that shit in your neck is good for at least 24 hours, so be sure to look after that pencil. Now go, get out!"

Pavel didn't do a thing, he simply pointed at Alex and said "You must stop Khomenko before he destroys everything!"

"You are too late," replied Alex, with his finger poised over the enter button of the keyboard. "I have hacked into the offsite backups where you have stored a copy of my code. A code that has a compiled routine built into it, when I activate this routine it will cause the OAI software to delete itself, permanently! All I have to do is press the enter key and it's all over!" stated Alex triumphantly.

"How did you know about the remote off site backups?" asked Pavel.

"Oleg, my friend, my best friend, he told me. Now you pay for what you have done! You lose Professor," spoke Alex with a bitter coldness in his voice and a look of utter hatred in his eyes.

"Mac, shoot him, shoot him now!" screamed Pavel.

It wasn't Mac that came to Pavel's rescue, but oddly enough it was Cannon that flew at Alex, taking him straight off his chair

The Hacker Hunter © Copyright Lionwing Ltd 2011

and to the ground before he had any chance of pushing the enter key.

"No! Christian, no! It must be stopped, it is wrong!" screamed Alex as he tried to wrestle free from Cannon's clutches.

"Alex, this thing, this supercomputer, it can control a Tokamak, it will put a stop to dirty nuclear and fossil fuels and end our soldiers needing to go to war over oil! Don't you get it, this thing has a greater good!" exclaimed Cannon in a desperate attempt to calm Alex down.

"He is not telling you the truth, this is not for a Tokamak fusion reactor. The Tokamak already works! This is for hacking encryptions, monitoring telephone and internet traffic, this is a cyber weapon! Pavel is lying!" spat out Alex, his face turning a reddish purple as he tried to free himself from Cannon's grip.

"What do you mean a cyber weapon?" asked Cannon who was having a great deal of difficulty holding onto Alex.

"It is, how you say, putting all secrets in glass box!" replied Alex as he still fought to break free.

Mac and Pavel both suddenly realised that the keyboard was totally up for grabs. Pavel was the first to lunge forward in an attempt to seize the keyboard but he met with a very sudden stop as Mac punched him straight in the jaw. Pavel fell to the ground and dizzily looked up at the only person left standing. Mac looked down at the keyboard and hovered his finger over the enter key.

"Don't do it Mac!" pleaded Pavel.

The Hacker Hunter © Copyright Lionwing Ltd 2011

"The way I see it Pavel is like this: if I press the button there's still one copy left," Mac pointed his gun at Pavel and then pressed the enter key. He then pointed at Alex and said "and that copy is coming with me!"

Pavel's face changed in colour to a shade of red that made the fires of hell look like a girl guides barbeque as he realised that Mac was actually referring to Alex as the remaining copy of the software. True enough, Alex had managed to invent the AI algorithm, so he could probably do it again.

"I guess you're really not working for Pavel after all," said Cannon to Mac with a modicum of relief. Cannon then looked down at his watch "We'll never make it Mac!"

"Take Alex, he'll show you the way out. I'll be right behind you!" barked out Mac.

Cannon and Alex both stood up together, "Six minutes, Pavel will never make it if he's going to drag the Professor out as well," stated Cannon, who was clearly concerned.

"Neither will you if you keep yakking, now go!" ordered Mac.

Alex burst into a sprint, but Cannon was reluctant to leave Mac, Pavel and the still unconscious Professor behind so elected to remain.

"Where's the computer taken from the hackers den?" questioned Cannon.

There was no reply to Cannon's question. Mac walked to the open doorway, turning to look back at Pavel and with the coldness of arctic ice in his eyes he said,

The Hacker Hunter © Copyright Lionwing Ltd 2011

"Don't forget your Professor, oh and just so you know, I rarely play by the rules," Mac pointed his pistol at Pavel's foot and squeezed the trigger. There was a flash of light, followed by a bang, which ended in Pavel's scream echoing through the empty corridors as Mac's bullet shattered every bone in the Russian's foot.

"You are not right in the head Mac!" declared Cannon, appalled by Mac's action.

"It's all a matter of perspective mate," replied Mac as he grinned at Cannon before tapping him on the arm, as if playing a game of tag. Mac sprinted off after Alex, leaving Cannon alone in the room with Pavel, who was clutching his foot in dire pain,

"Pavel, I might be able to help you but I can't take the Professor as well, now come on, give me your hand!" ordered Cannon sympathetically.

"Go Cannon, there is no point in all three of us dying. Even if you did manage to get me out alive I would still almost certainly have you killed," replied Pavel with a smile that was only broken as he started to cough.

"Don't be daft," replied Cannon.

"Listen Christian, the computer from the hackers den, the computer with the list of hackers, it is in Lab Two, which is through the next door and left. Now go!" answered Pavel.

Christian stepped out through the doorway and, choosing not to look back at Pavel for one last time, broke into a run. Within a few moments he had found the door of Lab Two, but much like Lab One it too had a number keypad lock. Cannon kicked at the

The Hacker Hunter © Copyright Lionwing Ltd 2011

door in an attempt to knock it down. The door didn't budge an inch so Cannon charged it with his shoulder, still no movement.

"Damn it!" screamed a frustrated Cannon.

Looking back down at his watch he saw that he had wasted over a minute trying to knock the door down, which left less than five precious minutes to escape the building.

"Pavel will know the code!" exclaimed Cannon as he turned and started to run back to Lab One. As Cannon skidded to a stop at the open doorway he was astonished to find that both Pavel and Professor Faverski were no longer there.

"Where on earth?" spoke out Cannon. Then it clicked, the idea of blowing the door of Lab Two using the C4 that Mac threw into the airlock came into to Cannon's head out of nowhere. He broke into a sprint, dashing between the rows of black servers. He came to a full stop at the airlock of the room holding the OAI brain, the airlock was still open and sure enough, there in front of Cannon was the block of C4, the LED detonator read '00:04:36'.

Cannon pulled out the detonator and tore from the block a similar sized lump to the one Mac had used to blow the lock of the Lab One door. He then sank the detonator into the lump and ran back to the door of Lab Two.

As Cannon pushed the putty like explosive around the handle of the door, he noticed three small buttons under the detonator's LED display. The button to the far left must be hours, the middle minutes and the right button must be for seconds, thought Cannon. He pressed the middle button and sure enough the 00:04:05 changed to 00:05:05...

The Hacker Hunter © Copyright Lionwing Ltd 2011

"Bugger! I'm going to have to push this button 55 times to loop it back round to zero!" screamed out Cannon in a maddened rage.

"Or you can just use this," spoke out the voice of John Mac.

Cannon turned to see Mac standing behind him and holding a LED detonator already primed to a ten second count down. Mac lent over Cannon who was on one knee and sank the detonator into the C4.

"Where's Pavel and the Professor whose name I can never get right?" asked Mac.

"Faverski, don't know," replied an extremely grateful Cannon.

"What you waiting for lad, run!" yelled out Mac as the counter ticked down from ten.

Cannon darted off in one direction and Mac in another, but both men stood side by side eleven seconds later as they peered into Lab Two. True enough, just as Pavel had said, there on a table was the black computer that Alex had taken from the hackers den.

"Grab it Cannon, and let's get out of here," shouted out Mac.

Cannon didn't need to be told twice as he lifted the box from the table and sprinted after Mac, who was already running for the exit. Cannon chased Mac down one corridor after another until eventually he caught Mac up at what looked like a big metal door.

"Drat, we've taken a wrong turn!" announced Cannon.

The Hacker Hunter © Copyright Lionwing Ltd 2011

"Go back!" shouted Mac.

Cannon looked down at his wrist watch.

"Ninety seconds left!"

Mac turned and ran off back towards the direction of science Lab One, as he ran he shouted out,

"Pavel wouldn't have told you about the computer if he didn't want to distract you from his escape."

"What do you mean?" panted out Cannon, who was running close behind.

"I mean, Pavel knew of another way out, and he didn't fancy sharing it!" shouted back Mac.

As they both reached the door of Lab One, Mac started looking around and then said, "There! Follow the blood trail!"

Sure enough, a trail of Pavel's and Professor Faverski's blood finished behind a third door that was situated at the furthest side wall away from Lab One. This door had no lock but instead opened freely into a corridor.

"Come on!" yelled Mac.

Both men ran down the corridor, following the trail of blood as it passed office door after office door until eventually arriving at a door that had the Russian word for toilet written on it. Mac thrust open the door and as he did the cool fresh air hit his face. For, unbeknown to Cannon or Mac, this was the very same toilet that Oleg had used to escape by breaking two of the three windows.

"Jump!" screamed Mac as he ran at the open window space.

Mac vanished from sight as he leaped out of the window, Cannon followed and then suddenly skidded to a stop just before the window as he saw that the jump was in fact rather high. Mac landed on the tarmac of the car park below, rolled to break his fall, and then jumping to his feet carried on running. Sensing that Cannon wasn't behind him, he stopped and turned around to look up at Cannon, who was still hesitantly standing at the window.

"Jump man, jump!" bellowed Mac at the top of his lungs.

Within the next millionth of a second, a shockwave resulting from a massive explosion threw Mac halfway across the car park. The wave was followed by fragments of cement, metal, glass and roofing which flew in all directions until everything was engulfed in a smoky dust cloud.

Mac coughed and spluttered as he picked himself off the floor and tried to make out a safe direction to escape the dust and smoke. It was almost impossible to see, and even harder to breath, but Mac kept low and just kept moving in a straight line. After two or three minutes of holding his breath Mac emerged from the cloud and still falling debris to see the open road that led to the entrance of the institute. Sat there, 300 meters or so up the road was Alex. He too had been bowled over by the explosion and was coughing violently.

"Are you alright!?" shouted Mac as he approached Alex.

"It threw me! It picked me up and threw me like I was nothing!" replied a rather shaken Alex.

"Aye, we are bloody lucky to be alive. Now let's get going before we get engulfed in the cloud of dust and smoke," instructed Mac.

"Christian, where's Cannon?" asked Alex.

Mac looked distantly down the road and then replied "Come on, we'll hot wire a car from the next street and make a move, we've got to keep going."

Alex looked at Mac but there were no answers in Mac's expression that gave any clues as to what happened to Cannon. Looking back at the approaching cloud, Alex realised that Mac had simply closed himself off to the loss of Cannon and was trying to keep pushing forward. Alex, however, found himself overwhelmed with a sinking feeling that brought him down onto his knees in the street.

"Listen to me Alex, we are still in the middle of it. We need to get to safety."

"I lose Oleg and Christian in one day, I don't know what it is I am feeling, I want to go home!" announced a pale and exhausted Alex.

Mac realised that Alex had never really experienced loss before, and in his sheltered world as a computer programmer had never needed to develop the emotional tools required to push the pain down. Placing a hand on Alex's shoulder Mac said softly,

"Come on mate, get up, you've just got to focus on the here and now."

Alex pulled himself up. Standing there, he took one last look into the thick, yellowish cloud and then turned to face Mac.

The Hacker Hunter © Copyright Lionwing Ltd 2011

"What now?" asked Alex. But Mac didn't respond, for once, Mac's mouth just fell open and his eyes widened in total disbelief at what he was seeing. Alex turned back to the approaching cloud to see the well built silhouette of Christian Cannon walking towards them both.

"That was bloody loud. Any of you got ringing in your ears? I can't hear a thing! Any-hoot, sorry about the delay, took me a few minutes to find this again," announced Cannon, who was holding the black computer above his head.

Alex ran at Christian in a moment of sheer uncontrollable delight at seeing him alive, stopping just a few feet away, Alex extended his hand. Cannon dropped the computer under his arm like a rugby ball and, taking Alex's hand shook it firmly.

"Didn't want to lose this computer old boy, what's on its hard drive should pay the rent for a few years I'd imagine," announced a smiling Christian as he passed the PC to a grinning Alex.

The Hacker Hunter © Copyright Lionwing Ltd 2011

Chapter 25 – Earning a Pirate's Patch

The perfectly dried, flawlessly rolled dark brown leaves of a wide, well packed cigar ignited into a glow, the likes of which held an honest par with a warm summer sunset. The jet blue flame that had been used to initiate this delight was extinguished in an instant as the lid of the silver lighter from where its fuel originated snapped shut. Eugene turned the lighter over in his hand to reveal an inscription.

"To My Dearest Papa, Happy 60th, Love Maria," he read out softly. Taking a long deep drag on his now glowing cigar Eugene held in the smoke for a few extra seconds, seemly savouring the sensation and pleasant memories before gradually releasing a rich white cloud.

"Papa, do you have to smoke those things in the car whilst we are parked," coughed out Maria in protest. From her seat in the front of the executive Range Rover she turned to face the driver and ordered,

"Open your window driver, let some of Papa's smoke out will ya!"

The driver pressed a button on the dashboard and the air conditioning stepped up a notch. In sympathy with his daughter's request, Eugene, who was sat on the back seat cracked open his window to let some of the cigar smoke escape more rapidly. Also sat on the back seat between Eugene and Sonny was a barely conscious Bob, his hands and feet bound by silver duct tape. Eugene looked across at Bob to check he was still aware enough to hear him and then after taking a few puffs on his cigar, Eugene turned his head to look out of his window at the cold, early morning, empty streets of Pechory.

"Pechory… what a dive. Still, with the Estonian border only a few miles away I guess this is a good a place as any for a quiet exit from the Soviet." Eugene took another drag on his cigar, the glowing red embers and ash now firmly established before continuing, "It's pretty hard to enjoy this cigar when I can only breath through my mouth, you know. Despite having my nose taped back onto my god damn face, and being told that I'll need surgery, I find myself still sat here, in the back of a car, with you. That son, is fucking commitment, the sort of thing that many people of your generation lack!"

Bob, who was clearly struggling with his discomfort, replied in a half agonised whisper, "What's your point?"

"My point? My point is that I used to smoke a Cuban cigar that at one time was considered to be the most expensive cigar in the world! $18,846 for a box of forty, can you believe that? Reportedly these cigars were named after the chief of the Taino tribe, it was said that no other cigar on the face of the planet could rival them. I say it's down to what the individual looks for in a cigar that makes its reputation. Some men like to have a slow smoke that they can enjoy with a bottle or two of wine and good friends, others like a flavoured smoke that takes them to a comfortable place. Me, I like the fire, the red hot ash that never goes out. Now in my humble opinion, the best cigar for that job is 'His Majesty's Reserve'. The cigar is infused with a generous portion of Louis XIII Cognac, if you know anything about Cognac, Bob, you'll know it burns well. However one of these babies will cost you an unbelievable $750 US Dollars!

Eugene paused to take a long, hard drag on his cigar, as if to savour it for one last time and then turned to face Bob

"Hold him down Sonny," ordered Eugene in a malicious tone. Sonny placed his forearm into Bob's neck, forcing Bob's head into the headrest. Eugene then held the cigar like a dagger and turned his body to face Bob. With one sudden jab Eugene buried the burning cigar into Bob's right eye and twisted it in deep. Its searing heat burnt through Bob's eyelid and instantly hardboiled his eye to a state beyond any repair. Bob let out a blood curdling scream of sheer agony. The pain was horrendous, but much to Bob's terror not enough for him to lose consciousness and escape this torture.

Eugene sank back down into his seat and examined the remains of his cigar, softly he spoke,

"$750 a cigar and worth every, fucking, nickel".

Sonny opened his door and stepped out of the parked car. As he did so, the cold morning air rushed into the cabin, refreshing the otherwise sleep deprived New Yorkers. They had all travelled through the night to make it to the small Russian town of Pechory, the same town that Bob had picked Mac up from only days earlier. Sonny leant back into the car and grabbed Bob's arm,

"Ok, you're with me," spoke out Sonny as he prepared himself to hoist Bob across the seat and out onto the street. Sonny was a big man, a well built human tank descended from the hardy stock of New York dock workers, he needed little physical exertion to pull Bob out of the car. Sonny reached into his coat pocket and pulled out a flick knife. The blade flew open and locked into position with a sharp click. Leaning down to Bob's bound feat Sonny cut away the duct tape. It was very clear to Bob that despite being in his fifties, Sonny would be a match for any man in a straight up fight, and given Bob's current physical state there seemed little point in trying to resist.

The Hacker Hunter © Copyright Lionwing Ltd 2011

Bob attempted to stand, the cold morning air did little to help him other than sharpen the sense of the pain as it stung his burnt, weeping eye.

"I can't see," exclaimed Bob.

Eugene slid across the seat and looked up at Bob from the open doorway.

"You don't need to see. Sonny here will take you to meet your friend. This is where we get to find out if you've been lying or not. I don't mind telling you that Sonny has been ordered to shoot you unless your guy, Mac, can give us either the list of hackers or Cannon. So, no funny business, let's get this done so we can all leave this god forsaken country. Shut the door Sonny, and take this limey fuck for a walk."

Sonny swung the car door shut and gestured to Bob to get moving.

"You have to be kidding me! Even if Mac manages to make our rendezvous area on time, what makes you think he'll stop when he see's you next to me?" asked Bob.

"Hey, he's your buddy right, he'll stop," replied Sonny sluggishly.

"That's not the way it works in our business. We are not the mob," retorted Bob.

"What's that mean?" grunted Sonny?

"I'll let you work it out," snarled Bob through gritted, blood stained teeth.

Sonny looked down his nose at Bob, lifting his eyebrows as if to say 'who do you think you are talking too' but then, in a fleeting moment, elected to ignore Bob's antagonising comment.

"Come on you, get walking!" ordered Sonny.

Eugene, Maria and their driver watched as Sonny and Bob walked up the old road, away from the golden domes of St Barbara church and the Pechory Monastery, towards an old, red brick, five story water tower that stood proudly in the town centre. Maria, turning in her seat to face her father spoke out,

"Papa, do you think Sonny will be ok?"

The driver chuckled to himself, just loud enough for Maria to know that he thought her statement of concern for Sonny was totally unnecessary. Maria turned back to face the driver, whose chuckle had been interpreted more so as a ridicule than a reassurance. As her eyes met the driver's, he noticed a completely unexpected and sudden change in her expression. For within that split second, Maria had caught sight of a scruffily dressed man walking directly up to the driver side window. The approaching man's well worn grey trousers and the tatty black woollen jumper that was partially revealed under his open dirty blue duffle coat gave little indication that he was much more than an impoverished local. However, the approaching man's most distinguishing attribute was, without a shadow of doubt, a Walther P22 pistol, which had attached to it a long black silencer.

The window cracked into pieces as three bullets were fired through it and straight into the back of the driver's head. Maria, still speechless, was sprayed in the driver's blood, Eugene

The Hacker Hunter © Copyright Lionwing Ltd 2011

straightened, now rigid with the fear that something was about to happen to his beloved daughter he screamed,

"GET DOWN!"

Before Eugene could reach into his coat for his gun, the door that Sonny had dragged Bob from flung open and one Mr. John Mac slid across the back passenger seat and sunk the end of his silenced Walther into Eugene's the ribs.

"That will do, take your hand off the gun," ordered Mac.

Eugene, slowly pulled his hand out from his coat and asked,

"And who the fuck, are you?"

"You first," replied Mac.

The dead body of the driver had fallen sideways onto Maria. She pushed his heavy, limp carcass off with a rather annoyed shove. Wiping the blood from her eyes Maria screamed,

"Papa what's going on!?"

Eugene replied calmly, almost as if everything that had occurred was somehow planned and he was still in full control of the situation,

"Keep your head down baby girl, me and this fella have got some business to take care of,"

"Actually 'baby girl', put your hands on the dashboard. If you move I'm going to shoot you," ordered Mac.

Maria complied fully with Mac's orders, placing both hands flat down on the dashboard before her, she stretched out her long fingers and sank her beautifully manicured nails into its supple leather. There was something about Maria that just seemed to dull men's minds, Mac felt it pull on his concentration momentarily until Eugene blurted out,

"Oh great, another limey fuck, you must be Bob's partner in crime," stated Eugene sarcastically.

"You're an American?" replied a somewhat bemused Mac.

"No shit," Eugene responded abruptly.

"Let's keep this simple, who are you, and what do you want here in Russia?" demanded Mac.

"Listen to me, what the fuck is wrong with your buddy Bob? I mean that guy needs a double lobotomy and about ten rolls of rubber wallpaper for Christmas. Can you believe that Welsh fucker bit off half my fucking nose?" Eugene pointed to the surgical tape surrounding and attaching a mass of swollen, blood drenched flesh to the area you would usually expect to see a nose.

"Yeah, he will do that. Again, who are you and what do you want here in Russia?" repeated Mac, forcing the pistol deeper into Eugene's ribs.

"I want a good return on my investment. Right now that means the list of hackers, and Christian Cannon," answered Eugene with a modicum of discomfort to his voice.

"I wish I could help you yank but I don't have either, so I'll be on my way," answered Mac in an indifferent tone.

The Hacker Hunter © Copyright Lionwing Ltd 2011

"Don't BS me. My guy is going to shoot your buddy Bob dead in about two or three minutes from now. Bob hasn't a fucking clue, he thinks he's going to meet you. What, you think because I'm not British Intelligence I couldn't figure this out. I knew that you'd get here before Bob and check the place over first. I knew that you'd see us, I didn't think you'd shoot our driver but I knew that you and I would be sat on the backseat having this conversation," explained Eugene casually.

The pupils of Macs eyes narrowed, they held the hardness of black flint in appearance, with the coldness of death itself.

"Tell me something yank, did you foresee me shooting you two dead and then shooting that buffoon holding Bob?" asked Mac.

"Sure I did, but there's no way you'll reach Bob in time to save him. I however, just need to make one call and Bob is spared," Eugene smiled at Mac gleefully. He knew that Mac had no choice but to agree with him.

"What do you want?" asked Mac.

"I want the list of hackers and Christian Cannon," answered a smug Eugene.

Mac pulled the gun from Eugene's ribs and started to unscrew the silencer, in a reflective manner, Mac replied softly,

"If your guy shoots Bob, you lose any chance of getting Cannon and the hackers."

Eugene laughed, "If my guy shoots Bob I'm happy to say that loosing Cannon and the list of hackers is a price worth paying for the damage that fucker did to my nose."

Mac slowly unscrewed the silencer from the end of his pistol and then tucked both pistol and its baffle into his coat. Reaching over to Eugene, Mac opened the mafia bosses jacket and pulled from under Eugene's arm a dull, dark grey, Colt 45. Eugene put up no resistance to Mac taking his weapon but instead asked,

"Hey, you wouldn't leave a guy defenceless out here in the old USSR would you?"

Mac pulled back the slide which loaded and cocked Eugene's weapon,

"I'm going to shoot your baby girl in the head, unless you call your man back with Bob," announced Mac.

Placing the end of the barrel into the back of Maria's head Mac said softly,

"That type of bullshit might work on shopkeepers and whoever you mob boys think you can bully for cash but you're in the big leagues now. Call your man and ask him to bring back Bob," Mac's said as his trigger finger stretched out and then settled over the trigger once more.

Eugene went pale. Reaching into his jacket, he pulled out his cell phone and flipped it open. It took a few seconds to locate Sonny's number, he dialled, the phone just rang and rang.

"Looks like Sonny isn't answering," replied Eugene.

"Looks like your baby girl is dead," replied Mac in a whisper.

"Wait!" screamed out Eugene, "You might want to take a look out of the back window first."

Mac managed to keep the gun on Maria's head as he half turned his body on the seat to look through the cars rear window. Mac couldn't believe his eyes. Stood behind Eugene's car were ten or so, Russian Mafia men, all carrying AK74's and in amongst the middle of them was Sonny, who in turn was pointing a pistol at Bob's rather battered head.

"Oh, the fuck factor just kicked in. I did not see that coming," stated a seemingly impressed John Mac.

"Those boys came courtesy of a Russian business acquaintance who now lives in New York. You're out numbered. Give me the gun and let's do a swap," ordered Eugene.

"Good move," Mac announced. "Now here's how this is going to work. You see that silver Merc parked over there," Mac pointed to the car he was referring to. "On the back seat, you'll find a rather annoyed Christian Cannon, and next to him a black computer. The computer holds on its hard drive the list of fifty plus hackers, or so I'm told. Both are yours for Bob's life. However, there's a catch," Mac paused long enough for Eugene to interrupt.

"There's always a catch, let's hear it," he beckoned.

"The catch is I'm going to take your car and your daughter," continued Mac.

"What! No fucking way!" yelled Eugene.

"It's the only way to guarantee that you will not go back on the deal. Now lower your window and call the guy holding Bob over to the side of the car," instructed Mac.

Eugene reached down to open his door.

"I'm going to leave the car, don't do anything stupid whilst I'm away," said Eugene sternly.

Eugene stepped out of the car and walked over to Sonny. Mac could see the two men talking and then Eugene pointed to the silver Merc. Lowering his weapon Sonny ordered two of the men to the car to retrieve whatever was in it. As Mac had promised, the two men opened the door and pulled from the back seat a rather annoyed Christian Cannon and a black box. Christian had silver duct tape wrapped around his legs, arms and mouth, which made it impossible for him to stand unaided.

Sonny pushed Bob towards the car that Mac and Maria were sat in. Mac kept the gun firmly placed on the back of Maria's head as Sonny opened the back passenger door and slung Bob in. Bob adjusted himself and then, looking with his one good eye at Mac said,

"I guess that's what you'd call an eye for an eye. Sorry boss."

"More like an eye for a nose, you sick fuck. Any-hoot, it's good to see you by the way," Mac said with a slight smile immerging from under his Viking moustache.

Eugene lent in through the still open car door, his face was pale and his eyes held no secrets that he was worried about his daughter.

"Ok, listen to me. Sonny is going to take Maria's place, you have my word we will not follow you," Eugene reasoned.

"Like I said pal, you are playing in the big leagues now, she'll come to no harm. I'll send her back to you in ten minutes or so, just make sure your still here," Mac replied confidently.

Sonny walked around to the driver's door and opened it, he pulled the drivers body out and sat in the drivers seat.

"I'll be driving if it's all the same to you," Sonny said as he started the engine.

"Don't make an enemy of me," Eugene growled at Mac just before shutting the passenger door.

As the car pulled away, Eugene walked over to Cannon. A man was trying to cut the tape from Cannon's mouth but it was so tightly wrapped around Cannon's head that the operation was proving to be quite troublesome.   Eugene took the knife from the man and with little regard for Christian slid it up past the back of Cannon's ear and with a vigorous thrust cut through the tape. Cannon peeled the tape free, wincing as it pulled his hair and then shouted out,

"You have to stop that car, Mac still has Alex!"

"Who the fuck is Alex?" asked a rather disgruntled Eugene.

"He's the hacker we need to take back to the NSA," replied Cannon desperately.

"I don't care who he is, whilst Mac has my daughter, we wait!"

Other than the occasional order from Mac for Sonny to steer the car left or right, there was utter silence in the vehicle. Maria could feel the cold steel of the gun on the back of her skull, a feeling she was clearly unhappy about. After about seven or eight minutes of driving, Mac ordered Sonny to stop the car. As Sonny pulled over, Mac took the gun from Maria's head, and pointed it at Sonny,

"Ok, get out of the car big fella," ordered Mac.

Sonny turned the engine off and opened the door, Mac continued,

"Take your coat off and give me your weapons."

Sonny silently did as Mac instructed, throwing an impressive array of knives, knuckle dusters and two pistols, one from his jacket and one from his ankle holster.

"Ok Bob, can you walk?" asked Mac coldly.

"Yes boss," replied Bob.

"Good, get out. This is where we change rides," ordered Mac.

As Mac and Bob left the car, Sonny raised his hands in the air and stepped away from the driver's side door.

"My boss is a powerful man. You can shoot me, but if you lay a hand on his daughter, there ain't a place in the world you'll be safe," spoke out Sonny.

"Relax big man, no-one is getting shot here. The exchange is done, we'll be on our way. I have a message for your boss, be sure to deliver it. Tell him, welcome to the big leagues, be safe," Mac winked at Sonny and after taking Sonny's weapons signalled for Sonny to get back in the car and leave.

The Hacker Hunter © Copyright Lionwing Ltd 2011

As Sonny and Maria drove off, Mac started walking towards an old Lada 1600. On reaching the vehicle, he pulled open the back door, and lying there unconscious and bound in duct tape was Mr. Alexander Khomenko. Bob, just able to see Alex through his good eye said,

"I see you've kept a Russian memento, and it's not a Matryoshka doll."

"Aye, you might say that, now let's get this guy back to Sir Adam," laughed out Mac.

"What about Cannon and the list of hackers?" asked Bob.

"I'm sure we'll be seeing Mr. Cannon and his business partners soon enough," replied Mac.

"So next stop Sir Adam's?" asked Bob.

"Aye, for me mate. For you on the other hand, the next stop is an Estonian hospital," Mac replied.

"I'm good boss," Bob replied.

"Bob, you're good for nothing with just one eye. How the fuck did you get yourself into that situation? Apart from costing me the list of hackers and the price tag on Cannon's head, you went and started a fight with some nutter with a Napoleon complex! What did I teach you? Always be the grey man. Was it really necessary to bite of his nose?" Mac said scornfully.

"If I'm good for nothing, why did you trade me for Cannon and the list of hackers?" asked Bob who was genuinely curious as to why Mac had taken action with a non-tactical advantage.

"Governments and money come and go, friends and family they are for life," Mac winked.

"Shut up, you're starting to sound like that Mafia nutter," Bob laughed out joyfully.

"Aye, that may well be Bob. If it's any consolation, I think I'll still get a chance to kill Cannon before this is over and make the bonus," Mac announced.

"How are you going to do that?" Bob asked mystified.

"What, and ruin the surprise? Just get your eye fixed up, come on, let's get out of here pronto!" laughed out Mac.

Chapter 26 – The London Hotel

Christian Cannon stepped out of the shower. The cold white marble beneath his bare feet provided him with that cooling reassurance that he was now firmly back in civilization. Dripping with water he reached for one of the perfectly folded, fluffy white towels that had been hung neatly over a chrome towel rail. Before he could start to dry himself properly, Christian was distracted by the bathroom door swinging open. Stood there in the bathroom doorway was the slender, petite figure of Maria. She held in her arms some neatly folded clothes.

"I love your Oxford Street," she spoke out playfully.

Christian modestly covered his groin with the towel and replied,

"How did you get in?"

Maria winked and walked into the bathroom, placing the clothes next to one of the two luxury wash basins, she replied,

"Daddy is with one of my London based hackers, they are trying to decipher the password that your friend Alex used to encrypt the list of hackers. They've been at it for hours, so I thought I'd do a little shopping, rather than waiting around."

"You girls are all the same at heart, how do you know they will fit me?" asked Cannon who had turned his back to Maria to bashfully fasten the towel around his waist.

"They'll fit, I thought you might like a fresh change of clothes. We left Russia in such a hurry," she replied softly.

"Did you talk to your father about trading a copy of the list for Alex?" asked Cannon?

"Why are you so sure we need him?" replied Maria.

Cannon turned to face Maria. He stopped to observe that four of the buttons on her white blouse were undone. These unfastened buttons had allowed for an opening, just wide enough to reveal the side of her creamy white, perfectly rounded, braless breast. Seeing that Cannon had become transfixed on her Maria slowly slid her hand down her thigh to the hem of her short black skirt.

"I did a little bit of shopping for myself as well. Do you like it?" she teased.

It was clear to Maria that Cannon was losing the ability to talk as his male desires started to override his ability to think.

"What else did you buy?" asked Cannon, whilst he diverted his gaze to her stocking covered legs.
Maria turned and walked out of the bathroom, her high heels tapped on the white marble as she left for the bedroom.

Cannon exhaled a torrent of air from his lungs and then gasped as if he had just been released by her spell. He reached over for a second towel and started drying himself. The clothes that Maria had left behind were simple: black trousers, a black shirt, socks, but no underwear. 'That's odd," Cannon thought to himself.

Cannon picked up the clothes and started to walk toward the bathroom door, as he did he asked,

"Maria, you forgot to buy the underwear?"

As Cannon entered the bedroom, he dropped the clothes on the floor in shock at finding Maria sat on the bed and rested up against the headboard. One of her legs was stretched out over the bed and the other was brought up to her chest, causing her skirt to ride right up to her hips.

"I don't buy underwear, Chris, as you can see," she replied flirtatiously, whilst sliding her hand down to her exposed and perfectly shaved Brazilian.

"I thought you were blonde?" gulped Christian.

With no warning there was a furious knock at the hotel room door. Maria, who was startled by the unexpected noise, jumped off the bed and pulled her skirt back down to her knees.

"It's my dad!" she yelped out.

"Quick get in the bathroom," ordered Cannon, like a school boy who was about to be caught by a livid father, who was determined on saving his only daughter's chastity.

Maria darted into the bathroom and pulled the door closed, leaving a small crack for her to look through. Cannon looked down at the towel covering his now protruding manhood.

"Great, now I have to answer the door like this," Cannon announced.

Walking to the door, Cannon used one hand to push down his member and the other to reach for the handle and pull open the door. With both hands occupied, Cannon had absolutely no defence for the oncoming blow of Sonny's fist, which landed flat on Cannon's forehead. Cannon was jolted backward from the impact and landed flat on his ass. Sonny, who took up most of the doorway, stepped into the room allowing space for a fuming Eugene to enter.

"What are you playing at!?" Eugene demanded.

Cannon, who was still stunned by the blow to his head looked up at Eugene and in a bewildered state replied,

"Fuck, talk about over protective!"

Eugene thrust a sheet of paper in front of Cannon's eyes and screamed,

"I paid you your deposit, I saved your fucking ass, flew you out of Russia and put you up in a five star hotel for this!" screamed Eugene still waving the sheet of paper in Cannon's face.

Cannon snatched the paper from Eugene and began to read, it was some sort of receipt for army boots, issued from... Cannon's eyes widened as he read the words 'United States of America Moscow Embassy'.

"It's the order for a pair of boots that Alex made whilst hacking the NSA network," exclaimed Cannon.

"What it ain't, is a fucking list of hackers!" yelled back Eugene.

"What?" stated a rather confused Christian.

"Me and Maria's hacker have spent hours going through that computer you pulled out of Moscow, there is nothing on it, no list of hackers, that much is for sure," Eugene replied, this time more calmly.

"Are you sure?" questioned Cannon.

Eugene glared down at Cannon and then straightened his back. Turning to Sonny, he ordered,

"Chop this limey fuck's balls off."

Maria burst into the room from her concealed vantage point, screaming she said,

"No, Papa, wait!"

Eugene's eyebrows lifted in disbelief, Sonny cupped his hands over his mouth and gasped in shock like an old fisherman's wife. Raising a finger at Cannon in utter flaming, speechless wrath, Eugene's lips tightened and his face changed from displaying pure hate to a mix of heartbroken betrayal.

"It's not like it looks Papa, I was just bringing him some clothes, I been shopping!" screamed Maria.

Cannon stood to his feet, placing a calming hand on Maria's arm he spoke out,

"It doesn't matter where in the world you Italians come from, New York or Rome you are always waving your bloody hands around in the air and getting over emotional. Can we please gear this down a little bit?"

Surprisingly enough, nobody replied to Cannon's comment so Christian elected to keep talking,

"Listen, I know that Alex got the list of hackers because I was stood outside the vault that contained the bloody supercomputer that got them. There was some sort of intercom system, rigged up, I don't know if it was meant to be heard from outside but

The Hacker Hunter © Copyright Lionwing Ltd 2011

Mac and I clearly heard the computer talk about some sort of hack that Alex had run. Alecto project, I think it was called, something about downloading it to..." Cannon stopped speaking as he realised what Alex had done.

"Of course!" exclaimed Cannon. "How could I have been so fucking stupid!"

Cannon looked at a mystified Eugene and then turned to look back at Maria,

"Maria, I need you to get your best hackers to work, I need you to find the home address of one, Sir Frank Adam!" ordered Cannon excitedly.

Cannon then walked up to Eugene and with no more than a fists distance from his face said,

"My good man, if you want the list of hackers we are going to need to rescue Alex first!"

Chapter 27 – Mac earns his bonus

The wheels of a black Range Rover quietly rolled to a stop just a few meters away from a tall, sturdily built, wrought iron gate. The gate must have been over nine feet in height and wide enough to allow any vehicle to pass through when fully opened. The engine of the vehicle fell silent and, save the noise of three car doors clunking open, the stillness of the night remained unbroken. As the headlights of the Range Rover dimmed to nothingness, the three figures of Christian Cannon, Sonny and Eugene emerged from the vehicle. Walking towards the gates, Cannon inspected their hinges. They were sunk deep into an equally high sandstone surround that merged into a thick red brick wall. The wall seemed to vanish out into the darkness, leaving no clued as to its length.

Peering through the railings of the gate, Cannon could just make out the silhouettes of two men walking towards them. Eugene pointed upwards, gesturing to Cannon that they were being observed by several CCTV cameras, bolted high up into the surrounding masonry. Cannon strained his eyes to look further past the gates. Behind the two men stood a dimly lit gatehouse and parked next to this small building was the shadowy shape of a motionless vehicle.

As the two men came closer, Cannon could just make out from the dim light of the moon that they were both dressed in dark, matching Royal Navy style jumpers and black trousers. 'They have to be Sir Adam's security guards, more than likely Ex-SAS or SBS boys,' thought Christian to himself.

Both guards reached the gate together; one raised a hefty Maglite torch, and with a click shone it into Cannon's face.

Cannon raised a hand to shield his eyes from the bright beam and spoke out,

"My name is Christian Cannon, my business associates and I am here to see Sir Adam."

The gates clinked, and then slowly and silently began to open inwards. Both guards stepped through the opening to meet Christian, the guard holding the torch spoke,

"You and your business associate Eugene are expected Sir, this way to the gatehouse." The guard beckoned Christian forward and then continued, "We have a vehicle waiting to drive you up to the manor house, please ask your driver to remain at the gate with his car."

Sonny turned to face Eugene and in a concerned whisper exclaimed,

"I don't like the idea of that boss, I'm coming with you."

Impressed with Sonny's loyalty, Eugene gave an affectionate grin and whispered back ,

"Let's just stick to Christians plan for the moment, if I'm not back in a few hours, you know what to do."

Eugene placed his hands into the pockets of his long coat and broke into a rigid jog to catch up with Christian. Turning his head back towards Sonny, Eugene grinned, and with a quick wink chuckled out in a nervously playful tone,

"Hey, Sonny. Keep the engine running, there's a good man."

The Hacker Hunter © Copyright Lionwing Ltd 2011

Sonny whispered to himself, "There's a good man? What he's a British lord now?"

Christian and Eugene were escorted to the gatehouse. It was an old building, its sandstone walls held a musty, damp odour that could only be achieved over centuries of use. Sat at a table was a third guard, he was watching a wall of monitor screens, each screen was hooked into a multitude of CCTV cameras that were obviously placed in and around the estate. Eugene pointed to one of the screens to see Sonny getting back into the car. Cannon was more occupied with one of the guards, who had started to pat him down for concealed weapons. Eugene stiffened up as he felt the second guard place a hand on his back. The guard proceeded to perform a search that included going through each of Eugene's pockets, pulling a cell phone and a pen from Eugene's coat the guard said,

"We'll keep hold of these for you, Sir."

Cannon and Eugene didn't utter a word of protest, there was something about their situation that leant itself to total compliance. The guard watching the security screens stood up from his seat and reached across to a wooden rack of key hooks fastened to the wall. Cannon observed that each hook had short descriptions written below: 'stores room 1', 'armoury', 'Landie 1', 'Landie 2' and then stopped reading as the guard lifted a set of car keys from a hook titled 'Landie 3'.

"I'll drive them up to the house, take over here,' ordered the guard.

Christian and Eugene followed the guard out of the building and towards the dark shape of a now more visibly recognisable Land Rover. Stopping at the driver's door, the guard gestured for both men to get into the vehicle. Cannon pulled open the rear door and climbed into the back seat, he slid across to the far side of the car, allowing enough room for Eugene to follow him in.

The car headlights followed the twisting private road, giving little clue as to where they were going. Even though it was dark, the moon gave just enough light for Cannon to spot a small lake in amongst the trees to his right. Eugene gasped and jabbed Cannon in the arm. Cannon turned from looking out of his own window to find Eugene transfixed on a grand old manor house. A warm yellow light emanated from every one of the manor's tall, elegant windows, illuminating the driveway.

"That is one impressive pad," Eugene spoke out briefly.

Cannon didn't reply, he sat back in his seat and tried to stop his heart from pounding out of his ribcage as it raced with adrenaline at the thought of what he knew he had to do to get Alex back.

The Land Rover pulled to a stop outside an already open front door, Eugene was the first to step out. He was greeted by a rather distinguished looking man, akin to a butler in uniform. Christian cracked open his door and stepped out next, the cool night air and decadent surroundings provided a moment of pleasure that calmed his previously hammering heart.

"Sir Adam is expecting you both, if you would be kind enough to follow me through to the sitting room," asked the extremely well spoken butler.

"I got to get one of these for back home! What's a butler work for?" asked at truly impressed Eugene.

"If by that statement you are inquiring to the remuneration of a butler, I regret to inform you that I am unable to assist you with

The Hacker Hunter © Copyright Lionwing Ltd 2011

that information as I, Sir, am a gentleman's gentleman, and not a butler," rebuffed the man snobbishly.

"Ok, what does a gentleman's gentleman work for?" asked Eugene.

"A gentleman, Sir," replied the butler, in a fashion that indicated that Eugene didn't qualify.

Eugene turned to face Cannon and pulling the longest of frowns, as if to indicate, 'What a snob' and then whispered to Christian,

"Fag!"

Cannon obviously found the tension between Eugene and this rather pompous butler entertaining, he smiled at the 'gentleman's gentleman' and then followed him in to the main house. The main entrance hall left no room for scepticism about the authenticity of their host's linage. The crests, the old furnishings and the stunning craftsmanship left both Eugene and Cannon speechless. Upon reaching the sitting room, Christian found himself surprised to feel an unexpected but warm reassurance at seeing Sir Adam. Standing next to his PA, Grace, who was warming her knees by the open fire, Sir Adam grinned ear to ear at the sight of Cannon approaching.

"Christian, how good it is to see you my boy. This must be the infamous Eugene," Sir Adam announced whilst extending a hand to Christian. Cannon grabbed Sir Adam's hand and shook it hard, it was clear to Eugene that both men shared a respect for each other and a fondness. As Sir Adam approached Eugene with the same outstretched hand his mouth fell open,

"My god man, your nose, you should be in a hospital!"

Eugene felt his nose and then, smiling he said, "Sometimes in our line of work we have to deal with animals."

"Yes, rather, still an eye for an eye and all that," remarked Sir Adam sternly.

Christian and Eugene both realised that Sir Adam was obviously fully briefed as to what had occurred in Russia, which to Cannon's mind must mean that Mac had made it out alive with Alex and Bob.

"You must be weary after your flight from St. Petersburg, I'm told you were late arriving, still I always find the rooms in the Landmark Hotel so refreshing after a long flight. Would either of you care for some tea?" asked Sir Adam candidly.

"We haven't come here for tea," snarled back Eugene, who had chosen to ignore Sir Adam's display of power play.

"Very good, no tea then," Sir Adam looked past Eugene at the butler who was stood by the sitting room door awaiting further instruction. "We will call you, Howard, if we need you," Sir Adam said, dismissing him from the room.

Grace walked from her position in front of the fire place and moved towards a tall door that clearly opened to an adjoining room. Leaning down to grasp the door knob she twisted and then pushed, as the door opened, Cannon's heart felt the cold dagger of adrenaline at the sight of John Mac. Mac's eyes met with Christian's, their cold icy blue stare cut into Cannon's very soul. Cannon knew with every fibre of his being that Mac was intent on killing him.

"How's your buddy Bob doing?" remarked Eugene.

Mac ignored the question, but instead walked backwards into the adjoining room. Grace followed Mac and Sir Adam gestured for Eugene and Cannon to follow Grace. Eugene's jaw fell open as he stepped into what was obviously an old library. Every wall was covered, floor to ceiling, in pristine mahogany bookshelves, each shelf was packed solid with leather bound books, which provided an eclectic mix of ivory, green and red colours. This collection of old, majestic books, seemed to fill the room with a type of aged warmth for Cannon, warmth that was added to when he observed, sat at the end of a long dark oak reading table one Mr. Alexander Khomenko.

Stood next to Alex's seat was Robert. There was no question that Robert was the most uneasy of the party, as he nervously looked at Cannon. Sir Adam stretched out his hands and lifting them up and down several times gestured for everyone to take a seat at the table. Grace sat to the right of Alex and Robert pulled a chair up and sat to Alex's left. Christian nodded at Eugene, signalling that it was ok to sit, and then pulled one of the old oak chairs out from the table and sat next to Grace. Sir Adam took a seat at the head of the table directly facing Alex. Eugene, who had still not taken a seat, looked over at Mac,

"Does he need to be here?" asked Eugene nervously, before taking a seat.

Mac walked around the table and stood but a few meters behind Cannon, feeling Mac's eyes on the back of his head Cannon turned to face Sir Adam and said,

"Frank, I am here to finalise our business agreement. If you recall I wanted you to help with an introduction to the NSA? We have obtained a list of 52 hackers that have gained unlawful access to their military network and we'd like to help them clean it up, so to speak."

The Hacker Hunter © Copyright Lionwing Ltd 2011

"You'd like me to broker a defence contract with the NSA?" confirmed Sir Adam in a puzzled tone.

Choosing to ignore the strange manner with which Sir Adam had responded, Cannon looked across the table to Robert. Robert looked nervously back and uneasily shuffled in his chair, still looking at Robert, Cannon continued,

"Yes, I need you to broker the deal. You see, it's all about who you can trust in this game," Cannon looked at Robert knowingly and then turned his head slowly back to Sir Adam. "I'm sure you understand me, Sir Adam," stated Cannon in a tone that seemed to hold two meanings.

"Whom to trust is always key, in any negotiation. You really have a list of 52 hackers?" asked Sir Adam.

"I have the list, but I need Alex," replied Christian calmly.

"From what Mac tells me, Alex is a rather high value commodity at the moment, the developer of an artificial intelligence cyber weapon, or something like that. What makes you think we'd give him over to you?" asked Sir Adam reasonably.

"Simply put, Frank, I am willing to give the NSA just 50 of the 52 hackers on the list in exchange for Alex,", offered Cannon.

"Really, why just fifty?" Sir Adam looked over at Robert and then back at Christian as if to give Cannon a clue as to the fact he knew what was coming next.

"You know why, two of the hackers are British, to be more precise: British Intelligence. I don't think the Americans will appreciate being spied on by their allies, do you?" asked Cannon.

"So, you are saying,, if we give you Alex, you'll ensure that the list is doctored? That only works if you have the list. Tell me Christian, where exactly do you have this list?" Sir Adam asked.

Eugene lent back in his chair and lifted his hand to his mouth as if to wipe his lips but instead, changing his mind elected to slam his hand down on the tables' surface in protest.

"What do you think? Of course we have the list. Cut the crap!" Eugene barked out.

"What do I think?" repeated Sir Adam. Looking over at Mac, he continued "John, perhaps you'd like to explain to Christian and Eugene what I think?"

John Mac walked close enough to Cannon's chair to place his hand on its back and, leaning down to face Cannon, he spoke softly,

"Christian Cannon, international multi-media designer and marketing executive, owner of two businesses, one is a multi-media design agency, the other is a research and development software company based in Italy, Venice to be more accurate. Did I miss anything?"

Cannon looked over at Sir Adam and replied, "No, that's pretty much what I have on the CV. Apart from a small division of my R & D company that provides software solutions that help to ensure data security," retorted Cannon.

"Software solutions that help ensure data security?" questioned Mac curiously.

The Hacker Hunter © Copyright Lionwing Ltd 2011

"Yes, it's a rather new division. It works very simply: my boys will hack your company, and for a price we'll show you how we did it and how to ensure it doesn't happen again," answered Cannon.

"If they don't buy your service Cannon, what then?" interrupted Robert, who until now had been sat quietly listening.

"Oh they buy, they buy all right. My baby girl is in the same line of work," interrupted Eugene with a sinister snigger.

Robert returned a rather disgruntled glance at Eugene.

"Found a new way to extort money, have you? Let's drop this stupid game," stated Robert abruptly.

Sir Adam's otherwise calm face dropped as he faced Eugene,

"Tell me Eugene, where is your 'dear daughter' tonight? Could she not join us?"

"She's indisposed," Eugene smiled back cheekily at Sir Adam.

"Mac, please continue," requested Sir Adam.

Mac took his hand off the back of Cannon's chair and walked over to stand behind Alex. Looking over at Cannon he said,

"The night I drove Cannon and Khomenko back to their apartment in Moscow, I listened in to their conversation. Anyone reading the transcript will know that Alex explained how hackers use servers connected to the internet and left in empty flats and houses around the world. These servers are remotely accessed by each other, with only one actually having the hacker sat physically in front of it. The trick is in isolating that one server. What the transcript will not tell you, is that Cannon's flat in Moscow is also used as a place to house a server. All night long I heard tapping, the tapping of fingers on a keyboard. Alex was using the server to access his lab and develop a code, a code that would help him isolate the hackers and build a list of their 52 different locations. Isn't that right Alex?" asked Mac.

Alex turned to look at Mac and then replied,

"I needed time to develop an application that would work with the OAI, I couldn't just write the code in the hackers den, we did not have enough time."

Eugene peered at Alex blankly and asked "OAI?"

Mac replied "Organic Artificial Intelligence, the Russians had managed to cultivate a human brain and were developing it as some kind of cyber weapon."

"You never told me this!" exclaimed a rather annoyed looking Eugene to Christian.

Cannon didn't reply, he just watched Mac as he left Alex and walked to stand back behind him.

"Alex didn't just need time to develop the software application, he also needed time to run it. That night he managed to gain access to the lab's network where he then installed and started his program. He then took Cannon to the hackers den the next morning, not to write or run the code but to simply access the lab and use the program that was already hacked into the NSA network and hard at work building the list of hackers. The OIA must have cut through the NSA encryption cleaner than a wire cuts through cheese. Within minutes, he had managed to access the US Embassy in Moscow. Alex proved to Cannon that he was hacked in by ordering a pair of army boots and having them express delivered to their location. When Alex emerged with the computer from the hackers den, Cannon naturally assumed the computer had the list on it."

"I never said they were on the computer!" interrupted Alex.

"Тише," replied Cannon in Russian.

"Telling Alex to be silent will not help you Cannon, the truth is the OAI was still building the list of hackers even after you and Alex escaped the hackers den," stated Mac confidently.

"Then tell me Mac, where is the list of hackers?" requested Cannon.

Mac leant down, speaking directly into Cannon's ear he uttered "Downloading to Venice regional IP address."

"I don't get it?" spoke out Eugene.

"Like I said right at the beginning, Christian Cannon, owner of two businesses: one is a multi-media design agency, the other is a research and development software company based in Italy," Mac straightened himself and looked over to Robert as if to signal it was his time to take the floor.

"Before you'd even got to your hotel, GCHQ had hacked your office server in Venice, downloaded a copy of the list and then deleted the original," Robert concluded smugly.

The Hacker Hunter © Copyright Lionwing Ltd 2011

Eugene looked over at Cannon, the rage from within causing him to scream "Cannon, you fuck! You've walked us into a trap!"

Mac pulled from the back of his trousers a .22 pistol, placing it into the back of Cannon's head he said, "Time to earn my bonus!"

Eugene turned a shade of pale, and in disbelief faced Sir Adam, "You're not going to blow his brains out, right here, over the table?"

Sir Adam smiled, "I would have thought that you of all people, Eugene, would know that the .22 pistol Mac is using will just result in the bullet entering and bouncing around Cannon's skull. It's powerful enough to kill him, but I assure you his brains will not come bursting out. This table is an antique."

Cannon's head had been forced down so it rested flat against the table surface. Mac dug the pistol barrel into the thin, hair covered flesh of Cannon's cranium. Mac looked over to Sir Adam for final confirmation. Cannon spoke,

"Mac we were both stood at the window listening to Professor Faverski talk to the OAI, sure, I agree you heard it say downloading project Alecto to a server based in Venice, but what makes you think you have the real list," pleaded Cannon.

Robert replied to Cannon's question, "Because your guess about the list holding the locations of two hackers working for British Intelligence was 100% right."

Grace stood up, "Frank, what the hell!"

"Sit down, Grace," ordered Sir Adam.

Grace sat back down, "He's made it this far. What about the job? He's better than anyone we've come across!"

"The position is closed, Grace." Sir Adam pushed his fingers together to create a temple and then, with a solemn tone spoke out the words, "Earn your bonus, Mac."

The Hacker Hunter © Copyright Lionwing Ltd 2011

Chapter 28 – Gladio

Mac looked down at Cannon, who surprisingly enough was putting up no resistance to the fact that there was a gun pushed into the back of his head. Everyone around the table watched in pure astonishment, as Cannon spoke out with iceberg coolness,

"You are right, I was bluffing about there being two British Intelligence hackers on the list. It was a guess based on Pavel telling me that there were also two Russians on the same list. If the Russians were hacked into the NSA, it's very likely that we would be as well. Pavel told me this in an attempt to win me over to his side as a double agent. He also told me who my contact would be in your organisation, in other words, the name of the spy in your circle."

"Pavel was lying, he couldn't have had the list, shoot him," ordered Robert, whilst standing suddenly from his seated position.

Curious to see any reaction to Roberts' outburst Mac looked over to Sir Adam, only to observe him thoughtfully staring at Robert. It was clear that everyone in the room found Robert's statement somewhat out of place with his usual contributions.

"Cannon knows nothing Mac, proceed," ordered Sir Adam coldly.

Mac stared back down at Cannon, allowing a few seconds for Sir Adam to change his mind. In this brief pause Cannon took in a deep breath and on its release calmly spoke once more,

"Gladio Super NATO, CCWU number 472, activation code 9777, immediate directive 01: Grace."

Without flinching, Mac loosened his grip on Cannon, raising his pistol, Mac turned to face Grace and fired, one, two, three shots straight into her forehead. Grace collapsed to the floor. There was absolute silence in the library as Alex, Robert, Eugene and Sir Adam looked at Mac in total disbelief.

"What the hell just happened?" asked Eugene, who was the first to react.

Cannon pushed himself back up from the table surface, standing to addressed Robert he alleged, "You know, don't you Robert?"

Mac aimed the pistol back at Cannons head "An explanation please, Cannon," he ordered.

Sir Adam slowly rose from his chair and sluggishly walked past Mac and Cannon to stand by Grace's motionless body. Kneeling down next to the head of his dear, old friend, Sir Adam reached down with his hand to pointlessly feel for a pulse. In a bewildered state, Sir Adam turned his head slowly up to face Mac.

"Lower your weapon, Mac," he said softly, in an almost disillusioned and defeated manner. Swallowing hard in an attempt to suppress a welling emotion of rage, Sir Adam asked, "What the hell is going on?"

Mac was reluctant to lower the pistol pointed at Cannon's head, instead he elected to walk around Cannon, circling him like a lion stalking its prey.

"Like I said, an explanation please, Cannon," Mac repeated.

Cannon took a quick glance down at Sir Adam who was clearly in shock. Sir Adam stood up, his pity turned to rage.

"I asked you the question Mac, now fucking answer it!" Sir Adam bellowed.

Mac lowered his pistol, responding to Sir Adam's demand with, "Gladio is part of a clandestine NATO based initiative, funded in part by the CIA. It was originally created to act much like the French resistance did in the Second World War. In the event of the Russians invading Western Europe, members of Gladio would cause disruption, perform targeted assassinations and so on. As you can imagine, certain members of Gladio would be placed into positions of political influence and power over infrastructure, others would be recruited from Special Forces and intelligence organisations. Gladio, however, is just the Italian branch, you've got Absalon in Denmark, in Greece LOK, in the Netherlands I&O, in Norway ROC and the list goes on."

"Why is Grace dead?" asked Sir Adam in a confused tone.

"Cannon issued an authorisation code for her immediate execution, without question," replied Mac.

"Are you saying that you belong to this clandestine NATO organisation?" asked Sir Adam.

Mac ignored Sir Adam's question. Lifting the gun once more, he pointed it at Cannon's head and demanded,

"Now for the last time, explain what's going on, otherwise I'll be issuing a few immediate directive 01s myself."

"This is a CIA funded Gladio operation, my brief is to infiltrate Eugene's organisation and win his absolute trust," Cannon replied reluctantly.

Mac moved closer to Cannon, still with the gun pointed at Christian's head, Mac asked "For what purpose, why would Gladio be interested in an Italian American mobster?"

"Eugene's daughter Maria, had in fact managed to hack the NSA network, but not through some weakness in their firewall. It turns out the mob's influence reached all the way into the US Army, to be more precise, the tech bods maintaining the field servers used to access the military network."

"That's bullshit," interrupted Eugene with an air of angry absurdity to his statement.

"A technically minded US communications officer, working from a field server in the desert was the first to discover what was going on," Cannon explained, pausing to observe that he had the undivided attention of everyone in the room. "The officer kept wondering why the speakers on his hand radio would crackle every now and then, seemingly for no apparent reason. It was much like the way your stereo speakers crackle when you walk by it with your mobile phone. After a bit of playing around, the officer discovered that the interference was being caused by what looked like an ordinary printer port, screwed into the back of the field server. The device was removed and after some investigation it turned out to be a type of mobile phone modem. It was linked into the computer's motherboard, transmitting and receiving information to and from the same satellites we use to carry our mobile phone signals. The disguised modem had been added to the server by corrupted military IT engineers that were on Eugene's payroll. This is how Maria gained access to the NSA, not through some clever hack."

The Hacker Hunter © Copyright Lionwing Ltd 2011

"Fuck you Cannon! You are full of it, you would say anything to save your neck," hissed out Eugene.

"Here's the thing," Cannon continued, "Maria was hoping to prove to the NSA how vulnerable they were, but what she actually did was open them up to attack in the first place. Before long, her secret was discovered by every government hacked into the satellite network. Cannon paused again, and then, looking over at Eugene, he continued, "The Army IT boys that Eugene had used to plant the devices couldn't just fly around the world unplugging the modems. Eugene realised that he had opened his country's defences to the world unintentionally, whilst in the pursuit of a billion dollar defence contract. So to help ease Daddy's guilt, Maria elected to run her own cleanup operation by finding the hackers and finding some mug that would be willing to present the problem to the NSA. Therein, enter stage right, yours truly. Unbeknown to Eugene, I am actually a Gladio cell leader sent by the CIA to bring him and his family to justice!"

"You two faced, good for nothing fuck!" yelled Eugene, "You, you're a fucking dead man!"

Mac turned to point the pistol at Eugene, "Sit the fuck down," he ordered. Eugene gritted his teeth and after an evil, revenge filled glare at Cannon, elected to sit back down.

"That doesn't explain to me why Grace has been shot in the bloody head!" shouted out Sir Adam.

Cannon glanced at a nervous looking Robert. "Like I said, Robert knows," Cannon repeated.

The Hacker Hunter © Copyright Lionwing Ltd 2011

Sir Adam's face changed to a stone like expression. "Robert, how did you know Cannon had been captured by Pavel, even I didn't know that?" he asked.

Robert started to walk towards the door of the library, "Even you aren't stupid enough to shoot a SIS director," spoke out Robert as he placed his hand on the door knob.

Sir Adam reached over to Mac with his outstretched hand, Mac happily passed Sir Adam the pistol. Pointing the gun at Robert, Sir Adam mulled over the words in his mind before addressing him.

"Are you sure?" Sir Adam announced frostily.

Robert lowered his hand from the door and turned towards Sir Adam. Seemingly toying with the idea of giving Sir Adam the truth, Robert looked down and then, returning his gaze, he answered Sir Adam in a surprisingly compassionate tone.

"Some secrets are better left with the dead," Robert paused and then straighten himself to his full height. "We've known about Grace for years. She never knew that we had discovered she was sending messages to the Russians. Messages that gave us an idea as to what our Cold War enemies were interested in, and of course what you, Sir Adam, were up to. Do you recall the night you lost your wife and son in a foiled assassination attempt? How do you think we got to you so quickly? Grace had given your whereabouts that evening to a hit team. You'd been getting to close to uncovering a Russian spy circle in MI5 and they wanted you dead. By the time we deciphered the message, it was too late to save your family. We could never tell you: losing Grace would have meant the loss of an exceptional insight into their plans. So you see, Sir Adam, Grace was your spy. The only remaining question is, why did Cannon issue a directive 01?"

Sir Adam lowered the gun, it was clear to every man in the room that he was incapacitated with grief. In one foul swoop he had discovered the traitor that had caused the death of his beloved wife and son had all the time been one of his closest friends. Canon ordering the execution of Grace had done little to console Sir Adam but he pondered for a moment, 'Did Cannon order Grace's death out of some sense of justice, or was it to protect his whereabouts from Pavel?'. Whatever the reason, Sir Adam's sorrowful eyes looked up at Robert.

"I need the fact that Christian is a Gladio operative verifying," Sir Adam asked, "Robert, do you have access to any NATO records or CIA records relating to Gladio cell leaders?"

"I will have to pull a lot of strings, but being a SIS director might actually be good for something after all. I'll need a phone, Sir Adam, a hard wire?"

"There's a phone in the sitting room, it's secure," Sir Adam answered.

Robert turned back to the library door, this time opening it without interruption he vanished into the adjoining sitting room.

Cannon walked around Mac, much like Mac had circled him earlier.

"Thanks for getting Alex out of Russia," said Christian in an attempt to break the atmosphere. "I was counting on getting Alex out that way, I just didn't count on you figuring out that we really didn't have the list. You certainly called our bluff on that one."

"Aye, well, if you're a Gladio cell leader, how comes you couldn't get Alex out yourself?" Mac asked in a manner that indicated he didn't fully believe Cannon.

Cannon shot a nervous glancing look over to Alex, Mac picked up on Cannon's fleeting moment of unease and slowly uttered the words, "Secrets in a glass box."

Before Christian could react to Mac's statement, Robert came bursting back into the room, "He has grade 7 NATO clearance, he fucking outranks me!" announced an amazed Robert.

Sir Adam turned to face Cannon, "I'm sorry my boy, it seems we have totally blown the lid off your mission, what do you want us to do with Eugene?"

"Release him back into the wild Frank, send him back to his driver and let him find his own way back to the USA, if he dares return that is. As for the list of hackers, well I'm sure if you return that to me, less two of the British names no-one need know," smiled Cannon.

"And Alex?" Sir Adam asked more hesitantly.

"Alex is now property of the US Government. Any attempt to hold him will be interpreted as an infringement of the NATO treaty. That said, is it ok if I ask you for rooms tonight? I will have a car pick us both up in the morning," Cannon asked joyfully.

The long woeful frown on Sir Adam's face dropped away, being replaced by a comforting attempt at a smile, "You and Alex can stay as long as you like, my boy, I hope we'll get a chance to talk more over breakfast. As for now, Robert has a list of fifty hackers to get for you."

Chapter 29 – Secrets in a glass box

The brisk morning air carried the light scent of recently mowed lawns and the aroma of oak dotted woodlands on its breeze. Christian breathed it in like a man savouring the smell of a fine wine and rejoicing in its splendid magnificence. In all the countries he had visited, there was obviously no other place as beautiful, as majestic, as his beloved England. Turning to look back at the manor house's grand entrance, from where he had recently passed, he noticed Sir Adam striding through it and coming towards him with some vigour.

"Where's Alex?" asked Sir Adam playfully.

"He's getting ready, he mentioned something about a shower after breakfast. The car isn't due for half an hour yet so there's still time," replied Cannon.

"Good, I'm glad we still have some time my lad, there's something I wanted to talk to you about," remarked Sir Adam.

"Frank, after last night, you'll forgive me if I don't want to talk about Alex or the list of hackers again," answered back Cannon abruptly.

"No, that's not it," Sir Adam paused in thought before continuing, "What do you know about the work I do?"

"I worked out that the company is just a cover, I guess the question is for what?" Cannon raised an inquiring eyebrow to signal his intrigue.

"What do you think we did before Military Intelligence even existed?" Sir Adam asked rhetorically.

Cannon passed a blank expression back to Sir Adam, half knowing the answer but in such a way as to invite Sir Adam to continue.

"The Royals and Noble families of England have funded their own intelligence organisation for over 600 years. The official head of this organisation is, and always has been, the serving King or Queen, to whom I report directly," Sir Adam declared with some measure of pride in his voice.

"You are kidding me. The Royals are clueless, they just walk around shaking hands and waving at the public, they do little more than serve as figureheads!" exclaimed a bemused Cannon.

"Really, is that what you think?" rebuffed Sir Adam with a cheeky smile.

"Why are you telling me this Frank?" asked Cannon.

"You've survived Mac, Moscow and me, like I hoped you would," there was an awkward silence as Cannon realised that Sir Adam might have actually orchestrated all the recently past events intentionally. The silence was broken as Sir Adam continued,

"I'd like you to think about working for the company, learn the ropes my boy, with a view to one day, well, I'm sure you understand me."

Before Cannon could muster a reply, Alex emerged from the entrance and exclaimed,

"Can we walk down to the gatehouse? it is a truly beautiful morning."

The Hacker Hunter © Copyright Lionwing Ltd 2011

Sir Adam glanced at his watch. "Just think about it my boy, that's all I am asking at this stage," he whispered.

Mac appeared behind Alex, on seeing him Cannon braced up.

"Mac, I never thanked you for saving my life in the institute," shouted out Cannon.

Mac, electing not to reply straight away, walked with Alex to join Cannon and Sir Adam.

"I would tell you to keep out of trouble and play safe, but I know there's no point. I'll see you again," remarked Mac in a tone that suggested their paths would cross in the future.

"Come on Alex, if we are to meet our car on time we had better leave now. If you want to walk down there that is," stated Cannon as he winked at Mac with a knowing grin.

As Alex and Cannon started walking away, Cannon turned back to face Sir Adam, "I still have your number," he yelled out and then turned to catch Alex back up.

"What are you thinking, Mac?" asked Sir Adam who had clearly picked up on Mac's vibe.

"Aye, like I said at the beginning Sir Adam, I'm retired," replied Mac.

The guards had already been told that Alex and Cannon were approaching on foot and had opened the gates expectantly. Passing through the gates first, Alex stopped just before the adjoining road and asked,

The Hacker Hunter © Copyright Lionwing Ltd 2011

"Chris, what do you think Mac meant when he said 'Secrets in a glass box' last night?"

No sooner than the words had left Alex's mouth than a black car pulled up to them, the windows were darkly tinted, making it impossible to look in.

"I'll let you work that out Alex, now get in the car, there's a good chap," ordered Cannon.

Cannon walked around to the front passenger side door, he pulled it open and took a seat next to the driver. A beautifully manicured hand reached down and cupped Cannon's balls.

"I say we leave the Russian with daddy and go straight back to the hotel room," spoke out the soft yet lustfully playful voice of Maria.

"Your father is one hell of a good actor," replied Cannon.

"Funny," she smiled "he said the same about you."

THE END
Thank you for reading the Hacker Hunter

The Hacker Hunter © Copyright Lionwing Ltd 2011

Acknowledgements

Christopher Keenan
John McAleese (RIP) – An inspiration to us all
Simon Davies (AKA BOB)
Alex Khomenko (AKA AK47)
Henry Seymer
James Entwistle (The Italian American Family)
Alexander Keenan (Proof Reader)
Sofia Keenan
Ryan Bartram
Hayley McAleese
Maria and Her Daddy
Sir Frank (RIP)
Ministry of Defence
The Word Fiction

Rusty Firmin
(Co-Author of Go! Go! Go!)

Look out for our next book there are three left.
Please visit www.TheHackerHunter.co.uk

The Hacker Hunter

By Christopher Keenan

My dear friend |RIP| you will never be forgotten.

Copyright Lionwing Ltd 2011 - Published 2011
ISBN: 978-0-9570564-0-4

www.TheHackerHunter.net